Y0-BXG-341

CRY OF THE FIREBIRD

BY AMY KUIVALAINEN

THE MAGICIANS OF VENICE
The Immortal City
The Sea of the Dead
The King's Seal

THE FIREBIRD FAERIE TALES
Cry of the Firebird

AMY KUIVALAINEN

CRY OF THE FIREBIRD

A FIREBIRD FAERIE TALES NOVEL

bhc
press™

Livonia, Michigan

Editor: Chelsea Cambeis
Proofreader: Tori Ladd

Published by BHC Press

Library of Congress Control Number: 2020936737

ISBN: 978-1-64397-189-6 (Hardcover)
ISBN: 978-1-64397-190-2 (Softcover)
ISBN: 978-1-64397-191-9 (Ebook)

For information, write:
BHC Press
885 Penniman #5505
Plymouth, MI 48170

Visit the publisher:
www.bhcpress.com

For Fox,
who encouraged me during the first draft
of this story, and every draft since.

CRY OF THE FIREBIRD

PART ONE
THE GIRL WITH NO MEMORY

PROLOGUE

LOOK THROUGH THE HEAVY pine forest and see a fire glowing. Beside it sits a bear of a man, knife in one hand and a clay bowl on the ground in front of him. It has been a long time since he last shed blood for his gods, and this will satisfy them a little longer.

The screech of the doomed animal in his clutches is broken off, and the bowl fills with its steaming blood. He puts the bowl on a flat stone by the fire before cutting his scarred wrist and letting his own blood drip into the mixture.

For many days, he has thrown his runes, trying to discover the meaning behind his dreams. He has marked each one with his blood, yet still, they reveal nothing.

A tune starts deep in his gut. It stretches and twists like an unborn child, traveling up like a snake through his chest, setting his bones to shake. He grinds his jaw shut to keep it from escaping as it creeps up his throat.

His lips vibrate as the magic tries to force its way out. The man is well learned in the ways of the song and knows how to control it. The bowl steams, and he leans over to breathe in the blood fumes that will give him visions.

The magic of the blood song works through him, pulling him under the power of the trance, dragging forth memories that he always does his best to keep buried. The visions hit him thick and fast.

The secrets in his blood demand to be heard, each turning over in his mind like rune stones spelling out his past and future: the lost princess, the witch, the game, the bloodline, the curse, the gates, the firebird. Over and over, they turn. Lost past, broken present, and a future that will burn the world in an inferno.

The magic tells him that the war he's been waiting for is almost there. But he's not ready.

This man's name is Vasilli, and he is searching for his brother. Yvan has the magic he needs to survive what is coming. Vasilli will possess it and break the threads of fate around him.

Even if he has to wade through a sea of blood to do it.

1

WHEN ANYA WOKE ON a drizzling early autumn morning, she had no idea that she was about to meet the God of the Dead.

After downing painkillers for her hangover, she headed into the village on unsteady but determined feet. The lady who ran the grocery store gave her a once-over glance, from her muddy boots to her fair, crookedly braided hair, and frowned in disapproval. Even with a blazing headache, Anya still managed to lift her lips in a partial sneer in reply. Anya had a sneer that could cut you in places you didn't know you had, but only if she deigned to notice you at all.

This wasn't an uncommon exchange when she bothered to walk the few short kilometers from her farm. Anya knew what they all thought of her, and she made it known that the feeling of dislike was mutual.

Thankfully, the only café wasn't busy with forestry workers in high-vis gear or local farmers midmorning. She'd been forced to partake in a weekly visit to the café when her grandfather, Eikki, was alive. Since his death three months prior, she'd found she still wasn't able to let the ritual go. It was also fun to remind people that she hadn't left the farm like they all told her she should. According to most, a woman running a farm by herself couldn't be done, no matter how small it was.

Liisi, the café owner, gave her a guarded smile as Anya ordered eggs and coffee before retreating to a booth in the corner. She fought the urge to rest her head on the cold countertop to soothe her burning head.

God, she was hungover. She hadn't planned to drink so much the night before, but she'd been having nightmares every night for the past week, and the vodka helped get her back to sleep. Last night, she'd relived the car accident that killed both of her parents. Anya hadn't forgotten the sound of her mother's blood dripping onto the dashboard as she had waited for someone to come rescue her from the back seat. It had been years since she'd dreamed of the crash, and now her PTSD was bound to flare up all over again. She'd only just gotten it under control enough that she wasn't seeing Eikki dying every time she shut her eyes.

"Here, you look like you need it." Liisi put a steaming mug of coffee down in front of her.

"Thanks," mumbled Anya. She waited until Liisi disappeared into the kitchen before she took a flask from her pocket and topped the mug up with vodka. Anya sipped, then stared out the window so she wouldn't look at Eikki's empty seat in front of her and feel the gaping hole of his loss.

Anya had always thought boredom would be the thing to kill her in the small village on the borders of Russia and Karelia, but now she knew it was going to be loneliness.

Just another reason you should sell the farm and start a new life somewhere else.

It was all Anya had thought about since she'd put Eikki in the ground months before. Every time she'd go to act on it, the guilt came crashing down over her like a tidal wave. Her ancestors had always farmed the land next to the ancient forest, and she was the last one left. It would not only be an ending for her, but of her family history and the promise of their land. Anya had another big mouthful of the spiked coffee. The heat and alcohol burned a hole in her empty stomach.

The loneliness wasn't the only problem. The feeling that something was missing in her life—in her—had only grown since Eikki's death, and in the last month, it had become almost unbearable. Every day, the pressure inside of her grew. She was twenty-seven years old and had barely seen anything of the world. Instead, she lived in a place where time seemed to stand still. *There has to be more than this.*

Liisi put a plate of eggs on the table in front of her. Anya smiled even as her stomach roiled. She couldn't keep living off vodka and coffee, but still, she stared at her plate with apprehension until someone cleared their throat.

"Excuse me. Is this seat taken?" the person asked in English.

Anya started in surprise and looked up at the tall man standing in front of her. He wore an immaculate black suit and stared at her like he knew her. Black hair framed the cheekbones of his handsome, pale face and intelligent black eyes. He was close enough that she could smell his aftershave—a strange blend of cypress, winter ice, and ash.

Anya glimpsed down at his shiny, black shoes. There wasn't a speck of dust or dirt on them. *Definitely not a local, that's for sure.* She looked around the café—still empty—then back to the man, who was waiting for an answer.

"No, it's not taken," she said, thoroughly confused. Tourists tended to be few and far between, and Anya hadn't seen anyone so polished since she'd lived in Moscow for a brief time. "I'm Anya." She fought the urge to fix her hair.

"Yes, I know." He sat down across from her.

"And you are?" Alarm bells went off in Anya's brain, not only because he knew her name, but because he smiled at her—a dazzling smile that turned his already handsome features into something gorgeous and dangerous.

He held out a hand to her. "You can call me Tuoni." His voice deep voice rattled her bones. "That's what Eikki knew me as."

"Like the God of the Dead?" Anya took his hand to shake it. Tuoni, in Karelian mythology, ruled the Land of the Dead with his children.

"Oh, good. You've heard of me. That will save us some time."

Anya's palm tingled as he tightened his grip. Black shadows shivered around their hands. She pulled hers away and rubbed at her eyes.

You must still be drunk. Eikki had loads of weird friends. She thought of the fortune teller with gold teeth. Tuoni was probably just there to pay his condolences.

Sudden, cold pressure built behind her eyes, and Tuoni laughed.

"Perhaps you are still a bit drunk, so let me clarify to put you at ease. I really am *that* Tuoni."

Despite thinking the guy was a nutter, sweat prickled the back of her neck. "Even if you were, how is that supposed to put me at ease?"

"I'm here to talk to you, Anya, not frighten you. Unless you can see my true form and that's what's disturbing you?"

True form. The words brought an old memory hurtling to the forefront of her mind. Eikki used to tell her stories about magical creatures and beings that used glamor and guises…usually to lure gullible humans to violent deaths.

"Not unless your true form is wearing a suit far too nice for this place," Anya replied, trying to hide her growing anxiety. She didn't scare easily, but the longer she talked to him, the more uncomfortable she became. As Tuoni stared at her, the hand he'd shaken burned with the imprint of his touch.

"Strange. I'm sure Eikki once mentioned you could see things," he said.

"Yeah." She scoffed. "Maybe in my PTSD-induced nightmares after watching my parents die." PTSD symptoms that had returned after she'd seen Eikki mauled by wolves in the forest. Anya put her hands under the table to hide their shaking.

"I'm not talking about nightmares, Anya." Tuoni watched her with a predator's interest, searching her features. "A shame. It's a useful talent for a shaman to have."

"I bet. So, you're here to pay your condolences to Eikki or something?" Her patience was running out. *Just play along, then he'll leave you alone.*

"Or something. I've come to talk to you about Eikki and your family legacy."

"Legacy? You mean the farm?"

Liisi came back to refill their coffees. "Who is this man you are talking to, Anya?"

Tuoni's brilliant smile returned. "I'm Eikki's lawyer from St. Petersburg, here to talk to Anya about her inheritance."

"I knew you were no farmer," Liisi said in shaky English.

Anya cringed at her pronunciation. Her parents—a schoolteacher and a lawyer—had taught her English, Finnish, and Russian in hopes that they would all travel when she got older. After their deaths, Eikki had continued their lessons.

Much good it did me, seeing how I've never traveled anywhere.

"A tragedy what happened to that old man. Attacked by wolves in the middle of summer. It's unnatural—"

"Sorry to interrupt," Tuoni shot her an apologetic smile, "but Anya and I do have a lot to discuss before I leave today."

"Of course! It's just so nice to see a new face, especially a handsome one."

Anya rolled her eyes. *And you were lying through your teeth anyway.* No one gave a shit about Eikki except her. Liisi just wanted someone to flirt with.

"Let me know if you need anything else," Liisi said, touching Tuoni's shoulder before bustling away.

"You said *legacy*." Anya lifted a brow.

"Yes, your legacy as a gatekeeper and shaman, like Eikki was."

Anya choked on her coffee. "You think he was a shaman? I mean, he was a *joiking* enthusiast when the Sami performers came through, but—"

"I am many things, Anya, but I'm not a liar. There was a lot Eikki kept hidden from you—his magic included. He wanted to protect you by making the world believe you were as devoid of magic as your father was."

"Stop. I don't know who you really are or who put you up to coming here to piss me off, but don't talk about my grandfather like he was crazy, and never, ever talk about my father." Anya had endured enough teasing about Eikki over the years. The village loved gossiping about him—that is until something terrible happened, and then he was the first person they called. The nearest doctor lived an hour away, and Eikki was handy with a needle and knew what herbs would heal and bring down a fever.

Cold radiated from Tuoni as his lips lifted in a sneer. "Do you really think I'm going to obey a sad little mortal like you?" Anger brewed in his eyes. "I'm here to help you, so shut up and listen so I can get back to what I'm meant to be doing."

"No, I don't think I will." Anya went to get up, but Tuoni made a small gesture, and she remained locked in her chair. "What the fuck? Let me go." Her heart pounded as she tried to wriggle free, panic racing through her.

Tuoni didn't seem concerned. "I don't want to frighten you; I just need you to sit still and listen. As I was saying, Eikki was a shaman and a gatekeeper. There are only a few places in the human world that touch an otherworld, and your farm borders on one of the strongest in Russia. Eikki protected this gateway into Skazki his entire life, like your ancestors before him."

The forest at night is their domain… Eikki's warning words rushed back to Anya. He had said that to her parents the night they died. He'd tried to convince them not to leave. How could Anya have forgotten that?

"What do you mean by a gateway to Skazki?" Anya asked. In the fairy tales, Skazki was the name of the land of heroes and myth, while Mir was the human world.

"A gateway is a place where two worlds touch. Sometimes, people and creatures with magical abilities can cross through, which means those gateways must be guarded. Your family have always been gatekeepers, and because of that, Eikki had enemies. Unless one has a lot of power, they need a gatekeeper to world-walk, so people like Eikki would be petitioned. He was particular on who he let through. The night your parents died—that was a disgruntled petitioner lashing out because they wanted to hurt Eikki."

They were murdered? Anya shuddered against the invisible bonds holding her as she remembered the shadows surrounding the car, blacking out the windshield as she and her parents screamed. Then the deafening silence when they hit the ditch.

She held back a sob. "Why are you telling me this?"

"Because despite his misguided efforts, Eikki can't protect you anymore. You're lucky word spreads so slowly between the worlds, because when the creatures and magic users in Skazki find out he's dead, they are all going to try to break through. You need to learn to be a gatekeeper and keep them out. You have a great power hidden inside of you, Anya. That power needs to be unleashed, because if you don't keep the gates closed, anyone and anything will be able to get in. Like the skin-changers that killed Eikki, for example." Tuoni studied her. "You saw them that day, didn't you?"

Anya thought she'd imagined seeing the skinny, humanoid forms hidden under the wolf furs. By the time she'd reached where they were attacking Eikki, they had disappeared into the forest, leaving him to bleed out from the deep wounds they'd ripped in his stomach and chest. Anya squeezed her eyes shut in an attempt to block out the bloody images.

"If Eikki was guarding this gate, how did they get in to kill him?"

"I can't be certain, but my guess is that one of his enemies from Skazki helped the skin-changers. He'd been having premonitions of his impending death as the cancer ate through him. Maybe they, too, knew he was weakening. The last time I saw him, he was determined to lay down a ward that would protect you long after he was gone, hopefully for the rest of your life, but he was murdered before he figured out how." Tuoni's tone softened ever so slightly. "He could never understand that he couldn't shield you forever. He couldn't stop the supernatural war that is coming, and neither can you. Now that he's no longer here to renew the gates' strength, they will weaken and fray. You don't have much time before they are ripped apart—and probably you along with them."

"Why me too?" Anya was struggling to believe any of what he was saying, and if it wasn't for the fact that she still couldn't move, she wouldn't believe him at all.

"Because you have untrained magic, and there are Powers in this world who will want it once it begins to manifest. As for the gates, you probably have six months at the most. Gate protection spells are usually renewed twice a year at the summer and winter solstice to strengthen them. You'll want to master your power and seal them before your time is up."

Anya was quiet a moment. She shook her head. "Why do you even care enough to tell me any of this?"

"I have my reasons, the main one being if this world is flooded with the monsters from all of your stories, it will be a massacre," Tuoni snapped. "It's not only them you need to worry about. There are other powerful magic users in this world and Skazki who will seek to take the gates from you. They want control of them and unlimited access between here and there. Stealing your magic and killing the last of your bloodline will just be an added bonus."

"Say I believe you. How am I meant to learn how to close—or even *find*—this magical gate before I get murdered?"

"Don't be sarcastic with me, child. You know I speak the truth, even if you were made to forget it," Tuoni said. "I suggest you start by looking through some of Eikki's books. Most shamans don't believe in writing things down, but he did. You can learn a lot if you keep your mind open." He gave her a chilling smile. "Now, I really must be going. I hope to see you again soon."

Anya rolled her eyes.

Tuoni sighed and got to his feet. "At least try to stay alive and make it a challenge for me."

Anya ignored the comment and glared up at him. "I would like to be let go now."

The weight holding her limbs down lifted, but he blocked her way out of the booth.

"Another thing—Eikki asked me to give you this before he died." Tuoni reached into his pocket and pulled out a smooth black-and-red stone.

Anya didn't want a damn thing from him, but she asked, "What is it?"

"It has been in your family for a long time. All you need to know is that it's dangerous—and your destiny." Tuoni took her hand and slapped the stone into her palm, then held her hand tightly. "I have a parting gift for you. You've been made to forget a lot about your life, Anya. It's time you woke up."

Anya stopped breathing as his handsome face shivered and slipped away. Underneath, his black eyes burned in a face of impossible, horrible beauty swathed in shadows. Anya struggled as a bolt of static snapped between their palms. Pain shot through her head, tearing something inside of her, and she cried out. The taste of salt and ash and blood swirled in her mouth as the sound of wings beat about her ears. Tuoni held on until the pain eased. Anya gagged and gasped for breath.

Tuoni's face changed back to normal, and he smiled down at her. "Take my advice and stay sober for the next few days. Things are going to get strange. *Hyvää päivää,* shamanitsa," he growled. Then he vanished.

"Where did he go?" Anya scrambled out of the booth.

Liisi gave her a disgusted look. "Are you drunk again? You're the only one in here, idiot girl."

Anya threw some money down on the table, clutched the stone to her chest, and ran.

✦

See a man in the forest. He is dressed in a long black trench coat, and water clings to his curly hair. Some days, he curses the shaman and the promise he made to watch over his family. Other days, he wonders what it would be like to step into the light and let her see him. But he's not there to talk to Anya. Only to protect her.

Sharp pain scratches at the pit of his stomach and back of his throat. He needs to feed but is reluctant to leave Anya when she is so alone.

And then there she is, running as fast as she can, clearing the village buildings, stumbling over the boundary fence, and cutting across a field. He snaps to attention but stays hidden in the tree line. There's nothing chasing her, but something had to cause such fear. He relaxes as soon as she passes through the farm's wards, then stares at the sky. It's a few hours till nightfall. Then he will hunt down whatever made her so afraid and tear it to pieces.

2

ANYA'S LUNGS BURNED AS the village rushed past her in a haze of dark brown timber and brick houses, stores, and the *tsasouna*. The priest called out to her to watch where she was running, and the kids on the corner pointed and laughed, but she didn't stop until she was over the boundary fence and on her own land again.

Anya bent over, hands on her knees, and spat out the ash-and-blood taste lingering in her mouth from whatever Tuoni had done to her. He'd said she had been made to forget things… But how was that possible? What did he mean? She shut her eyes and breathed in the earthy scent of pine, birch, and cold rot that rose from the forest looming beside her.

The back of Anya's neck burned. She spun around. There was nothing there, as always. Certainly not the terrifying God of the Dead going on about magic gates and monsters. She rubbed the warm stone in her hand, using the repetitive action to ground herself. Tuoni had wanted her to know, without a doubt, that magic was real, that what he said was the truth. He'd said he hadn't wanted to frighten her, but the terror of his real face wasn't something that would leave her anytime soon.

Cold rain crept under the collar of Anya's black jacket, and she shuddered. She needed to get warm and think this through properly. Anya headed for her small house at the bottom of the field, her grip on the stone tightening and her palm still stinging from the static of Tuoni's touch.

Breathe and think. First, Eikki had apparently been a shaman and gatekeeper. When Anya looked back, she had to admit there'd been signs to suggest he was into the old ways. He would whisper rhymes to the trees, plant during particular phases of the moon, write and draw strange things in journals, and whistle songs to birds. When she was little, he would sing to her all the old tales of heroes and magic. When Anya was older, she told him they hadn't been tales for children.

"They are tales for you, though," Eikki had said. *"They will teach you about life."*

Anya's lips lifted in the smallest of smiles. She had forgotten about that.

Second, if Tuoni was right and she only had months left before the gates in the forest opened—and people came looking to murder her—she would have to find someone to buy or rent the farm if she was going to have time to learn how to keep them closed. Running the farm by herself over the past months had taken its toll. She was exhausted, frustrated, and had no time to grieve for Eikki, let alone learn magic. A bitter laugh escaped her lips.

Learn magic. Sure. Was she actually considering that Tuoni was telling the truth? The bloody ash taste grew stronger in her mouth, almost like a reminder that she *had* seen real magic that morning. There was no way she could dismiss or deny it.

Not like she had in Moscow.

Anya fought the urge to dry wretch again.

In the short time she lived there—only months—Anya had seen doctors about her nightmares. Even her boyfriend had suggested she get medicated after they broke up. They'd been out drinking one night, and she thought she saw a leshy in Zaryadye Park. She panicked and couldn't stop screaming. Her boyfriend, sick of the nightmares and the stories, left her soon after.

Fuck him and the doctors.

And the third thing Anya took away from her conversation with the God of the Dead: Tuoni's comment about being made to forget. That one worried her more than the others, because if it were true, how would she get her memories back? How would she know what was missing? Anya rolled the stone in her pocket, drawing comfort from its warmth, and crossed the sludgy road to home.

It was a simple house with a porch and small, square glass windows. Her grandfather's grandfather, Ilya, built it, and it had been added to by every generation. The barn was a hundred meters from the house and made of the same weathered wood.

Anya kicked off her wet boots, took out a large iron key, and opened the front door. She locked it behind her. Her nausea eased as she breathed in the comforting smells of split pine blocks, beeswax candle smoke, and coffee.

Bright rag rugs covered the floors; ornaments sat on the shelves; and battered books took up many of the flat surfaces, stacked in uneven piles. Dried herbs had always hung in the little kitchen, and the belongings of the people who had lived there filled every nook and cranny. Despite the clutter, she never had the heart to throw any of it out.

Anya took the stone out of her pocket and studied it. There was nothing peculiar about it, except for the lines of red amongst the black. How could a rock be her destiny?

Shrugging, she placed it on the small shelf above the fireplace where she wouldn't lose it and went to find something to drink. Tuoni's warning about staying sober itched at her. However, if she was going to start believing in gates to Skazki and shamanism, she would need vodka to help her.

Anya retrieved a bottle of vodka she'd made in an ancient still from down in the cellar.

Maybe Eikki had left her a helpful how-to guide in one of his journals. *Be realistic. Your luck has never been that good.*

Anya had never gone through the shelf of journals in Eikki's bedroom. They'd always been respectful of each other's privacy, and since his death, she hadn't even gone into the room. She opened the door and tried to ignore the squeeze of grief in her chest as her eyes wandered over his things.

An overflowing bookshelf stood in one corner. Anya scanned the spines, taking note of just how many books on mythology and folktales he had. Anya had never asked Eikki what he wrote about in his journals, even when he sat in the kitchen, scribbling away until midnight. Feeling like she was about to cross the line and betray his privacy, she randomly selected a few of the notebooks and headed back to the warmth of the fire.

Anya ignored the tremble in her fingers as she opened the first one and flicked through it. Drawings and symbols filled the pages. The words were written in English, Finnish, and Russian.

She sipped her vodka straight from the bottle as she spent hours trying to make heads or tails of the journal. There was a lot of useless information, like a poem about Baba Yaga playing some magical game with another witch, and the best time to hunt for mushrooms. There was nothing about gates or strange black stones.

Anya read until the writing and drawings on the pages swam. She fell asleep, holding her sore hand to her chest and thinking of fire.

Anya woke with a start, sending the journal flying from her lap. She'd dreamed of a man with odd eyes who smelled of autumn. He'd been having an argument with Eikki that she couldn't hear. And she'd dreamed hazy images of a lake and red-stained boulders. Everywhere there was fire, the world burning in an inferno around her.

That'll teach you to read a shaman's journals before bed.

The sun was already up. With a groan, Anya dragged herself to her feet. She grabbed a piece of bread from the kitchen on the way past and munched it as she put on gum boots, then headed to the barn to feed the animals.

Anya was collecting more wood from the shed—and looking out for spiders—when she noticed smoke coming from under the house's back door.

"Shit. Not again." Anya dropped the wood and ran. As she opened the door, a cloud of smoke poured out. She hurried through the house, hoping coals hadn't rolled from the fireplace and burned the mat like last time.

Anya checked each room, but there was no fire. Where had all the smoke come from? She went into the sitting room, thinking the flue on the fireplace had closed by accident. Something crunched under her boots. She lifted one foot to find fragments of the broken black stone. Her stone—her *destiny*—had rolled off the mantle and smashed on the floor. Anya bent down to gather the pieces of glossy rock with a sigh.

"That's great, Anya. You have the family heirloom for a day, and it's already broken. Destiny my ass."

Something rustled in her bedroom. Anya froze. She grabbed the iron poker beside her and held it above her head. No one in the village would be stupid enough to break into her house, but kids would occasionally throw rocks at her roof as a dare.

Anya kicked the bedroom door open, ready for a fight. Instead of a thief or delinquent, a small bird with bright gold feathers fluttered in the middle of her bed.

"Stupid bird. How did you get in here?" Anya hadn't left any windows open, so she could only guess it had somehow gotten in through the chimney. She took an old shirt and wrapped it around her hand before reaching for the bird. The chick didn't cry or struggle as she picked up its shivering little body. Anya carried it to the sitting room and placed it on the floor next to the fireplace before adding some more wood and coaxing the coals to life.

"There you go, little one." She contemplated what to do with it. Anya didn't like people, but she was hopelessly soft with animals. The wind outside had blown up into an icy gale, so she couldn't just put it in a tree. If she weren't so soft, she would have taken it outside and hit it over the head with a brick. It cooed at her, and she knew she couldn't do it.

Another animal to take care of was the last thing she needed. Especially a chick that would require constant feeding and attention.

What did a bird that size eat? She was frying herself fish for dinner, so she figured it could eat that or die. It didn't take long for her to fillet the trout and fry it in butter and salt. She couldn't remember how many days it had been since she'd eaten a proper meal. Her breakfast at the café the previous day had went untouched.

"I need a drink," Anya muttered. She placed a hand on the cellar door, then hesitated.

Stay sober, Tuoni had said. Reluctantly, Anya made herself a cup of coffee instead. When the God of the Dead told you to do something, it was probably wise to listen to him just a little bit.

Back in the sitting room, Anya got comfortable on the mat in front of the fire, her plate of food in her lap. The chick made chirpy sounds at her. With a sigh, Anya took a tiny piece of fish from her plate and offered it to the little bird. It pecked at it straight away and looked to her for more.

"First you're sleeping in my bed; now you're trying to steal my dinner. You aren't a very polite bird, are you?"

The bird chirped more forcefully, and she relented, feeding it as much as it would eat.

After it was satisfied, the chick climbed out of the shirt and hopped on unsteady feet. It looked so ridiculous that Anya had to laugh at its feeble attempts.

"Careful, now. Don't get too close to the fire," she warned. "You'll get burned, and I won't rescue you."

It gave her an incredulous look before jumping into the flames.

"Shit!" Anya rushed to get it out before it caught fire. The bird's little head turned, and it crowed with delight. The fire exploded, and Anya jerked backward, shielding her face. The bird shrieked again, then flapped its wings before launching itself up the chimney.

"What the fuck?" She scrambled to her feet and ran outside just as the bird streaked out of the chimney stack in a flash of orange light. It flew higher and higher before exploding like a firework, then swooped back down to earth, full-grown and made of living flame.

Anya stared, eyes wide. "Holy shit."

It looked something like a peacock with its long, curling tail. It cooed softly, its burning feathers shimmering, and walked toward the house.

"You'd better be able to turn your flames off if you think you're coming back inside," Anya said, feeling more hysterical by the second.

The bird tilted its head as if it were listening to her. Then it stamped one foot, and the flames disappeared, leaving only silky gold and red feathers.

"Oh...I suppose you can."

Anya followed the bird back inside. She'd thought her week couldn't get any weirder. Turns out she was wrong.

See the man in the forest and the bowl of blood he holds. Vasilli breathes in the steam rising from it. His eyes snap open as the bowl explodes in flames, searing his face and hands. The bowl shatters, and he is thrown back into the leaf litter. Vasilli laughs aloud.

"Finally, I will get to kill you!" Vasilli knew the shaman had the stone. Now he will get the firebird, kill his brother, and be done with that cursed family of gatekeepers once and for all.

"Vischto! Vischtan!"

His minions come bounding out of the trees, their wolf pelts filthy with dried blood.

Vasilli's smile is vicious. "We're going hunting."

3

A NYA LAY IN BED the following morning staring at the pine knots on the ceiling beams, trying to process the past few days.

The previous evening, the firebird had curled up on the floor in front of the fire and went to sleep. Anya had woken a few times in the night and checked on it, still struggling to believe what she had seen. The stone Tuoni had given her wasn't a stone at all. Had he known it would hatch?

It's your destiny. How was a firebird going to help her with everything she needed to learn?

Anya got dressed and crept out to where she'd left the bird sleeping. She froze in the doorway. A very tall, very naked man was stretched out on the mat beside the fire. She tiptoed around him and grabbed the poker, then demanded, "Who the hell are you?" and nudged him with the end of it.

The man woke with a surprised jerk. His eyes filled with alarm before flames licked up along his brown skin. He twisted on the carpet, crying out in pain as fiery feathers pushed and burned their way out of his arms and chest. His huge body folded in on itself with a crunch of bones, and suddenly, he was the firebird, squawking irritably as flames dripped onto the rug.

"Stop that! You're going to burn the house down." Anya dropped the poker and grabbed a blanket off the back of the couch, ready to beat the flames out.

The firebird hissed at her, and Anya jumped back as it began to shift again, the flames and feathers sucking in, arms spurting from its wings. With a frustrated shout, it transformed back into a man. He sucked in a breath, bracing himself on hands and knees. Long, dark hair hung around his high cheekbones and eyes that glowed with a strange amber light.

"Can…can I have that blanket?" he asked in a rough, deep voice.

Anya tossed it to him, too stunned to object, and he wrapped it around himself. The smell of ozone—of storms and wildfire—emanated from him as he pushed his hands through his hair and groaned.

Anya sat down before she fell down. "Are you okay?"

After meeting the God of the Dead and a firebird hatching in her home, a naked man didn't seem so frightening. At least, that's what she told herself.

"I think so." He hugged his knees to his broad chest. "Who are you?"

"Anya Venäläinen. And you are?"

He frowned at the question. After a moment, he said, "Yvan Tsarevich. At least, I used to be."

"I'm going to make some coffee. Would you like some?" she asked, not knowing what else to do.

He nodded and pulled the blanket tighter around himself. Anya stumbled into the kitchen, gripped the countertop, and took five deep breaths. *You have a shape-shifting firebird in your sitting room.* She spilled grounds everywhere as she tried to make coffee with shaking hands. Tuoni's voice rang through her head: *Things are going to get strange.* He couldn't have warned her about this?

"You bastard," muttered Anya.

Back in the sitting room, Yvan had managed to get off the floor and was on the couch, his eyes dancing over her as she offered him a mug of coffee.

"Venäläinen." He said the name carefully. "As in Ilya Venäläinen?"

Anya's brows rose in surprise. "Yes. He was my grandfather's grandfather."

"So many years." Yvan's vocabulary seemed to come back to him as he let out an impressive list of expletives. He rubbed a hand over his face. "You are Ilya's heir, though? A shamanitsa and gatekeeper?"

Anya shook her head. "Not even close. I didn't even know about the gate until two days ago when Tuoni told me."

"Tuoni was here? That can't be good. If you are not a shamanitsa, who is guarding the gates to Skazki?"

"No one, apparently. My grandfather, Eikki, was the last gatekeeper, and he never taught me about any of this."

Yvan's dark brows rose. "No one is watching the gates to Skazki? Are they even shut?"

Anya nodded. "Tuoni said they will be closed for months yet. Plenty of time for me to go through Eikki's books and learn how to close them," Anya said with far more confidence than she felt.

Yvan set his coffee down and put his head in his hands. The scent of ozone grew as he muttered under his breath.

Anya's mouth fell open. "Did you just call me an idiot?"

"You can't just learn gates magic in a couple of months," Yvan said. "Forget it. I need to leave. Now that I'm reborn, Vasilli will find me and kill you because you've sheltered me, and according to you, you have no idea how to defend yourself with magic."

"Vasilli?"

"Yes, Vasilli, my brother. He may already know that I'm here…" Fear flashed in Yvan's strange eyes, and his skin began to flicker with flames as his panic mounted.

Anya hesitated, wanting to comfort him, but she was still unsure of him. She reached over and patted his warm shoulder. The fire did not burn her as it danced across her fingers. "Breathe, Yvan. If you change back into the firebird, we can't figure any of this out. And if we don't figure this out, I can't help you." She used the same tone she did with distressed animals. "Maybe you should sleep?"

"I've slept long enough, and you can't help me," he snapped.

Anya pulled her hand away, her patience tapped out. "Fine. Figure it out on your own. I've got animals to feed. The kitchen is through there; the bathroom is that way. If you set my house on fire, I'll shoot you."

She didn't know if Yvan was disorientated or crazy, but she wasn't about to fight with someone who didn't want her assistance. She dumped her cup in the sink and headed for the barn, hoping that by the time she went back inside, he would be gone.

Anya spent the next hour doing chores and cursing Tuoni. She didn't want to deal with gates or magic or men that turned into mythical birds, no matter how handsome they were.

But Yvan seemed to know things about Eikki and Ilya. Maybe he could help her.

Anya dismissed the thought immediately. Yvan didn't want her help, and she didn't want his. Mostly because he apparently had a murderous brother after him who would kill her too. What the hell had her family been doing with a firebird's egg, and how did Yvan know Ilya? He could leave, but she needed answers first.

Anya left the barn full of determination. She charged through the back door and slammed directly into Yvan. He cursed as he half turned into the firebird, feathers and fire pushing through his skin and sucking back again in seconds, leaving him smudged with black ash.

"I'm sorry!" Anya reached to steady him but then pulled her hand back, thinking better of it. He'd already proven that he was prone to bursting into flames. Yvan was taller than she realized, dressed in pants of Eikki's, which barely brushed his ankles.

"It's okay." Yvan sighed. "The bird is quiet again." He pushed a plate of fresh bread at her. "Are you hungry? I baked because there was no food and also to apologize. I was…not polite to you before. I was in shock—I still am—and I'm sorry."

"I'm not hungry, but thanks." Anya didn't know what to make of his apology. She fixed herself another coffee and sat down at the table. Yvan sat opposite her, his strange eyes glowing as he watched her.

When she was unable to take the silence any longer, she asked, "How did you know Ilya?"

"I met him once. How do you know Tuoni when you have no magical training? And how did you have the firebird's egg?"

Anya had a seconds-long internal debate before she told him about Eikki's death, her unexpected breakfast guest, and the "gifts" he had given her.

Yvan rubbed at his stubbled chin. "Then that settles it. I'm going to try to cross into Skazki tonight. Maybe the firebird will be strong enough to cross through without the help of a gatekeeper. The longer I stay here, the more danger you're in."

"Right, because your brother wants to murder you—*and* me for fun?"

Yvan frowned at her tone. "Exactly. Your lack of training will get us both killed. I'll probably die trying to protect you. If I'm gone, Vasilli might leave you alone. That way, you can continue to drink the rest of your life away. Then, when the gates break open and the end of the world arrives, you won't notice or care."

Anya pulled back as if he'd slapped her. "What's your problem? You know nothing about my life."

"I know enough. The only stores in the cellar are vodka, which tells me that if you don't die soon from alcohol poisoning, you'll kill yourself, leaving no point in stocking food for the future." Yvan carried on relentlessly. "What you don't understand is that as much as you want to deny it, you do have magic in your blood, and if it decides to rise when you're drunk, you could hurt yourself and anybody around you. Right now, that includes me."

Anya's hand clenched around her mug, the ash-and-blood taste rising in her mouth again the angrier she became. "Look, asshole, I haven't been storing anything because I've been trying to decide whether or not to sell this place and get out of here—something that's appealing to me more and more. I've been drunk every night for months, and you know what? My "magic" hasn't risen once, so why don't you fuck off back to Skazki. Then you won't have to worry that I'll fry you with my so-called powers." She stormed outside before she really lost it and threw her coffee at him. His brother could come and gut him for all she cared.

Yvan Tsarevich was not naturally a mean-spirited person, but finding out that he'd spent over a century trapped in a firebird's egg pissed him off and confused him even more. Finding out that an untrained shamanitsa was the person who'd woken him—accidentally at that—made everything worse.

Yvan picked up Anya's mug and tipped it over. The coffee that had been steaming minutes before spilled onto the plate beside him in frozen, slushy lumps. He smiled grimly.

Yvan felt a bit guilty for upsetting her, even if it did prove his suspicions. Anya's magic was waking up, whether she wanted it or not. For now, it seemed she had to be angry for it to be released. Yvan didn't want to be a prick to her, but seeing her big green eyes fill with confusion every time she looked at him made him panic inside.

Unintentionally or not, Anya had saved him from the egg's prison, and now he owed her a life debt. He could honor it by getting out of her life as quickly as possible, and Yvan had always tried to be honorable.

The firebird shifted irritably under his skin, making him want to scratch all over. Yvan didn't know what monstrous mistake had happened for them to be stuck sharing the same body or what he could do about it. He needed to find a way to control the firebird, especially with Vasilli surely closing in.

I could just burn my way out through your skin, Prince, and be done with you, the firebird whispered in his mind.

What would that achieve? If you kill me, it could very well kill you too. We're stuck with each other.

This girl could help separate us. She has power. I can feel it radiating through her, even if she cannot.

She is untrained and afraid. Vasilli and the Powers would destroy her in a heartbeat and steal her magic. If we take her with us, she could get us both killed.

Or you could stop upsetting her and make her an ally. You know this family has the power to stand up against Vasilli.

She doesn't know how to use it, and I can't protect her.

Yvan wasn't sure he could even defend himself. If he could get to Skazki, maybe he could find out if any of his friends were still living. Ilya had been dead for generations, which meant most of his friends would be dead too…except Trajan. *Maybe he could help us.*

A sharp prickle of magic danced across his skin. Yvan stilled. He knew that power.

He rushed to the window to see Anya talking to a man he knew far too well. Fear seized him again, and the panicking firebird tore itself free.

4

ANYA HIT THE LOG in front of her, grinning when it split cleanly in two. The ax in her hands and the strength in her shoulders felt like one easy line of burn as she took out her frustration on the woodpile.

Thuck.

Fuck weird firebird men.

Thuck.

She was not a shamanitsa.

Thuck.

She was not—

"Dobryj vecer."

Anya stopped mid-swing and spun to find a man upon a horse. He flashed her a charming smile. He had a thick black beard that had grown out from its manicured state and long black hair tied at the nape of his neck. He slid off the horse, and Anya gripped her ax a little tighter. He was the biggest Russian she had ever seen and smelled unpleasantly of horse sweat, camp smoke, and… blood. Anya took a step back.

"Can I help you?" she asked in a tone that suggested she wasn't interested in helping him at all. Her famous glare didn't seem to work on him.

"I hope so. I'm trying to find my brother," he said.

"Try the village. All sorts of people wash up in a place like this." She gave him a helpful smile and hoped he would go away.

He didn't.

Instead, his black eyes looked her over. Cold pressure—similar to what she'd felt during her conversation with Tuoni—crept through her mind. She shook her head, but the sensation only squeezed tighter. Anya lowered the ax when she meant to grip it tighter. She waited for the man to say something, anything, until her own mouth opened. "I'm about to cook something to eat. Would you like to stay the night?" She rubbed at her forehead. She *had not* just said that. Had she?

"Thank you. I'd appreciate that." He extended his hand to her. "I'm Vasilli."

Run! a voice cried out in her mind, but the cold pressure silenced it, and she grabbed his hand, giving it a friendly shake. Static snapped between their palms, and she let him go with a laugh.

"I'm sorry. I didn't mean to zap you! Static. I'm terrible for it." She smiled and shook her head. "I'm Anya Venäläinen. There's an empty stall in the barn if you want to put your horse away. I think there's a storm coming tonight."

Vasilli laughed—a joyful sound that could have charmed the devil. "There certainly is."

Anya waited until he'd disappeared into the barn before hurrying inside to find Yvan. Now that she wasn't standing in front of Vasilli, a wave of cold sweat swept over her.

"Yvan? Where are you?" she whispered as she searched the house.

A soft cooing came from the fireplace, and then the firebird tumbled out of hiding. In the smoothest transition she'd seen yet, it transformed into Yvan.

"Anya!" He grabbed her shoulders. "That's Vasilli!"

"I know, and I invited him to dinner." She flinched at the horror in his expression. "Yvan, I swear I didn't mean to. It just came out!"

He turned her hands over and studied them. "The firebird can feel Vasilli's compulsion on you. You're not trained to fight it. The best thing you can do is play along. Let's hope that if I remain hidden, he'll grow bored and leave you alone." Yvan squeezed her hands, eyes full of unspoken emotion. Anya's worry mounted. "It's going to be okay, Anya. Keep him entertained, and I'll escape the farm as soon as he's sleeping." He let go, then transformed again and jumped back into the fire.

"I was wondering where you had gone." Vasilli stood in the threshold.

Anya grabbed another log and began to build a wall in front of the firebird. "I wanted to get the fire going. It's going to be freezing tonight."

Vasilli didn't look convinced, and Anya's smile widened until it hurt.

She was so screwed.

+✦+

Anya had never understood why Eikki taught her to be polite to the people who hated her, but now, she was silently sending thanks to him in the afterlife. She managed to keep calm as she and Vasilli ate together before settling by the fire in the sitting room. She regretted getting a bottle of vodka from the cellar, because now, she was torn between drinking out of politeness and wanting to avoid getting drunk enough to tell him about the firebird hiding in the chimney.

"Venäläinen," Vasilli said, rolling the name over his tongue. "A strange name. It means *Russian* in Finnish, doesn't it?"

"Yes." Anya laughed a little. "The Finns who ended up living on the Russian side of the border sometimes took as a surname. It's what my ancestor, Ilya, apparently used to get called because this part of Karelia didn't have many Russians back then. When he settled here, he dropped whatever his Russian name had been and took Venäläinen instead. I don't even know what the old name was."

Stop rambling, Anya. She couldn't help it. The more Vasilli studied her with his glittering black eyes, the more secrets she wanted to tell him.

"Names are funny that way. They can shape us and change our identity," Vasilli said. "They are good things to hide behind."

"Do you think that's what your brother is doing? Hiding under a different name?"

"Perhaps. Though Yvan was always very proud of who he was and the place he came from." Vasilli's lips curled into an unpleasant smirk. "Plus, he would lack the imagination to think of changing it."

"Can I ask why you're trying to find him?" Anya seized the opportunity to get answers out of Vasilli that she had yet to get out of Yvan. She wasn't entirely sure she trusted Yvan much more than Vasilli at this point, and the last thing she wanted was to be in the middle of a family feud. Though Vasilli *was* the one who'd put a compulsion spell on her, not Yvan.

"We had a disagreement many years ago. You know how brothers fight over stupid things."

"No, not really. I'm an only child, though I always liked the idea of having a brother." Anya's parents had been talking about trying for another baby before they died. They had even asked her how she felt about being a big sister. Her father had never hidden his disappointment that she was a girl very well, and he'd been determined to have a boy who could carry on the family name.

"You are better off without them. Trust me. I was the middle son. Dimitri was the eldest. He died a few years ago. The youngest and most favored was Yvan. They were both incredibly disappointing, but family is family, and I need to find him."

"What was the fight about?"

Vasilli smiled. "A woman of all things."

"Oh? Have you asked her if she's seen him?" Anya tried and failed to imagine these two intense men besotted enough over a woman to want to kill each other over her.

"She died long ago."

Anya's brow furrowed. "I'm sorry. It's the worst feeling in the world losing someone you love." It was odd for her to say something so vulnerable, but she didn't need to fake her sincerity.

Vasilli laughed, jarring her. "I didn't love her. She was just the thing we fought over." He looked her over in a way that made her want to shower. "You know, you actually look like someone I did love once. Same winter-white hair, same spring-green eyes." He reached over and brushed a thumb over her cheek.

Anya pasted a smile on her face. "Thank you, I think. She sounds lovely." She pulled gently out of his reach as something deeply female inside of her assessed him as a threat more significant than she'd sensed before. She sipped her vodka, fighting to keep herself in the chair beside him, but she couldn't.

"You know, tomorrow, you really should ask around the village about any newcomers. We get a lot of seasonal workers here." She stood. "There's a small spare room in the barn that you're welcome to use. As for me, I need to get some sleep. You know us farmers—in bed at dusk and up at dawn."

Vasilli took the hint and rose to his feet. In an unexpected gesture, he bowed, took her hand, and kissed it. "Thank you for giving me hospitality tonight, Anya Venäläinen. You would make your ancestors proud."

Anya followed Vasilli through the house to the back door and watched him disappear into the windy, dark night. As quickly as she dared, she shut the door and locked it for the first time in years. Back in the sitting room, she pushed the half-burnt logs out of the way to check if the firebird was still in the fireplace. It ruffled its feathers at her, as if to say it would not be budging.

"Fine, stay in there. I'm done entertaining surly Russians for one day."

⁺⋆⁺

Anya got in the shower and groaned as the hot water warmed her body; she'd felt cold since Vasilli arrived. She tried not to laugh at the absurd day she'd had. She had a firebird *and* a psycho in her house, and she was…in her bathroom with no lock on the door. *Shit.* Anya rinsed off the soap and wrapped a towel around herself, feeling like the dumb girl who was always killed first in a horror movie.

She stepped into her room and was about to drop her towel when she spotted Yvan sitting at the end of her bed. She clutched the towel tighter. "What the hell are you doing in here?"

"I'm making sure Vasilli doesn't climb through your window and murder you. You need to get dressed, and we both need to get out of here before Vasilli returns." In his hands was the heavy stick that Anya kept hidden under her bed.

Anya scoffed. "Don't tell me what to do! Why should I go anywhere with you? Besides, he doesn't seem interested in killing me, only finding you." She pointed to the door. "You said that you would leave as soon as he went to bed. You know where the door is."

Yvan shook his head. "You don't get it. It's too late for that. Vasilli had a compulsion spell on you that not only forced you to welcome him into your home, but also allowed him to feel if what you've been saying was truth or not. He will know you've lied to him, Anya. He's playing with you like a demented cat and bloody mouse. Trust me, he likes to play sick games with his victims. If you stay here, you'll die."

She scowled at him. "Why do you even care?" Yvan had been angry at her since he hatched, and the thought that he would go out of his way to protect her was laughable.

"Because I owe you, that's why. I'm going to keep you alive, whether you like it or not." There was an earnestness in his voice that made Anya pause. His eyes flickered with worry as he looked at her. "Please trust me on this. If you keep thinking he won't kill you for the sake of it, I'll be putting you in a grave earlier than I anticipated, and I don't want to have to bury you."

"Well…I can't get dressed with you in here, can I?"

Yvan's shoulders loosened with visible relief. "Dress warm and pack a bag. I'll be guarding the door."

Anya pulled on a pair of jeans, a gray long-sleeved shirt, and tied her boots tight, but she didn't pack a bag. It didn't matter if he once knew Ilya. Anya didn't know Yvan. She couldn't just abandon her family home and go traipsing into the forest with him.

Yvan was pacing outside the door when she opened it, looking edgy and irritated again with Eikki's old fishing bag slung over his shoulder. "Why haven't you packed?"

"About that… I'm not going to run off in the night with you—"

"Yvan!" Vasilli's voice echoed through the walls. Anya's bones vibrated. "I know you're in there, you coward! I can smell you and that damn bird! Come out, or I will burn this fucking house down."

Anya hurried to the window and peered through the curtains. Vasilli stood in the yard with a burning torch in one hand. The barn was already a flaming mass behind him.

"The animals!" Anya went to the door, but Yvan grabbed her.

"They're already dead. You can't save them, Anya. If you go out there, you die." He pulled her back. "Pack. Now!"

Anya ran back to her bedroom and stuffed jeans and shirts into a backpack. She pulled Eikki's favorite coat on and reached for the pistol and bullets he stored behind it.

"Hurry up!" Yvan shouted as she grabbed Eikki's journals and put them in her pack. "Is there any way out of here besides through the front and back doors?" Yvan steadied her as the house shook again.

"Come out, Yvan, and I might be persuaded to spare that lying whore who's hiding you!" Vasilli called. "Now! Or I will kill her slowly in front of you."

Anya loaded her pistol. "Like hell you will."

"That won't do much good against him." Yvan lowered the barrel. "Is there a way out?"

Anya glared through the window at the burning barn. She was furious now, and still being a little drunk wasn't helping. "The cellar."

Yvan grabbed her hand and pulled her toward the kitchen, down the steps, and into the dark. "Now what?"

Anya took two bottles of vodka off a shelf. One went in her bag, and from the other, she took a long swig. "Now we pull this shelf back and get out of here."

Yvan took the bottle from her. "No more vodka. You are no use to me drunk and scared."

She raised her chin. "The only reason I'm letting you push me around right now is because I *am* drunk."

"You can fight with me later when we both survive." He gestured to the shelf, and they pushed it out of the way to reveal a tunnel.

Anya grabbed an old, dusty flashlight from where it hung on an iron nail. They used a handle on the back of the shelf to pull the secret door shut behind them.

She turned on the flashlight, grateful the batteries still worked. "This way."

Above the surface, Vasilli's power and anger twisted together in his veins.

"Yvan!" he shouted again to no reply.

Focusing his mind, Vasilli raised his huge arms and released his rage. The earth shook as a wave of magic surged forward and buckled the house in half before sending it up in flames.

Vasilli stood watching the house burn. A wolf trotted up and sat down on his heels next to him. Then the sickening sound of bones snapping mingled with the crackling sound of fire, followed by a piercing yowl of pain.

Vasilli looked to the bony man sitting on his haunches where the wolf had just been. "You made it finally. I hope you're in the mood for tracking."

"Are you sure they survived that?" Vischto asked, nodding toward the pile of glowing coals.

Vasilli smiled. "We'll find out soon enough. Yvan has the firebird inside of him. It might have been feeling generous and protected them."

Anya had been a surprise. Vasilli knew a great deal about this particular family and the magic in their blood. It looked like she was the only one left. She seemed to be no threat; he had only touched a little magic coming from her—likely useless remnants of power passed on through her bloodline. She hadn't even suspected it when he bespelled her to invite him inside her house. He was pleased that Ilya's spawn had fallen so far from greatness, and soon, the gates would fall too with only this useless girl left of the gatekeeper bloodline. Watching his enemy's house finally burn had its own kind of satisfaction.

"Let's hope the firebird doesn't immolate itself again like last time—"

Vischto yelped as Vasilli backhanded him, sending him sprawling to the dirt.

"Don't you dare mention it again, or I'll skin you," Vasilli hissed. "I've waited over a hundred years to get this fucking bird and its power. Getting it before anyone else is all that matters now. We will wait until this place is in ashes to see whether it's here or not."

Before the firebird hatched just days ago, Vasilli had been on another job, hunting a magical bloodline that Ladislav needed for gods knew what. When Ladislav sent him a message earlier in the day, requesting that he return to Moscow, Vasilli had to tell him about the firebird's rebirth to get the old prick off his back. Ladislav wanted the firebird far more than any untapped members of magical bloodlines, but Vasilli would never give such power to a fool like him. He just had to play second-best for a little while longer yet.

Vasilli smiled. He would take the firebird's magic for himself and finally eradicate the threat of it and his brother once and for all. No more would he have to worry about the legitimacy of Ilya's vague old prophecies. No more would he have to hide his power from lesser men like Ladislav.

He watched the last of Ilya's line burn…and his smile widened.

5

THE TUNNEL STRETCHED OUT like a black void in front of them. Anya had expected it to be filled with spiders and broken beams, but it was the opposite: dry and well maintained. When she found the tunnel when she was only little, Eikki had been furious.

"They were built in the war and are dangerous from disuse. Never go in there," Eikki had cautioned her. He told her all about cave-ins to frighten her into never daring it again. But it seemed they weren't dangerous at all. He had obviously been taking care of them. She bit her lip, trying not to scream at the discovery of yet another secret Eikki had hidden from her.

Dirt and rock broke free and rained down on them. Yvan grabbed her, using his body to shield her until the shaking stopped.

"What was that?" she asked from underneath his shoulder.

"Vasilli just destroyed your house."

Anya put a hand against the tunnel wall, trying to stay upright. Her whole world had been destroyed in a just few days. *What am I going to do?*

Yvan's warm hand rested on her shoulder. "Anya, I'm sorry, but we have to keep going."

"I don't want your pity." She shoved his hand away. "You brought this nightmare to my door."

Anya hurried down the tunnel. She needed to get outside so she could breathe and think. Where did the tunnel even lead? She didn't want to consider that they might find a cave-in farther along. She began to feel light-headed, the panic taking over her. Anya broke into a run.

"Anya!" Yvan called, but she could barely hear him over the roaring in her ears. "Wait! You need to be—"

Something struck her hard in the head, and then she was falling down into the yawning darkness.

When Anya came back into consciousness, it was to the smell of ozone and wild-fire. She swayed a few inches one way and then the other before realizing that Yvan was carrying her up a flight of wooden stairs.

"Think I bumped my head," she murmured.

"You hit a low beam at a considerable speed. I did try to stop you from running off." Yvan was smiling a little—the first she'd seen him give—and Anya had to admit that he had nice lips.

You must've hit your head harder than you thought.

"Put me down. I'll be fine," she said, feeling more awkward by the second.

Yvan lowered her onto a dusty old couch and shone the light around. They were in a hunting cabin with a small camp bed and a wooden chest in the far corner of the room. A table, chair, small cupboard, and the couch she sat on took up the rest of the space.

It came back to her in a rush—Eikki's hunting cabin. She hadn't thought about it in years…or was it another memory that he'd taken from her like Tuoni said? If that was the case, what was it about the cabin that was so dangerous for her to know?

"We should be able to hide here for the night. Vasilli will be weak after destroying your house and won't have the magic to track us," Yvan said. He turned up some matches and lit an oil lamp.

Anya rubbed at her throbbing skull. "Are you sure that he won't just assume we're dead?"

"He's not stupid, Anya. He'll check the rubble, or his minions will, and they'll learn soon enough that we escaped. Our only hope is that we can get a few days head start."

"You mean *you*. There is no *we*."

"There is. Vasilli knows you lied to him and that you were sheltering me. He won't stop until you're dead too. If I can sense your magic, he certainly would have and will be able to follow it no matter where you run."

Anya put her head in her hands. She had no farm, no animals. All she had was the cabin she was hiding in. "But if I leave, who will shut the gates? I need to learn how to close them."

"We can figure that out once we get away from Vasilli. I know people in Skazki who will be able to help you. You won't have restrictions on your power there, as you have in Mir. Even an untrained shamanitsa in Skazki is better than none at all." Yvan sat down opposite her. "Eikki really never taught you anything about this world?"

Anya shook her head. "No. Though I don't think he could have foreseen a firebird hatching on my farm and a maniac setting it on fire. What the hell did you do to Vasilli? Why does he hate you so much?"

"I don't want to talk about—"

"I don't care. You want me to trust you? I need to know you're better than him."

Yvan's eyes flashed with fire. "I *am* better than him! Don't glare at me like that. I was trying to get away from you to prevent this very thing from happening. Vasilli got here early, and for that, I'm sorry, Anya. You have to come with me, or you'll be dead within a day. Trust is earned, and I can earn yours with time."

Defeat washed over her. "Okay. I'll go with you." Anya tried not to cry as she gave in to the inevitable. "It's settled." Now that she had no home, she couldn't just live like a crazy person in the forest. If Yvan really did have friends that could help her with her magic, there was no way she could turn that down.

Yvan took out one of the bottles of vodka and drank a large mouthful. He offered it to her, and she had a few sips. "You really want to know what happened with Vasilli?"

"Of course I do. It must have been pretty bad for him to want to kill you."

Yvan shook his head. "It's not really me he wants. It's the firebird. I can tell you the story, but I don't know if you'll believe me."

Anya barked a laugh. "In the past two days, I've had breakfast with Tuoni, learned that my grandfather was a shaman and keeper of a gate to Skazki, *and* watched you turn into a firebird. I'm reevaluating everything I believe right now."

"I suppose you have a point." Yvan bent down to put small logs in the fireplace. Fire leaped out of his hand and ignited the dry wood. He looked at his fingers in amazement for a few moments before sitting down in front of the flames. "It's been a long day for both of us, so I'll try to keep it short."

Anya had a large mouthful of vodka before offering the bottle back to him. "Shot of courage?"

"I'm a very famous prince. I don't need a shot of vodka to give me courage." But then he took it from her with a grin. "I'm going to need at least three shots."

"Look at that—you *can* smile."

"Do you want to hear this story or not?" Yvan drank from the bottle before setting it down between them. "My father was Tsar Vyslav of a country in Skazki, and he was immensely proud of his apple orchard. So much so that when he found out that the firebird—a legendary creature who hadn't been seen in our lands for centuries—was stealing them, he decided he would capture it and hold it prisoner for its crimes.

"He told my brothers, Vasilli and Dimitri, that whoever caught the firebird for him would get half the kingdom straight away and be made the other half's official heir upon his death. I begged to try too, but he wouldn't let me. My brothers set out to watch for the firebird, but boredom struck, and Vasilli and Dimitri ended up getting drunk and missed out on capturing the bird. This was before Vasilli really knew the power the firebird could give him. That and he was always reluctant to do anything Vyslav asked him.

"My father was so angry at them that he offered me the same deal. As the youngest of sons, I was about as far away from the throne as you can imagine, so of course, I jumped at the opportunity.

"I hid in the orchard that night and saw the firebird when it came on its next visit. I startled it and managed to get a feather before it took off out of the kingdom. Because I'd only managed to capture a single feather and my brothers had failed on their own, my father sent all of us after it. Dimitri and Vasilli always liked to work together on their schemes, so I snuck around them while they camped at crossroads and went my own way."

"Wait, I think I remember Eikki telling me this story," Anya said.

"No doubt the incorrect version that made the rounds afterward."

"The brothers set out, and they came across a large marker stone—the crossroads you mentioned," Anya said, ignoring his tone. "It said whoever took the first road would know hunger and cold; on the second road, his horse would die; and on the third road, they would die, but their horse would live."

Yvan snorted, but Anya continued. "The two older brothers didn't know which to take, so they camped by the road until they could come to a decision.

The youngest brother—you, apparently—crept past as your brothers slept. After taking the second road, a wolf ate your horse."

Yvan grinned. "Close enough. The wolf was Koschey the Deathless. You know who he is, right?"

Anya searched her memory. "I think he's like a trickster god who can't die?"

"That pretty much sums him up. He's a shape-shifter and, for the most part, a total prick. But every now and again, he's okay." Yvan grinned again. "To make amends for eating my horse, he offered to carry me on his back to the kingdom next to ours. Koschey had heard the gossip on the wind and knew the firebird had taken a liking to a golden cage in the neighboring tsardom. He was up for some mischief, so he offered to help me steal it."

Anya gripped the bottle of vodka between them. "What could possibly go wrong with that plan?"

"A lot, as it turned out. The golden cage the firebird liked to roost in was enchanted. When I unlocked the door and tried to steal it, alarms sounded throughout the whole kingdom. We were caught and dragged before the tsar."

Yvan stretched out on his side and propped his head up with his hand. "The tsar planned to execute me unless I acquired for him his heart's desire. That turned out to be a horse with a golden mane that one of the neighboring tsars had refused to sell him for years. Koschey was more than happy to participate in another attempt at thievery. When we crept into the stables to steal the horse, he warned me not to touch its golden bridle. I thought he was playing a trick on me, but as soon as I touched the bridle, an enchantment activated, and I was frozen to the spot."

"And you got caught again." Anya laughed.

Yvan nodded once. "Koschey bailed as my lookout, and I was dragged before the tsar. Inspired by my last failed attempt, I offered to get this tsar his heart's desire, which happened to be a princess from the next tsardom over. Koschey found me afterward and was especially keen to accompany me this time because he loved beautiful women."

"Helena?" Anya guessed. She was never a pro-princess child, preferring the other tales Eikki told of magicians and forest gods, but she recalled the princess from this particular story.

"Yes, Helena." Yvan hesitated, his face lost in memory. "She was stunning. Sweet and compliant."

Anya snorted. "Sounds boring to me."

"I suppose she was, but she was raised to be the perfect princess."

"I bet. Let's skip the mushy bits. I think I remember what happened next anyway. You captured Helena, but then you fell in love with her, and when the time came to hand her over, you couldn't do it. So Koschey shape-shifted into her form, and you exchanged him for the golden-maned horse instead. That must've made for an interesting wedding night." Anya imagined the lovely princess transforming into a hysterical trickster god in the tsar's bed and smirked.

Yvan nodded. "Koschey escaped the angry tsar that night and traveled with us to the previous tsardom. He'd had such a laugh tricking the last tsar that he offered to do it again. While Helena waited in the forest nearby, I offered Koschey in the form of the golden-maned horse in exchange for the firebird. The tsar was so overjoyed to finally have the horse that he fell for the ruse.

"Helena, the firebird, and I made it back to the safety of my own lands upon the golden-maned horse. Later, Koschey met us at the spot where he'd eaten my horse, declaring his debts to me repaid. Personally, I think he came along to make some mischief rather than to make amends. Helena and I camped there that night, making plans for when we presented our prizes to my father the next day. That night was the first time I died."

Yvan had another drink of vodka, his face clouding over. "I don't know how they knew where I was, though I assume Vasilli did a tracking spell. He and Dimitri came into the camp that night and killed me in my sleep. I still don't think Dimitri wanted to do it, but he was always afraid of Vasilli and followed wherever he led. We all knew Vasilli was different. He had a dark soul and a cruel nature, but I never thought he had it in him to kill his own brother. I was wrong."

Anya wrapped her arms around herself, suddenly cold. "Eikki said they chopped you up and threw you in the river. They threatened Helena into making her say that they, not you, had retrieved the horse, firebird, and her. Your father bought the tale, believing that you had died on your adventures as they said, and Vasilli got half the kingdom."

Yvan sat up, shaking his head. "No, that's where the other stories get it wrong. Dimitri was to get half the kingdom. Vasilli wanted only Helena and the firebird. Koschey found my body and caught the crows that were about to eat my dead flesh. The mother crow pleaded for her children, and he agreed to let them live if she went and stole from the gods the Water of Death, which made my body whole again, and the Water of Life, which revived me." Yvan's brow wrinkled. "I don't remember any of this. Koschey told me after, and honestly, I don't know whether it was the truth or not…

"After I woke, Koschey took me to my family, where Vasilli was about to wed Helena. My brothers were to be punished by my father for their betrayal, but they managed to escape through Vasilli's tricks. He'd always had talents with dark magic, and my father never tried to stop Vasilli from using them. Maybe if he had, he would have turned out differently."

"And then you married Helena and lived happily ever after, right?"

"Hardly," Yvan muttered. "Yes, I did marry Helena, and for a time, I thought we were happy. Then one night, about two winters later, I couldn't sleep. I went for a walk to clear my head and spotted Vasilli and two of his minion shape-shifters, Vischtan and Vischto, sneaking into the palace. Vasilli released the firebird from its cage and began the spell that would enable him to steal the bird's magic. I engaged them, and while I was fighting Vischtan, Vasilli killed Helena as the human sacrifice required to make his spell permanent. I tried to stop him from completing the spell, but as I grabbed the firebird, it exploded, and we were both reduced to ashes."

Yvan pushed his hands through his hair. "Now we're stuck together. I think it has to do with the moment of resurrection. When a firebird dies, its ashes are carried on the winds to a sacred temple. The priests make a new egg, and when the time is right, the bird re-hatches once more. My guess is that my ashes were carried on the winds as well."

"And you and the firebird were made into one egg," Anya finished in awe. "That's why you keep changing."

Yvan nodded. "Yes. The bird is argumentative as ever."

"Wait, this is a fairy tale that's been passed down for years." Anya looked Yvan over. "How *old* are you?"

He shrugged. "I don't know."

"If you knew Ilya, that's at least a hundred years. After all this time, Vasilli still wants the firebird's magic? No wonder he's so impatient. That would be a long time to wait to get revenge on the person who foiled your plans."

Yvan's face crinkled with unease, and Anya felt guilty for making him relive it all. To have died and come back to life twice would be rough on any person. Morning light trickled through the trees outside, and she yawned. "Thanks for telling me. I guess I'm not the only one confused about the last few days."

"It was your magic that sparked the egg to hatch, Anya. We can't dismiss that as mere coincidence."

"Tuoni said it was destiny. But you know what? Destiny can wait. We can figure it out tomorrow. Go to sleep. I'll take the couch."

"You should sleep too." Yvan got up and stumbled over to the small camp bed. "We have another long night ahead of us tomorrow."

Anya scowled. "Can't wait." She stoked the fire high again before curling up underneath her warm coat. She traced the Sami figures—little animals and trees—that had been stitched into the outside of it like she had when she was little. Eikki rarely wore the coat, but it was her favorite.

"Anya?" Yvan murmured. "Do you trust me now?"

"Maybe a little bit. Not enough to go to sleep before you."

Yvan let out a sound that may have been a laugh. "Good enough."

Anya tucked her hand under the coat and rubbed her palm where Tuoni had shocked her. She could still feel the burn under her skin. The itch of it was getting stronger. The vodka had numbed it, but now that she was sobering up, it was coming back with a vengeance.

Anya glanced across at Yvan. It had taken him minutes to fall asleep. Now, he was shaking violently as nightmares claimed him. *What horrors are you dreaming about, Prince?*

She got up, picked the faded blanket off the end of the camp bed, and folded it over him. Her fingertips brushed against him, and images flooded her mind: Helena covered in blood, a palace burning to the ground, Vasilli's dark eyes following her everywhere. Anya stumbled backward, shaking so forcefully she thought she would collapse. Yvan, on the other hand, had settled into a peaceful sleep.

"What trouble are you going to get me into next, Yvan Tsarevich?" Anya whispered.

6

ANYA WOKE MIDAFTERNOON TO the sun streaming through the cabin's dirty windows and a cloudy head. She pulled on her coat and boots and stepped outside, then brushed aside a damp lock of hair and tried to steady her breathing. Her mouth tasted weird again, like ashes and tears and blood, the same as when Tuoni had grabbed her. Maybe Yvan would know what he did to her. Except the shape-shifting prince was nowhere to be seen.

"Yvan?" Her stomach clenched, wondering if he had left without her. *Why do you even care? He's the one who brought Vasilli to your farm.*

Despite that, Yvan was growing on her, and it was a rare thing for her to like anyone. Suffering made people interesting, and after his story last night, there was no doubt that Yvan had suffered.

Now that Anya was outside, lost childhood memories of the hunting cabin hit her hard: Eikki teaching her to glean the forest for berries and mushrooms, and how to track foxes and rabbits. The blood-and-ash taste in her mouth resurfaced, but she barely noticed as grief pierced her low in the gut. She wished he were there with her, if only for a moment.

Anya followed an overgrown path down to a small, clean stream and drank handfuls of water to rinse the taste from her mouth. She washed her face and tried her best to re-braid her hair without a comb or mirror. As she wandered back to the cabin, she spotted Yvan coming through the trees with freshly caught trout dangling in one hand and fishing gear in the other.

"I thought you might have left for Skazki without me," Anya said, trying to disguise the relief in her voice.

"Sorry to disappoint. I was hungry." Yvan shifted on his feet. "I also went back to the house to see if I could spot Vasilli."

"The animals?"

Yvan shook his head. "I'm sorry, Anya. He really left nothing, and there was no sign of him. He could be hiding out until tonight when he'll check the house ruins for our bodies."

Anya sat on the porch steps, the wind knocked out of her. Yvan went inside, then came out with his fish on a frying pan and set about making a fire underneath the trees.

"Do you want to talk about it?" he asked, not looking up from what he was doing.

"The animals were the only things I cared about in the world." Anya brushed a tear off her cheek before he could see it. "It might sound dumb to you, but they were the only things that got me out of bed some days. They were my friends, even before Eikki died."

"I understand that. I always found animals easier than people too." Yvan gave her an understanding smile. "Except for the firebird. He was always an asshole."

Anya let out a soft laugh and sniffed. "Yeah, I can imagine." She seized the opportunity to change the subject. "Hey, do you think the firebird would be able to tell if Tuoni left some kind of magic on me? He said I had been made to forget things and that it was time I 'woke up.' Since then, it's like I keep having all of these memories appear. I get a weird taste in my mouth."

Yvan stoked the building fire. "What kind of memories?"

"Well, last night, I dreamed about a dog I brought back to life after it got hit by a car." She felt stupid saying so. "Then about a boy teasing me. I gave him a rash. I know it sounds weird, but both things felt too real to be a dream." She didn't mention the man who smelled like autumn, whose smile filled her chest with warmth. This time in her dreams, he hadn't been arguing with Eikki but talking with her. How could she forget someone like him?

Yvan set the frying pan over the fire, washed his hands in a bucket of water, and walked over to her. "Give me the hand Tuoni touched."

His eyes glowed, and Anya figured the firebird was in a helpful mood. She gave Yvan her right hand, and he rested his large palm on the back of it as he turned it over.

After a quiet moment, Yvan nodded. "The firebird says he can feel the God of the Dead's power still residing here," he said in a metallic timbre. He rested fingertips on her forehead. "And here. He also says there's another shaman's magic resting on your mind. Maybe Eikki really did take some of your memories away." Yvan stepped back.

"I don't understand why, though. We were always so close." Anya looked down at her palm. "At least, I thought we were."

"Maybe he didn't want you to know about this world." Yvan got the fish out of the pan and onto plates. He offered her one. "As soon as the sun goes down, we run, so eat."

Anya took the plate from him. "Has anyone ever told you that you're incredibly bossy?"

"Yes." Yvan sat back down in front of the fire, and Anya rolled her eyes when he wasn't looking. When she was finished with her fish, he snatched her plate and set it aside. "Good, now I have something to show you—a sauna and washhouse. Do you remember them?"

Anya did, but the images were fuzzy in her mind's eye. "Maybe a little? Eikki came here by himself more than me. Why? Do you feel like a sauna?"

"I do actually, but I don't think it's going to be possible. I'll show you why."

Anya followed Yvan through the trees. Snatches of memory of the sauna that sat next to where the stream deepened into a pool drifted back to her. A small log shack came into view through the trees, and Anya smiled, remembering Eikki showing her how to make *vasta* out of birch branches.

"The shamans of my people often used *banyas* to perform their magic," Yvan said as they walked around the building. "And Norsemen used saunas to invoke visions."

"That was probably due to dehydration. As you can see, there is no evidence of magic here." Anya pulled open the sauna door with a flourish.

Yvan cleared his throat. "You were saying?"

The benches had been pulled out and replaced with a small stool and a table. Dried herbs hung from the roof, and paintings and symbols covered the blackened walls. Blood rushed to Anya's head as the smell of the herbs hit her. The signs on the walls pulsed, and her vision swam. The blood-and-ash taste hit her mouth again, and she gagged.

Eikki really had been a shaman... A part of Anya hadn't really believed it. Still, there was evidence of her grandfather's secret life right in front of her.

Yvan put his hand under her elbow to steady her as she bent over and tried to get air back into her body.

"Oh god, Yvan." She spit the ashy tears from her mouth. "He lied to me so goddamn much."

"I'm sure he had his reasons. Come on. I haven't looked inside, but there could be things in there that could help us in Skazki." He squeezed her shoulder as she straightened.

They went inside, and Anya sat down on the small stool, feeling out of place and confused as she stared at the walls and objects around her.

Yvan examined the paintings and curious objects around the room. Anya toyed with some smooth stones she found in a clay bowl on the table in front of her. She picked one up and dropped it. A ripple passed through the tabletop and rustled the leaves outside the sauna door.

Yvan froze and looked outside. "Did you feel that?"

There's no way that was me. Anya picked up the stone again and dropped it against the pine table. The same ripple occurred but stronger. Yvan turned to look at her.

"What? I didn't do anything," she said.

Yvan strode across the room and snatched the stone off the table. "These are rune stones! You don't drop these against a surface unless you're casting them. Who knows what you've just attracted to us!"

"How was I supposed to know?" Anya stood up, getting in his face. "You know what? Take whatever you want. I don't even care."

Anya was almost back at the cabin when Yvan came up behind her and grabbed her by the shoulder, stopping her in place.

"I'm sorry for snapping at you. You should take these rune stones with you." Yvan held a small leather bag out to her with a soft expression on his face. "They are precious, and I can feel their power. We'll just have to hope they don't generate a bigger aura once we get to Skazki, because they might act as a beacon for Vasilli."

"Why don't we leave them here? It would save us any additional trouble." Anya's hand burned as she took the bag.

He shook his head. "Rune stones are rare, useful, and important. They could help us in Skazki."

"Only if we can hide them."

"It's worth the risk. Trust me on—" Yvan choked on his words as the firebird's feathers pushed through him. His bones cracked, and he screamed. He collapsed to the ground as his arms became wings. Flames licked up his back, burning his clothes. Yvan's form fought between bird and man.

"Yvan? Are you—"

I want to see the world. I want to be free. The voice touched Anya's mind. It was old and angry with a terrifying metallic timbre.

"Stop it! You're going to hurt him. Find a compromise or let him be." Not knowing what else to do, she grabbed the bucket of water and doused him with it.

Yvan started to seize. Anya rolled him onto his side to keep his airways clear. Colors danced along his skin, flashing back and forth. Finally, with a cry that seemed ripped from his throat, the colors settled. Inked on Yvan's entire torso was the firebird—in living tattoo form, made of bright oranges, reds, and yellows. Its wings stretched up over his shoulders and cascaded down his back. To Anya's horror, the firebird winked at her. Yvan groaned and coughed.

Anya leaned over him. "Are you all right?"

"No." His voice was hoarse. "What happened?"

"The firebird tried to get free of you. I—well, I yelled at it to leave you alone," Anya said, feeling like an idiot.

"It listened to you?"

"It said it wanted to see the world, so I guess that's why—" She gestured at his fresh tattoo.

Yvan ran a hand across his front. "It feels so bizarre." He took her hand before she could protest and ran her fingers along the wings on his arms and down his chest. It felt incredibly soft, just like a feather.

Anya became aware of how naked Yvan was. She reddened and pulled her hand away. Yvan's eyes had changed from gold and red to a deep blue that was almost black in the fading afternoon light. His expression shifted from her to something over her right shoulder.

"Vischto," he growled.

Anya whipped her head around just in time to see the wolf disappear into the forest. "Who?"

"One of Vasilli's minions. We need to go." Yvan climbed to his feet and hurried into the cabin.

Anya followed him. "Are you sure? It looked like a normal wolf to me." She grabbed her bag and tried to keep her eyes focused on his neck up as he dug about in Eikki's things and pulled on some more clothes.

"I'd never forget the skin-changer who almost tore my throat out," Yvan spat. Anya went to grab the pistol, but he stopped her. "Don't bother. Guns don't work in Skazki." He took Eikki's fishing knife from a shelf of gear and passed it to her. "If Vischto gets anywhere near you, don't hesitate to use it."

"You're freaking me out."

"Good. You should fear them, because they *will* kill you."

"You suck at comforting people." Anya took the knife, made sure it was secure in its leather scabbard, and shoved it into her coat pocket next to the bag of rune stones.

"No time for comforting." Yvan looked outside the cabin before waving at her. "Come on. He's gone for the moment. Probably to find Vasilli."

"Awesome," Anya said. The darkening forest suddenly looked a lot more menacing than it ever had before.

Yvan startled her by taking her hand. "Don't get lost and try to keep up."

Anya ran blindly behind Yvan as they bolted through the forest. She held tightly to him, putting her other hand out in front of her to knock away branches, hoping they wouldn't crash straight into a blackberry bush. He must've been able to see in the dark, because he never tripped, while Anya struggled to keep up. It didn't help that his legs were twice as long as hers.

She panted. "Where are we going?"

"Right now, we're getting as far away from the cabin as we can before Vasilli gets there. As for passing over into Skazki, I'll know the crossing when I see it. The main gateway is on the farm's land, but the weak place between the worlds is farther into the forest."

Sweat froze on the back of her neck as a howl echoed through the trees. Anya quickened her pace, running close to Yvan.

"Don't overexert yourself," he told her. "Vischto has to wait for Vasilli before he can do anything. If Vasilli were close, we would know. If we cross into Skazki tonight, hopefully we can get a head start while they're still searching the forest for us."

"That is if he doesn't catch us first."

"Don't even joke about that. We were lucky last time. I doubt it'll happen again."

"Thanks for reminding me." Anya skidded to a stop as vibrations rolled through the air and static snapped over her skin. "What was that?"

"You can feel the power in the air. This part of the forest shifts as it connects with Skazki. That's what you can feel. I've never been able to pass through the gates without a gatekeeper's help. The firebird's power should change that."

Anya reached for Tuoni's summary of gatekeeping, but her brain had turned to mush since that conversation. "I assumed only a gatekeeper could open the passages."

"A proper opening, yes. A strong magic user like Vasilli can sometimes cheat by finding weak spots in the border. Think of them as back doors that only the powerful can use. Even then, the pathways can be fickle and refuse them without a gatekeeper."

Yvan helped her over a fallen tree. Another howl shook the trees, close enough for Anya's breath to catch.

"*Yebat*! He's getting closer." Yvan dragged her into a run. "Vischto will try to delay us from entering so Vasilli can catch up to us. If he attacks, be ready to fight back."

Anya slowed at the sight of a blue ribbon of shimmering light snaking through the trees. "What's that?"

"That's our way in." Yvan headed toward the light.

"It looks like an aurora," Anya said when they stopped in front of it. Her skin prickled with goose bumps as the light pulled at something deep inside of her.

Vischto jumped through the trees, landing only meters from them, and let out a blood-chilling growl of warning. Yvan burst into flames as the firebird took charge of him and launched itself through the aurora.

"Thanks for waiting for me!" Anya shouted. She rushed to follow him through, but the wall of blue light held, resisting her.

Vischto growled again as he moved in on her.

"Let me in, damn it!" Anya cursed the aurora with all her might. Sharp, hot energy streaked through her arm and zapped the wall, burning a hole through it like it were paper. Anya tumbled through the wall of light, and it sealed with a snap behind her. She hung suspended in the air for a heart-stopping second before slamming onto the forest floor.

Yvan helped her to her feet. "I thought it wasn't going to let you through." He picked the leaves out of her hair, his face pale.

"It wasn't. I think I hurt it." Anya brushed off her pants and hissed at the fresh scrapes on her palms. There was no sign of the power that had burned through the aurora, only blood and dirt.

"Look," said Yvan.

On the other side of the sheer blue light, Vischto threw himself against the wall and howled in frustration.

"We need to keep moving. He'll report back to Vasilli, and he'll know exactly where we crossed over. We need to throw him off our trail as much as we can."

Anya rubbed at her arms, her skin tingling all over as if she were covered in ants.

Yvan's hand found hers in the dark. "Don't get lost." Anya just caught the flash of his smile through the gloom.

"Don't lead me into any ditches." Her fingers tightened around his, and she followed Yvan into the darkness without looking back.

Look through the autumn glade to where two exhausted travelers sleep. A fox pads through the leaf litter toward them. He is curious; humans are rarely seen in this part of the forest.

The fox sniffs the young woman. She smells strongly of Mir. Colors swirl around her. There is strong, raw magic inside of her, but it is buried deep.

He sniffs the man but smells a bird. Curious, he sniffs closer to the opening of the man's shirt. A fiery-colored bird leaps out and pecks the fox's nose with its sharp beak.

"Gods!" The fox jumps out of harm's way.

Be gone. The menacing voice touches the fox's mind.

With his tail standing on end, the fox turns and bolts from the glade. A firebird has returned to Skazki! He knows who would pay for such a shocking revelation.

See the old bent crone who stands in front of a bubbling cauldron in a cottage made of rotting bones. She stirs her soup and hums with pleasure. It had been a long time since a child wandered through to Skazki and across her path. It had been a petulant creature. She cackled with delight that the Mir people had stopped telling their children the old stories about her. Hopefully, more unsuspecting children would come, and she would grow fat on their dreams before getting fat on their flesh.

Baba Yaga could never have such fun in Mir. Too many rules there, too many people watching her. Plus, she had dreamed of fire, the bloodline, and the game starting again at last. She left Mir and came home to Skazki, needing to be where her magic was most potent to see if she could discover the time of the war's beginning and what destiny would push into her path. The coming battles deserved a celebration and a forbidden meal.

"Hey, Old Iron Teeth!" The voice carries up and through the window. "I have information for you! Let down your house, and I shall share it with you."

Baba Yaga continues to stir before finally relenting. The cabin wobbles as it lowers its chicken legs and comes to rest on the ground. The shiny black nose of a fox appears around her door before the rest of it creeps inside and across the wooden floor to where she's cooking.

A pile of children's clothes lay discarded in the corner of the room. The fox holds back a shudder. There are some things even foxes know better than to eat.

"What is it you wish to tell me?" Baba Yaga asks. "Be warned, little fox, if you lie to me, I shall eat another of your cubs."

"There are Mir visitors in the forest." His words come out all at once.

"And?"

"There is a woman. She has power." The fox licks his lips as the old witch stops stirring. "And there's a man from Skazki with her. He is split in two."

Baba Yaga turns to face the fox. "How is he split in two?"

"He shares his body with a firebird."

Baba Yaga stares at him, and he feels her moving in his mind, searching for the lie in his tale. He thinks of the bird, how it bit his nose.

She laughs hysterically. Her carefully laid plans are coming to fruition. "Finally! He has been reborn, and he brings the girl to me at last."

"My debt?" asks the fox, hopeful.

"It has been paid. Now leave, before I change my mind and add you to my stew."

The fox doesn't need to be asked twice. He bolts through the door just as it snaps shut, taking part of his tail.

Baba Yaga shuffles over to her loom and checks through her weave again. Her gnarled hand strokes the lid of a wooden crate, sensing the power of the game board inside of it.

"Yes…" She grins with iron teeth. "It is almost time for it to begin again."

7

BACK IN THE GLADE, Anya was caught in a nightmare she couldn't break out of. Like the one in which she revived the dog, it didn't feel like a dream, but rather a memory.

An army was camped in a snowy forest around her. The smell of iron and horse sweat lingered in the air. Warriors stamped their feet to keep them warm as they watched her expectantly. She turned to where a small black goat was waiting on a blood-stained altar, its liquid pupils wide from whatever drug it had been given.

Anya pulled a knife from her belt. The handle was carved like a snarling bear. She cut the goat's throat. Its hot blood warmed her frozen fingers as she smeared it on her rune stones.

"Shamanitsa…" The deep voice rumbled behind her, a warning to hurry up.

Anya ignored the tsar. He was impatient, and she didn't care. He'd raped her every night since he captured her. His lust was his biggest weakness. She'd promised herself that she would watch him die.

Anya took a deep breath and began to sing a song with no words. Power echoed around her as she clutched her runes. Finally, she let them go, and they scattered over the forest floor. She stared at them, reading what they wanted to tell her.

"Victory," she said. For the army, of course. He was destined to die, and she bit the inside of her cheek to keep from laughing in his stupid, doomed face.

"Thank you. You are free to go, but if you've lied to me, I'll kill you," said the tsar.

Anya nodded, keeping her eyes downcast as she collected her rune stones and headed into the forest. As she reached the top of a cliff, she paused to look at the clashing armies. Tuoni appeared beside her, wearing black leather armor with a sword on his back. He smiled down at the bloodshed below them.

"Kill him for me. As painfully as possible. I want him alive enough to feel as the crows pluck out his eyes," Anya said, her bloody hands clenched in rage.

Tuoni put his hands on her shoulders and turned her to face his merciless, beautiful black eyes. "Remember this, Anya. Dreams have power. They show old truths you are too blind to see on waking. They uncover memories that are lost in the blood flowing through your veins. Remember her magic. Remember what she did when you wake." Then, with a smile, he pushed her off the cliff.

Anya jerked awake and desperately sucked air back into her tight lungs. She was drenched in sweat, and her shoulders ached where Tuoni had pushed her. The smell of burning flesh collected in her nostrils, and her brain hummed the tune of the song with no words.

"What's happening to me?" Anya whispered, staring at her dirty hands. She started as Yvan came crashing through the trees and pulled her to her feet.

"We have to go," he said. "What just happened?"

"I don't know." She wiped the sweat from her face. "I—I was dreaming."

"You were projecting your magic everywhere is what you were doing. It's pulsing off you." Yvan tossed his bag over his shoulder. "Dreams have power in Skazki, and yours just sent out a magical beacon saying, 'Here I am!' Gods know what it's going to attract."

"What does it matter who it attracts? There's no way Vasilli could've caught up to us yet." Still, she was unable to keep the tremble out of her voice.

"You don't understand," muttered Yvan.

Anya stopped moving. "Then explain it to me."

Yvan grabbed her arm and forced her to jog alongside him. "Skazki isn't like the human world. It has fewer rules. There are immortal old gods, monsters, and magic users that control the otherworlds. We call them Powers. Those that live here in Skazki have allegiance to one Power or another to gain favor and protection. When someone with magic enters the realm of a Power, they know, and they will try to make you obligated to them. It's a lifetime bond if you owe them a favor. "

"Oh, come on! They wouldn't be interested in me because of a nightmare! If they want anyone, it's you and that fucking bird."

"You have magic! You just don't know how to use it, which is worse, because they could mold you any way they like."

"They can go to hell. If I can't use it, no one can."

"Grow up, Anya! Think. These beings are so powerful they could make you believe anything. One spell, one cantrip, and you would be their willing slave. You have no way to protect yourself, as you proved with Vasilli and his compulsion. You are defenseless against them, and I won't be able to stop them from taking you."

"It's not like I can help it, Yvan."

"I know. That's what makes this even worse."

Anya turned her attention to the endless forest surrounding them. "Do you even know where we are?"

"As soon as we find a road or a village, I'll figure it out. Skazki tends to change when you aren't paying attention, just like the rest of the otherworlds. I'm focusing on getting us as far away from here as possible. Thanks to your dreaming, who knows what will be following us."

"I'm not going to apologize for something I had no control over, but I'm sorry for yelling at you. Angry is better than scared, and I'm terrified." She bit her lip. Admitting fear wasn't really her thing.

The hardness in his eyes shifted, and he loosened his grip on her hand. "I know. I am too. I'll try my best to get you through this, but you're going to have to be patient with me. I've got no experience dealing with untrained shamanitsas."

Anya smiled up at him. "Me neither, but I'll try not to fight you too much. Deal?"

"Deal."

Anya followed Yvan until they stumbled through the trees and onto a dirt road. There wasn't a single house or person in sight.

"Which way?" Anya asked. Her ribs ached from trying to keep up with Yvan's long strides.

He stood rigidly, staring at something past her left shoulder.

The hair on her neck rose. "Should I turn around?"

Yvan shook his head. "Get behind me."

Anya did as she was told, turning back around as a rider on horseback moved from the edge of the forest and stopped in the middle of the road.

He had a shaggy, long beard and hair the color of dried blood. He was filthy and matted with gore, his red eyes glowing in the fading light. In one hand, he held a long, crude spear covered in old blood and rune marks. His horse was massive and the same bloody red.

"The Red Rider," Anya whispered. Her hand tightened on the back of Yvan's shirt. She remembered enough of her fairy tales to know who the three riders served.

"We have no quarrel with you or your mistress," Yvan told the Red Rider.

"You have been summoned nonetheless, Yvan Tsarevich. She doesn't like to be kept waiting. I've been instructed to take you by force if necessary."

Yvan bowed. "Lead the way. We would be honored to meet your mistress."

The Red Rider steered his horse in the opposite direction. "Don't even think of running. The Black Rider is waiting in the woods, and he isn't as polite as I am."

Yvan tightened his grip on her hand. "Anya, please tell me you know who Baba Yaga is…"

She did. And she had no intention of ending up in a soup pot.

Anya had never seen an uglier house than Baba Yaga's. It was made entirely of moldy bones in the same interlocking design as a log cabin. A thorny garden grew as high as the fence, and skulls, bleached white by the sun, capped each fence post. Two enormous, scaly chicken legs covered in lichen extended from either side of the house.

Anya snorted in amusement and disgust. Yvan had turned an attractive shade of gray. *Be brave, Anya. Or be angry.*

Anya pushed her fear down and hung on to her anger. "Come on. Let's get this over with."

"You should be more afraid," Yvan muttered.

Anya *was* afraid, but she wasn't going to show it. In her experience, anger was always better when dealing with bullies. "Why would I be afraid of a shitty old house and a gnarly old witch?" she shouted.

"By all means, do come in, loud-mouthed girl!" Baba Yaga—Anya presumed—called out.

The gate and the door to the house opened for them. The smell of rotting meat reached Anya's nose. She gagged.

"No, thanks!" Anya called. She leaned close to Yvan. "I know the stories. If we go in there, we won't ever come out."

Baba Yaga appeared in the garden. She looked Anya up and down with her beady black eyes. She had messy gray hair, a wrinkled face, and an iron-toothed smile. Cold pressure built behind Anya's eyes, and she fought the sensation, imagining the firebird's heat melting it away. After dealing with Tuoni and Vasilli, she wasn't about to let another compulsion spell take hold of her. The old witch shuddered once, and the pressure let up.

"Ah, Yanka." Baba Yaga cackled. "I thought you were still dead. I should have known it was you in my vision."

"Sorry to disappoint, but my name isn't Yanka," Anya said. *Yanka.* The name sounded so familiar, but Anya couldn't place it.

Baba Yaga made a frustrated growl in the back of her throat. "A bloodline brat. I heard Yanka had crossed into Mir and bred with a filthy human to have Ilya. And here's her weak spawn, in the company of Vyslav's son and a firebird."

Yvan opened his mouth, but Baba Yaga held up her hand to stop him. "Don't even bother to deny it. I can smell the bird's magic from here."

"What do you want?" Anya asked, but her mind was elsewhere, churning over the name of Ilya's mother. She groped for a memory of Eikki telling her about Yanka but came up with nothing. She rubbed at her head as her mind shuddered—Tuoni's magic tearing away another piece of whatever spell Eikki had put on her. *Yanka.* She could feel the answer close, but something stopped her from reaching it.

"Yanka's blood, what makes you think you can give me what I want?" Baba Yaga clucked her tongue to get Anya's attention. Her eyes sparkled. "As it happens, I have something *you* want."

"I doubt it."

"You've no idea who you are and what powers you have. I could tell you. I could show you."

"And for what price?" said Yvan.

"It's cheap for knowledge of her magic and destiny." Baba Yaga offered a gray smile. "I want Yanka's rune stones."

"I'd rather not know who I am. Ignorance seems like bliss," Anya lied, hoping the witch would get bored and let them go.

"How about you give us the directions we need?" Yvan said. "As beautiful as it is, we would like to leave your forest."

The witch scratched her nose. "For the stones?"

"It's a different thing we bargain for, and it has a different cost."

"What do you offer?" Baba Yaga still hadn't taken her hungry eyes off Anya, and it was starting to annoy her. She remembered what Yvan had said about the Powers wanting to mold and use her and moved closer to him.

"What about a feather from the firebird?" Yvan suggested. "You know what it could be used for, and you know I'll be overpaying for a simple thing such as directions."

The old witch rubbed her hands together. "Where do wish to go so desperately, Yvan Tsarevich?"

"We want a straight passage through Skazki. One that doesn't involve getting waylaid by any of the Powers."

Baba Yaga grunted. "I don't know all the ways of the otherworlds, but I have an item in my possession that does. You better make it a good feather, princeling." She turned and went back into the cottage.

"I hope you know what you're doing. I don't think we can trust her," Anya whispered.

"Not even for a second."

Anya turned as he began to remove his clothes so he wouldn't destroy them.

Yvan whimpered as the transformation began, and Anya turned back around just as he burst into flames. The firebird launched up into the sky, letting out a joyful cry. It danced on the wind like a kite of fire.

"I never would've believed it if I hadn't seen it." Baba Yaga stood outside the cottage again, craning her neck to watch the firebird fly. "Two creatures sharing the same body is a tricky business, especially when one is more powerful than the other. The firebird will get frustrated and try to take over. And people will come after it, wanting its magic, including Yvan's idiot brother. You're better off letting him leave on his own and staying here as my pupil."

Anya raised a brow. "Is that what Yanka did?"

The old witch spat on the ground. "She should have. She had too much power in her that she didn't know what to do with. I heard she blew herself up." She grunted. "The magic isn't as strong in Mir. It was a waste for her to go there. Yanka never had enough sense to know what was good for her."

"Perhaps the magic here got to be too much for her. Maybe in Mir, she could live a normal life."

"Why would you want to be normal when you could be extraordinary? I suppose that explains why you're such an untrained, bad-mannered nuisance." Baba Yaga's expression grew sly. "You will have the same problem. The magic will start to consume you if you don't learn how to control it. You look like her, you know. Yanka. The same eyes, same white hair. Same magic, I wonder?" She stretched a bony hand out to touch her, but Anya sidestepped her.

"I don't think so. I only learned I have magic a few days ago."

"They probably didn't want to train you in case you were another bad apple. You should stay here and let me protect you. Let the prince go. He doesn't have the power to look after you."

Anya blinked as the cold moved behind her eyes again. She slammed it back as it started to grow, popping her ears. "Stop it. Stay out of my head." She clutched at the pressure in her skull. "Yvan didn't leave me behind, and I won't leave him."

The old witch's smirk disappeared. "He's already clouding your judgment, foolish child. I can't believe Yanka produced such an idiot."

The cold vanished from her head, and Anya inhaled a painful breath.

The firebird cried out in warning and landed softly on the ground beside her. It ruffled its feathers and pulled one out, then screeched as Yvan pushed his way back through. Feathers melted back into his skin until he was naked and shaking, clutching the feather in his hand.

Anya handed him back his clothes, and he dragged them on slowly, as if his body were sore from the transformation. The firebird tattoo settled back into place, and Yvan held out the feather to Baba Yaga. She handed him a round leather bag the size of a small plate.

"Cast *Raidho* from Yanka's runes on the drum, ask it for guidance, and it will show you the way." Baba Yaga tucked the feather away in a fold in her robes.

"There's a village not far from here. I suggest you get there as quickly as possible. If you are still in my forest come nightfall, I'll get my Black Rider to kill you." Baba Yaga looked Anya over one more time, then spat a ball of phlegm into the dirt. "Until our next meeting, shamanitsa."

Vasilli had searched the forest around the farm for Yvan without success until his minions called to him, confirming that both he and the girl lived, no doubt with the firebird's help. In his haste to get to Skazki, his horse had tripped over a rotting log and broke its leg. He'd liked his horse, but he still cut its throat and continued on foot.

Vischto trotted beside him. "There is a camp up ahead with a horse you can use."

"Good. Make a distraction." Vasilli stopped outside the camp to watch and wait. When he saw the Red Rider cooking by a fire, he grinned. A horse and chance to piss off Baba Yaga at the same time? The day was looking better and better.

Vischto's howl broke through the still night, and Vasilli rushed into the camp, grabbed the rider's spear, and drove it deep into his gullet.

"Not again," the rider mumbled, then sagged into the dirt.

"Give the witch my thanks." Vasilli twisted the spear in farther.

The rider choked on a bloody laugh. "You'll be able to thank her yourself."

Vasilli ignored the threat, pulled himself into the saddle, and disappeared into the night. He could sense the firebird's magic, and if he hurried, he would have them by dawn.

8

ANYA'S LUNGS BURNED AS she struggled to keep up with Yvan. They hadn't stopped running since they were dismissed by Baba Yaga, and the only thing that kept Anya going was the fear of meeting the Black Rider.

Yvan slowed his pace. "I can't believe she didn't strike you down for being so disrespectful to her. This is so much worse than I thought."

"Why? She seemed helpful enough when we offered her something she wanted."

Yvan shook his head. "That was too easy, Anya. She offered to teach you, which means she wants you."

"If she's so powerful, why didn't she just take me?"

"Because she wants you to join her of your own volition. Something's coming that she wants allies for, and with Yanka as the matriarch of your bloodline, she knows what your potential could be. Fuck, I forgot all about Yanka. Ilya had fallen out with her, but never explained why." Yvan pushed his hands through his hair with a hiss of frustration. "I've been asleep too long. I don't know what's happening in the worlds."

"Okay, so we find out. Let's worry about it when we get to safety." Anya hurried him along. She didn't need him freaking out. He was the only one of them who knew how to navigate Skazki.

Now that they were away from her, the meeting with Baba Yaga seemed surreal. How many shocks could somebody take in one week?

Anya shook her head and followed Yvan until he paused in the middle of a dirt road.

"Look there. We're close." He pointed to the village in the distance.

"Let's hope they have hot water." Anya laughed in relief, refusing to turn back to the dark, watchful forest behind her.

The village was quiet as they approached a tavern and hurried inside. It was filled with drinkers who reminded Anya of the old men from home. They were rough farmers and tradesmen, their overalls and heavy woolen jackets stained with dirt. The room had a smoky air of filthiness, a product of the small clay pipes they were smoking.

"We need a room," Yvan said to a man behind the bar. "We also need hot food if there's any left."

"Where are you coming from?" He eyed them suspiciously.

"Through the forest. We've had a rough few nights. Please, a room."

The barman looked like he would argue, but likely saw the look in Yvan's eyes and thought better of it. He grunted. "Up the stairs, first door on the right. There's a washhouse if your woman needs it."

Anya made a little snort of disgust at the comment before disguising it as a cough. The barman yelled at a petite woman, who hustled them upstairs and let them into a small room with one bed, a pine chair, and a fireplace.

"I'll bring food up shortly." She handed Anya a towel, then curtsied to Yvan before hurrying from the room.

Yvan sat down on the edge of the bed. "I wonder if there's a seamstress in town. We're going to need clothes and some supplies. With the village being this close to Baba Yaga's forest, it might be better supplied than most places since travelers and merchants likely stay here on their way to petition her."

Anya nodded vaguely. She needed some space. Her head was filled with snarls, and she hadn't been able to think straight since her dream in the forest. A dream that had left her shoulders feeling bruised. She could still feel the pressure of Tuoni's palms before he pushed her.

How could anyone do that in a dream? Unless it wasn't just a dream, which was the most frightening thought of all.

"I'm going for a bath. I need to think some of this through alone."

Yvan gave her a serious look. "Be careful."

Anya found the small washroom downstairs and scrubbed herself raw. In the past months, when she'd daydreamed about traveling, she thought of exotic, warm countries, not fairy-tale worlds full of new responsibilities and deranged villains. Her mind hadn't caught up with the reality of where she was, and if she let it, it would send her hiding under the nearest bed.

God, I need a drink. When she was finally clean and dry, she made her way to the bar.

The men in the room stared at her, but Anya had been graced with plenty of disapproving glances in the past, so she gave them one back before sitting down at the bar.

"Vodka," she said to the barman.

"I don't think your husband—"

"What my husband thinks is no concern of yours. Vodka."

With a shrug, the barman handed her a large cup and left her be. The vodka was almost as strong as the stuff she brewed herself, and soon, the warm mist began to roll in. It calmed the incessant tingling under her skin that she'd felt since coming to Skazki, and it was like she could breathe again.

It didn't take long for a man with a bushy beard to sit down beside her. *No matter what world you're in, men are all the same.*

"What makes you think you can drink in this place, woman?"

"Because there's nowhere else to drink," Anya said. She gave the barman a meaningful look, and he refilled her drink without argument.

"It's going to be cold tonight," the drunk mused. "How about I keep you warm?" He reached out a grubby hand to touch her shoulder, but Anya grabbed it and crushed his fingers.

"Back off," she snapped. Heat rushed through her hand, and the drunk yelped in surprise. He pulled away from her, then flexed his fingers and stared at her wide-eyed. Where she had grabbed him was now bright red like her touch had burned his skin.

Had she really done that?

"Witch," the drunk hissed.

He made another clumsy grab for her. Anya aimed a kick between his legs, but her boot caught the edge of the seat instead, unbalancing the man and sending him backward with a crash. A roar of laughter rose from the other drinkers as the man, red-faced and angry, struggled to his feet.

"You're going to regret that." He raised a hand to hit her, but someone grabbed his arm from behind. As he turned, Yvan punched him—hard.

"You don't hit women, especially not mine," Yvan said, his voice like ice.

The man slumped to the floor, blood pouring out of his mouth and staining the floor red.

The bar fell silent. Yvan grabbed Anya around her waist to steady her, picked up her bag, and walked her back to their room.

"Yvan, I…I think I burned him."

He helped her sit down at the end of the bed. She leaned down and made a feeble attempt to pull her boots off.

"Whatever you think you did to him was nothing compared to the damage he could've done to you. You could've been hurt, Anya. Why don't you ever think?" He knelt to help her untie her boots.

"He started it."

"Doesn't matter. You can't draw attention to yourself in these places. The people that live here are mortal and subject to the will of the Powers. When Vasilli comes after us, he'll hear whispers of the two strangers who came to town and caused trouble." Yvan clenched his hands into fists, and Anya placed her own hand over them.

"I'm sorry, Yvan. I was upset, and I wanted a drink and…"

Yvan moved his hands from hers. "I know. Maybe try to rest for a while. I'll keep the first watch."

Anya lay down and tried to get comfortable, but her mind refused to rest even though her body ached from exhaustion. Yvan dozed off in the chair near the fire, so she went through her bag and took out one of Eikki's journals.

Like the others Anya had looked through, it was filled with scraps of paper, strange symbols, and small pictograms. There were sketches and occasional paragraphs in his tight, neat handwriting. Not every page was dated, but one in particular caught her eye—her thirteenth birthday.

Today would have been the first day of Anya's initiation. It is hard not to start her training. She is already so talented, but she is too much like Yanka. She has darkness in her since her parent's death, and I worry that nothing will temper her if she learns her power. If I knew how strong Anya would grow, it would be different, but Zosi looked into her future, and she saw blood and fear and power. I can't let this happen to her, not after all she has already been through. And so, I will take the memories from her to stop it from happening. It is the right thing to do. I love her too much to lose her now.

Anya slammed the journal cover closed, startling Yvan awake.

He shifted in his chair and rubbed at his face. "What is it?"

"Baba Yaga was right. Eikki didn't want to train me because I'm too much like Yanka."

"Why would he think that?"

"It says it here." She pointed at the journal. "I was too much like her. He also mentions some woman called Zosi, but I don't remember her." Anya opened the book again to point out the paragraph she'd just read.

Yvan scanned the lines, his frown deepening as he did. "It is possible to take memories away, but only some are skilled enough to do it. He must've trusted this Zosi to allow her to evaluate you. If Eikki was anything like Ilya, he would've been reluctant to share things that were too personal." He scratched at his chin. "Back then, there wouldn't have been many who were still alive who knew Yanka."

"But why would it matter if I was like Yanka? What the hell did she do to make them fear her so much? I can't even remember what I did to make Eikki go to Zosi. It's just another thing I feel like I should know that's missing."

"Yanka's history is sketchy at best. She was a Power here in Skazki, and her battles with Baba Yaga were known from one side of Skazki to the other. Ilya stayed out of any wars between Powers, even though he was probably asked more than once to ally with them. He was determined that his family be neutral. It's possible Eikki didn't want another war and thought you might start one if you came completely into your power."

Anya brought her knees up to her chest, trying to breathe and ease the ache inside of her. Eikki had been afraid of her? She couldn't remember anything she could have done to upset him. What other memories had he taken from her?

"How did Tuoni know about the memory spell? He did something to break it, Yvan, because I felt it... I'm *still* feeling it every time I get a memory back. What if I did something really horrible, and it's better that I don't know?"

Yvan sat down beside her and rested a hand on her back. "I don't know much more than you about what's going on, but I'm going to take you to someone who might. His name is Trajan. He's an old friend of mine, someone who also knew Ilya. It's possible that he knew Eikki too. He's going to be able to help us."

"Yvan, you've been asleep in that egg for over a hundred years. He's going to be dead, not helpful."

"Trajan doesn't age like the rest of us. If he's in Skazki, I know where to find him. We will get to the bottom of this, Anya. I promise." He brushed the hair from her face. "Hey, look at me. I've only known you a few days, but I know for sure that you aren't evil or malicious. A pain in my ass, sure, but not evil. I doubt there will be any memory that comes back that you can't handle."

Anya managed a smile. "Thanks. You're a pain in my ass too, but you're okay."

"Stop reading this for tonight and try to sleep." He closed the journal and put it on her bag, then moved back to his chair.

Anya stretched out in the bed, hoping that for one night, the dreams would leave her alone.

Yvan stayed up and watched as Anya tossed and turned in her sleep, debating whether he should wake her. Anya was certainly dreaming again, but she wasn't producing a magical beacon, thank the gods. She was already attracting too much trouble, but leaving her to fend for herself was unthinkable.

Yvan was going to need help protecting her, and with any luck, he would find Trajan soon. He paced the room, considering his options. On the other hand, he didn't know if bringing another person into their mess would be a good idea.

They will hunt her mercilessly once her potential is known, the firebird whispered through his mind. *Whatever your misgivings, you will need help.*

Let me out, and I will cry tears of pearls to pay for her protection if it comes to that.

Why are you so concerned about her well-being?

It was her touch that woke us from our long slumber, her power that broke our prison. That's not a debt quickly repaid. Besides, you will not leave her. You are too honorable for that, Yvan Tsarevich. Remember, what affects you also affects me. You are becoming too fond of her already.

Yvan didn't reply but looked over at Anya's tangled mass of fair hair. Maybe the bird was right. It stretched itself underneath Yvan's skin, impatient and waiting to be let free. Yvan shut his eyes and braced himself for the pain.

9

A NYA WOKE AT DAWN and looked blearily around the room. Her head pounded when she tried to sit up, so she sagged back down with a groan. After a few minutes the door opened, and Yvan appeared carrying a tray of food.

"Good morning." He placed the tray on the edge of the bed. Anya grunted in reply. "Here, drink this. You'll feel better." He waved a small cup of black coffee under her nose.

Anya sat up, resting her back against the wall. The coffee seared her mouth and throat before flooding her stomach with warmth. "God, that's hot," she said, screwing up her face.

"It will give you an appetite." Yvan smiled as he drank his own.

"You look terrible. Didn't you sleep at all?"

"A wooden chair isn't the most comfortable thing to sleep on."

"You could've pushed me over the other side of the bed."

Yvan shrugged his big shoulders. "It would've been inappropriate. A gentleman would never presume to fall asleep beside a lady without her permission."

Anya grinned. "Ah, those princely manners are coming through. I'm hardly a lady, Yvan."

"True, but I *am* a gentleman. Eat something. I've found a seamstress in town. We need to get some supplies, including clothes to blend in and gear to camp. It's at least two days' walk between here and Trajan's place."

"Yay, more camping."

"You'll get used to it."

Anya really doubted it, but the alternative was waiting around for Vasilli to catch them, so camping it was.

Outside, the predawn morning was chilly and damp. Yvan led the way to the goods store on the other side of the village. The seamstress was waiting for them with two more cups of steaming coffee.

She narrowed her black eyes. "It isn't often we get strangers visiting." Her round, creased face looked grim wrapped in a gray scarf.

"We're just passing through. Thank you for opening so early for us." Yvan gave her a charming smile Anya had never seen before.

"Call me Unä," the woman said. She looked Anya over and grunted. "You clearly need another woman's guiding hand, child. You come with Unä. She will look after you." She linked her arm around Anya's and led her through the store. Yvan made to follow, but Unä held up a hand. "You stay. Women's business."

"Fine. I'll get my own gear, but we don't have time to dawdle." He shot Anya a meaningful look.

"We know, hero," Unä muttered. She had a matriarchal type of authority about her that Anya didn't dare disobey. Unä placed her hands on her generous hips. "Now, where are you going, and what will you need?"

"I'm not sure exactly. We're traveling to visit a friend, and it's shaping up to be more dangerous than I thought." First Vasilli and now Baba Yaga, she didn't know who would jump out next.

"Heroes." Unä rolled her eyes. "They always seem to find a woman to drag along with them. They need us. For the brains." She tapped Anya's temple to emphasize her point. "You'll need as much as you can carry, which means four shirts, two pants, two vests, two boots, one light coat. You have a winter coat on you, and it is very fine indeed." She ran her weathered fingers through the fur of Eikki's coat collar. "You need one brush and one balm, but first you need a haircut."

She was right. It had been a long time since it'd been cut and hung almost to Anya's waist.

"You sit." She pointed, and Anya sat on the wooden stool. From one of the folds of her apron, Unä produced a pair of scissors and a small comb, and proceeded to cut Anya's hair. "You need a weapon too. All women need a weapon."

"I've got a knife."

Unä stopped cutting. "Show me."

Anya hunted around in her bag and produced her knife. Unä took it from her and flipped it over a few times in her hand with dexterity. If Anya tried that, she would've sliced her hands to pieces.

"Mir rubbish," Unä muttered, and before Anya could stop her, she threw it at one of the hardwood poles supporting the roof. The knife blade snapped under the impact, breaking off at the handle.

"Like I said, it's Mir rubbish! You need a proper weapon."

"So it would seem," said Anya as she looked at the broken knife pieces.

Unä resumed cutting and chatting. She braided Anya's hair and made her promise to take better care of it, then showed her to a mirror.

Anya barely recognized herself. She looked at her reflection mostly with indifference, but detected a spark of something akin to delight too.

"Now clothes."

Unä provided clothes that fit perfectly to Anya's shape. She wore a soft, maroon cotton shirt with fine black embroidery around its collar and bell sleeves. A dark brown vest went over the top and was buttoned tightly but not uncomfortably. She also wore dark brown pants that were snug along the curves of her legs, and boots made of reindeer leather and fur.

They gathered up the last of Anya's Mir clothes and tossed them into the fire. Anya picked up all the hair from the floor and threw it in too. It was strangely both terrifying and liberating to watch her old life be done away with.

There was something familiar about Unä, but Anya couldn't put her finger on it. She reminded her of the grandmothers in the village, who used to cross themselves whenever Anya walked past.

"Come, let's find the hero," said Unä.

Anya wasn't the only one who had gone through a radical transformation. Dressed in clothes that fit with his hair combed and ordered, Yvan looked like he could be the imposing prince of legend. His eyes swept over her, and a small smile appeared on his face.

"You look like you belong here."

"I see you have organized yourself without my help, hero. That is good. I could not have been bothered."

Yvan handed Unä a small leather pouch. "I'm no hero."

"So you say, but you have the look of one." Unä tipped the bag into her hand, and pearls flooded her soft palm. "This seems to be a lot for what you've taken. Was there something else you wanted?"

"Your silence. People may come looking for us, and we were never here. Understand?" Yvan smiled.

Unä rolled her eyes. "Heroes! So dramatic. It will be done."

"We have to go. We've got a long day and night ahead of us," he said, then held the door open for Anya.

Anya shoved her new knife down the side of her boot. "Thank you for all of your help," she said to Unä.

The old woman looked Yvan over with a warning glare. "You watch that girl. There is more to her than you can imagine."

"I will," Yvan promised, and Anya couldn't help but smile. It had been a long time since she'd had a friend.

As they cleared the village and ducked into the forest beyond it, Anya asked, "Where did you get those pearls to pay for all these clothes?"

Yvan scanned around the woods with wary eyes. "The firebird."

Anya screwed up her face. "Did he lay them?"

"No. Don't you know any of the old stories? Firebird tears turn into pearls. While you were sleeping last night, I transformed, and when I went back to being myself, there they were."

"What? Like you just cried a whole bunch, and there were pearls?"

"Yes."

"Huh. Well, I suppose that's probably more comfortable than laying them."

Yvan's mouth twitched. Anya would win the grumpy bastard over yet.

Unä hummed as she walked back through the store to where she'd cut Anya's hair. The girl had been wise to burn it, but one perfect platinum strand remained in the groove of the wooden floorboards.

Unä bent down, picked the strand up with her fingertips, and cackled with glee. She pulled a small black box from her apron and placed the hair on the satin lining within. When it was tucked safely in the folds of her clothes, she did a bandy-legged dance, her glamour melting away until she was Baba Yaga once more.

She'd placed a charm on the knife, so when thrown, it would always fly true. On the bottom of the boots, she carved the sign of protection so Anya wouldn't fall when running. And she had placed a tracking spell on both. She wanted to know precisely where the brat went.

Baba Yaga stepped through the back door of the shop and headed for the forest. She would be keeping her inner eye close on Yanka's blood. She needed Anya to return to her of her own free will, and there was time yet to wait her out.

Just as she stepped into the trees, she felt Vasilli's power cross over her borders. Just what she needed. Baba Yaga climbed into her enchanted pestle and mortar and flew swiftly through the forest, determined to get back to her cottage and make life miserable for the bastard.

Vasilli had been lost in the cursed forest for days. He sat on the large red horse with his two wolves running behind him, their heads down and wary of their master's mood. The horse seemed intent on fighting him every step of the way. Vasilli had given up, and now the horse was finding its way home.

The bone cottage came into view at nightfall on the fourth day. The old witch was already standing beside her gate, picking the grime out from under her fingernails with a sliver of bone.

"Baba Yaga. So this is your doing?" Vasilli called as he rode nearer.

"This is my forest, Vasilli. I know everything that goes on in it, even if you're arrogant enough to think you can cross through my lands without me noticing." Her black eyes flashed with menace. "The forest thinks for itself. Perhaps it didn't want to let you go straight away. I believe that horse belongs to me too."

"And has the forest produced anything of interest lately?" Vasilli worked to make his tone almost friendly. He didn't have the power to take on Baba Yaga. Not yet.

"Nothing worth mentioning. Why? Have you lost something?"

"Indeed, I have. Two very good friends of mine have gone astray, and I wish to find them."

Baba Yaga looked up at him and rolled her eyes. "*Byk der'mo*, Vasilli. I know who you seek, and I know they are not good friends of yours. It must be hard to have lost your brother again, especially now that he's with Ilya's blood."

"What business is that of yours, witch?"

Baba Yaga shrugged her bony shoulders. "None, but I'm not the one who is in danger from them. They came seeking help, and being full of stomach and generous of nature, I gave it to them."

Vasilli gripped the leather reins tighter. "Tell me what you gave them, Baba Yaga."

"Nothing of much value." Baba Yaga returned her attention to her nails. "Just directions."

"Where to?"

"Let's just say I gave them bad directions." She flashed her iron smile. "I'll tell you which way they went for a trade."

"What do you want?"

"I want my damn horse back! My rider told me what happened, and I'm not impressed that you stole from me on my land." Baba Yaga threw down the bone. Power rushed from her, and Vasilli relented, dismounting and pushing the horse away. It wandered into the yard and nuzzled the old witch.

"Fine. Which way?" he asked.

Baba Yaga's eyes lingered on the deep cuts in the horse's flesh where Vasilli had cut it to perform his dark magic. "They went east," she said through gritted iron teeth. "You had best hurry, Vasilli, before they fulfill Ilya's prophecy, heh?"

"Ilya was a stupid, raving farmer. I don't give a fuck about anything he said."

"I think you do. You've been hunting that firebird long enough." She stepped into the doorway of her house. "I hope it burns you up until your skin melts and you scream for mercy."

"One day, Baba Yaga, I'm going to kill you."

"You keep dreaming, little wolf. I know what blood flows in your veins, and if she couldn't kill me, you certainly have no chance." She clapped her hands, and the house rose on its chicken legs, high enough to drown out Vasilli's curses.

10

TWO DAYS LATER, ANYA was sick of the rain, no longer able to appreciate how beautiful it made the forest look. She was also tired, damp, cold, and over Yvan's melancholy company. He became more serious with every step they took. She had headaches from her constant nightmares and the shakes from not having any alcohol in days. If it wasn't nightmares, it was dreams of the past she lost. The man with strange eyes and autumn scent haunted her every time she shut her eyes. He was like a puzzle her mind kept trying to work out without coming up with a satisfying answer.

Yvan walked ahead of her with his hood over his head, likely deep in his own thoughts and memories.

"Are you lost?" Anya asked for the third time that day. "I thought you said your friend's house was only a few days away."

"I'm not lost," Yvan said, his temper barely restrained. "We're close. I know it. Things change in a period of a hundred years. In Skazki, things can change daily if they want to."

The only good thing that had happened was that Vasilli had not caught up to them by some miracle. Yvan had insisted on them splitting guard shifts every night to keep watch for Vischto and Vischtan. Instead of celebrating their absence, Yvan became more worried with each passing day.

"It's not right. Vasilli wasn't that far behind us," he'd kept saying, until Anya threw one of Eikki's journals at him and told him to count his blessings.

Now Anya was soaked to the skin and about to suggest they find somewhere dry to camp when Yvan let out a shout of triumph.

"Anya, quickly! I've found it."

Anya failed to see what he was so excited about. Beside the road was an oval block of slate. She flicked water from her hood. "It looks like every other rock we've walked past."

"No, this is it. Come on." He took her hand. "We're almost there."

There was barely a track through the woods, and night was falling fast, but Yvan managed to follow it, and Anya managed to keep her mouth shut and not provoke him.

The track widened, and there in front of them, hidden deep in the forest, was a house built of dark timber. Time had covered it with a light green moss. It was almost invisible as it blended into the shape of the mountain behind it.

"Well done, Yvan. Let's hope he's not dead."

"He'll be here," Yvan replied with an odd smile. "He can be temperamental, so please try to behave."

Anya gave him a mock salute but said nothing, and Yvan knocked on the carved wooden door. No answer. He knocked again. Still no answer.

"It's raining so heavily he probably can't even hear you," Anya said over the downpour. She stepped forward and beat against the door with her fists before adding a kick for luck. "Hey! Open the damn door!"

Yvan groaned. "You're trying to get me killed, aren't you?"

"If he's a friend of yours, I'm sure he'll understand."

The door opened. The man on the other side was tall and slender with curly, dark hair. His dark eyes widened in surprise as he looked Anya up and down in a way that made heat rush to her half-frozen face.

The stranger bowed and said, "Good evening, Anya. Would you like to come in?" His voice was smoke and honey.

Anya remained in the rain, shocked to hear her name on his lips. The scent of autumn drifted from inside the house—spice and crisp leaves and smoke.

It can't be.

This was the man she'd been dreaming about since Tuoni meddled with her memories.

"Thank the gods you're here." Yvan pushed past her.

"Yvan! This is a night for surprises. Come in. Quickly." He waved them inside. "I didn't think you were ever going to hatch."

"You and me both." Yvan slipped out of his coat.

Anya dripped water and mud over the threshold. "I'm sorry, but who are you, and how do you know my name?" She paused for a beat. "And why have I been dreaming about you?"

"This is Trajan, who I was telling you—wait, what dreams?" Yvan's brow crinkled in confusion. "Trajan, this is Anya. She's Ilya's—"

"I know who she is. There's a guest room upstairs, Anya. Second on the left. Do help herself to the hot water." Trajan's eyes flashed a wine red before going back to brown.

Anya opened her mouth to argue, but Yvan shook his head at her. "Uh, thanks," she murmured, then picked up her bag and headed up the stairs.

Before she was out of earshot, Trajan hissed, "You have ten minutes to tell me what the hell you think you're doing endangering Anya by bringing her into Skazki."

Their murmurings faded as she climbed farther upstairs. Anya didn't have the nerve to eavesdrop. Besides, she was so cold her toes were numb. Still, Anya didn't like being dismissed like a child. It reminded her of when Eikki got visitors. She was always sent away.

But Trajan *was* one of those visitors. Anya was sure of it. She'd been dreaming of him nearly every night. Realizing he was a real person made her question her other nightmares, like the one with the army and the dead goat.

Anya found the spare room and bathroom, then peeled off her wet clothes and boots. As promised, the water was hot when it came out of the taps, and

Anya hurried to wash and dress in dry clothes. Once she was dry and back in the bedroom, she draped her coat over a chair near the fire to dry. When she turned, Trajan was standing in the doorway, observing her.

She gripped her chest. "God, you scared me! Didn't Yvan tell you that we've had Vasilli after us for days? I'm a bit on edge."

"I'm sorry. I thought I'd better come up and show you how to turn on the lights." He reached for the nearest lantern hanging on the wall. He twisted something at its base, and the frosted glass filled with light. Anya got her first proper look at her dream guy. Trajan was dressed in Mir clothes: black jeans, boots, and a button-down shirt the same wine red that his eyes had turned.

Two things struck Anya when her eyes finally reached his face. The first was that, like Tuoni, there was an eerie perfection in Trajan's features. The second was that, in her dreams, she had known him when she was young, and yet he still looked exactly the same, right down to the dark, curling lock of hair that wanted to hang across his forehead.

He had to be a supernatural being. No one looked that good for that long, and Anya's insatiable curiosity wanted to know exactly what he was.

"Yvan has briefly filled me in on your adventures. You have gone through quite the ordeal in the past week. I'm sorry about that." Trajan's voice still sounded smokey, with an accent Anya didn't recognize.

"It's not your fault the God of the Dead decided to ruin my life, strip away a memory spell, and give me a firebird egg." Anya put her hands over her mouth to contain the hysterical laughter that had been threatening to bubble out for days.

"Would you like to come tell me about it?"

"Can you answer one question first? Just so I know I'm not losing my mind?"

Trajan put his hands in his pockets, a curiously human gesture that made Anya relax. "Sure. You can ask me anything you like."

"We've met before, haven't we? Like in real life, not just in dreams."

"Yes. Quite a few times, in fact." Trajan's small smile returned, and he added, "If you come downstairs and have something to eat, I'll be able to prove it."

"Are you trying to bribe me?" asked Anya, smiling back at him before she realized she was doing it.

"It all depends. Is it working?"

"A little. Are you going to hurt Yvan for bringing me here?"

"Eavesdropping is rude."

Anya folded her arms. "So is threatening my only friend."

"I'm not going to hurt Yvan. He's my friend too. I was shocked to see you both on my doorstep, that's all. Eikki would be turning over in his grave if he knew you were here."

"Yeah, well, if he were alive right now, I'd probably kill him myself for not preparing me for any of this." Anya flinched at the bitterness in her voice. She had never, ever spoken badly of Eikki before.

In the last few days, her anger had grown along with her fear. It was a deep, simmering kind of fire in her belly, and she wasn't sure when it was going to explode.

Trajan frowned, his eyes reading something in her face that she hadn't wanted to give away. "Come and eat, Anya. We can talk about Eikki and his reasons for things when you're warm again."

Anya nodded and followed him to the kitchen, where Yvan was waiting. He'd made some soup from what was left of their supplies and set the table for the two of them.

"You're not eating?" Anya asked Trajan. "Yvan's cooking isn't that bad, I swear." Anya shot the firebird prince a wink. He had taken over cooking duties after Anya tried to make him something to eat on their first night.

"I already ate." Trajan poured himself a wine instead. "I want to hear more about your adventures."

So Anya and Yvan told him about their week: the run-in with Tuoni, the firebird egg hatching, running from Vasilli, and Baba Yaga's interest in Anya. It felt so much longer than a week, and she quietly marveled how far they had come.

Yvan got up and cleaned his bowl. "I came here hoping you'd be able to help. I didn't know what else to do." *With her.* Yvan didn't need to say it for Anya to feel it.

"I've already sent for Izrayl and Cerise. Once they arrive, we can get to the bottom of this and make a plan." Trajan, twisted the stem of his glass between his long fingers. "As for what Tuoni did to Anya, we might have to find someone with more magical knowledge to confirm that he's damaged Eikki's memory magic."

"The firebird couldn't sense any harm from whatever Tuoni did. It seems he just broke what was already there."

"And you trust the firebird?"

Yvan nodded, already looking like a weight had been lifted from his shoulders. "Yes. Anya freed us, and it likes her more than it likes me. I'm going to turn in. Sleeping rough with this one complaining the whole time has taken it out of me." He nodded at Anya with a smirk.

She rolled her eyes. "Because your surly company and incessant snoring have been a delight to put up with."

Yvan smiled and lifted his middle finger at her, surprising a laugh out of Trajan.

"When did you learn that?" he asked.

Yvan grinned. "Anya taught it to me after I caught her doing it behind my back. She tried to tell me it meant *thank you*, but I knew better."

Trajan laughed even harder. "Oh, Anya. I've missed you."

Anya's chest filled with warmth. Even though she didn't know how exactly they knew each other, no one had ever missed her before, and it surprised and delighted her.

"So, how did you know Eikki?" she asked Trajan as she cleaned her bowl and cup.

"It's a long, complicated story."

Anya hazarded a guess based on his guarded tone: "One you aren't going to tell me?"

She turned and jumped, almost crashing into him. He was standing only inches from her, and the scent of autumn washed over her. It comforted her, and something buried deep in her psyche told her that was because she was safe with him.

Trajan moved passed her to wash his wine glass. "I'll tell you, but not tonight. It's not only my story to tell, and I don't want to keep you up later than necessary."

"You said you were going to prove that we've met before." There was no way she'd be able to sleep just yet. While the bed upstairs had a powerful allure after days of sleeping on the ground, it wasn't as powerful as the man in front of her. She had been dreaming about him all week, and her curiosity wasn't going to be satisfied until she knew why.

"I am a man of my word," Trajan said, his smile wide enough to make heat curl in her stomach. "Follow me, and I'll show you."

Trajan led the way through the house, then opened the door to a large sitting area. Anya bit back a gasp of delight. Bookshelves lined the walls, and a fire burned in the large, stone fireplace. There were heavy rugs on the floor, and paintings hung on any wall space the bookshelves didn't occupy. It was a real private library. She had never seen anything like it outside of movies.

"Wow, this is beautiful." She loved books but had rarely had time to read in the past months while she ran the farm.

"The real treasure is above the fireplace." Trajan pointed.

Anya walked toward the fire to get a closer look. Hanging in a frame was a crayon drawing obviously done by a very young child. The figure on the left had messy brown hair and held hands with the figure on the right, who had yellow hair and green eyes.

"Did your kid draw this?" Anya asked. She hadn't picked him as the father type, but she'd been wrong before.

Trajan shook his head, a half smile tugging at the corner of his mouth. "You drew it for me when I came to visit. This is proof that we've met."

"And that's why I've been dreaming about you. After Tuoni zapped me, I swear I've dreamed of you every single night." She looked back at the picture, trying to find the lost memory of drawing it. "I was quite a terrible artist, wasn't I? I'm surprised you still have it."

"When a fearless mortal girl draws you a picture, you don't just throw it away."

"Fearless?" She scoffed. "Hardly. I was always afraid when I was a child."

Trajan folded his arms. "Not of me. It was quite a surprise for a little girl to want to be my best friend, even though I was a stranger. You refused to let my hand go."

Anya cringed. "I did? Well, I was afraid of things in the darkness more than people, so I wouldn't have been afraid of you. Why was that a surprise?"

Trajan hesitated, like he was weighing up his reply. "Because I am the thing in the darkness. Every mortal fears my kind. It's deeply ingrained in them—except for you. You held my hand that day, not knowing you were touching a monster."

Anya stared at the man sitting in front of her. He looked like he belonged in a *GQ* shoot, not a moss-covered house in Skazki. "So what kind of monster are you, then? I mean, I've met a death deity, an immortal witch, and a firebird prince. Even I'm meant to have some kind of secret magic. We can all be monsters together."

"You aren't a monster, Anya. If you were, Yvan would have left you to Vasilli."

"Why don't you stop dodging the question and just tell me?"

"Because he's a demon."

Anya spun toward the deep voice. Her jaw fell open as a giant wolf stalked into the room. It had shiny black fur, smelled like rain…and had just spoken.

11

ANYA'S STOMACH CLENCHED AT the sickening cracking and snapping as the wolf changed. When his skin started to melt, she had to look away before she threw up her dinner.

Trajan raised a brow. "Izrayl, couldn't you have done that outside?"

"And miss the look on her face?" Izrayl chuckled as he stretched out his back with a final crack.

Anya looked back to the massive man standing by the fire. He had dark brown skin and black hair that fell to his waist in a braid. He watched her with amber wolf eyes and stood there naked and proud, like it was utterly natural to meet people in such a manner. Anya had to admit that, recently, it had been. She did her best to keep her eyes above his waist, but damn, was he built.

"Cover yourself, beast." Trajan tossed him a blanket off one of the couches. "Anya has had enough surprises this week without seeing your junk hanging everywhere."

Izrayl smirked. "Yes, big brother." He wrapped the blanket around his waist before holding his hands up to the fire. "I was on my way here to tell you about this one walking around loose in Skazki." He jerked his thumb toward Anya. "Her trail is bright red with magic. Anyone could follow her."

"Hello? I have a name. Why were you following me?" She and Yvan had been keeping lookout, and there'd been no sign of a black wolf.

"This time, it was pure accident. I thought my nose was playing tricks on me. I've followed you on and off in Russia, so I knew the scent." Izrayl stretched out on the carpet in front of the fire. "I was coming to see Trajan, and then boom—a nose full of Venäläinen magic. I've been trailing you, making sure nothing followed you and Yvan."

"So what are you, some kind of werewolf?"

Trajan bit back a laugh at Izrayl's horrified face.

"No, I'm *volk krovi*. I could eat a werewolf for breakfast."

"No way! I thought you guys were made up." *Volk krovi,* the wolf blood people, were pure myth—or at least that's what she'd thought. Eikki had told her that they were both shape-shifters and warriors.

"I'm the realest thing you're ever going to meet, sweetheart. What are you doing wandering about Skazki? And why weren't you"—he gave Trajan an accusatory look—"watching over her like you're supposed to?"

Anya turned on Trajan. "What does he mean?"

"Oh, hasn't the thanatos told you about that yet?"

"I was building up to it." Trajan's eyes flashed red.

Izrayl only shrugged. "If we waited for you to tell anyone anything, we would all die of old age."

Anya felt more confused by the second. "What's a thanatos? Is it like a demon?"

Izrayl laughed, and Trajan's glare intensified. "You can tell her this one. I'm going to get some clothes on." He strutted away like he hadn't just dropped two massive bombshells.

Anya turned back to Trajan and went for the more troubling question: "Have you really been watching over me?"

"It's a long story, but the short answer is yes. Since Eikki died, I have been watching over you."

"Well, you did a pretty shit job of it recently."

"I had no idea you'd met with Tuoni. I saw you run from the village, but that night, I couldn't find a trace of what had upset you. I thought I could leave you alone for a few days, and I was wrong." Trajan shook his head. "When I returned, the farm was in ashes, and there was no trace of you. I came back to Skazki and reached out to friends to join me here and help me find you, and then you and Yvan suddenly arrived at my door."

Anya sat down on one of the armchairs. She had felt someone watching her that day after Tuoni's visit, but she'd thought it was her imagination. Not once since Eikki's death had Trajan knocked on the door to give his condolences. She didn't know it then, but she knew it now, and if he had been watching over her that entire time, he had left Anya to grieve on her own.

"I'm going to need the longer version," Anya said finally.

"Yvan should be here for it. It involves him too."

"Okay, then what's a thanatos? Tell me that, at least."

Trajan walked over to a drinks cabinet and poured two vodkas, handing one to Anya before he sat down. "A thanatos is a part of Greek legend. In the stories, we are Death. In reality, we merely provide the service of taking the dead's souls to Elysium or the Underworld. It's why humans get nervous around us. They can feel death."

Anya sipped her drink before asking, "Why aren't you doing that now?"

"Ilya helped me break my bond to my old mistress, Eris. Now, I can take a human form if I can maintain it."

"Your human form…" Anya stretched each word as she mulled them over.

"Yes, I don't naturally look like this. I have to feed to have the power to hold this form."

"Feed on what exactly?" *Please don't say blood. Please don't say blood.*

"Death," Trajan said. Anya didn't know if that was better or worse. "When someone dies, their body releases their life's essence. Thanatos feed on that energy, and when the soul is released from the body, we ferry it to where it needs to go."

Anya took a steadying breath. If she could deal with a shape-shifting firebird prince, she could deal with this. "So Ilya saved you from having to ferry these souls?"

"Basically, yes. I escaped servitude with his help."

"How do you feed now?"

"Hospitals are always good places. When I'm in Skazki, I can usually find a village where someone is dying."

"What happens if you don't feed?"

Trajan shifted uncomfortably in his chair. "I revert to my true form—something I have no intention of doing again. You have nothing to fear from me, Anya. I would never hurt you. I promise."

"I'm not scared of you." She meant it. She didn't have all her memories back yet, but she knew she would find Trajan in them. He felt like a friend, and she needed those right now, no matter how strange their true natures were.

"Oh, Trajan, please tell me you haven't developed a taste for damsels in distress." A stunning woman stood in the doorway on the other side of the room. "You know how tedious they can be." She had a silken voice and rich, cherry-colored hair that matched her lipstick. She was, without a doubt, the most beautiful woman Anya had ever seen.

"This is Cerise," Trajan said as the woman strolled into the room. "She's the other friend I contacted to help me find you and Yvan."

Cerise released a husky chuckle that rolled down Anya's spine. "Looks like you didn't need me after all. So, you're the girl who's had Trajan all tangled up in a panic?"

"That's me," Anya said. "Are you another thanatos or *volk krovi*?" Cerise had the same accent as Trajan and the same unnaturally perfect features.

She laughed even louder and sat down on a couch. "I know I've been traveling the last few days, but a wolf?" Cerise wore a black corset, leather pants, and knee-high boots—the most unlikely traveling ensemble Anya could imagine. "I'm neither, dear."

Trajan got up to pour Cerise a drink. "She just met Izrayl. He decided to change in front of her as an introduction."

"Oh, goodness. No wonder you look so rattled. Izrayl with his dick out would shock anyone." Cerise let out another big, bawdy laugh. "No, darling. I'm a keres. My kind are Greek war spirits that hang around battlefields to take souls to the Underworld."

"Like Valkyries?"

"Those winged women don't drink the blood of the dead. My kind does."

"You drink blood?" Anya swallowed hard. This night was fast going to the top of her list of the weirdest shit ever.

"Yes, but luckily I don't have to chase battlefields anymore to get it." Cerise shrugged as she lit a cigarette. "There are lots of lovely morgue assistants these days who are happy to oblige a lady."

"Well, you learn something new every day." Anya drained her vodka. She had an overwhelming urge to go wake Yvan up so she had one familiar face to ground her. She almost laughed aloud—he, the firebird prince, was now what she considered normal.

Footsteps and masculine grumbles echoed in the hall. Izrayl appeared, and then, as if he'd read her thoughts, Yvan joined him. The prince's clothes were rumpled, and his hair was tousled from the small amount of sleep he'd gotten before their visitors arrived.

"Cerise! Come and kiss me, you red-haired harpy!" Izrayl bellowed, and Cerise all but flew into his arms. She squealed as he picked her up in a massive embrace and kissed both of his cheeks.

"How goes it, old dog?" she asked.

"Still alive." He grinned salaciously at her. "And still young enough to learn some new tricks if you're the one doing the teaching."

"Try it, and I'll neuter you." Cerise tugged on his braid. "You dogs, all you think of is hunting, fighting, and fucking."

"What else is there?" Izrayl growled in the back of his throat and raised an eyebrow at her.

"The cries of men in battle, sword and shield clashing as steel and bronze drink the blood of heroes?" Cerise replied, making Izrayl laugh louder.

"Fucking war spirits. Let's move this party to the kitchen. I'm hungry, and Anya's looking confused." Izrayl set Cerise back on her feet. "If we're going to play story time, I need protein."

Cerise's attention landed on Yvan, and her smile turned atomic. "Who ordered the hot Russian?"

"Stop that," Izrayl said. "You'll make poor Yvan blush."

Yvan gave her a polite bow. "Yvan Tsarevich. It's a pleasure to meet you."

"Cerise." She put her hand in his. "Feel free to kiss it."

Yvan chuckled and did just that. "My lady."

That made Izrayl laugh even louder. "Don't let her fool you."

Cerise shot Yvan a wink before letting Izrayl put an arm around her shoulders and steer her toward the kitchen.

"Your taste in friends is as interesting as ever, Trajan," Yvan said.

"Be careful. She likes to drink men's blood," Anya told him. A small barb of jealousy stung her unexpectedly, but Yvan gave her a smile that vanquished it in an instant.

"I swear... I was asleep for ten minutes, and the house erupts."

"At least it wasn't literally this time."

"I did tell you that I had called for backup," Trajan reminded them. "How are you taking all this, Anya?"

"Oh, fine. Just fine. I'm going to need another few of these, though." She held up her glass of vodka.

"Me too," said Yvan. He nudged Anya's foot with his. "Come on, shamanitsa. It looks like we're going to get caught up on the world tonight, whether we want to or not."

12

IN THE KITCHEN, IZRAYL devoured what was left of the soup Yvan had cooked, and Cerise had another cigarette. Anya sat next to Yvan and offered him what was left of her vodka. He took it and drained it before passing it back. Trajan stood in front of them with his arms folded. His eyes narrowed, then he opened a cupboard and placed a bottle of vodka and an additional glass on the table in front of them.

"Okay, you two, where do you want to start?" asked Izrayl.

Both Trajan and Yvan looked at Anya.

Trajan took a seat on the other side of her. "Ladies first."

"I want to know about Eikki and why you were watching over me when he died."

"Well, I wasn't stalking you," Trajan hurried to explain.

Izrayl grunted. "Close enough. Eikki called on Trajan more than once to keep watch on you. Hell, even I got dragged to Moscow that one time."

"Moscow? What do you mean?" Anya had always thought it was Eikki who'd found her freezing to death in the park. He'd taken her home to the farm, and she never left again. Until now.

"Eikki got a message to Trajan and me. He was freaking out because you'd run away and he had no way of protecting you. And where did we find you? Dying in a park with a group of Darkness operatives closing in." Izrayl drained his soup, then put his bowl down. "Man, that was a fight."

Anya dimly recalled a fight that night, but she'd thought it had been drunks brawling.

"What is the Darkness?" asked Yvan. "I've been asleep a long time, remember? And I have questions of my own about what the Powers have been up to. Baba Yaga was too interested in Anya for my liking."

Izrayl looked between them. "Wait, you guys have already tousled with Baba Yaga?"

Anya wanted more answers but instead found herself updating Cerise and Izrayl on the past week.

Cerise swore. "This is so much worse than I thought, Trajan. You're lucky I owe you a big favor."

"And I'm calling it in."

"Back to the Darkness, please?" Yvan prompted.

"The Guardians of the Dark, they used to call themselves. Now they're simply known as The Darkness," Trajan said. "They're run by an ancient blood sorcerer called Ladislav. Vasilli is one of his generals."

"Of course he is." Yvan ran a hand through his hair.

"The Illumination keeps them in check." Izrayl let out a cynical laugh. "Well, sort of. They like to think they're the do-gooder police of the supernatural world. Guardians of the Light and all that shit. Really, they're both the same. Both organizations want supernatural creatures and magic users on their side, just like the crap the Powers pull in Skazki and the otherworlds. The supernaturals that refuse to join either side are neutral, but it's damn hard to stay that way, trust me."

"And what was Eikki?"

"He was neutral to the core like Ilya. Most gatekeepers are unless they are indoctrinated young. Why do you think Eikki freaked when you left the farm? You were under his protection there, under wards that kept you safe. I always wanted to know why you'd give that up for Moscow of all places."

"I didn't know there were wards keeping me safe, though that explains a lot about what happened when I got to Moscow." Anya twisted her cup between her hands. "I left because I felt trapped living in the middle of nowhere. It's as simple as that. The bus I got on was going to Moscow. I was there for maybe a month before all my PTSD symptoms flared up. Do you think the wards kept them under control?"

"Undoubtedly," Trajan said. "Eikki wanted you to feel as safe as possible, even if that mean a boring life for a young woman. He was distraught when he realized you were gone."

"I know," she whispered. "I thought I was doing him a favor by leaving." When Anya got back, she'd seen how much she'd hurt him and how selfish she'd been. She promised to never leave again.

The nightmares had disappeared as soon as she was back at the farm, and now she knew it wasn't just because she was home. If the wards were keeping her PTSD symptoms in check, it would explain why they had come back with such a vengeance when Eikki died.

"Your grandfather had good reason to panic," Izrayl said. "In Moscow—the heart of the Darkness's power—you were ripe for the picking. An untrained person with a touch of magic is a prize worth fighting over. They'd been told by Eikki that you didn't have any, but of course they could sense it in close proximity.

On top of that, Eikki was neutral, and they wanted him on the Darkness's side. They could've used you to press him into service. That's why, when you disappeared, Eikki reached out to us and called Trajan back to his duty."

"What duty?" Anya and Yvan asked at once.

Trajan glared daggers at Izrayl. "To watch over Ilya's family."

"You were meant to be protecting Anya?" Yvan stared at Trajan, incredulous. "Then where the fuck were you when Vasilli attacked us?"

"I had gone to feed if you must know." Trajan's eyes flashed red.

Yvan backed down, but his knuckles were white with restrained anger.

"Look, I thought Anya would be safe for a few days under the farm's wards. When I got back two days later, the place was ash. There was no sign of her, and the stink of Vasilli's magic was everywhere. Anya's trail led to the forest, then disappeared, so I knew she must have made it into Skazki. I panicked and sent out messages to Izrayl and Cerise to meet me here so that we could track Anya down. Then you turned up on my damn doorstep."

Yvan dropped his hands in his lap. "I had nowhere else to go. There was no one I could trust. What was I meant to do? Leave Anya in the woods? I could never do that to one of Ilya's kin."

"You knew Ilya, but you've never told me how," Anya pointed out.

"We've been a bit busy, and I didn't want to scare you more than—"

"Well, we aren't busy now. I want all of the stories. Right now. So out with it, Tsarevich. Eikki had your egg. How did my family know you, and how do you know Trajan and Izrayl?"

Anya's brain was already spinning, but she didn't want any more secrets, and she'd had it with the vague comments they kept making because of their shared history.

"I would like to know that too." Cerise tapped her scarlet nails on the table. "More to the point, I want to know precisely how deep the shit that I've just landed in is."

Yvan refilled Anya's vodka without looking at her. "It all started after my quest for the firebird. I was living back in the palace and was out hunting when I first met Izrayl. He scared me half to death. Of course, I knew *volk krovi* existed, but I didn't think they lived in our forest."

"Vasilli had been stealing our children to use their blood in his magic." Izrayl's eyes went feral. "We knew the youngest of Vyslav's sons had more sense than his father, so we approached Yvan about it."

Yvan leaned back in his chair and folded his arms. "Since Vasilli and Dimitri had disappeared after killing me and lying to our father, I'd already been worried that without anything to check him, Vasilli would fall deeper into his fascination with dark magic. I also knew that he would be too powerful for me to stop alone and that I would have to find someone with power to match him."

Yvan fell silent, so Izrayl took over. "The only person we'd ever heard of powerful enough to take on Vasilli was Yanka. It took us six months to find any trace of her, and when we did, we learned she was dead. That was when we crossed into Russia and found Ilya, her son. We first met Trajan there too."

"I was visiting Ilya for the first time since we met," Trajan explained for Anya's benefit. "Long story short, he saw me feeding off someone on a beach in Greece and had never met one of my kind before. We became fast friends, and he offered me a place to stay whenever I wanted it, so I took him up on it."

Izrayl shot him an annoyed glance. "Enough interrupting! As I was saying, even though Ilya was ridiculously talented, especially when it came to prophetic visions, he didn't have half the strength it would take to fight Vasilli. But he *did* tell us he'd had a vision, and according to him, the firebird could defeat Vasilli, but it had to agree to do it willingly, which turned out to be quite the hurdle. The bird was stubborn as shit and resented us for holding it captive. Before we could convince it to help us—"

"Vasilli attacked the palace and bound the firebird's power until Yvan interrupted the spell and died a fiery death along with the bird," Anya finished.

Izrayl nodded. "It seems the prince has told you some information, at least."

"I'm interested to know how my egg ended up with the Venäläinens," Yvan said. He looked queasy and frustrated. Anya could understand not wanting to dredge up a painful past, so she reached under the table and took his hand. He didn't move away, so Anya left it there.

Trajan rested his arms on the table, swapping silent confirmations with Izrayl, who nodded. "Izrayl and I went to Ilya to tell him what had happened to Yvan, and Ilya convinced me to help him to find the firebird's egg. As payment for releasing me from Eris's servitude, I led him to the temple in the Greek otherworld where a firebird's ashes go to be remade. On that trip, Ilya spoke again of his recurring vision of the firebird fighting Vasilli. He'd seen it fighting alongside a woman who looked like Yanka, but with Yanka already dead, we never understood it."

Anya's stomach fluttered as Baba Yaga's words came rushing back to her: *You look like her, you know. Yanka. The same eyes, same white hair. Same magic, I wonder?*

"And then what happened?" she asked, her voice cracking.

"We recovered the firebird egg, and Ilya vowed that his family would keep it safe until it was reborn. Before he returned home, he charged me with looking after his wife and his son, Ahti. I didn't think much of it, until I returned to the farm sometime later and learned that he had been murdered. Looking back, I realized he must have seen it coming." Trajan's eyes glazed, lost in the past. "I never found out who did it... Luckily, Ahti was old enough that Ilya had already had the chance to teach him the gates magic. Ahti took Ilya's mantle as the gatekeeper."

"Then many, many years later, you were born." Izrayl's voice rumbled. "Eikki knew about Ilya's prophecy, and even as a young child, you looked like Yanka. Naturally, he grew worried and crossed over to tell us about you."

"Eikki didn't have copies of Ilya's prophecies, so he was never sure of the vision's precise details, but he was cautious about it," Trajan said. "He took one look at you in your crib, born with Ilya's white hair and green eyes, and decided to tell your parents everything. They didn't believe him, and your father didn't have a drop of magic in him, so he never understood Eikki's concern. He wanted to raise you like a normal human and insisted on keeping you as far away from as Eikki as possible. It wasn't until you were nearly six years old that they decided to visit the old man—the first time since you were a little baby and he voiced his concern."

"And then they crashed the car," Anya whispered, her hand going to her chest where a ball of pain was growing.

"When your parents were killed, Eikki blamed himself completely. He decided he wouldn't let the same thing happen to you. Their deaths, combined with your striking resemblance to Yanka and Ilya's prophecy looming, frightened him. He asked me if there was a way to suppress the magic already inside of you. That was when I made the decision to come see you for myself." Trajan smiled a little.

"He was concerned about your lack of fear of me. Not only were you unafraid, but you also took an instant liking to me. I tried to tell him he had to teach you to protect you, that the line of gatekeepers couldn't end with him. I told him it could be your destiny to stop Vasilli once and for all, which he didn't love hearing. Vasilli has wreaked havoc for far too long now. If he and Ladislav got hold of the firebird's magic or yours, the Darkness would start a war with the Illumination for dominance and tear the worlds apart again. The Illumination has had the upper hand on them for centuries, and they would love a chance to change that."

"What do you mean, tear the worlds apart *again*?" asked Yvan. "What has Vasilli been doing all this time?"

Izrayl laughed bitterly. "I guess you missed the last two World Wars. The Darkness kicked off both of them. Supernatural wars were going on behind the real ones. Humans were puppets or cannon fodder while the Illumination and Darkness fought for control of the human world. They've had a tentative peace treaty since the fifties, but it's only a matter of time before they kick off again. They can't help themselves, and if Vasilli gets the firebird's magic? It's guaranteed."

Anya took a big mouthful of vodka. A whole world existed in the shadows that no one knew about, and she didn't know whether to laugh or cry about it, but she'd hit her mental wall, and it was going to be one of the two. She laughed—a mirthless sound that made the rest of them pause.

"So what you're all saying is that because of some vision Ilya had years ago, you think I have enough power to stop Vasilli for good? I'm not trained to act *normal*, let alone magical. I don't even know how to control the gates on the farm!" She wasn't a prophecy material.

"If Vasilli were sure you're the woman from the prophecy, he would've grabbed you when you first met," Izrayl said. "Because your magic was so dormant, he must not have considered you a big enough threat to worry about. He'll realize soon enough." He curled his lips like he had a bad taste in his mouth. "He's always been smart and vicious. He'll figure it out, and then you'll be hunted more fiercely than Yvan and the firebird ever were because of Yanka. She was so powerful that tsars, gods, and kings from all of the otherworlds sought her counsel."

Anya sucked in a breath. "It must have been Yanka in the dream about the tsar. Tuoni said that there are memories lost in the blood flowing through my veins…"

"What dream?" they all asked at once.

Anya looked at Yvan. "The one I was having when you woke me because I was sending out a signal or something. I was dreaming about Yanka and a battle."

Trajan fixed Yvan with a glare. "How could you have let such a thing slide past your attention?"

"She never told me what the dream was about! We were in Baba Yaga's forest, and Anya was sending a beacon in every direction. All I could think of was getting her out of there as quickly as possible."

Trajan looked unimpressed but turned his attention back to Anya. "Tell us what the dream was about. It's important."

"I dreamed I was her," Anya tried to explain. "She was predicting the outcome of a battle for a tsar who had kidnapped her. She told him the army would win, but she didn't say she foresaw his death. Then I was on a hill with Tuoni until Yvan woke me up. I don't know who the tsar was."

"I do. It was Yvan's great-grandfather," said Trajan.

"What are you talking about?" Yvan asked with an edge to his voice.

"Ilya's prophecy has bothered me for centuries, so I researched Yanka as much as I could. Most stories say she was the daughter of a king. Her sister was sent to marry your great-grandfather as part of a peace treaty. The tsar, your great-grandfather, had wanted Yanka, but her father refused to give her up because of her magical gifts. When the tsar went warmongering once more, he must've captured Yanka and forced her to predict his battles for him. I'm only guessing, though. There's no way to verify it because none of the stories I dug up were the same."

"He raped her," Anya added quietly. "That's why she hated him so much."

Yvan's hand clenched in hers. "Did she fall pregnant from it?"

"There's no way to know," Trajan said. "I'm sure if she had fallen pregnant, she would have aborted it. None of the stories mentioned a bastard child."

Yvan buried his head in hands and groaned. "I don't think I can take any more of this. My mind feels like it's splitting apart."

"Good to know I'm not alone." Anya patted his back. Tears had built up in her throat, and if she drank any more, she would spend the next day throwing up. Her head spun with so much information that she regretted demanding they tell her everything at once.

Yvan got up. "We've been running for days, and I can't…I can't do this anymore without sleep."

"I agree with Yvan. I'm going to bed," Anya said. She was exhausted, emotional, and wanted to be alone.

Cerise grabbed what was left of the bottle of vodka. "I'm getting drunk."

"Do you have everything you need?" asked Trajan, his dark eyes filled with worry.

"I'll be fine. Thank you, everyone, for telling me what I needed to know." Anya got to her feet.

Yvan put a steadying hand under her elbow as she swayed. "Let's go, shamanitsa, before you pass out on the floor." He helped her up the stairs.

"What a night."

"I have a feeling tomorrow isn't going to be any easier."

"Can't you lie to me just once?"

"No. You've been lied to enough. That's why life is so hard now," Yvan said, ever the voice of reason.

When they got to her room, Anya hesitated, then hugged him awkwardly, her face pressed against his chest. "Thank you for not leaving me in the forest. What happened between Yanka and your great-grandfather doesn't matter. You're still my friend. Nothing they did can change that."

Yvan's shoulders relaxed, and his arms went around her. "Thank you, Anya. For what it's worth, I'm glad it was your house I hatched in."

"Even with Vasilli chasing us, weird prophecies falling into place, and my cluelessness about magic?"

Yvan let her go and reached for his bedroom door. "No one said friendships were meant to be easy."

13

"YOU CAN'T SEND ME *away, Eikki, not now that her magic is getting stronger. You're too old to hold back the people the Darkness and Illumination will send to recruit her."* Trajan stood in the barn with Eikki. *"I swore an unbreakable oath to Ilya to protect his family."*

"And you have served that oath. I'm releasing you of it. Do you think Anya will believe she's normal if she has a protector shadowing her every step? She is already too attached to you, and she's becoming a woman—that will only confuse her more." Eikki put a hand on Trajan's shoulder. *"Once her memories are gone and her magic is suppressed, we won't have to worry about anyone coming for her. I'll make it known that she is like her father. They won't want her, and you won't be needed any longer. It's a chance for you to have your own life. That's what you wanted to be free for, isn't it?"*

"I don't agree with this. I respect you, but locking away this part of her is wrong. She's a magical child," Trajan pleaded. *"She won't know who she is!"*

"But she will be safe."

"If you don't send me away, she will always be safe. I swear it, Eikki. I won't let anything happen to her."

"My mind is made up. Go, Trajan. I release you of your duty," Eikki said, his voice stern.

Trajan took a step back from him. "Very well, Gatekeeper. Just promise me that you'll reach out if you ever need me."

"I will, old friend."

Trajan left the barn without looking back, long coat streaming behind him. Twelve-year-old Anya leaped from her hiding place in the hayloft and tore after him across the paddock.

"Trajan! Wait!" she called, then latched onto his waist to stop him from going any farther. "You can't go."

Trajan crouched down beside her. "I have to, little one. I'm sorry, but your grandfather thinks it's for the best, and I have to obey."

"You're going for good? Like forever?" Anya had been taught not to cry, but the thought of never seeing her friend again hurt too much.

Trajan took her hand in his. "You'll see me again one day, I promise. In the meantime, you listen to your grandfather and stay safe."

Anya nodded, then wrapped her arms around his neck. "I'll miss you."

"I'll miss you too, little one. Be safe for me."

The dream tore away from her, and she jolted into wakefulness. Anya's cheeks and pillow were damp with tears. She sat up and placed a hand over her aching chest as the lost memory settled in her mind.

Trajan. Her special friend. She'd barely talked to Eikki for weeks after he sent him away, until something happened and all memory of Trajan faded away. *Oh, Eikki, why did you take my memory of him away?*

It was as though a floodgate had been opened. Memories and feelings rushed over her, emotion for the thanatos she only just met. He had always been her friend. That's why she felt safe with him. That's why she knew in her bones that she could trust him.

Anya got out of bed, showered, and dressed in clean clothes. Her mind was on fire from all the stories told the previous night, but something had also calmed inside of her. She knew that the strange bunch of people she'd fallen in with wasn't going to let her figure out her new and confusing world on her own.

Anya's need for coffee, the smell of which drifted up from the kitchen, drove her out of her room and downstairs. When she arrived, she found Yvan, Trajan, and Izrayl already awake. Trajan was brewing coffee in a plunger, and when he smiled at her, a flush of renewed memories rose to the surface.

"I had a dream about you last night," she blurted.

"A sexy dream?" Izrayl asked from where he was scrambling eggs at the stove.

Yvan stopped buttering his toast and smacked him in the back of the head. "Don't talk to her like that."

Trajan offered her a steaming mug, his smile widening. "Don't mind them. Was it a good dream, at least?"

Anya shook her head, and his lovely smile slipped. "No, it was horrible. It was the day you left." She accepted the coffee and sat down at the table, then exhaled heavily and laughed.

"If it was horrible, why do you look so happy about it?" Trajan took a seat beside her.

"Because it was a real memory. That must mean whatever Tuoni did to me is working, even if it's happening gradually. In a few days, I could remember who you are—properly." Anya rested a hand on his arm. He looked down at it curiously, and she went to move it, but he put his warm palm over her hand.

"That's good news. It's been rather terrible having you look at me like a stranger."

Heat flushed her cheeks, and Yvan interrupted them by placing a plate of breakfast in front of her. "You better eat, Anya. We need to discuss leaving while we still have a lead on Vasilli." He sat down on the other side of her.

"And go where?" Cerise breezed into the kitchen, looking like a million dollars with her vibrant red hair in a long, intricate braid. "I don't want to have to deal with Vasilli anytime soon."

"Baba Yaga gave us a drum. She said it would show us the way through Skazki if I cast Yanka's rune stones on it, but I haven't tried it out yet," Anya said.

"I've been thinking about Paris," Trajan said. "I have a townhouse, and unlike in Skazki, you'll be able to hide your magic there."

"Because here, that red magic trail is everywhere you go," Izrayl reminded her.

Yvan looked skeptical. "But won't Mir make it harder for Anya to learn her magic?"

"Not if Tuoni really did something to remove the blocks on Anya's memory." Trajan turned back to her. "You were already a natural with your magic before Eikki hid it away. It was like you could use it intuitively, without any practice. If you remember those times, you might be able to access that power more easily and pick up where you left off."

"I have Eikki's journals, but I can start with the runes and the drum." Anya sounded way more confident than she felt.

"Baba Yaga said that the drum would give us safe passage. If we decide to go to Paris, hopefully it will lead us to a gate that's outside of Russia," Yvan said. He squirmed in his seat, then cursed, his fingers going to the buttons on his shirt. He undid them, gritting his teeth, and then released a breath as the firebird stretched his wings along his skin.

Anya reached for his shaking shoulder. "Are you okay?"

"It wanted to see." Yvan rolled his eyes. "Damn thing won't shut up." The firebird's feathers gleamed. It blinked, then turned so that Yvan looked as if he had a bird's head growing out of his chest.

Izrayl laughed. "I thought I was a freak. That's just gross."

Yvan sighed. "It's draining having this extra voice in my head. It's like having a wife again."

"Then it's settled. We head to Paris," Trajan said, seemingly unfazed by the firebird on Yvan's chest. "Anya, you should have a look at the drum and runes this morning. See if it gives you some useful directions while we pack."

Anya bit her lip. "I can try, but I can't promise anything magical will happen."

"Of what I've seen of magic, you need talent or instincts, and you have both," said Yvan. "Have you felt any different since crossing over?"

"My hand still burns sometimes where Tuoni zapped me, and sometimes I feel like I have static running under my skin. Vodka dulls it down enough that I don't want to scratch myself to pieces."

The magic is building inside of you, child, the firebird warned her. *You must release it, or it will start releasing itself.*

"That's not helpful," Anya told the bird on Yvan's chest. "It says it's the magic trying to get out." The firebird stretched its wing down Yvan's arm, curled out of his skin, and brushed against her, sending warmth flooding up to her arm. "Wow," she whispered, stroking the feather with one finger.

"Using the drum could help release some of your magic," Trajan said.

"You don't think using magic will attract Vasilli?"

"If it does, at least you have some fierce protectors," said Cerise. "And a sexy guard dog."

Izrayl grunted. "Don't push your luck with the dog jokes."

"You should try using the drum outside," Trajan said. "That way, if you release too much power, you won't destroy the house."

Anya nodded. "That's probably a good idea. Just don't expect any miracles."

Cerise clapped her hands. "All right, then. You get started on the drum, and the rest of us will focus on packing what we need for when that miracle arrives."

The forest was cold and damp from the rain the night before. The scent of sweet pines and the thick earthiness of rotting leaves and moss filled the air.

Anya held the drum in one hand, the runes in the other, and Eikki's journals were in a bag beside her. Warm and dry inside her thick coat, she had been sitting on a rock for an hour trying to find the will to try out the drum.

Yvan hadn't been enthusiastic about letting her out of their sight, but she couldn't handle the thought of people watching her. She hadn't wandered far, just far enough to be out of sight.

Anya turned the drum over in her hands. It was a rough oval shape painted with the symbols of the Sami *nojd* drums. She'd seen such drums when Eikki had taken her to the Midsummer celebrations. There had been *joik* singing, which Eikki loved and left her brain buzzing. In the center of the drum was a large cross with a reindeer in the middle of it. Scattered around the drum were drawings of churches, birds, stick figures, trees, a wolf, a bear, and more reindeer.

I know I've seen these markings before.

It took Anya a few minutes of flicking through Eikki's journals before she found the small sketch of a drum. She read the scribbled note aloud:

"The drums are read from top to bottom. The top is north, most often crowned with a cross shape—the North Star. The next three layers represent the heavenly realm, the earthly realm, and the Underworld. Ask it a question and cast your bone to see your answers."

Anya reread it twice while checking her drum. On one of the four arms of the center crosspiece, there was a smaller cross, encircled with antlers—the north, the heavens. She didn't know what all the other symbols meant, but she understood how a compass worked. Maybe it would work that way too?

Anya placed the drum in front of her on the ground, took out her runes, and randomly picked one. It was smooth in her hand and had a scratching in it that looked like a slanted L. Her fingertips tingled as she sorted through them to find the one Yvan had shown her.

Baba Yaga had said to drop *Raidho* on the drum, and according to Yvan, it looked like a crooked R. She finally found it and turned it over in her palm until the stone turned warm. Silencing all the voices in her head, Anya stretched her hand out over the drum.

"Show me the path to Paris," she said. Heat rushed through her, making her ears pop, and she dropped the rune stone. It bounced once on a bird, then on a string of crosses before stopping on a stick figure wearing a dress. She ignored the thrumming under her skin and tried to imagine the same landing on a compass. Southeast.

"Okay, maybe that's the way…" Anya breathed out and picked up the rune, then placed it into the bag and tucked them into her coat pocket. She'd just stood up when a deep growl echoed through the trees. A gray wolf appeared in view, not ten feet from her, and her heart stopped.

"The master wants you," it rasped through its teeth.

Anya stepped backward. "So which one are you? Vischto or Vischtan?"

The wolf growled. "I am Vischto, and I'll be the one honored for finding you."

"My friends know where I am."

"The master knows where you are too, and he's coming for you." Vischto crouched down, and Anya turned and bolted.

In the same instant, a huge, black blur sped past her, followed by a yelp. She stopped and turned as a black wolf far bigger than Vischto wrestled him with brutal ferocity. Vischto bit at Izrayl's back, making him buck in an attempt to throw him off. Panic mounted in Anya. Her body tingled, and searing pain streaked down her arm.

"No! Stop!" Anya held out a burning hand, and the heat rushed thick and fast from her. It hit Vischto in the side, sending him to ground screeching and howling. Izrayl fell back as the wolf transformed into a skinny, naked man with black eyes filled with agony. He writhed, scratching deep, red gashes into his pale flesh. His breath hissed out of him, and then his body exploded, showering them in ash.

Anya's hand was still outstretched as her legs gave way. She crumpled on the ground. Izrayl morphed back into his human body, which was covered in Vischto's bites and scratches. He lifted her into his arms, but she couldn't move or speak, her face and lips completely numb.

"Bloody Yvan is going to kill me," he muttered. He moved swiftly through the forest back to the house.

When Izrayl stepped inside, Trajan asked, "What happened?" Without waiting for an answer, he said, "Give her to me and get Cerise to help you with your wounds. You're bleeding everywhere." Izrayl passed Anya to Trajan, who carried her up the stairs to her room.

"I'm o-okay…" Anya mumbled through numb lips. "Vissto."

Trajan wrapped her in a blanket and held her tight.

Yvan stormed into the room. "What the hell happened?"

"Go and see Izrayl. They were attacked. And get Anya something to warm her up. Coffee. She's shivering." Trajan left no room for further conversation.

Yvan glared at him but did as he was told.

Trajan rocked Anya. "We should've never let you go into the forest alone."

"Just cold…" Anya managed as she rested her pounding head in the groove of his neck and breathed in his warm autumn scent. *Trajan.*

He shook her gently. "Don't go to sleep."

"Why?"

"Because you might not wake up." Trajan moved her to check that her eyes were open, his own filled with worry. "And I need you to wake up. I only just got you back."

"Nice." Anya touched his face. "I remember…"

"What do you remember?"

"Missed you."

Yvan stormed back into the room with Izrayl following close behind, holding a wad of bandages to his chest.

"I followed Anya to make sure she didn't get lost, and Vischto appeared out of nowhere," Izrayl said. "I managed to intervene before he attacked her. Then she screamed, and all of a sudden, Vischto was off me and on the ground. He burned from the inside out. She used her magic on him. Turned him into ash in seconds. It was the freakiest shit I've ever seen."

I killed someone. Anya curled her fingers into Trajan's shirt as the horror of it hit her.

"The firebird says the use of magic has drained her. She used too much at once." Yvan crouched down beside her. "You just need to rest."

"Is that all?" Trajan breathed a sigh of relief. "You can go to sleep now if you want to, Anya."

With her head still resting on him, she closed her eyes and swallowed down her unexpected tears. The first time she'd used her magic, and she had used it to kill.

Is this why Eikki was afraid?

"Vischto said Vasilli was coming for her. We need to leave as soon as she can move," Izrayl said.

"Then make sure you're ready. I'll stay with her," Trajan replied.

Anya opened a bleary eye as Yvan touched her cheek. She tried to smile at him, but her mouth still wouldn't cooperate.

"If her temperature drops, find me. The firebird will help," he told Trajan. "And watch where you put your hands."

After they were gone, Trajan lifted Anya onto the bed and removed her boots. He placed another blanket over her.

"Don't go," Anya croaked. She held out the hand the magic had come out of. It was burning while the rest of her froze, as if all her energy had been pulled to one place.

Trajan sat down next to her. He placed his cold hand in hers, and the burning pain eased. "I'm not going anywhere. Every time I do, something happens. I dropped my guard to feed, and Tuoni gave you Yvan's egg, and now this time, you were attacked by Vischto."

"At least m-magic worked."

"A little too well. Don't worry. We'll find someone to teach you. Just rest now." Trajan stroked the hair back from her forehead. "And just so you know, I missed you too."

Vasilli threw his rune stones across the forest floor, hoping they would give him some kind of direction. He'd sent Vischtan along the trail ahead of him to scout and Vischto in another direction in case the witch was telling lies. He didn't trust the Powers, which is why he had killed as many of the lesser ones as he could and siphoned their magic when he did, growing his own.

He hated Baba Yaga most of all.

When Vasilli first entered Skazki, he could taste the magic residue Anya had left in a glade. She had seemed so unimportant the night they met, and yet Baba Yaga had helped her.

Vasilli tried to clear his mind as he surveyed at the small bone runes. Nothing. Just gibberish yet again. Vasilli raged until he ran out of breath.

Finally, he sat down next to the fire. He cursed himself again for not slitting Anya's throat when he had the chance. She'd seemed so ordinary that he hadn't thought of her as a threat, much less connected her to Ilya's ramblings about his bloodline allying with the firebird to destroy Vasilli.

There had been no sign of a trail for days now. Baba Yaga had played him. Of course, she would've seen Anya for what she was in an instant. All of Skazki knew of the feud Baba Yaga had with Yanka. The old witch never did anything out of the kindness of her black heart. She wanted Anya on her side, which meant she sensed something in her that Vasilli had missed. Perhaps she'd seen visions of the coming war, same as him.

Vischtan screeched, jolting Vasilli out of his thoughts.

"Master, h-help me." The skin-changer howled and twisted before coughing out a cloud of ash as he died.

Vasilli bent down beside the body but was too shocked at first to know how to react. He placed a hand on Vischtan and whispered words of power. In his mind, he saw Vischto fighting a *volk krovi* and Anya raise her hand against him. She had killed him, and Vischtan too through their twin bond.

"Fucking gods!" Vasilli hissed. He scratched symbols in the dirt before cutting his arm and letting the hot, red drops stain the earth. He knew he was at least a day away from her, but he wouldn't let her escape again. Anya might've had Yvan and a *volk krovi* protecting her, but her dreams were another matter entirely.

14

I N THE DARKNESS, ANYA dreamed she was a little girl again, playing in the forest, flowers in her hand, blackberry stains on her lips. Through the trees, she spotted a man sitting by a stream.

"I've been expecting you," the man said, his voice a deep thrum. "Come closer so that I can see you."

Anya couldn't disobey an adult, so she went to stand in front of him just out of arm's reach. The man's face was dark from the sun, and his eyes were deep and old.

"Yanka's blood, you've grown so big." He moved his hand and presented her with a red rose. "My gift to you, to honor your beauty."

Little Anya took the rose and smiled at him. "Was that magic?"

"No, my love. I simply asked the rose to appear in my hand. Some might call it magic." He studied her a long moment, and she held his gaze. "I could teach you magic if you want. If you take my hand, I will show you the most amazing things in the world." He stretched out his hand, and Anya studied it. He smiled at her.

"I shouldn't trust strangers," she said.

The warmth drained out of his black eyes. "Come with me, Anya, and we could rule the world. This one and the one we will build together."

"I don't want to go." Her bottom lip turned out in a pout.

He frowned at her. "Leave them. You and I will have a new family. One so strong and powerful it will make the world quake," he said. "They don't want you, Anya. You and I belong together. If you come with me, you will stay beautiful and powerful forever. I will love you and never leave you. We will crush our enemies into the dust."

"I don't want to go with you." Gone was the childlike voice. Adult Anya spoke through her child form.

"What chance do you think you have? You and my useless brother?" he growled through his teeth. "Do you really think I won't find you? You've only gotten as far as you have because I have willed it. I could crush you right now, even in your dreams. You have no idea of my power, child."

"Then why are you afraid?" she asked, this time in her sweet, little girl voice.

He backhanded her across her face, and she fell back onto the dirt. Despite the pain, she laughed. She struggled to climb to her feet. "You're so powerful, and yet you resort to hitting me," she said between giggles. "I'm going to destroy you, Vasilli."

"You say that now, but when all your friends are dead, and no one can help you with the power that is surely destroying you from the inside out, you'll come to me. It's only a matter of time." Vasilli rotated his hand in a twisting gesture, and the rose in her hand crumpled. The pieces trembled in her hand. "A parting gift for you. Never forget, roses are beautiful, but they have thorns."

Anya screamed as the thorns buried deep in her flesh. She tried in vain to scratch them from her palm as bright blood rushed from the wounds.

Vasilli laughed as she screamed and screamed.

"Anya! Wake up!"

Trajan's voice startled her awake. She glanced around the room, trying to center herself back in the real world.

"Oh, no. Trajan, he's coming. He's coming!" Anya pulled on the sleeve of his shirt. "Go wake everyone. We need to leave."

He didn't question her, only hurried from the room to do as she asked.

Anya looked down at the palm of her hand. Raised pink scars had appeared on her skin where the thorns had buried themselves in. Swallowing her rising horror, Anya got out of bed and dressed.

Yvan burst in as she pulled on her boots. "What happened?"

"Vasilli is coming. We need to go."

Yvan took her firmly by the shoulders to halt her flurry of movement. "How do you know?"

"I met him in a dream."

"Anya—"

"Don't say it was just a dream! Look at this!" She held her palm up to his face.

He took her hand and ran his thumb over the raised bumps, then dropped it as if she had burned him. "There's something in there. Something alive."

"I know. They're thorns. We need to get away from here. We can worry about cutting them out later."

"You must promise to tell me if you feel sick or strange in any way. We don't know what will happen with those things inside your body."

"Deal. Go get your things. I'll be downstairs."

Anya did up her pack and slid her knife down the side of her boot just as Trajan reappeared. He wore a black leather jacket and sunglasses that were pushed up into his dark hair.

"They are ready and waiting for you," he said.

She nodded and went to move past him, but he grabbed her and held her tight. When the shock of his embrace wore off, she wrapped her arms around him, the fear inside her easing just a little.

"Yvan told me about your hand. Whatever it is, we will fix it, Anya."

"I'm sure it's nothing," she lied, stepping away from him. "We need to go."

Yvan, Izrayl, and Cerise were waiting for them outside in the midday sun. Cerise was dressed in a long fur coat with a cigarette in hand. She looked at Anya's hand but didn't mention the scars.

"Izrayl, I'll carry your clothes in my pack," Trajan said.

The *volk krovi* grinned. "Always looking out for me, big brother."

"I don't think the ladies will want to see your nakedness when you change back."

"Their loss." Izrayl shed his clothes, then bones began to snap, and black fur burst from his brown skin. His long hair formed into a ridge of fur down his back. In a matter of seconds, a large wolf had taken his place and was looking at Anya with big amber eyes.

"God, that doesn't ever stop being amazing," she whispered.

The wolf sniffed the air once before trotting off into the trees.

"Shall we?" Cerise followed Izrayl with a swish of her fur coat.

"Please tell me if you start feeling unwell," Trajan said to Anya.

"I promise." In front of her, Yvan gave her a nod, and she knew he watched her too. With an inward sigh, she set off after Cerise.

They kept a quick pace through the massive birch and pines. Anya slipped on pine needles and wet logs, but each time, Yvan or Trajan was there to catch her before she went down. Her hand had begun to itch terribly, but she refused to scratch it so no one would fret.

"So, how did you meet Trajan? Did you know each other in the Underworld?" Anya asked Cerise, hoping conversation would distract her from her palm.

"Oh god, no. The Greek Underworld isn't exactly a social place." Cerise's delighted laugh echoed in the outdoors. "Should I tell her, Trajan?"

He was walking in front of them, and with every memory that returned to her, Anya liked him more. *And just so you know, I missed you too.* Anya had been awake enough to hear that, and she wasn't going to forget it anytime soon.

Trajan shot an amused look over his shoulder. "There's no way I can stop you."

"True," Cerise agreed. "Okay, Anya, picture this. I had finally worked off my debt to Eris and was released from my servitude. I popped up to the surface and woke in an alley disoriented with the worst headache. I hadn't taken on a human form before, and I had no idea where to start. I rendered myself invisible so I wouldn't scare the life out of anyone I met and began to search for my perfect form. I hadn't even gone a block before I saw her—the most beautiful woman in the whole world, Ava Gardner. She was on a movie poster for *The Killers* outside of a run-down old theater, and she was divine. This form I wear now is an inspired recreation of that picture." Cerise flicked her long red hair with pride.

"I found her a few months later. I'd sensed something from the Underworld had surfaced, but by the time I found her, she'd been caught and charged with murder." Trajan grinned.

"The man was already dead, darling. I wasn't willing to let a good meal go to waste." Cerise stepped over a fallen branch. "Long story short, Trajan arrived and saved my hide. He taught me how to feed in a less obvious way. We both have a penchant for hospitals and morgues, so it worked out quite well. Now we will use what power we have to save your hide the way he saved mine. I'd never hear the end of it if I didn't help out. Pouty Trajan is the *worst*."

"I can imagine." Anya laughed, looking between them. "I like your matching sunglasses. They are adorable." Both Cerise and Trajan were wearing wayfarers, but Cerise's had dark red frames to match her hair. With Trajan's tousled good looks, leather jacket, and lace-up boots, he was far too stylish to be hiking in a muddy forest in Skazki. Anya was doing her best not to check out his ass, but she was only human, after all.

"We aren't twinning it or anything," Cerise said. "We are creatures born in darkness, and the light hurts our eyes. Trajan is practically blind even inside. That's why he wears contacts or glasses." She tugged on the back of his coat playfully. "Wait until you see his reading glasses. He looks so nerdy."

"Don't listen to her, Trajan. Nerds are hot," said Anya.

"Thank you, Anya." He swatted Cerise's hand away, then smiled. Trajan in his glasses was at the top of Anya's list of things to see.

After hours of walking, they stopped for a quick drink of water and a rest while Izrayl backtracked to make sure they weren't followed. Anya risked a glance at her hand, and a cold sweat broke out on the back of her neck. The scars were redder now, with tentacles of purple spreading from them like veins.

Izrayl burst through the trees and shook his head, a low growl rolling through his body.

"Vasilli has found the house," Trajan said.

"Is Vischtan with him?" Yvan asked.

Izrayl shook his big head before taking off through the trees. He'd been circling their general vicinity all morning, keeping a lookout for Vasilli or anything else that could hinder them.

"Are you okay, honey?" Cerise asked Anya. "You're looking awfully pale."

"It's nothing. I'm more worried about you trying to make your way through the forest in those boots," Anya tried to joke. Cerise was wearing impossibly high-heeled boots that came up past her knees. She looked like a gorgeously impractical femme fatale.

Cerise raised a perfect red eyebrow. "Don't worry about my boots. I've had loads of practice walking in them. Just worry about yourself."

Anya pulled her hair back in a high ponytail to get it off her sweaty neck. Her hand stung, and she tried not to wince as she fastened her hair tie.

They started moving again, heading southeast as the drum had instructed. Anya pondered the symbols the rune stone had landed on. Bird, crosses, woman. Bird, crosses, woman. It rolled around and around her head like a mantra to distract her from the ache spreading up her arm.

The next time she fell down, Anya didn't have anyone there to catch her, and her world flooded with darkness.

Vasilli found the house near where Vischto met his end. He wanted to destroy it, to rip it apart with his magic like he had Anya's farm, but he couldn't afford the massive loss of power, not when he was gaining on his quarry.

Anya had fallen for a child's trick in the dream, and he had planted his own unique way of tracking her deep in her flesh. The thorns would fester deep in her body, spreading through her, paralyzing her. It would make up for the lost time and damage her enough to make her compliant.

Ladislav was becoming impatient. Vasilli needed to collect the girl and get her back to Russia. If he offered Anya, Ladislav would be too distracted to worry about what Vasilli was doing with the firebird. In truth, the discovery of the girl couldn't have come at a better time. She'd serve as the perfect diversion. All he needed was time and a human sacrifice to tear the magic from the bird forever. There would be no more following orders after that.

Vasilli pulled off his heavy coat and the shirt he wore underneath. Tattooed on his muscled abdomen was a vicious black dragon. He didn't want to release this pet—it would've been useful in the fight against Ladislav when everything finally came to a head—but sacrifices had to be made.

Clearing his mind, Vasilli took his knife, cut his palm, and smeared his blood over the tattoo.

"Rise and waken, dark slave.

Break free from bonds of magic and flesh.

I call you forth, I call you out.

Slave of mine, caught by my hand,

rise from your trappings of blood and bone.

Take form and shape.

Rise and waken.

I call you to do your master's bidding."

Dark magic poured through his body, filling the tattoo as it twitched. With a shout of pain Vasilli couldn't hold in, the creature pulled itself from his skin and flopped bloody as a newborn onto the ground. It cried as it stretched its wings and grew to the size of a horse, then turned to Vasilli and lowered itself in a bow.

"How may I serve, Master?" it rasped through a mouth of venomous fangs.

"Find the girl and my brother and bring them to me. Slaughter whatever gets in your way."

"As my master wishes." The creature bowed its head in servitude before launching itself into the air. It flapped its enormous wings and disappeared into the distance, hunting for blood.

15

ON THE OTHER SIDE of the forest, a hunter hid in the long grass. She brushed aside her shaggy black fringe and zeroed in on the deer through the trees. Her eyes narrowed as she aimed and fired. The deer bucked once, then fell. She lowered the bow and straightened. One shot. One kill.

Come home, Yakaterina. Her sister's voice echoed through her head.

I'm hunting.

We have trouble.

Katya knew that tone and was in motion, leaving the kill where it lay.

What have you seen? she asked as she ran.

Strangers are coming. They are going to need your help. Dark forces are hunting them. Get home as quick as you can. Baba Zosia has seen them too.

I'll be there soon. She quickened her pace.

It took Katya less than an hour to get back to the camp. Painted wooden caravans formed a circle, hidden amongst the oak and pines. Children playing within the circle were watched by the women at the cooking fires. The smell of smoke, red paprika, and other spices filled the air. Old men playing chess bickered. Katya greeted everyone by name as she passed and sent a few young men back for her deer. Winter was coming, and the meat needed to be dried and stored.

She ran up the wrought iron steps of her sister's caravan and pushed her way through the heavy red curtains.

"Aleksandra?" she called.

Her sister stood by the small stove, boiling water for tea. They were sisters but didn't look very much alike in Katya's opinion. They both had olive skin, burgundy lips, and black hair, but Aleksandra was the more beautiful of the two. Her ebony hair reached her waist in full, shining curls. Her features were softer, fuller, and more delicate. Her eyes were a vibrant blue, and they saw far into the future. Katya's eyes were the color of jade. She was shorter, thinner, stronger, faster, and blunter in her manners. A thin white scar cut through her left eye but was hidden by her fringe.

"What's so important?" Katya asked.

Aleksandra frowned at Katya's mud-covered boots, which she had failed to take off. A line of muck covered Aleksandra's clean mats from the door to where Katya stood.

"I had a vision. I saw a small group traveling with a black cloud following them. There's a young woman with fair hair. She has magic pouring from her. You need to help them. Bring them here if you have to. The woman is important, but I can't see how." She scooped sugar into a delicate teacup and a large metal mug. "Baba Zosia came to me. She had the same vision, and she looked nervous."

"What's hunting them? Please tell me it's a big monster, because I'm getting bored hunting animals. I've been sitting around Skazki for too long."

Aleksandra frowned, and Katya felt a lecture burning on the tip of her sister's tongue. "There's something evil on their trail. Just because you enjoy the fight doesn't mean you should be craving it, Yakaterina."

"I can if I want, little mother. What's the point of wasting the gifts God has given me? You see the monsters, and I kill them. That's how it works."

"The gifts should only be used to protect the tribe. That's why we inherited them. If Father were alive, I'm sure he would tell you the same." Aleksandra poured steaming tea into the cups.

"If Father were alive, he would still be cursing his luck that I was born a girl instead of a boy." Katya scowled. "I'm a warrior. That is my gift, and I will use it the way I want." The little kitchen suddenly felt too crowded.

Aleksandra sighed and handed Katya her mug. "You don't have much time. Drink your tea, then go find them. I'm hoping Baba Zosia can help the young woman rein in some of that magic before she hurts herself or others."

Aleksandra's gifts included compassion. If there were a baby bird with a broken wing within a hundred kilometers, she would find it and spend weeks tending to it until it could fly away, leaving her weeping with joy. The soppy side of her sister's character always made Katya roll her eyes. A killer and a healer living under the same roof wasn't always easy.

"Did you see what I'm meant to be hunting? Just so I have some idea of what weapons to take." Katya sipped her tea—black and sweet, with a twist of aniseed the way she liked it.

"I couldn't see what it was, exactly." Aleksandra's brows drew together in frustration. "But it was big, and it had great wings. They aren't far away. You should encounter them by this afternoon."

"I'll see you at dawn at the latest. Or if I get killed, not at all." Katya barked out a laugh when her sister's face crumpled with worry.

"I don't understand your humor some days, Katya."

"There's a lot you don't understand about me, *soră*. Don't worry so much. I'm not dead yet." Katya winked, then stepped out the door.

Anya drifted back into consciousness as daylight was fading within the trees. Trajan carried her, his profile gleaming in the afternoon sun. It was the nicest sight Anya had woken up to in a long time.

"What happened? Put me down," she said.

"We tried that, and you toppled over. Can you feel your toes again?"

Anya tried to move and couldn't. Hot panic rolled through her. "I can't...I can't move. Put me down. I'm going to be sick."

Trajan shifted her, holding her above the ground as she threw up green bile streaked with blood.

"Here, Anya." Cerise wiped her face and held a water bottle to her lips. "Try to drink. Trajan, we have to get those things out of her and soon."

Anya groaned. "I'm going to kill Vasilli."

Once she was cleaned up, Trajan had her back in his arms. He smiled, though his eyes were filled with worry.

"I'm sorry if I smell like vomit." She couldn't muster enough energy to be truly embarrassed. "I'm dying, aren't I?"

"No." His arms tightened around her.

"Liar."

"This is just some trick of Vasilli's to hinder us." His jaw clenched. "When we get a little farther, we'll find a safe place and get those thorns out."

"Doesn't feel like a trick." Anya shut her eyes, willing his smell and warmth to steady her. "I hated it when you left."

"I didn't leave. I was sent away."

"I'm sorry I forgot you."

"You have nothing to be sorry for, Anya. We simply have fifteen years to catch up on, and I intend to make sure we have a chance to do just that."

Anya tried to smile. Her head was the only part of her she could still control. "You've gotten better-looking with age."

"What lies. I was always this good-looking." Trajan looked down at her with a playful expression. "Are you trying to flirt with me right now?"

"It might be the only time I have left to flirt."

Trajan laughed, shaking his head. "You're not going to die. Rest now. You can flirt with me later."

"There will be no trying." Anya curled into him and let the swaying of his stride ease her.

"Izrayl has found a suitable place to stop," said Yvan as he fell back beside them. He brushed a warm hand across Anya's forehead.

"Don't look so worried, Tsarevich. You're not getting rid of me this easily," Anya said, her voice cracking.

"You wouldn't be you if you did anything the easy way."

Trajan set her down on the soft grass near a stream. Cerise was beside her in seconds, inspecting her hand.

"Are you a doctor?" Anya asked.

Cerise took off her coat. "I've had some medical training as a nurse. It makes it easier to get into hospitals." Her gaze followed the tendrils up Anya's arm and down her side. "This looks like blood poisoning. If we can get the thorns out and stop the infection, your body might be strong enough to heal the rest."

"You mean cut them from her?" Yvan asked.

"It's either that, or Anya worsens and possibly dies."

Izrayl appeared from between the trees and transformed into a naked man. If she were going to die, Anya decided it wasn't the worst thing to look at as she did. Trajan tossed him a pair of jeans, and Izrayl pulled them on.

"I don't know why I need to bother. I'm just going to have to take them off again in a minute."

"Anya is suffering enough. She doesn't need the additional shock," Cerise pulled a wicked-looking knife from her bag.

Anya's breath caught at the sight of it. "Maybe Anya needs the distraction." Cerise took her hand, and she let the breath out in a squeak.

Trajan put a hand on Izrayl's bicep to stop him from undoing his jeans. "Don't even think about it."

"Can you feel it when I touch your hand?"

Anya watched Cerise poke the scars but there was no accompanying sensation. She shook her head. "No, nothing."

Cerise looked to Trajan. "Hold her still just in case. Let's hope you don't feel the knife and that the thorns don't fight back."

Trajan sat down on the other side of Anya and pulled her close. "I'm sorry for the pain this may cause," he whispered, his lips brushing her ear, "but I can't bear the thought of losing you again."

Anya shut her eyes and nodded. "I'm ready. Cut the fucking things out."

Katya darted through the trees, thinking about her conversation with Aleksandra. Despite how much she hated him, Katya was like her father in many ways. He had been a hunter too. Usually, the men in the family inherited the hunter gifts, while the women inherited telepathy and divination. Being cursed with two girls, one of his daughters become the hunter. The tribe's hunters didn't just hunt animals but also put down supernatural creatures for preying on humans and those weaker than them.

Their tribe wandered between Skazki and Mir, and Katya had spent lengthy times in both. She only really came back to Skazki when Aleksandra's persistent nagging about her duty to the tribe became too much. Katya had an apartment in Moscow and one in Paris, and both were full of guns she couldn't bring over. It didn't bother her that much, because she never stayed in Skazki long. There were plenty of monsters to hunt in Mir, and it wasn't like the Illumination ever got off their asses to help the Neutrals. Dodging her targets *and* the authorities made

Katya's job as a hunter much more of a challenge, but she felt her skills went to better use in Mir. People in Skazki still taught their children about monsters and how to defend against them. The humans had forgotten about them, and that made them prey. Plus, the tribe had plenty of able-bodied men—not to mention Baba Zosia and Aleksandra—to keep them safe when she wasn't around.

The prior week, Aleksandra had contacted Katya with fierce premonitions of a brewing war and the world on fire. She'd insisted Katya to come back to protect the tribe. The promise of a fight had brought her back, not allegiance.

Aleki? Where are they? Katya had been running most of the day and was getting annoyed.

You are close. Keep going. Katya, the creature is dangerous. Be careful.

Tense voices drifted from the direction of a stream that was close by. *Ask and you shall receive.* She loosened her bow from where it hung concealed underneath her leather coat. Her coat also hid an impressive assortment of vicious weapons, including throwing knives and a short sword. In Katya's opinion, you could never be too prepared.

She spotted the small group at the tree line. Two women and three men. The blond woman among them oozed so much magic, Katya was surprised the trees weren't coming alive and dancing. A few of the group members held the young woman down, and a knife flashed in the hand of the red-haired woman.

Not on my watch. Katya nocked an arrow and released it.

Anya waited for the pain of the blade, but it never came. Her eyes flew open as an arrow thudded into the ground beside them. A woman appeared through the trees, loading another arrow into her bow as she ran. Izrayl morphed and charged her, dodging another fired shot.

"Oh, a *volk krovi*! It must be my lucky day," she said. The bow disappeared under her coat in a quick move, and a knife appeared in each hand. Izrayl launched himself at her, and she fell to her knees, sliding underneath him, her blade catching one of his legs. Izrayl landed and turned for another assault.

"Stop!" Anya shouted with her ruined voice.

Izrayl attacked the stranger with a growl, and she flipped over him, dodging his teeth. Izrayl managed to catch her coat with his claws, and she hit the ground with a loud thump. He stalked over to her, a deep growl rolling through him.

The woman waited until he was crouched over her before she swung her arm out and punched him in the nose. Izrayl yelped in pain and surprise.

"That's enough!" Trajan shouted, his voice echoing over the noise and confusion. "Izrayl, back down. You, woman, explain why you're attacking us."

She rolled to her feet and spat blood on the dirt beside her. "You were about to slice that poor girl up. I can't allow that."

"They're helping me. They are my friends." Anya wheezed. Even speaking strained her.

The stranger fingered the hilts of her knives as her eyes darted around the group. Finally, she lowered her weapons. "If you're her friends, why the hell were you about to cut her hand apart?"

Izrayl changed back into his human body. "She's been poisoned, you presumptuous psychopath." His nose was bleeding, and he had a deep gash on his thigh where she'd cut him with her knife.

"I'm sorry about the wound, wolf boy," she said, though she didn't sound sincere. "My name is Katya, and I'm here to help you too. Would you mind putting on some jeans?"

"I would, actually." Izrayl crossed his arms. "And we don't need your help."

"Really?" Katya pushed him hard, knocking him down to the ground.

A high-pitched, bloodcurdling screech sounded overhead. Not a second later, a black dragon swooped down, its claws snapping at them.

"What the hell is that?" Anya said as Trajan moved to shield her body.

"Get her under the trees!" Katya shouted. She nocked another arrow into her bow.

Trajan and Yvan grabbed Anya's arms, and Cerise lifted her legs. They carried her out of the way and positioned themselves where they could keep an eye on the dragon. Izrayl howled as it landed in the glade.

"Watch its head!" Katya yelled to Izrayl as he went for its long, snakelike neck.

A clawed foot caught him and brushed him out of the way as though he were a puppy and not a massive wolf.

Anya watched with wide eyes as Katya fired her bow and hit the dragon in the chest. It screeched in fury and lashed its head from side to side. Swearing, Katya pulled out a short sword. Izrayl was back on his feet and doing his best to damage the creature's wings by shredding them with his long claws.

"Look after Anya," Trajan said to Cerise.

Anya wanted to reach for him, but she was paralyzed. "Be careful."

"I'll be fine." Trajan smiled at her before heading into the fight.

Katya was fighting at the beast's head, while Izrayl bit at its legs and belly. As if in slow motion, Anya watched Trajan climb up onto its back behind its wings. He shimmered for a moment, like a mirage, and then the creature ceased fighting and sagged to its knees. It cried high and mournful as silvery smoke rose from it and seeped into Trajan, whose gentle protector visage shuddered as he opened his mouth and let out a sound of such otherworldly terror that Anya wanted to curl into a ball and cry. Cerise leaped in front of Anya to shield her from the sight and clamped her hands over her ears.

"Just breathe," she commanded, but Anya's body wouldn't obey. Instead, she sagged into Cerise's arms in a dead faint.

16

ANYA WOKE TO THE smell of acrid smoke and the musk of animal fur. She opened her sore eyes and found that she was slumped over Izrayl's back, with Cerise on one side of her and Yvan on the other.

"Cerise? Where's Trajan? What happened to him?"

"Try not to talk," she said. "You had a seizure and coughed up a lot of blood."

"Where's Trajan?"

"Shh! He's walking a little way back."

"Is he okay?"

Cerise rolled her eyes. "He's fine, just an idiot. He shouldn't have fed off that dragon in front of you all, and now he's embarrassed. He didn't want to carry you because he thought you might have been frightened when you woke. Just try to relax. Katya is taking us to her camp. Apparently, they have a wise woman who will be able to help you." Cerise did little to hide her skepticism.

"What happened to the dragon?"

"We burned it so Vasilli can't resurrect it. Don't worry about it, darling. Just sleep."

Night had fallen and Yvan's coat had been placed over Anya by the time she woke again. She could just make out the glimmer of fire through the heavy beech and pine trees.

"You'll have to change back here," Katya said to Izrayl. "My tribe doesn't look kindly on *volk krovi*." She spoke good English, but she had a thick Eastern European accent and rolled her Rs.

"Is it because we're so handsome?" Izrayl asked.

Yvan stepped forward and lifted Anya from Izrayl's back. She couldn't move her arms or legs and started to weep as fear overwhelmed her.

"Don't cry, *shalost*. All will be well, " Yvan whispered.

"Mischief? That doesn't sound like me."

He smiled and shook his head. "Ha! You can't go one day without getting into some kind of trouble."

"We have to hurry," Katya said. "Everything is prepared so my sister and Baba Zosia can work on Anya straight away."

Through bleary eyes, Anya saw flames and curious glances from strange faces. Spices and incense filled the air, mixed with the smell of Yvan's skin. If she could have moved, she would have clung to him and buried her face into his chest like a little child, breathing in his comforting scent of storms and fire.

"This way." Katya led them to a wooden caravan painted yellow and black. The door opened, and a short, squat old woman shuffled out. She gripped Anya's face with her bony hands. Her snapping black eyes looked deep into her before she muttered something in a language Anya didn't know.

"Come," she said in English. Yvan carried Anya up the iron steps and placed her on a narrow bed. "Go."

"But—" Yvan began, but he was already being pushed outside.

"You come."

Trajan complied, ducking into the caravan, followed by a beautiful woman with long black hair.

"Hello, Anya. I'm Aleksandra. Everything is going to be fine." She looked at Trajan, who stood in the corner. "What are you?"

"He come wit her," the old woman said. "He is *moartea spiritului*."

"Not anymore," Trajan said.

The old woman rattled a reply to Aleksandra.

"Baba Zosia says you are here to detect if we are about to lose Anya's soul," Aleksandra translated.

Baba Zosia got to work lighting the many candles in the cramped space, and Aleksandra moved to help her.

"Trajan?" Anya croaked. He knelt down beside her bed and pushed the damp hair from her face. "Can you feel my death yet?"

"Yes," he said grimly. "But I won't let you go just yet, not when I've finally got you back."

All the emotions that had been building the past few days, brought on by her renewed memories, bubbled to the surface. She knew what she wanted before she died.

"Can I have a final request in case I don't make it?"

"Anything."

"Kiss me. I haven't been kissed in five years, Trajan. I'm s-scared, and it will be a nice way to go." It was the first time in months that Anya realized she wasn't ready to die after all, but she wanted a kiss goodbye if she was going to.

His eyes filled with conflict. "Are you sure? Even after what you saw me do today?"

"Yes. You're still Trajan. Please."

"All right, Anya." Trajan stroked her face before pressing his lips softly to hers. They were gentle, warm, and sent heat from her lips to her chest. He tasted of autumn and darkness, spice and forbidden things. When he moved away from her, his eyes glittered with amazement.

"Thank you," Anya whispered, and then a fit of coughing overtook her.

"We need to get started now." Aleksandra maneuvered Trajan into the far corner of the hot room.

Baba Zosia crouched next to the bed and removed Anya's shirt. "This made by magic. Only magic can unmake."

Aleksandra passed a small pestle and mortar to Baba Zosia, and Anya caught the strong smell of spices.

"If I die, give my soul to Tuoni. The bastard got me into this mess, and I'm going to haunt him in the afterlife," Anya said to Trajan.

"I promise." He gave her a bleak smile.

"You quiet now. Both quiet," Baba Zosia snapped.

Aleksandra came forward and from a hessian bag poured salt in a circle around the narrow bed on which Anya lay. From the folds of her shawl, Baba Zosia produced small bells, which she rang, filling the tense air with their tinkling. Eikki had owned similar bells. He called them *bakterismasko* bells and had a set on a shelf in his room.

Baba Zosia crushed herbs and spice in the stone basin. The rich smell of cloves bombarded Anya's senses, making her magic spike uneasily as Baba Zosia started to hum a tune. Her heart raced, but she managed to find Trajan's face and focus on it.

I kissed him, she thought in a daze, and she had liked it.

Anya watched with grim fascination as Baba Zosia took her infected hand and with two quick flicks of a knife, opened the inflamed scars. Blood poured from the wounds, and Baba Zosia let it drip into the crushed herbs. Anya could no longer follow the tune she was humming, its rhythm reduced to a buzzing static in her brain. Aleksandra joined in and continued the rhythm of it when Baba Zosia spat into the mixture. A small leather bag appeared in her hand, and she tipped the contents in.

Finally, she lit a small bundle of dried grasses and dropped the ashes into the mixture, grinding it until it became a thick paste. She scooped some into her wrinkled hand, then spread it over Anya's wound. Anya screamed as a burning sensation burst up her arm. A thousand knives scraped through her veins as she twisted in pain.

Trajan's eyes flashed red as he rushed to her side. "She's fading to the afterlife! Do something!"

"Hold her down," Baba Zosia told Aleksandra.

Aleksandra gripped Anya's shoulders without even a pause in her incessant humming. Baba Zosia began an incantation in the gypsies' obscure language. She said it three times, her voice becoming more potent with each telling until she was shouting.

Anya screamed as her power flared hot and mixed with Baba Zosia's. It roared through her, burning and cleansing the poison from her body. With a final shout, the pain vanished.

Anya opened her eyes as Baba Zosia ran the rim of a small glass vial over her bloody palm. Then she held it to Anya's face so she could see the two rose thorns in the congealing mess of blood.

"Bind her," Baba Zosia said to Aleksandra.

"I'll be back with some water to clean the wound." Aleksandra helped the older woman down the stairs and out of the caravan.

Trajan moved to Anya's side, his cold hand resting on her burning head.

"Why is it so dark?" Anya whispered.

"Whatever you and that woman just did, it melted all the candles." His hands were shaking. "I thought I'd lost you for a minute."

"I'm not going anywhere. You wasted a kiss for nothing." Anya smiled sleepily.

"It wasn't a waste. And neither is this one." Trajan kissed her again, his long fingers twisting in her hair. Anya managed to move her good hand, gripping his shirt. His scent and the heat of his body warmed her. She should've been shocked, but all she felt was relief to be alive, to have him so close to her. His lips felt right against hers.

Aleksandra reappeared with a steaming basin of water and coughed politely. Trajan broke off the embrace at once. Dazed, Anya touched her lips, the sensation of him imprinted on them.

"I see your hands are working again, which is a good sign." Aleksandra took her place by Anya's side. "Once we get all of this blood bathed off, we'll stitch your hand and get you changed into fresh clothes." She gave Trajan a pointed look.

"I'll be close if you need me," he said and made for the door.

Yvan stood outside of Baba Zosia's caravan, arms folded and pissed that he'd been evicted. He had spent an agonizing amount of time listening to Anya scream, unable to help her. The sound of her cries had ripped the heart right out of him. Even the firebird was restless at the thought of Anya in pain.

Yvan was debating whether or not to barge in when Trajan came hurrying out.

"I see you've been kicked out as well," Yvan said.

"I served my purpose." He looked flustered.

"Which was?"

"To tell them if Anya was dying. She's fine now, just exhausted. You can stop looking so worried, Yvan."

Yvan gripped his hair in his hands. "No, I can't. Vasilli did that to her through a *dream*. How in all the worlds are we going to keep her safe from him?"

"Anya won't make the same mistake twice. She knows what Vasilli can do. We'll go to Paris, call others to help us." Trajan's voice had grown soft, and Yvan's frown deepened. He didn't like the way the thanatos had been looking at Anya.

She doesn't belong to you, princeling, the firebird reminded him.

Like he didn't know that already. He'd seen the way Anya had been looking at Trajan too.

"You should go eat something, Trajan. The body you have is still mostly human, after all. It can't live only off the energy you consumed from that creature. I'll watch over Anya."

Trajan hesitated. "I don't know if I should."

Yvan folded his arms and stepped between Trajan and the caravan. "She's important to me and the firebird too. You're not the only one with the power to protect her."

Without another word, Trajan relented and headed to where the others were eating.

When Aleksandra opened the door, Yvan ducked into the shadows, hoping she didn't spot him. He watched her walk past. The water in the basin she carried was alarmingly red. Once she was out of sight, he hurried up the stairs and into the dark caravan.

Anya lay on the bed, covered high with brightly colored crocheted blankets. Her green eyes flickered open, and she smiled up at him.

"I was wondering if you were ever going to come to visit me," she said.

He sat down on the small milking stool beside her. "I haven't been allowed to. I'm still not." Yvan took her heavily bandaged hand between both of his. His heart shattered seeing what Vasilli had done to her. "How are you?"

"I'm sore, but I can move now, which is a good thing."

Let me help her, the firebird said. It shifted on Yvan's chest, and warmth flooded down his arms and into her hand.

Anya's eyes grew wide. "That feels incredible."

"It wants to do its part in helping you. The firebird doesn't like to see you suffer either."

"Will you stay with me a little while?" Anya's eyes began to droop.

"If you would like me to."

"Stay. I don't want to be alone, Yvan." She rolled onto her side and cuddled into their hands before drifting off to sleep.

Yvan was nodding off too, until the door to the caravan opened. Baba Zosia shuffled in and grunted when she saw him. "I knew you be here," she said quietly, so as not to wake Anya.

"I'm not disturbing her."

"You and dat burd inside you." Her fingers brushed his face, and the fire-bird's power flared. "You make problems for her."

"I know that, but I can't leave her now that Vasilli is aware of her."

"He do this for fun." Baba Zosia held a glass vial in front of him. The bloody thorns were inside. Yvan flinched.

"I know he did. Anya didn't know he could harm her in her dreams."

"I will show her how to stop dat. I show her some more tings. But not for long. You all must go. He come for her."

"Thank you. We'll take any help you are willing to give, *chovihani*." He bowed his head.

"Dat other creature. He care for her." Baba Zosia's face tightened into a scowl.

"Trajan? Yes, he does." Yvan's chest tightened at the fact that a complete stranger had noticed Trajan's apparent interest in Anya.

"He fall in love wit her. Bad ting."

"Perhaps."

She tapped her temple. "I see it in a vision. He will. She will wit him too. It is already done. You still be there for her?"

Yvan flinched like someone had hooked him in the guts. He looked down at Anya sleeping beside him. He hadn't even known he was getting feelings for her until it was too late.

"She needs hero. You be her hero, and her lovers not matter." Baba Zosia waved her hand. "You be what she need. She love you different. She love you for-ever and true. Be her hero. Be her champion."

Yvan took in Anya's pale face and tangled mass of silvery hair. "I'm already her champion. I won't leave her, no matter what." The words cut him like broken glass. "Her magic woke me. She saved me. We are bound together, tighter than lovers, to whatever end."

Baba Zosia patted his shoulder. "Good boy. You grieve for wife?"

Yvan had no idea how she knew about Helena. The fairy-tale version of her had been told throughout both worlds, but only Yvan and Vasilli knew the truth of what really happened the night she died. He hadn't even told Anya the full version of events.

"A part of me was grieving the whole time I was in the egg, but now, other things are more important." Yvan looked back at Anya. He would protect her, even from herself, and maybe then he could leave the past behind.

17

RAIN PATTERED ON THE roof, and the warm, milky smell of cooking porridge and cinnamon filtered back to where Anya lay. She flexed her toes and was relieved to find they were working again. She sat up slowly and ran her hands through her hair. Her wounded palm was still tender but not throbbing as it had been. Whatever Yvan and the firebird had done, it had helped ease the pain. With her body protesting every step, she hobbled through the curtained doorway.

Baba Zosia, swathed in knitted shawls, stood in front of a cast-iron, pot-bellied stove, scooping thick porridge into painted wooden bowls. "Eat," she said and passed Anya a bowl.

She took it and sat at the small pine table. Muttering something under her breath, Baba Zosia sat down and glared at her.

"Thank you for getting the thorns out of my hand," Anya said, not knowing if the older woman would even understand her. "I would be dead without your help."

"Worse," said Baba Zosia. "Eat."

Anya scooped the gooey porridge in her mouth. Ever since she'd come to Skazki, she'd had a much stronger appetite than usual. Being sober more often probably had a lot to do with it.

"You have Papa's eyes." Baba Zosia tapped her temple.

"You knew Eikki?"

"Our path cross. He come to me when you born. To see destiny. He scared. I go to him when you older. Destiny still the same." Baba Zosia clucked her tongue.

Aleksandra came into the caravan, her black hair glittering with rain droplets. *"Bună dimineaţa."* She offered Anya a bright smile. "It's nice to see you up and eating already."

Baba Zosia said something long and complicated to Aleksandra, who she removed her soaked shawl and hung it near the stove to dry.

"Baba Zosia said I'm to translate for you." She poured them all coffee. "Her English is limited, and she says she has much to tell you."

"You speak English very well," Anya said.

"Yakaterina taught me. She spends a lot of time in the human world. Our language is only used by our particular tribe. It's a hybrid of many languages—

Rom, Russian, Egyptian, you name it. We have had many different cultures join us over the years, so it's tough to learn it unless you live with us."

"Do you live in Skazki permanently?"

"We are world-walkers; we travel in and out as it suits us. Lately, we've been in Skazki more, though. Trouble is brewing—"

Baba Zosia began firing off words Anya couldn't understand.

"She says that she looked into your future when you were a child, and she saw many things. She saw you being torn apart by dark and light. You were powerful and strong. She could taste the magic. Eikki didn't want that for you, so he said he wouldn't teach you. He thought that if he made people believe you had no ability, they would leave you alone like they did his son."

"Well, I'm disappointed that he didn't teach me."

Baba Zosia raised an eyebrow at her, and Anya shut her mouth. She said something to Aleksandra, who nodded and said, "When your parents named you, they found one so close to your ancestor's that it was as if destiny were forcing itself. A name like yours would draw suspicion, even if Eikki did lie about your abilities, so he shortened your name to Anya."

"But Anya is my whole name." She had been called Anya for as long as she could remember. She thought of Yvan calling her *shalost*—mischief—and smiled at the nickname. "Then what is my full name if it's not Anya?"

Aleksandra translated for Baba Zosia, who clucked her tongue before answering. "Anyanka."

"Anyanka." Anya's stomach dropped. Eikki had never called her that, not once. And this old woman—she had examined her twice as a child. Of course... Eikki's journal. "Zosi. You're the Zosi Eikki wrote about."

"He call me that sometimes," she said with a wave of her hand.

"It was because of you that he took my memories away." Heat rushed through Anya, her magic waking with her anger. Aleksandra translated, but Baba Zosia's eyes had already narrowed at Anya's tone.

"He took them so you hurt no one else," she spat.

"What are you talking about? I never hurt—"

Baba Zosia slammed her hand down on the table. "You almost drown boy!" She broke off into an angry conversation with Aleksandra, who grew paler with every word.

"Tell me," Anya demanded.

"She said that you'd been playing down at the lake while Eikki gleaned the forest. A group of boys came down and started to tease you. You...summoned the water, wrapped it around the boys, and held them with it. You pushed the water into their mouths. Eikki only just managed to stop you from drowning them. He had to change their memories, made it so that they thought they'd been tangled in the weeds instead."

"I—I did that?" Anya shook her head. "I wouldn't have."

"You did." Baba Zosia stood.

Part of Anya wanted to sprint from the caravan and things she'd done, but she remained rooted where she was. "I need to know," she whispered. "Tuoni—he came to my village, and since then, I've been having dreams—memories—but they're fragmented, like I'm missing pieces. I need to know all of it."

"You want past back, yah? Even hurtful past?"

Anya nodded. If she remembered her magic, she could better learn to use it again. She would be able to defend herself. If what knowledge she'd had in the past hadn't been taken from her, Vasilli would've never been able to trick her in the dreams. She would've been able to defend her friends against the dragon. She was tired of feeling powerless. "Yes, I want it all back. Right now."

"Fine! Come." Baba Zosia waved her over, and Anya moved to stand beside her. She held a hand out over Anya's head, and her magic tingled over her scalp. Baba Zosia clucked her tongue. "Stupid men. Only do half job. Tuoni know better than to get involved."

"Well, he did, and now I want it gone for good."

"You regret this."

"Better than not knowing."

Baba Zosia shook her head. "No, it not."

She flicked Anya hard in her third eye, sending a bolt of power streaking through her. Anya hit the floor. Heat and magic and memory bombarded her, and all she could do was lie still until it stopped. Aleksandra placed a pillow under her head.

"It's going to be okay, Anya," she whispered.

Anya couldn't form a word of reply as the magic pulled her further and further down. It tore down the walls in her mind so quickly, she couldn't make sense of what she was seeing. Tears streamed down her face as she shut her eyes and surrendered.

Anya had no idea how much time had passed before Katya's voice drifted through the noise in her head.

"I can't believe you killed her already." The hunter nudged her softly with the toe of her boot.

"We haven't killed her. She asked Baba Zosia to undo a memory spell, and it's taking a toll on her," Aleksandra said. "She'll be all right soon enough."

"You don't think you pushed her too hard? She almost died yesterday."

"We know that better than anyone," Aleksandra snapped.

Baba Zosia added something in their language, and Katya sighed, loud and sarcastic.

"I'm Anyanka," Anya whispered. She peeled her eyes open to find Katya peering at her, a teasing look on her face.

"I thought Yakaterina was a mouthful. May I call you Anya still? I think if I start calling you Yanka, it might cause a riot." She grinned. "Anya suits you better anyway."

Anya rubbed her eyes, trying to clear away the tears, the memories, the emotions. Magic danced under her skin, warming her fingertips. It seemed to be waiting for her to use it.

"So many memories... My magic... It was all pushed down and taken from me," she whispered.

Katya smiled down at her. "Aw, did they take the magic but leave the fun?"

Anya scowled. "Fuck you and your *Frozen* jokes."

Katya burst out in a big belly laugh. "She's going to be fine."

"My skin won't stop tingling." Anya flexed her hands in an attempt to relieve it.

"It's your magic. That's why you have to learn to control it, so it doesn't try to escape at unexpected times," Aleksandra said.

"That'd make you a real killjoy during sex." Katya smirked.

"Silly Katya go to Mir and tink she know everyting." Baba Zosia's accent became thick with scorn. "Leaves tribe to run with men and become harlot."

Katya rolled her eyes. "I've no time to be a harlot. I'm too busy killing things that stupid people can't see."

"You hunt in the human world? But how do you get in? I thought the gates were all guarded."

"They can't stop us, little Anya. We move between Skazki and Mir as effortlessly as you do. We've roamed since time began. We are of both worlds, and each world recognizes us as belonging to it."

"Where do you hunt?"

"I have an apartment in Budapest, one in Moscow, and one in Paris. It depends on where the trouble is brewing and how quickly I can get there."

Aleksandra shot her a disapproving look. "All you're doing is cleaning up other people's messes. You and your friends cause more trouble than the monsters."

"Wait, you know other hunters in the human world?" Anya sat up—slowly. Baba Zosia's magic had knocked her down hard, and her brain still felt like it was vibrating in her skull.

"A few. We're loners by nature, but there are people I can call if I ever need back up."

"You were amazing yesterday. You're half the size of Izrayl, and you were kicking his ass."

Katya grinned. "Thanks. I could show you a trick or two."

"I could show you both a trick or two," Cerise said as she appeared in the doorway. "I was wondering if you were up yet. I came to check on you, being your nurse and all. What are you doing on the floor?"

"I'm fine," Anya said but let Cerise help her up and into a chair.

"I talked to the boys, and they said you're heading to Paris," Katya said to Cerise.

"What of it, hunter?"

"I was thinking of heading back that way myself, and from what Trajan said, you lot have Vasilli after you." Katya flashed a bloodthirsty grin. "Hunting the Darkness is my favorite kind of sport."

Anya's brow furrowed. "You want to come with us?"

"If you'll have me. Trouble is following you, and you could use an extra warrior in your group. Not that Fido doesn't do an okay job."

Anya smiled and wondered if Katya would ever have the guts to call Izrayl 'Fido' to his face. One look at her sharp, scarred face, and Anya suspected she would.

"I have contacts in Europe. If Vasilli and the Darkness are rumbling, the hunters will know what activity is going on," said Katya. "Vasilli will likely have his allies looking everywhere for you, and he will have alerted the Darkness throughout Russia. You killed Vischto, and you added insult to injury by turning him down in that dream of yours."

"Because that turned out so well for me." Anya waved her bandaged hand at her. "He's going to know the thorns are out."

"Not necessarily. Baba Zosia said that if they remain in your blood, he may not be able to tell," Aleksandra said.

"Well, that's something, at least."

Cerise tapped her long nails on the arm of her chair. "We can train Anya how to defend herself against soldiers in combat. It's the magic she really needs a trainer for, and we don't know any shamans."

Katya nodded. "I have some friends who might be able to help, seeing how you can't stay here with us and learn like Aleki."

"You know gates magic?" Anya asked, turning to Aleksandra.

"Not in a way that would be useful to you. We are a world-walker tribe, which means we know of many back ways into the human world and other worlds. I can do magic to find those weak places, but I can't open and close them on command, especially not established ones. It's more like scrying than what a real gatekeeper can do," Aleksandra explained. "Baba Zosia doesn't want you to stay with us. We won't risk our people if Vasilli comes for you."

"I understand." Anya didn't want Vasilli anywhere near innocent people, especially not because of her. She could only imagine what kind of damage the black dragon would have done to these people to get at her.

Aleksandra looked at Katya, lips pursed. "What about the twins? They might be able to show her some things. They walk the dream worlds and understand boundary magic. They could help."

"I'll see if I can get in touch with them when we get to Paris. We should teach her something easy for now, so she's not trailing so much magic everywhere. It's like breadcrumbs for Vasilli and any Power in the area. If I'm going with them, I don't want that kind of heat after us. How about scrying? She's got her own runes."

"That will be a useful skill. If you're serious about going with them, I suggest teaching her to mind-link with you too." Aleksandra directed a pointed look at her sister.

"No. I don't need another voice in my head. You breaking into my thoughts is bad enough."

Baba Zosia scolded Katya in their language. The hunter threw up her hands, then snapped back at Baba Zosia before storming out of the caravan. Aleksandra sighed and went after her, while Baba Zosia went back to the tiny kitchen and lit a pipe.

Cerise blew out a breath. "Well, I'll leave you to it, Anya. I'll let the boys know you're doing okay. They're worried senseless. Yvan keeps igniting."

"Literally or figuratively?"

"Both. His skin was dripping flames last night, and the bird wasn't even trying to push its way through."

Anya's brows shot up. "Really?"

"He says the firebird is troubled as well."

"Aren't I lucky to have all of these people worried about me all of a sudden?" Anya reached back and tried to braid her hair.

Cerise moved her hands away, and after they found Anya's brush in her pack, she braided it tight for her. "I haven't seen Trajan this anxious for a mortal before." She wove the remaining strands together. "It concerns me."

"Why?" Anya didn't know if Trajan had told Cerise about their kisses the night before and wasn't about to share if he hadn't.

"Our kind and your kind are on different sides of reality. It's unheard of and discouraged for us to get attached to mortals."

"Why?"

"Because they die, or we kill them."

"Accidentally or on purpose?"

"Pick one, honey. It's our job and our very nature. You saw what Trajan did to that creature. Doesn't that frighten you?"

"He wouldn't hurt me." Trajan was the one person in the world she could say that about with certainty. *And Yvan.* The previous night, he had stayed with her, and the firebird had eased her pain. His presence had meant more to her than she could articulate.

"He wouldn't do it intentionally, but in the heat of the moment, he could lose control."

"Well, nothing has happened for you to be so concerned about any heated moments." Anya wanted to reassure her, but she couldn't stop thinking about the kisses the night before. Maybe he'd done it because she had been dying. *The first one perhaps, but what about the second one?* She had no answer for that.

"It doesn't matter if they haven't happened yet. I still feel like I need to warn you. I've known him sixty-five years, and I've never seen him look at anyone the way he looks at you."

How does he look at me? Anya bit her tongue to stop herself from asking. She was saved from answering by Aleksandra's reappearance.

"I'll be back later." Cerise gave the end of Anya's braid a playful tug. "Have fun learning magic."

Baba Zosia turned to offer Anya another cup of coffee. She reached to take it, but nausea hit her. Baba Zosia said something, but her voice was drowned out and far away. Memories rushed through Anya's mind. She tasted blood and ash, smelled mud and lake weed, as images flashed before her.

Humiliation prickled her skin as a boy with blond hair picked up another handful of mud. The first one had hit her in the face, bruising her cheek and filling her mouth with blood.

The three boys had been teasing her about her tits, which had begun to grow two months prior. When she'd ignored them, they started throwing things at her. Anya summoned magic to her fingertips, and the next time the boy raised his arm, water surged out of the lake, grabbed him by the arm, and held him tight. His friends screamed as the reeds stretched out and pulled them into the water. The blond boy cried as he struggled. Anya stepped toward him as her fingers curled, sending water into his mouth. He tried spitting it out, but he couldn't keep it up and started to gurgle.

Anya had smiled, watching as he pissed himself. As he stopped struggling.

"Anya! Stop!" Eikki shouted, and then Baba Zosia's strong hand was shaking her.

"Anya!"

The memory vanished, and she was in the wooden caravan again.

"I—I remembered the boys."

Baba Zosia let her go. Anya got up and stumbled past her. Neither Baba Zosia nor Aleksandra tried to stop her as she hurried out of the caravan. She ran for the forest, the camp around her blurred by her tears.

18

B IRCH BOUGHS SLAPPED AGAINST Anya's arms and face as she ran farther and farther into the woods. Horror clawed at her throat. She dry heaved but managed to keep her breakfast down.

Anya sat down on a fallen tree and put her head between her legs, her breath coming in tight, panicked gasps as sweat broke out over her skin. *You almost killed those boys.* And she had sat back and smiled while she did it.

"You know running off on your own would be considered unwise—"

Anya's head jerked up.

Trajan took one look at her tear-stained face and was crouched beside her in a blink. "Anya, what happened? Are you hurt?"

Anya shook her head and wiped the tears off her face. "I asked Baba Zosia to remove Eikki's memory spell."

Trajan swore in Greek. "Which incident did you see?"

"There's more than one?" she asked, her voice rising in panic.

"You're okay. Talk to me, Anya. What did you see?"

"The boys at the lake. I almost murdered them. I...I liked seeing them powerless."

Trajan moved to sit beside her, resting his elbows on his knees. "I remember when that happened. It was the reason Eikki decided to go through with his plan to take away your memories. I told him he was overreacting, that you were young and hurt. Your magic had tried to protect you, that's all."

"I know what I felt, Trajan. I wanted to make them feel as humiliated as me." Anya's face twisted with disgust. "Maybe Eikki was right to not teach me if I was willing to kill."

"Anya, you were afraid and alone. Those boys could've hurt you a lot more than what they did. You defended yourself. It was a lesson the little bastards needed, in my opinion. That's why I convinced Eikki to leave their fear of you in place so they knew to never mess with you again." Trajan grinned sideways at her, making her heart trip. It prompted a fresh memory and surge of emotion: she'd had a massive crush on him at twelve.

His smile slipped. "What's the matter? Your face just changed to horror and back again."

"Nothing. I was...thinking about what other horrible things I did that I'm inevitably going to remember and freak out over."

"The lake was probably the incident that scared Eikki the most." Trajan's smile grew bigger. "Well, apart from when you were nine and told him you were going to marry me when you grew up."

Anya buried her head in her hands. "Shut up. I did not."

"You did. You were very vocal and insistent about it too." He pulled her hands away from her burning face. "Eikki had a heart attack, but I thought it was cute."

"Well, can you blame me? You saw the village I grew up in; any man with a full set of teeth is a prize."

They both laughed. Trajan kept hold of her hand, and she didn't mind.

"How about this, whenever you have a bad memory, come talk to me about it. I wasn't there for all of them, but it might help." He brushed his thumb over her palm. "I was out of your life for a long time, but you can talk to me about anything, and I won't judge you. Don't let the memory of those boys make you doubt yourself. You weren't a murderer then, and you're not one now."

"Thanks." Anya's tongue tied as his thumb circled against her skin again, the small touch sending a wave of goose bumps up her arm. His eyes were warm and golden. Her eyes drifted to the curve of his lips, and she couldn't help but think of them against hers.

"Trajan? About last night—" She paused to summon her courage. "Thank you for being there for me and giving me one last kiss. You didn't have to, and I don't want any weirdness between us—"

"Do you feel weird with me here right now?" His brows drew together.

"No. But I thought maybe you would. Cerise told me that your kind doesn't mix with mortals."

"Did she now?" Trajan said, frustration tinging his gentle tone. "It's true that I haven't 'mixed' with a mortal before, but I wouldn't have kissed you if I didn't want to."

"Oh." Heat flooded Anya's cheeks. "That's good, then."

"I'm glad you think so." Trajan's small, pleased smile returned.

Anya was filled with so many butterflies, she was surprised they weren't bursting out of her bright red ears. Before she could reply, a sharp whistle cut through the trees.

"Anya! Do you want these magic lessons or not?" Katya shouted.

Trajan squeezed her hand, then let it go. "You'd better go. That hunter doesn't seem to be the patient type."

Anya jumped to her feet. "I'll catch up with you later?"

He nodded once.

Without another word, Anya trekked back through the woods with rosy cheeks and sweaty palms, feeling like she was walking on air.

Anya was calmer after her talk with Trajan, but she still needed something to distract her. Her head swam with memories and kisses and Trajan's irresistible grin. Aleksandra made them fresh cups of coffee and sat down at the scrubbed wooden table.

"Is Katya okay? She sounded angry just now," Anya said, hoping that they would all overlook her running off. She was embarrassed and hated it.

"Katya's fine. Just stubborn. She doesn't really care for magic and has no wish to learn it. How are you feeling?" Aleksandra placed her hand on Anya's forehead.

"I'm okay. Overwhelmed, but okay."

"Memory magic is tricky. It will take a little while for things to come back to you. Be patient, and don't panic when it happens. It will take some time. Now, show me your runes."

Anya found her pack at the back of the caravan and dug out her runes and the shaman drum. "I have no idea how to use either of these properly." She placed them on the table.

Aleksandra didn't touch the drum as she leaned in for a closer look. "Where did you get this? The magic on it is strange."

"Baba Yaga traded me for it."

"I don't know anything about drums, so we'll have to ask Baba Zosia about it. It's pulsing with power." Aleksandra went to touch the leather bag containing the runes but jerked her hand back with a yelp.

"What happened?"

"I'm not sure. They zapped me." She cradled her hand to her chest.

"Sorry. I'm not really sure how they work either." Anya tipped them out. "They didn't zap Yvan when he touched them."

"I'll let you handle them from now on."

Anya turned the runes over so they lay faceup, their symbols all showing clearly. Slowly and with extreme patience, Aleksandra named them one by one and explained what each represented. After the fourth rune, Aleksandra gave Anya a battered notebook and pencil to make notes.

Aleksandra soon had her repeating them back to her: *Fehu, Thurisaz, Ansuz...*

After an hour of study, Baba Zosia hobbled in and put more coffee on. Aleksandra spoke to her, and Anya heard Baba Yaga's name mentioned more than once. Baba Zosia replied to her in angry tones. She sat down next to Aleksandra to inspect the drum, careful not to touch it. She spoke, and Aleksandra translated.

"She says this drum is magic in many ways. It changes with each user. For example, if I were to possess it, the symbols on the skin would change so they were most right to me."

"When I first used it, the rune stone landed on this bird, the crosses, and this figure here." Anya touched the skin of the drum. "Could you tell me what that means?"

Aleksandra translated, and Baba Zosia cackled before giving her reply.

"She said if you can't figure it out, you are an idiot." Aleksandra's cheeks pinked a little.

Anya shrugged. "When it comes to magic, I definitely am. Could you tell me how to use it, at least?"

"This drum is Sami. It's not our magic. Baba Zosia knows the basics, but as for using it traditionally...well, you'll need a Sami shaman for that."

"I'll take any information she can give me."

"Very well. Drums are read in all directions, from the front and from the back, from top to bottom. Your eye should move from the highest world to the lowest one, reading the markings counterclockwise. This is north, south, east, west," Aleksandra explained with Baba Zosia prompting her. "This is the North Star. The top half of the drum is usually the heavenly realm, especially the northeastern section. This is a church, representing God or divine beings." She pointed. "This bear is the god Ukko. The rune here is *Algiz,* if you remember."

Anya glanced at her notes. "Protection, defense, and warding off evil."

"That's right. This bird, I can only assume, is the firebird. Look at its tail, long and beautiful, and its home is the sky. This northwestern section is also heavenly things or higher knowledge. You have Yggdrasil, the world tree, from your northern tales. Also, you have Odin's ravens, Huginn and Muninn—Thought and Memory."

"And that symbol is *Ansuz*, a symbol for Odin, God, insights, truth, vision, and the power of words." Anya looked closer, secretly proud that she had remembered it without her notes this time.

"This whole middle section is the earthly realm. Right here, you have a warrior or hunter, then a forest, salmon. Here is *Uruz*—physical strength, speed, courage, and sex. Here is its female counterpart, *Pertho*, which is the symbol of women, mysteries, and fertility. This is a male shaman with his drum and a female shamanitsa on the opposite side." Aleksandra pointed toward the lower part of the drum. "Now, this last end of the drum is the Underworld, especially this southeastern section. These crosses are a graveyard or death. We have Fenrir and Cerberus, hellhounds of the Underworld. This is *Thurisaz*, but it is *merkstave*—backward—so the meaning is the opposite now. Here it represents evil, hate, lies, rape, and torment. It's all bad."

Anya pointed. "What's this one? It looks like a funny little house."

"That's a winter storage hut, but in this case, I believe it's Baba Yaga's house. Those are not traditional tree trunks holding it up."

Anya rubbed a hand over her face. "Great. I really can't escape her, can I?"

Baba Zosia shook her head. "She watches you."

Hours later, Anya's pounding head was full of magic and symbols and rune stones. She stumbled out of Aleksandra's caravan and into the cold, misty rain. She was exhausted, and they had barely scraped the surface.

"Hale and whole I see, shamanitsa." Yvan stood under the awning of a caravan, the collar of his jacket turned up to keep the rain out, his black hair wet and glossy.

"Thanks to you and my other helpers, I'm doing okay." Anya joined him. "Have you been standing here long?"

"A while. I was hoping your bodyguards would've freed you long before now."

"They've been teaching me the ways of the great shamanitsas!"

Yvan grinned and leaned against the caravan. "I'm happy to hear it. I'm looking forward to seeing what you can do with all that magic. Are you learning anything useful?"

"Bits and pieces. They're going to teach me how to mind-link with Katya this afternoon." She sucked in a breath and blew it out. "Baba Zosia seems to think I have the capability."

"Even a blind man can see your potential, *shalost*." His eyes were soft yet severe, and Anya was acutely aware of the weight of them when he looked at her.

"Where's everyone else?"

"They're around. Trajan and Izrayl went on a scouting trip. Cerise, I have no idea, but I saw her a little while ago. Katya disappeared with her bow and sword. I get the feeling that being in the tribe and around so many people makes her uncomfortable."

"It's certainly a change for me too. Our little group is growing every day. I swear I'm going to start handing out name tags so I can keep up."

Yvan chuckled. "Katya told me her intention to join us. I don't see the harm in it. She can take care of any threat that comes against her. I've never seen a woman warrior like her."

Anya felt a pinch of jealousy at the admiration in his tone, but she buried it. "Cerise tells me you were lighting yourself on fire last night. How's that going for you?"

Yvan shrugged. "Fine, now I know that you are well."

"You were that worried?"

"Are you surprised that I would worry about you?"

"I'm surprised when anyone gives a damn. It's a new experience for me."

"Of course I give a damn. If you had died yesterday, I never could've forgiven myself." Yvan wrapped her cold hands in his. "That my own brother was the one to hurt you—"

"Hey, stop. What Vasilli does has nothing to do with you. You carry too much guilt as it is. Don't shoulder me as one of your burdens."

"You're a burden I don't mind shouldering."

"Just don't let it become so heavy that you can't carry it and leave." The pain of losing Trajan the first time around was fresh. She couldn't handle losing Yvan after all they'd been through.

Yvan squeezed her hand before letting it go. "Don't worry. I'm not going anywhere, Anya."

19

TRAJAN PACED ACROSS THE forest floor. Every few minutes, he would stop and touch his lips, the sensation of kissing Anya still imprinted on them. Talking to Anya in the forest had only made it worse. The way she looked at him, the way she talked to him was changing. The spark of recognition and affection now in her eyes filled him with warmth. He'd caught up with Eikki here and there over the years and knew that Anya had grown into a unique, beautiful woman, but experiencing it firsthand was a different matter. He'd never kissed a mortal before; he had never even been tempted to until now. Anya tasted of magic and fire, and he couldn't stop thinking about it.

Izrayl sat on a rock with an amused expression on his face. Cerise appeared through the trees, her red hair standing out against the forest's greens and browns.

"Relax, Trajan. Anya's fine, but I'm not. Whoever thought camping was a good idea needs to have their brain examined. Baba Zosia and Aleksandra are training our girl as we speak, so we have some time to talk."

Trajan let his hands fall to his sides. "I'm such an idiot. Eikki used to speak about Baba Zosia and this tribe. He called her Zosi, and I never put it together. He never even told me Anya's real name is Anyanka." He resumed pacing. "And now that Anya is getting all of her memories back, she's going to be hurt by how much Eikki took from her."

"For goodness sake, between you and Yvan, there's enough worry to smother the poor girl to death," said Cerise.

"It's not like she hasn't been through enough already. She could've died yesterday!"

"But she didn't, so get over it," Izrayl said, then raised a brow before adding, "And thank God she didn't die, because she's rather extraordinary—but you already know that, don't you, Trajan?"

Cerise hit Izrayl across the back of the head. "Take your mind out of the gutter. Trajan damn well knows better than to think about going there with a mortal. Right, Trajan?"

Trajan became very interested in cleaning the water droplets off the lenses of his glasses. "None of your business. It's not like you've never had a relationship with a mortal before."

Cerise's gaze lingered on him for a moment before she changed the subject. "Once we get to Paris, we can come up with a real plan in five-star accommodation. With any luck, Vasilli won't find out that his stunt with the thorns hasn't worked until we're long gone from here."

"At least in the human world, Anya won't be trailing magic all over the place." Izrayl picked leaves out of his hair. "Paris is a good idea, considering all we have are rubbish options. Can't go back to Russia. They still have a bounty on us for that time we rescued Anya in Moscow. They're still touchy about all their operatives you killed, Trajan. Last time I checked, the bounty on your head was close to five million euro."

"They had it coming. Anya was alone and defenseless," Trajan said without an ounce of remorse.

Cerise tapped her nails against her chin. "Katya could teach Anya how to defend herself while she learns magic. She's great with a blade."

"Just as long as Katya doesn't teach her any of her bad manners." Izrayl grunted. "That girl has some serious issues with *volk krovi*."

"Sounds to me like you're sulking because she hasn't looked at you twice." Cerise smirked.

"Please, like I give a damn."

Trajan stopped pacing and looked between them. "If you two would get back to the problem at hand..."

Cerise lit a cigarette. "Relax. Anya is going to learn some magic today, and then tomorrow, we go to Paris. Your house will be able to hold us all, and it's a veritable fortress with all the security. Anya can learn her magic there and prepare to shut the gates."

"The gates aren't going to hold forever." He began to pace again. "We're going to need to figure out a way to get her back through to her farm when the time comes. At least if she has a little time to explore her talent, she may be able to use the gates without killing herself..."

Izrayl stood up and stretched. "We can't leave it longer than another day here. We're putting these people at risk. Vasilli won't be fooled for long, and he will kill these people for sheltering us out of spite."

Cerise stubbed out her cigarette on a rock. "Well, I don't think I could handle much more of this trudging through mud and lack of hot showers anyway. Also, my supplies are running low. I only have three vials of dead man's blood left." She gave Trajan a disapproving look. "We all know that you'll be fine for weeks, thanks to that unfortunate incident with Vasilli's pet."

"Let it go," Izrayl warned.

"Don't worry. Anya isn't scared of him because of it. Though, in my opinion, she should be." Cerise poked Trajan in the shoulder. "Careful there, old friend."

Trajan was smart enough not to bite Cerise's bait.

They hadn't even made it out of the forest before they heard Anya's laughter. Trajan smiled and went to find her. She sat on a wooden stump, surrounded by some of the tribe's children, teaching them scissors, paper, rock. Yvan stood among them, laughing. Anya looked more carefree than he had ever seen her, making her even more beautiful.

"She's very patient with them."

Trajan turned to find Katya leaning against the side of a caravan.

"Yes. She's always had a kind heart, even though she hides it." He turned back to watch Anya.

"That trick you did with the dragon—any chance of it happening again by accident?" Katya asked, her eyes still on the children.

"None at all. I'd never hurt anyone here. You have my word."

"Good." Katya didn't push him for anything more than that. "When we get back to the human world, I don't know what kind of reception we're going to get. Probably a bad one knowing the Darkness. Vasilli and Ladislav will have their operatives looking everywhere for Anya and Yvan."

"You're not afraid of a fight, are you?" Izrayl asked.

He and Katya eyed each other up like gunfighters.

She hooked her thumbs in her belt, close to the sheaths holding her daggers. "I live for it." Katya tossed her shaggy black hair. "I'm worried about an old dog like you taking on the big boys, that's all."

Izrayl grunted. "Settle down, pup. Those teeth aren't sharp enough to take me on just yet. I'll give you a rematch if you want, but right now, we've got bigger problems."

All three of them turned and looked at Anya again. She gave them a puzzled glance but was interrupted by one of the children clamoring for her attention.

"Aleki tells me she learns remarkably fast. She thinks too fast, but I think Anya's just a natural. She certainly has enough power to throw around, that's for sure," Katya said. "Kind of surprised the Darkness hasn't tried to take her already."

"They tried once in Moscow. They were suspicious of what Eikki had told them about her lack of abilities and thought to find out for themselves when she was ripe for the picking." Trajan could still feel the rage he'd released that night, could taste the blood in his mouth.

"The Darkness do love a press-gang when they are keen to recruit, don't they? What happened?" Katya looked at Trajan uneasily. "Anya only told me that you two found her in a park in Moscow."

"Izrayl and I had been tracking her for days, trying to get her back to Eikki. The Darkness had been following her too."

Katya frowned, her fingers tapping against her arm. "How did they find her? Wasn't she living as a normal?"

"From what I learned afterward, Anya was spotted by a Darkness member—someone who recognized her as being of Ilya's bloodline—then flagged her and alerted Ladislav." Trajan didn't mention what he did to get that information or how good it felt to remind them what was still protecting the Venäläinens.

"We found the Darkness closing in on her," Izrayl continued, his eyes flicking over to Trajan. "Trajan kind of lost it. He raged out, tried to kill all ten of them. They had backup; we didn't. It was a messy fight. Trajan almost died, but we got Anya back to Eikki in one piece."

"They would've found it a hard task to kill me," Trajan said. That night was still a sore spot between them. Izrayl didn't like to kill unless he had to, but Trajan was his best friend, so he'd excused his behavior.

"I won't say the Darkness didn't deserve it. I know what they do to people with magical abilities." Katya crossed her arms. "Sounds like a good fight."

"The problem is that we're now high on their shit list. I'm happy to go back to the human world, though. I've missed the girls there for a number of reasons." Izrayl gave Katya a wicked smile.

She rolled her eyes. "I'm sure. You two having a bounty on your heads is going to create even more trouble."

"I'm sure you can handle some trouble." Izrayl's smile only grew wider.

"I can handle a lot of trouble." Katya's mouth twisted into a grin. "And I could certainly handle you."

Izrayl laughed. "Keep telling yourself that, hunter."

Night fell in the forest. Katya tipped back yet another drink as everyone sat around the cooking fires eating and talking. She stood outside of the fire circle, leaning against one of the caravans.

Katya's eyes slipped to where Izrayl was chatting with Cerise, then quickly looked away. She didn't know what had gotten into her. Flirting with a *volk krovi* was just plain dangerous, no matter how cute he was. He had a shitty attitude, but it kind of heightened his appeal.

Katya groaned inwardly at her stupidity. It had been drilled into her to kill his kind, not flirt with them. Maybe Baba Zosia was right…maybe she was turning into a hussy. Or maybe there was a *volk krovi* walking around with amazing black hair, wicked amber eyes, and a killer smile who could loosen a seven-ty-year-old nun's morals just by walking past.

Focus! Katya decided to blame her current dry spell, the golden firelight, and the vodka singing in her brain. It would be really great if he would stop smiling at her, then looking away. *Bastard men.* Katya took another sip of vodka.

Trajan and Anya were sitting next to each other, their sides just touching. They reminded Katya of nervous high school kids who didn't know whether to hold hands in public or not. Cute, in a bizarre way. A Grecian death spirit crushing on a mortal Russian shamanitsa? That was a world of drama waiting to happen.

"You seem lost in thought."

Katya stumbled backward, and Izrayl placed his hand on the small of her back to steady her. "Big thinker I am."

"Easy there, hunter." He chuckled. "I never picked you for a big thinker. You're more like me. You're a doer."

Katya turned around to face him. His long braid hung over his shoulder, and she fought the urge to touch it. "Won't do you."

She would've thought that would offend him, but Izrayl laughed. "I bet a one-legged leper could do you right about now."

Katya shook her head and groaned.

"I can't imagine a leper would be your type, though. Or a *volk krovi*, for that matter. You've made it pretty clear what you think of them."

"You wouldn't know what my type is." She took another drink.

Izrayl fixed his golden eyes on her, and her legs swayed. He reached out and took the red mug out of her hands without taking his gaze off her. "You've had enough of this for one night. We have a big day tomorrow. You should think about going to bed."

"I will have someone escort you to your kennel."

"So you're spiteful even when you're drunk." Hurt crossed his face, and she regretted the joke immediately.

"Shit, I'm sorry. I'm kind of a bitch most of the time. Don't mean to be. I just don't play well with others. Plus, I'm supposed to hate you. If my father were alive… Fuck, I'd be in *so* much trouble."

"Lucky he isn't, then."

"Doesn't matter. I can feel his disapproval from the afterlife." Katya tried to walk forward and ended up tripping right into Izrayl.

Izrayl laughed as he caught her before she hit the grass. "You're kind of adorable when you're off your face." He propped her against him.

"You're nicer when I'm drunk."

"Don't tell anyone." He winked. "You really should go to bed. I can help you—don't give me that look! No funny stuff, I swear. Believe it or not, I don't take advantage of girls when they're drunk."

Katya gave him a wonky smile, then it fell from her face. "Izrayl?"

"Yakaterina."

"See that tree? Head for it, because I'm about to throw up."

He carried her behind the tree, and as she fell forward to vomit, his warm hands held the hair back from her face.

Katya groaned. "This is so embarrassing."

"It's amusing for me, though. Now when you're being standoffish, I can go, 'Hey, Katya. Remember that time I held your hair while you threw up?' and you'll *have* to acknowledge me."

"You could just say hello," Katya said, then heaved once more.

"That hasn't worked so far." Izrayl helped her up. "Let's take you home." Katya lost her footing, and Izrayl swung her up in his arms. "Let's do this the easy way, and don't even think about fighting with me, or I'll dump you on the ground and leave you there."

"Okay," she mumbled.

Izrayl walked up the stairs of Aleksandra's caravan and placed Katya on her bed. Katya clutched her head and squeezed her eyes shut. When she opened them, he was holding out a cup of water.

"Thank you."

Izrayl gave her the cup before folding his arms and leaning against the doorframe. Katya took a few sips and placed it on the nightstand.

She lay back on her pillows. "Will you please stop looking at me like that?"

"Like what?" Izrayl asked.

"Like you're laughing at me. It's rude."

"Only because you aren't in on the joke."

"Because I *am* the joke." Katya grabbed the quilt, and he helped her pull it up to her chin.

"Can I ask why you're meant to hate *volk krovi*?"

"'Cause my father said they killed my mother. So he made me...kill them back."

"Did you find her murderers?"

Katya shrugged. "He told me the *volk krovi* killed her. Made me hate them. I don't even know if that's true anymore."

Izrayl's golden eyes softened. "I'm not like other *volk krovi*."

"I *know*, and I hate it already."

Izrayl's smile turned mischievous, and heat zinged through her blood. His smile widened as if he sensed the change in her. "I would give you a kiss good-night, but I'm not keen on vomit breath."

"What makes you think I'd want you to kiss me? I'm not *that* drunk."

Izrayl leaned down toward her face. He was so close she felt his breath on her lips. "Despite your prejudice against my kind, I think you're curious," he whispered. "Goodnight, little hunter."

He disappeared out the door, leaving her staring stupidly after him.

20

ANYA SAT IN THE caravan kitchen with Aleksandra, Baba Zosia, and Katya, doing her best to coax her magic to life. She'd woken that morning with a buzzing under her skin that she was beginning to identify more and more as her magic. When she closed her eyes and focused, she could sense the strange shape of it, like flickering flames inside her. She blinked back tears as she realized that *this* was what had been missing from her life. It wasn't only about her masked memories, but this magic inside of her that had been smothered to ash. Together, they made up the lost part of her, which had been restored, ready for her to learn and embrace like she should have been able to do fifteen years ago. *Oh, Eikki, I love you, but you have no idea the damage you've done.*

"You need to relax, Anya," Aleksandra said. "Everything is fine."

"I *am* relaxed," Anya insisted with closed eyes.

She listened to each person breathing and the rain hammering on the wooden sides of the caravan. To her right, the pot-bellied stove ticked and popped. She could smell dust, incense, Aleksandra's perfume, and the coffee dregs in the cup in front of her. Anya opened her right eye. Katya, who she was meant to be mind-linking with, sat opposite her. Her eyes were shut, but she was smiling cheekily. Anya stifled a giggle. Baba Zosia hissed at her, and Anya worked to regain her composure.

"Calm your thoughts, Anya," said Aleksandra. "Think of a vivid memory and focus on it. Block out everything else around you. Find that quiet space in your mind."

Anya took a deep, steadying breath and tried to focus on the flames inside of her. Instead, the firebird, rising from her chimney and across the blue-black sky, soared through her mind. The fire on its body lit the darkness with an inferno of bright light. The white stars blinked behind it. She remembered how the night had smelled: the scent of pine, the muskiness of the animals coming from the barn, wood smoke from the house, and the smell of the firebird itself. It reminded her of ozone—the way a thunderstorm smells, hot and charged, crackling with energy.

Across the table, Katya gasped so loudly that Anya jumped.

"I'm sorry. It's just—the firebird. I've never seen anything like it," Katya said.

Anya smiled. "You should have been there. It was…incredible."

Aleksandra cleared her throat. "This is good. It means Anya can find the focus she needs. Try it again."

And so they tried, and they tried, and they tried. Anya was ready to give up entirely when, finally, heat and the adrenaline rush of her magic shot through her and reached out of her body and across the table.

Katya's voice rolled through her mind: *How much longer can they expect us to try? And why in the hell are they pushing her so hard? Poor thing has had a lifetime of surprises in the last couple weeks… Okay, Katya, focus.*

I'm sure I will live to see many more surprises, Anya thought.

Katya clapped her hands. "She did it! It worked."

Baba Zosia grumbled. "Too much magic. Could taste it in the air. Small, small."

Now that Anya had touched it once, the power purred softly through her, and this time, she managed to just lightly brush Katya's mind. She was thinking of Izrayl, who'd apparently gotten her some water when she was drunk the night before. Anya felt Katya's fresh wave of embarrassment.

Don't feel that way. Izrayl was just trying to do a nice thing, Anya thought.

Yeah, but I shouldn't have been drinking at all. I'm meant to be protecting the tribe.

"It's working," Katya said.

"Good! Good!" Baba Zosia clapped her hands as Anya opened her eyes. "Now, again!"

✦

For Anya, the day was spent inside with the three women, but outside was a flurry of activity. The tribe would move on that night, leaving little trace that they were ever there. Baba Zosia had decided it was time for them to move to the winter grounds. No word was mentioned of Vasilli.

By nightfall, everyone from the youngest infant to the oldest grandfather was ready to leave. Anya dressed in warm clothes and shouldered her bag before stepping out into what remained of the camp. Horses were being hitched to caravans. The small bells sewn onto their harnesses rang as they fussed. Yvan stood to one side of all the commotion, and Anya hurried to join him.

He moved her out of the way of a man carrying a large roll of carpet. "Be careful you don't get trodden on in the madness."

"Madness is the name for it."

"How did your lessons go today?"

"Better than I expected. I can talk to Katya in her mind."

Yvan frowned. "That sounds complicated."

"It is. Apparently, I have problems focusing and finding the inner peace required." Anya laughed.

"No surprise there. How did you manage the magic?"

"I focused on a memory that makes me happy—the night you hatched and the firebird flying for the first time."

"This is a memory that helps you find inner peace?" A faint pink tinge rose up his neck. "I'd think you'd see it as the moment your peace ended."

Anya shook her head. "If not for you, I probably would've been dead by alcohol poisoning or a drunken farming accident sometime soon. Hatching in my house was a good thing, despite what came after."

Yvan opened his mouth to reply when Trajan, Cerise, and Izrayl appeared, and he closed it again. Anya's stomach flipped as Trajan spotted her and smiled.

The caravans moved off one at a time. Within thirty minutes, they had all disappeared except Baba Zosia's. It stopped just on the outskirts, and after checking no one was left behind, she moved to a nearby tree.

"Watch this," Katya said.

Baba Zosia pulled a small knife from her belt. Squinting in the darkness, Anya could just make out a strange, curving symbol scratched into the bark. Baba Zosia scored a line through it, disfiguring the symbol.

Anya sensed something in the air change and give out, like the forest had let out a breath it'd been holding. Static pricked the back of her neck as Baba Zosia cut her finger and smeared blood on the tree. The strange symbol melted into the bark, and the tree healed as though nothing had been carved into it.

Lifting her hands toward the campsite, Baba Zosia chanted in the complicated language of the tribe. Magic thrummed through the air, making Anya's flare and itch under her skin. Around her, a breeze picked up, and the campground, with its tracks in the mud and stains from the fires, all melted away until there was nothing but autumn leaf litter and debris left in its place. It looked like it hadn't been disturbed for years.

"Amazing," Anya said, eyes wide.

"That's magic, baby." Katya winked. "Come on. She wants to see you before you leave."

Baba Zosia stood with Aleksandra supporting her by the arm. Whatever she had just done had clearly taken it out of her.

"Thank you for all of your help, Baba Zosia. I hope one day I can repay you for it," Anya said.

The old woman pinched her chin. "You pay me by not dying. Be smart." She tapped Anya hard on the forehead. "You learn from dis. You…" Baba Zosia said something to Aleksandra, who continued, "You guard your dreams and guard your heart."

"I will. I promise you."

Anya thanked Aleksandra, who hugged her, and they said farewell to the rest of the group. Baba Zosia was helped into her caravan, and they made their way after the rest of the tribe, leaving behind an unmarred forest and taking with them any evidence that they were ever there.

Katya was alert and on edge as they moved through the forest in the opposite direction. She hadn't spoken to Izrayl all day and wondered if ignoring him like this would make the situation worse.

I wouldn't worry about it now. Anya touched her mind before opening her mouth. "I'm sorry about that. I've been tuning into you all day, and it just happened."

"It's fine, Anya. I would rather you be the one reading my thoughts than the others, if you know what I mean."

"Don't worry. I'll keep out."

"You girls do realize I can hear everything you are saying?" Cerise walked up beside them. Katya couldn't believe she managed to walk so far in those ridiculous boots.

"You aren't the one I'm worried about. It's the wolf boy, wherever he has gone." Katya glanced over her shoulder.

"Trajan and Izrayl decided to do a quick scout ahead to make sure Vasilli isn't hiding somewhere ready to ambush us."

"I wouldn't put it past him," Yvan said. "Vasilli is the slyest, slipperiest, most cunning man ever created. It would be nothing for him to wait for days until we left the protection of the camp."

Cerise gave him a faux smile. "Always cheery and optimistic, aren't you?"

"Unlike you lovely ladies, I know my brother. I know what he's capable of. If you think he'll show any mercy, you're wrong. If he's quiet, be even more worried. It means he's organizing something worse." It was quite the speech for Yvan, who'd been quiet since arriving at the camp and always seemed content to let everyone else do the talking.

"The Darkness has a base in Moscow. If he needs help or counsel, that will be the first place he'll go," Katya said. "Paris will put some decent distance between us for the time being."

"Can I ask a question?" Anya asked as Yvan stopped her from tripping over a tree root. "The Darkness was after me in Moscow when I had no idea about magic, but I was rescued. So what happens to the people like me who don't know they have magic and the Darkness *does* get them?"

"They reeducate them," Katya replied, darkness coating her tone.

"What does that even mean?"

"You don't want to know. Believe me, it's not something you want to talk about in the dark. "

"What about the Illumination? Are they any better?" Anya pressed.

Cerise and Katya both laughed.

"It doesn't matter. Illumination or Darkness, they're all assholes, and you should stay as far away from them as you can, shamanitsa." Katya ducked under a tree branch.

"We seem to be clear." Izrayl emerged from the trees in a pair of dirty jeans and covered in mud. "You make a terrible lot of noise. It must be a woman thing."

Yvan coughed meaningfully, but Izrayl ignored him.

"There's a gate not far ahead." Trajan appeared at Anya's side and took her hand. Anya's eyes widened in surprise, but Katya wasn't surprised at all. "Watch your step. The ground is uneven."

After a few more minutes of climbing over fallen logs and navigating slippery loose rocks, the soft light of an aurora glimmering among the trees came into view.

"There it is," Anya whispered. "I can feel it more intensely than last time."

Yvan moved to the left side of her and took her other hand. "Let's hope you don't have to scream at it again for it to let you through." They shared a smile.

"Cut me some slack. Vasilli's minions were getting ready to attack us. Screaming was my only option."

"You can take your time now, Anya. We've made sure that the coast is clear, and Izrayl can smell trouble from far away, even in his human form," Trajan assured her.

"That's why I have to keep away from Katya," Izrayl said.

Katya shifted her bow from one hand to the other. "Keep it up, and I'll buy you a muzzle."

"Another dog joke. How original."

Katya opened her mouth for a scathing retort, but Yvan cut her off.

"Do you want to see if you can open a doorway in the gate?" he asked Anya.

Anya's ashen eyebrows drew together. "I can try. It's reacting to my magic. It's like a tugging sensation. I think it's calling to me…" She let their hands go and approached the wall of light. She placed her palm on the aurora and shut her eyes.

Katya's breath caught as the light seemed to burn away and a tear in the wall appeared.

"I can't believe I did that," Anya whispered.

"Well done, Anya." Yvan flicked her braid. "You see, you're a natural gatekeeper just like Ilya was. Now you won't have to lose your temper and punch it to gain access."

"Very funny, Tsarevich. Let's go. I don't know how long it will last."

The group lined up and moved as one through the glimmering wall of light, back into the human world.

Not for the first time in the last few days, Vasilli found himself ready to burn the forest to the ground to find Anya and Yvan. He knew magic was at work, shielding them from his tracking spells, but he couldn't find the source of it. The usual revealing incantations weren't producing any results. This was old magic—much older than him, which was very old indeed.

He could sense Anya was close; the thorns were still giving off the same magical signature he had been tracking for days. The previous night, a shudder had rolled through the forest, and whatever had been blocking his passage was suddenly gone. Without wasting a moment, Vasilli had packed up his camp and homed in on the location of his thorns.

By midday, he found the glade where the signal was coming from. He pulled out a knife as long as his forearm, ready to slit the bitch's throat. The magical pulse came from behind a large birch tree, not even a hundred meters from him. He looked about for Yvan's tall frame, but he was nowhere to be found. Perhaps his fool brother had been cast aside by the growing shamanitsa. Yvan had no problem attracting women, but keeping them had never been his strong point.

Vasilli charged forward, his knife lashing out around the tree. It met with bark and nothing else. He swore viciously and dropped his gaze. The ground amongst the roots had recently been disturbed.

He fell to his knees and dug in the mud like a dog until his fingers brushed a small glass vial. Vasilli rubbed the mud off with his filthy cloak and found his thorns submerged in half an inch of blood. He gripped the vial so hard it shattered in his hand. As he opened his mouth to scream, an invisible force slammed into him. He clutched his head, smearing blood in his hair.

Ladislav forced his way into Vasilli's mind. *Vasilli, you have failed again. They have already crossed. Come to Moscow. Now.*

Vasilli gritted his teeth against the pain burning behind his eyes. *When did they cross?*

Last night. Our people are tracking them. Come to Moscow. Do not go after them. That is an order. You will be held accountable for your recent failings.

Without waiting for a reply, Ladislav severed the connection, leaving Vasilli on the ground, still clutching his temples. Blood dripped from his eyes, nose, and ears, but he didn't bother to wipe it off.

When he could finally stand, he cursed Anya, Yvan, and Ladislav until he was breathless. For now, he had to find the closest gate and get to Moscow. Ladislav was not a creature to be kept waiting, and it wasn't time for Vasilli to shrug off the yoke that bound them. He thought of how good it was going to feel to pull the old prick's magic from him and cut off his fucking head when he was done making him scream.

Soon, Vasilli promised himself. He just needed to be patient and gather the power he needed to overthrow Ladislav and take control of the Darkness for himself.

PART TWO

THE WORLD BEHIND THE WORLD

21

KATYA TRIED AND FAILED to sleep in a cramped train carriage, which smelled of boiled cabbage, dust, and mildew. The interior was painted a dull gray to match the gray curtains, gray bed sheets, and dirty gray carpet.

The color of joy, she thought miserably. They had been traveling for days, and she longed for a hot bath and a clean bed.

They'd journeyed on foot until they reached a village not far from Baia Mare, Romania. From there, they had hitched an uncomfortable ride in the back of a truck to the closest train station. The places they'd passed through since then had been a blur. They were heading to Paris, and that was all she cared about. Her mind had been on Anya's talent to read her mind if she wasn't careful. Katya tried not to dwell on it too much and considered the bright sides. She was the only one with the talent to connect with Anya, and maybe it could be useful in a fight. And a fight was coming; Katya could feel it in her hunter's bones.

Katya was finally drifting off to sleep when the door to her carriage opened and someone slipped inside. She gripped the knife under her pillow and was ready to use it, but warm hands pinned her arms down. She took a deep breath, readying a scream, but hot lips smothered her cry with a kiss.

"Please don't use that knife on me, Katya. It will ruin the mood." Izrayl loosened his grip on her arms as his lips found hers again. His hands slid down and rested on the sides of her small rib cage. She buried her hands in his thick hair as he kissed her again. His hand slid under her shirt and stroked her stomach, achingly slow. Katya's breath caught in her throat. His exploring hands began to move south until Katya fell out of bed onto the hard carriage floor.

"Fuck," she muttered. Her eyes snapped open, ending the dream.

Sunlight shone through the dirty curtains, and Katya groaned in frustration and embarrassment.

As if on cue, the door slid open, and Izrayl stuck his head in. "Are you awake yet? What are you doing on the floor?"

Her cheeks burned. "I fell out of bed."

"Was it a nightmare or a sex dream?" He grinned at her. Katya fought the urge to bury her head under the blanket. "So a sex dream? Must've been juicy by the look on your face." He laughed as she struggled to get up, her legs and arms twisted in the sheets.

"You're delusional."

"Here, let me help." Izrayl picked her up and dropped her down on the bed. "At least you could get enough sleep to dream. I hate trains. They make me itch."

Katya adjusted the blanket to cover her bare legs. She only ever slept in a T-shirt and underwear, and while she wasn't ordinarily shy, she was now. "Are the others up?"

"No, I was bored, so I thought I'd see if you were awake." Izrayl sat down on the carriage floor and rested his back against the door.

"What time is it?"

"About 6:30 in the morning."

"I should kill you for waking me up this early." Katya buried herself deeper in her blankets.

"You were awake already. I didn't wake you." Izrayl grinned mischievously. "Or did I?"

"Don't flatter yourself."

"I told you, you're curious—"

Izrayl tensed and let out a low growl.

Katya sat up, gripping her knife. "What is it?"

He held a finger over his mouth, and she shut up. Izrayl stood, pulled her off the bed, and put her on the floor. He shielded her with his body as a dark shadow passed over the window.

"Don't move," he whispered. "We have company."

"Vasilli?"

"No, something else."

Katya reached for her bag and rummaged around in it.

"What are you doing?"

She found the sleek weight of the revolver she always carried with her, even in Skazki. "My good luck charm."

"Get dressed and we'll go find the others. They have to be after Anya and Yvan." Izrayl helped her to her feet.

Katya dragged on her jeans, weapon holsters, jacket, and boots. She slung her bag over her shoulder and met Izrayl in the corridor.

"I thought it would take Vasilli a lot longer to send his cronies," Izrayl muttered. "You can bet he has gone straight to Ladislav."

"Let's just pray that Ladislav himself doesn't come after us."

"I *am* praying. I hope Trajan is awake, because we're about to have a fight on our hands."

As they neared Trajan's sleeper, he emerged disheveled and tense. "Can you feel it?" he asked Izrayl, who nodded. "Wake Yvan and Cerise. I'll get Anya." He hurried a couple of doors down and knocked before entering. He came out carrying Anya's bag as she shrugged on her heavy, fur-lined coat.

Yvan stumbled out from his room farther up the aisle. He rubbed his eyes. "What's going on? The firebird is panicking."

Anya glanced around. "My magic is flaring too."

"Trouble is what's going on," said Katya. "Get your gear, Prince."

Yvan went back into his room just as Cerise appeared, moving through the carriages, holding a handkerchief to her bloody nose.

"What happened to you?" Izrayl asked.

"Some bastard jumped me when I was sneaking a cigarette. I managed to throw the prick off the train, but there are at least six others." Cerise produced a phone. "He was carrying this."

Katya leaned in for a closer look. The case was engraved with the Darkness's insignia: a sword with a snarling black dragon wrapped around it. "So the Darkness is onto us already. I'm guessing there were cameras at the last train station we were at, which means they're going to have all of our faces now. Who knows how many others will be waiting for us at the next stop? We're going to have to jump and find another way to Paris." Katya readjusted her weapons so none of them would hurt her when she rolled.

Trajan pulled Anya close. "Hold on to me. I'll heal faster than you if we land rough."

"Good idea. I'd rather you break some bones than Anya." Yvan took off his coat and shirt. The firebird moved about on his chest, its long, fiery wings stretching down his arms.

Anya's eyes lingered for a moment, then she blushed and looked away. Katya didn't. Yvan had a hot body, and it had been a while since she'd seen some skin other than Izrayl's occasional and unavoidable nakedness. Yvan rolled his shoulders, and feathers pushed through his skin like silken spikes. He bit back a groan, and Anya took a step toward him.

"Yvan…" Anya's voice was tight with concern.

"I'm fine, Anya." His dark eyes flashed gold and red. "Hold close to Trajan."

Izrayl nudged Katya with his shoulder. "Are you going to be okay by yourself, little hunter, or would you like a strapping man to hang on to as well?"

"If you can find me one, I'll gladly hang on to him." She smirked. "I'll make do on my own. I wouldn't have suggested jumping if I didn't think I could do it."

"Then you'd better go before I push you out."

Cerise sighed over their bickering. "Trajan, be a dear and get the door."

Trajan slid the doors open, and as he turned for Anya, something swung itself through, claws outstretched. Katya fired three shots, and the creature collapsed on the carriage floor. Black blood oozed from the bullet holes, and Katya squeezed a fourth bullet into its head.

Anya clung to Trajan. "What the hell is that?"

Katya looked down at it, unfazed. "I'm not sure. It doesn't like silver, though."

It was man-shaped but utterly hairless with pale gray skin. Instead of hands, it had claws like a bird and a mouthful of sharp, long-fanged teeth.

"Its body is the Darkness's problem now. We have to go before their companions arrive." Without waiting for them, Katya strode to the door and jumped. She hit the ground harder than expected, rolling three times before the long grass slowed her to a stop. She looked up in time to see Yvan glide through the air and land gracefully. Then the golden feathers melted back into his skin like they'd never been there to begin with.

Izrayl's cursing drew Katya's attention to a blackberry bush. She tried not to laugh as he ripped himself free. His shoulder hung at an odd angle.

She straightened her holsters. "Is it broken?"

"Dislocated."

"I can put it—"

"Stay back." He backed away with wide eyes, but he didn't see Cerise moving behind him.

"I've done it before. Are you afraid or something?" Katya provoked him to keep him from turning.

Cerise reached for his shoulder.

"I'm afraid of no wom—*fuck*!" He gripped his shoulder and spun around.

Cerise grinned. "Good as new, sweetie."

"We have to keep moving," Trajan slipped on his sunglasses. "It won't take them long to find their dead companion, and we need to be far from here when they do."

They arrived in Paris a week later. After the train incident, they had walked for nearly two days before they managed to catch a series of buses and hitchhike across countries.

Anya had never been to Paris before, so despite being so tired her eyes were falling out, she remained glued to the window, trying to take in all of the beautiful buildings, hum of cars, and stylishly dressed people. She was impressed when Trajan directed the cab driver to his townhouse in Neuilly-sur-Seine in fluent French.

"You speak French?"

He shrugged. "When you're immortal, you need things to occupy your mind."

Their trek to Paris had given them the opportunity to talk about Eikki and the years they'd been apart. Trajan was as sweet and funny as Anya remembered. She had always found it difficult to let people in and talk freely with them, but it was easy with Trajan. Every time her hand brushed his, she fought hard not to have an internal meltdown. It wasn't like she hadn't dated before, but there was something about Trajan's touch specifically that made her body short-circuit, similar to when she used her magic.

Trajan's townhouse was built of pale gray stone and had long Gothic windows. It was one of the only mansions in the area not attached to another. A high wrought iron-and-stone fence surrounded it.

Trajan approached the front gate. "I called my maintenance people a few days ago, so everything should be uncovered and ready for our arrival." He punched in a code, and the gate glided open. Inside was a well-tended garden and lawn.

Katya, Izrayl and Yvan's taxi arrived. Yvan looked around warily, as if he expected something to jump out at them at any moment.

Katya let out an appreciative whistle. "Goddamn, Trajan. I think I'm going to move in."

"I was going to suggest that anyway," Trajan said. "If we're going to work together, it will be better if we stay together as a group." He nodded at Izrayl. "You can help grab her stuff tomorrow."

"My pleasure." He shot Katya a wink.

Anya moved out of the way to join Yvan. "How are you coping?" He had been wide-eyed and cautious ever since crossing over from Skazki. Modern technology and the sheer number of people had proven to be enough to stress him out.

"I'm sure I'll get used to it, but everything is so...loud."

"I know what you mean. I've spent most of my time isolated on a farm, remember?" Anya nudged him with her shoulder. "We can be the sheltered, technologically-challenged people together."

"Indeed. How's your magic?"

Anya flexed her fingers. "It's still there. I thought once we left Skazki, it would change, but it feels the same. Like flames under my skin."

"Good. That means learning should be easier for you."

"I have to get a teacher first."

"Don't worry. I'm sure they'll find you one soon enough." Yvan smiled at her—the first she had seen in days—and they followed Trajan and the others inside.

22

TRAJAN WENT STRAIGHT TO his wing of the house, shutting the doors behind him and sighing with relief as silence enveloped him. He hadn't been around so many people for such a long stretch of time before, and he'd been desperate for a quiet moment.

Plus, a little separation from Anya was also a good idea, he decided. Not that he didn't want to be around her. On the contrary, he wanted to be around her *too* much, and that was problematic. He couldn't look at her and not think about kissing her and wanting to do it again. He groaned and headed for the bathroom.

Trajan shed his filthy clothes and went for a long, hot shower. Showering always reminded him of the night Ilya helped free him from Eris. It had been cold and raining, and he'd stood in the downpour, naked as a babe, marveling at the touch of water against his skin. Even the sensation of cold had held a special kind of fascination.

In the last few weeks, Trajan had wondered just how much Ilya had seen in his visions. Did he see Trajan developing feelings for his descendant? Surely Ilya would have said something if he had.

Trajan rested his head against the cold tiles. He didn't have any experience with emotions like this. Until a few weeks ago, he wouldn't have believed he was capable of feeling this much. He felt like kicking himself for not approaching Anya after Eikki's death. *So much time wasted.* And time *was* a factor. Anya was mortal, and that was a complication he couldn't ignore. He didn't know what his control would be like with a human, and the thought of accidentally feeding on her filled him with a special kind of horror.

After Trajan had got out of the shower, he looked at himself in the mirror to check that his fading energy wasn't starting to show in any of his human features. The life he had taken from Vasilli's dragon was almost spent, and he didn't want to have cravings while Anya was near him. He would have to feed soon, but for now, he would go and check on his guests.

Anya was drinking vodka and laughing with the others when Trajan decided to join them. He was dressed in a collared shirt rolled to the elbows, a waistcoat, and pressed trousers. He hadn't shaved in a day or two, and Anya liked it. God, she wanted to kiss him to know what that stubble felt like against her skin. Her mouth went dry, and her hands sweat just at the thought of it.

Get it together, Anya. He's not the first guy you've had a crush on.

"Stop staring," Katya said, and Anya snapped herself out of it. She sipped from the glass in her hands, cursing herself for being so obvious.

"I thought you'd drowned." Cerise sipped her martini where she reclined on a chaise lounge. She was wrapped in a painted silk kimono and, much to Anya's amusement, wearing fluffy pink slippers.

A war spirit in slippers... This new world you live in is something else.

"We were just about to send Anya in there to give you mouth-to-mouth," Izrayl said.

Trajan raised a brow but didn't rise to his teasing. Anya flipped Izrayl off and wished the carpet would swallow her whole.

Cerise rolled her eyes. "Oh, do grow up. Let's get back to the topic at hand. We were actually discussing some American friends of Katya's who might be able to help Anya develop her magic."

"They'll be hard to track down this time of year—they like to get off the grid—but I'll try to get in touch with them after I get my stuff," Katya said to Trajan. "Okay, I'm starving. I need something cheese-loaded."

"I got you, hunter." Izrayl waved his phone in the air. "What do you want?"

Anya's experience with cuisine was limited, so she let them order for her while she did her best to stay out of everyone's way. Her gaze jumped from face to face, and she couldn't help the smile stretching across her face. She had always wanted a bigger family, and despite the less than pleasant circumstances, they were becoming hers. Her determination to master her magic put steel in her spine. If the prophecy was right, she could protect them from Vasilli, and at this point, she would do anything to keep them safe.

Later, full of pasta and vodka, Anya said good night to everyone and went upstairs to her room. It was the nicest room she'd ever seen, with blue-gray walls and elegant antique furniture. She flopped down into an armchair and stared at the ceiling. She was too wound up to sleep, but she'd needed to stop drinking and get away from Trajan so she could think straight.

You have bigger things to worry about than your lascivious thoughts about a thanatos.

There was a soft tap on the door, and Cerise's red head poked in. "You got everything you need, Anya?"

"Yeah, I think so. This place is kitted out like a hotel."

"It's a safe house for Trajan's friends, so he keeps it full of spare toothbrushes and whatnot. We can do some shopping and get you some clothes. We can't have you wandering around Paris dressed like a Skazki cosplayer." Cerise opened one of the glass doors leading to the balcony outside and lit a cigarette before turning to studying Anya. "Don't let Izrayl's teasing get to you. He can be a prick, but it's not malicious."

"It doesn't bother me, and if it annoyed Trajan, I'm sure he would get Izrayl to cut it out." Anya shrugged, but Cerise's frown only deepened. "What's wrong, Cerise? I'm getting the sense that you didn't come up here just to check that I have enough toothpaste."

"It's this thing you and Trajan have… Anya, you have to understand our kind and your kind aren't compatible."

Anya laughed. "I know I'm not compatible with Trajan. I don't think I'm compatible with a normal man, let alone a thanatos." Each of Anya's dating experiences had been a nightmare. But if she were being honest, being around Trajan felt more natural and effortless than anyone else she'd ever dated. He knew her, and she would never have to pretend to be anyone she wasn't with him.

"That's not what I meant. There's nothing wrong with you. It's what's wrong with him." Cerise exhaled a stream of smoke. "You saw what Trajan did to that dragon of Vasilli's. He did it in minutes. Imagine how quickly he could do it to a human. If he loses control with you, for even a second, and accidentally kills you, he would never, ever get over it. He's never been with a human before, and there are reasons that our kind and yours don't mix."

"What? Like ever?"

"Not that I'm aware of. I don't see how it could end well, no matter how careful you are."

Anya chewed her lip. "I don't think that's enough to scare me off. I know you mean well, but I can't help what I'm feeling. I...kissed him, and I want to do it again. Badly."

"I knew something must have happened by the goofy way he keeps looking at you." Cerise stubbed out her cigarette. "Trajan's old enough to make his own decisions, as are you. Just know that if you're looking for a normal relationship, you aren't going to get it with him."

"I know that. Plus, I can't say I'll be a much easier partner. You know, with all the magic and impending doom stuff."

Cerise narrowed her gaze, then sighed. "You're starting to look all sad and lovesick. You should talk to him. But don't say I didn't warn you." She paused by the bedroom door, her hand resting on the handle. "He's my best friend, Anya. It doesn't matter how much I like you; if you make him take this chance with you, and you hurt him, I'll kill you."

Anya stood outside Trajan's door, trying to summon the courage to knock. She'd tried to talk herself out of going to him, but after Cerise's visit, Anya knew she wasn't going to sleep until she did. She smoothed her hair back, then rapped her knuckles on the door. Without waiting for an answer, she opened it a little to stop herself from running back to her room like a scared little *devushka*.

"Trajan?" She stuck her head in and looked around the dimly lit room.

"Anya? What's wrong?" Trajan strode out of his bedroom with a book in hand, his glasses sitting on the bridge of his nose. She'd been right: he was definitely nerdy hot in his glasses.

"Nothing's wrong. I was just...after a book. I can't sleep."

"There's a library downstairs you can help yourself to."

"Right, thanks." Anya turned back to the door, cursing her own cowardice.

"Would you like some company?" he asked.

Her hand froze on the door handle. "Yeah, if you aren't busy. Or tired."

Trajan smiled, and her toes curled in her slippers. "I'm not busy or tired. Take a seat. Would you like a drink?"

"Please." Anya sat down on one of the couches that were arranged around a carved oak coffee table.

Trajan turned on a tall lamp next to her and placed a glass of vodka in front of her.

"What are you reading?" she asked as he poured himself a scotch. She looked over at the deserted volume. *"Stories and Legends of Pagan Russia,"* she read aloud. "Are you catching up on Yvan's biography?"

"No, I was actually looking for references to Yanka." Trajan sat down beside her.

"I thought you knew Ilya. Wasn't Yanka his mother?"

"According to Ilya, she didn't stay with them for very long. He had memories of her until he was about five years old, and then she disappeared. I thought that if I could find out more about her, it might help you."

"You have all helped me too much as it is. I could never be able to pay any of you back." Anya sipped her vodka. If any of them were hurt protecting her, she would blame herself forever.

"We don't do any of it with the thought of being paid back, Anya. We do it because we know you're worth it, even if you don't think you are, so banish that ridiculous notion from your mind."

"I have a lot of ridiculous notions in my mind." The vodka warmed her and loosened her tongue. She shouldn't have accepted another drink, but she felt like she needed it for courage. "I talked to Cerise tonight."

"Oh, what about?"

"About thanatos-human relationships. She said you've never had one because you could accidentally feed on someone if you lose control."

Trajan's dark brows drew together in annoyance. "Did she now? And what are your thoughts on the matter?"

"You probably just need some practice."

Trajan's frown shifted into a grin.

"Is it true that a thanatos has never been with a human?"

Trajan hummed and took another drink. "That Cerise knows of, perhaps. I don't see how what has happened with others pertains to us."

"Well, for starters, she thinks there is an *us*." Anya swallowed hard, her pulse in her throat. "Is there?"

"So this is why you were pacing outside my door..." Trajan put his drink down. "Very well. Let's talk about facts first. Fact, I'm not human even though I look like one. I feed off life force and could very well feed off you if I lose control. That should worry you."

"It doesn't. You don't strike me as someone who loses control easily."

"I thought that too, until you turned up on my doorstep."

She smiled despite her nerves.

"Why would you even want to risk this?"

"Because I think you'd be worth it." Anya pushed her hand through her hair. "Look, I'm terrible at this kind of thing, but I like you. I literally think about kissing you every time I see you. Of all the crazy shit that has happened in the past few weeks, you feel like a surprise bonus. With all my memories back, I now know that you and my magic were the pieces that have been missing my entire life, and I've finally gotten you back. Talking to you, being around you feels like the easiest thing in the world, and I've never felt that way with anyone."

Trajan's wine-red eyes widened in surprise as he stared at her, speechless.

Shit, too much, Anya. Retreat. She put her glass of vodka back on the table and got up.

"So that's why I want to risk it. Come find me when you figure out if you are willing to do the same." She turned and headed for the door. Her fingers touched the handle, and then Trajan was suddenly beside her, his hand holding the door shut. Anya turned to face him. His eyes glowed with heat. Her heart stopped.

"You said that I might just need practice touching people." His voice went smokey.

"Y-Yes."

"Then I want to risk it. But you will have to be patient with me while we... practice."

"Okay," Anya said.

His hands moved to either side of her, and he pinned her against the door. Her breath caught as he ran his fingers along her cheek and down her throat.

Anya's hands went to his waistcoat, feeling the warm muscle underneath. Slowly, Trajan pushed his glasses to the top of his dark hair and bent his head.

"Can I kiss you?" he asked, his breath warm against her lips.

"Yes," Anya whispered, then rose on her toes to press her mouth to his. He tasted of spicy whiskey. Desire flushed down her body. Anya's grip on Trajan's waistcoat tightened, and as his long fingers pushed through her hair, tilting her head back so he could deepen the kiss. Anya melted into him as his other arm came around her waist and pulled her against him.

"Trajan, I—" Anya gasped as a sharp pain pierced her head. She cried out, and her knees give way.

"Anya, what is it? What's wrong?" Trajan held her up as visions bombarded her: Katya pounding down a sidewalk, shadowy figures running behind her. Katya's fear bloomed inside Anya's chest.

"Katya!" She gasped, clinging onto him. "Katya is in trouble!"

23

AFTER DAYS OF TRAVELING and being on high alert, Katya couldn't relax no matter what she did, so she thought she might as well be productive. Trajan had offered her Izrayl's help to move, but she was never going to take him up on that.

Katya's apartment was in Montmartre. It was neat and impersonal. The furniture and pictures hanging on the walls had come with the apartment, and it was precisely the way she had left it. Katya smiled with delight as she ran her fingers over her laptop. She'd missed it terribly and had felt completely lost without it. She shoved the few changes of clothes she had hanging in the cupboard into a bag, then opened the gun cabinet she'd secreted behind some coats and emptied the contents into another bag. After picking up the remaining weapons and books, she locked the door and gave the landlord back his keys.

"You in trouble with the police or something?"

"Of course not, *monsieur*," Katya said. "Why do you ask?"

"There have been people here looking for you. I assumed they were police from the questions they were asking." His eyes narrowed, and Katya gave him a smile she hoped was convincing.

"Do I look like I would be any trouble? It sounds like they've got their people mixed up." She laughed, though her heart was hammering in her chest. No one knew where she lived aside from a very select group of hunters.

Her landlord grunted as a way of saying goodbye, and she hurried down the stairs and out onto the wet street.

If people had been there looking for her, they would be watching her then too. Katya cursed herself for not asking someone to come with her, but she felt the reassuring weight of her guns at her sides. She walked casually along the street, intent on leading them away from Trajan's.

A few moments later, as she passed a Sacré-Coeur souvenir shop, she risked a glance over her shoulder. Two men were following her.

That's just great. Sometimes Katya hated being right. Their eyes caught the light of the shop fronts, and for a second, they flashed gold like an animal's. *Monsters, not men.*

Katya steadied her breath and restrained herself from bolting and giving the game away.

Anya! Katya reached out, trying to link with the shamanitsa's mind.

A tall man stepped in front of her, and Katya dodged the blade that he swiped at her stomach. She kicked him hard in the knee and brought her elbow up to crack him in the head. Then she turned and ran like hell.

Sweat soaked her back, and the butt of a handgun rubbed irritably against her hip. Pain shot through her thighs and lungs, but she didn't dare slow down to look behind her.

In the back of her mind, her father's voice came through unbidden and unexpected: *You've let yourself get slow and weak. You're supposed to train harder in Skazki, not waste your time hunting animals and flirting with a beast you should be killing.* She pushed herself harder to prove him wrong and looked for a place to make her stand.

Katya reached out with the spark of magic she possessed, searching for Anya's mind. *Anya! They're following me. I'm keeping them away from Trajan's, but I don't know how many they are. Hurry!*

Anya gripped her head, almost buckling over at the sound of Katya screaming inside her skull. "Oh god, Katya! We need to find her. We need to go now!" She ran out into the hallway. "Izrayl!" She didn't know which room he had taken, but she would need his help.

He stumbled into the hallway, buttoning up his jeans. "What's wrong?"

"Katya's being attacked. She left the mansion and is being followed." Anya grabbed his hand and dragged him toward the stairs.

"We'll take my car. Where is she?"

"I don't know. She said her flat was in Montmartre somewhere."

Trajan pulled on his coat. "I'm coming."

"I'm driving." Izrayl ducked back into his room to get his keys and pull on a black shirt.

Trajan pulled Anya aside. "I don't want you coming with us. The Darkness wants you, not Katya. You'll be playing right into their hands."

"I'm the only way to find her! I'll stay out of the way." She grabbed her coat and boots. This wasn't the way she had planned for the night to go, but she couldn't leave Katya to be captured either. Anya met them at the elevator just as Izrayl was tucking a gun into the back of his jeans.

"That stupid girl! She should've known better than to go out by herself," he muttered. "If they don't kick her ass, I will."

"Let's just get her home first. She probably thought she could handle herself," said Trajan.

"She's like all hunters—hot-headed and reckless."

The garage was huge and housed at least twenty cars, which all looked expensive and fast. Izrayl climbed into the driver's seat of a black muscle car. Trajan took the passenger side after opening the back door for Anya.

"Put your seat belt on. Izrayl likes to drive like a maniac."

Izrayl started the engine and took off up the curving ramp, which led out to the road. The automatic door was already open, and he roared out onto the street.

Katya. Anya had to concentrate hard on connecting with her as the lights flickering past distracted her. *Show me where you are.*

Anya! She saw Katya with her knives out, and for a moment, Anya could feel her fear as she ran past a lit carousel.

"She's running. There's a carousel—"

Anya didn't know close to enough about Paris to identify where Katya was, so she reached out and grabbed Izrayl's shoulder. Setting her teeth, Anya forced the image of Katya fighting for her life into his mind.

"Holy shit!" Izrayl swerved but kept the car on the road. "She's running through Square Louise Michel. Goddamn Darkness is on her trail." He changed up a gear, and the speed dial jumped.

We're coming, Katya. Hold on.

Izrayl wove through the streets, skidding and sliding with little regard for stoplights or other cars. Ten minutes and many curse words later, he slammed on the brakes and jumped out of the vehicle. Within a blink, he had shifted into his wolf form and was gone.

Katya had been cornered near the monumental fountains and was forced to make a stand. The creatures were similar to those on the train. Their fingers morphed into long claws and moved so fast she barely had time to block them.

Katya screamed as one of her attacker's claws ripped through her side. She fired her gun, and it clicked—a hollow sound that signaled she had finally used her last bullet.

Fuck.

The creature raised its clawed hand to strike her down when a black wolf knocked her aside. She fell to the ground, then rolled back to her feet as Izrayl tore through her attacker's throat. It still lay gargling as Izrayl padded toward her, his black face shiny with gore.

"Look out!" Katya screamed as another pale-faced creature appeared behind him.

Izrayl turned, but a clawed hand was already digging deep into his back. Katya pulled a long knife from the sheath strapped to her thigh, and the creature screamed as the sharp blade sliced through its hand, leaving five bloody fingers and claws embedded deep in Izrayl's flesh. The creature cradled its wrist and hissed at her before vanishing into the blackness. Katya stood over Izrayl's bleeding body, unwilling to lower her guard.

"Katya!" Trajan ran toward her.

"He's hurt," she said. Then she sank to her knees and passed out on the cold grass.

By the time they returned to Trajan's, the back seat was covered in so much blood, Anya thought their passengers must have been dead. When they drove back into the garage, Cerise was waiting, dressed in medical scrubs.

A part of the garage had been miraculously transformed into a makeshift hospital. Initially, Anya thought the stainless steel cupboards and drawers were storage for tools, but two of the metal panels had been folded down to make sturdy operating tables, and the drawers had been opened to reveal medical instruments and bright lamps.

"God," Anya muttered. "I see you two have dealt with this before?"

"More than we would have liked. Open the back doors, please, Anya." With the ease of the supernaturally strong, Trajan and Cerise carried Katya and then Izrayl from the car and laid them on the metal tables.

"Cut her coat and shirt off, Anya. I need to see what I'm dealing with." Cerise handed her a pair of scissors. "Trajan, try to wake Izrayl up so he can shift back. I'm a nurse, not a vet."

Katya didn't move or wake when Anya cut the sleeves of her leather coat. Anya gasped when she pulled back the first layer of material. Katya's back was covered in deep claw marks that oozed dark blood. She had no idea how anyone could live through that and keep fighting.

"Hurry up, Anya. Stop gawking."

Anya quickly removed Katya's arsenal of weapons and the tatters of her T-shirt, leaving her back bare. Amongst the wounds and blood, odd symbols were tattooed around Katya's narrow hips and up her backbone.

"You're going to be okay, Katya," Anya whispered. Tears built in the back of her eyes.

Cerise's eyes ran over Katya's wounds. "Trajan, she's going to need blood."

"What type?" He opened a fridge full of blood bags.

Cerise ran a gloved finger over one of Katya's wounds and popped it in her mouth with a thoughtful suck. Her blue eyes flashed black for a split second, then she said, "AB positive, my favorite."

Anya's stomach churned as Cerise smiled at her.

"Don't worry. I don't really like living blood, and Katya won't be a corpse for a long time yet."

Anya looked away just in time to see Izrayl's body shudder and change back into its human form. Pale, clawed fingers still stuck grotesquely from his bleeding back amongst the blood and other wounds.

"Be a dear and pull those out for me, Trajan," Cerise said.

Trajan did as he was told and gripped the first finger. Anya swayed as the elevator dinged, and Yvan stepped out.

"Perfect timing, Yvan." Cerise clapped her hands together. "Take Anya upstairs. She's about to pass out."

Anya's knees went squishy, and she started to rock just before Yvan's strong hands caught her.

"Easy there, *shalost*. Let's get you upstairs." He lifted her up into his arms and carried her to the elevator. Yvan managed to get her back to her bedroom before she threw up all over herself and his arm.

"Shit," Anya muttered. Yvan helped her into the bathroom, and she stuck her head in the toilet as her stomach rolled again. "I thought I had a stronger stomach than that. I'm so sorry."

"I'll live," Yvan washed his arm in the sink. Then he wet a cloth and placed it on the back of her neck. "Are you okay?"

"Yeah, let me get cleaned up and I'll tell you all about it." Anya waved him out. She looked at the mess in the bathroom and was mortified Yvan had witnessed it. She pulled off her soiled clothes and rinsed them in the sink before she climbed into the shower to wash the sour smell from her skin. She had stitched up wounds on animals before without blinking, but stitching up wounded friends, it turned out, was completely different.

Anya emerged a short time later wrapped in a robe. Yvan came through the door with two steaming cups of tea.

"I thought you'd need something to drink, and I don't think vodka will be your friend right now." He handed her a cup.

"Thanks," Anya said and sipped the scalding liquid. "I think I've had enough vodka for one night anyway. It's probably why I couldn't keep my stomach under control." They both knew it was a lie, but Yvan didn't call her on it.

"What happened?" he pressed.

"Katya was attacked in the park by a group of creatures like the one we saw on the train. We got there just in time. Izrayl tore into them, and then he was attacked too." Anya shuddered. "There was so much blood…"

Yvan sat down in the couch beside her. "It worries me that the Darkness managed to find her. What in the hell are these creatures? They don't sound like anything I have encountered before, even in Skazki."

"Whatever they are, their bodies are littering the park right now thanks to Katya and Izrayl, except a wounded one that escaped Trajan when he joined the fight."

"The Darkness won't allow humans to discover what happened. The bodies will be removed, and the wounded one would have reported back to them by now." Yvan's eyes danced over her face, his concerned expression turning uneasy before he shifted in his chair. "It was lucky you were with Trajan when you had the vision and could get to her in time. Should I ask what you were doing in his room so late?"

Anya tugged the ends of her wet hair. "Talking…and we kissed."

"I see." Yvan looked away from her to a picture on the wall above her head. "So, you're a couple?"

"I don't know about that," Anya replied, feeling more awkward than he looked. "I wouldn't know what to call it at this stage."

Yvan frowned. "It sounds complicated."

"Are you angry?" Anya wondered why she felt the need to ask.

Yvan's frown deepened. "Should I be?"

"No, it's just…never mind. I thought you would lecture me, warn me."

"I'm your friend, not your father, Anya. I don't need to tell you to be careful, and I won't try to make decisions for you. But I will be here for you if and when you make the wrong ones."

"Prince Yvan, my hero." Anya was rewarded with one of his rare smiles.

"We all need rescuing sometimes, Anyanka. All I ask is that you be careful with that heart of yours. You have so much to learn, and you don't need a broken heart on top of that." Yvan leaned back against the couch cushions. "And don't make me deal with jealous lovers when I want to spend time with you."

"I don't think Trajan is the jealous type." Anya dropped her head to his shoulder, letting the warmth of the firebird seep through her cheek. "Don't worry. My heart is big enough for both of you."

Look through the fog to a small campground deep in the North American mountains. Sitting in the closest tent is a man in the middle of a trance. His visions usually come to him unbidden and clear, but for days, he's been seeing bits and pieces that make no sense. His hunter friend is in trouble, but what kind, he can't tell. He hopes the magic of the Land of Dreaming will bring him clarity.

He follows the paths of the spirit world. The colors move in front of him to form a picture of Katya bleeding on the ground next to a wolf's body.

He sees a girl trailing bright red magic wherever she goes. Darkness hunts her. He is stunned and horrified as he glimpses the war that is coming for her. He knows she will need him and his brother.

Aleksandra? He throws the name to the wind. *Where is your sister?* He waits. He feels the trance wearing off, but he hangs on to the spirit world, waiting for her reply.

Paris. Black magic is following them. The firebird has returned. Aleksandra's voice is barely a whisper against his cheek.

Suddenly, his world is crashing, and he is being pulled backward. Air rushes through his ears, and he cries out in pain as his spirit slams back into his body. He opens bleary eyes. His twin brother sits across the fire, his grin wide and knowing.

"When do we leave?"

24

VASILLI PASSED THROUGH THE glimmering wall of light that took him from Skazki to Sokolniki Park. The guardian of the gate watched him closely with falcon eyes but allowed his passage. He was too old to care about politics. Only the gate mattered to him, and who he let through changed on his whim. That night, his whim worked in Vasilli's favor. Because of its location and the labyrinth built around it, the Sokolniki Park gate was the strongest in Moscow. It was no coincidence that Alexei Mikhailovich had loved hunting in the park or that his son Peter had put so much effort into maintaining it.

Vasilli breathed in the cold air and let his body readjust to Mir's rhythms. There was magic still there, but it was buried deep in the earth and the subconsciouses of the humans living there. Ladislav claimed that his rule of the Darkness would change that. Vasilli snorted; Ladislav was not a leader that inspired that kind of confidence. There was only one person who could have managed it, and with the princess gone, Vasilli would take on her vision when he had the power.

There were places in Moscow where mortals did not enter. A sinister malevolence touched them—not to mention the shadows—and they knew instinctively to turn and walk away. One of these places was a grand townhouse that had been the Guardians of the Dark's main Russian base for over four hundred years. Vasilli could feel the power radiating from it long before he could see it.

A homeless *babushka* sat on the steps leading down to the building's lower basements smoking a cigarette.

"Vasilli, Vasilli, what took you so long, *chernyĭ syn* of mine?" she asked.

"Hello, Zhenechka. Are you going to let me pass tonight?" She didn't look it, but she was one of the most powerful shamanitsas in all of Europe. She kept guard at the entrance to their headquarters with fierce diligence. The last policeman who had tried to move her along had been turned into a rat and squashed under her heavy boot.

"Of course, Vas'ka. You know you're a favorite of mine." Zhenechka pinched his bearded cheek, and Vasilli felt the burning power under her wrinkled hands. "Be patient tonight, eh? There's been no good news received, and Ladislav is not happy."

"Is he ever?" Vasilli patted her shoulder fondly. She was one of the people he would keep when he ruled, and he wouldn't waste her abilities by forcing her to guard the fucking steps.

Vasilli moved down the stairs and unlocked the door with a brief touch of his hand. Usually, he would have cleaned up before seeing the master, but if Ladislav was already in a bad mood, he wouldn't like to be kept waiting.

Ladislav was one of the strongest black magic users ever to have been born outside of Skazki. In Russia's older times, he had been worshiped as a dark god, and the blood sacrifices done in his name had granted him immortality. The men in his command still murmured the old ritual line before they killed in his name, and he grew stronger every day because of it.

Vasilli joined him at a polished ebony table. Ladislav had long, steel-gray hair worn in a thick braid interwoven with secret spells. It was said that those who could weave intricate braids could read the wearer's fate within its twisted strands. Within Ladislav's braid were smaller, tighter plaits, sometimes intertwined with colored threads, and these were the ones that held his spells. Vasilli had often wondered if the secret of Ladislav's power was, like Samson, contained within his hair...and what would happen if he shaved it off.

But why shave a head when you could cut a neck?

"It's good to see you, Vasilli, despite your recent failings. I expected a firebird on your return, and you have nothing," Ladislav said. "It would seem we underestimated Anya and your brother. We were convinced that she had no power, like her father. When we tried to take her in Moscow a few years ago, it was simply for leverage. We wanted to pressure Eikki to move from neutral to Darkness.

But then Ilya's pet thanatos retrieved her, and we considered it nothing more than a lost opportunity once she was back under Eikki's protection. She wasn't worth *that* much, after all. Yet now we find out that she does indeed have magic and that she has managed to outsmart you."

Vasilli shook his head. "I was at her house. I spoke to her, but even I only detected the slightest bit of magic in her—"

"And yet you let her slip right through your fingers!" Ladislav's gaze cut into Vasilli like a blade. "Even a *hint* of Venäläinen magic is valuable."

"It was miniscule. There must have been a spell masking her true potential. If there was, it was masterfully done." Vasilli trained his face into an impassive expression. "As to my recent failings, Anya and Yvan had help. Baba Yaga detained me, and a world-walker witch was assisting her as well."

Ladislav glowered but didn't press the issue. "We know about the tribe. We caught the hunter's image when she was traveling with Anya in Romania. We found her apartment, but the team we sent after her were wiped out. It's unsettling to think Anya has such protectors already, and we have to assume that the thanatos will be joining her if he hasn't already. Regardless, we want Anya now. I'm prepared to do what it takes to collect her. Capturing her will likely create an opening for us to acquire the firebird as well." Ladislav's eyes narrowed.

A small domovoi dashed into the room with a chilled decanter of vodka and two glasses. He placed it on the table between them and, with a short bow, vanished once more.

"She's just a hunter. Who did you send to get her?" Vasilli poured a glass of the vodka for Ladislav before taking one for himself.

"I sent Völundr."

"Shvedskii gryazi." Vasilli fought the urge to spit on Ladislav's fine carpet.

"Swedish filth he may be, but his loyalty isn't under question at the moment, and yours is."

"How could you say that? The princess—"

"The princess is dead, Vasilli!"

"We don't know that for certain. She's immortal."

"Then where has she been for the last hundreds of years? We must move on, Vasilli. The world has not stopped, and neither will we."

There was a knock at the door, and a pale, colorless man stepped in. In his hand, he held a bleeding crow.

"Völundr, thank you for coming. Is that the survivor?"

"Yes, my lord. Shall I change him for questioning?"

Ladislav nodded, and hot power rolled from Völundr. The bird in his hand struggled futilely as it began to stretch and change. Within seconds, a pale creature shaped like a man was lying on the floor in front of them. It clutched a bleeding, fingerless hand to its chest, and from its throat came a series of croaking, mewling sounds of pain.

"So this is why you let this filth contaminate our halls," Vasilli said as he looked at the pathetic creature in front of him. "You're letting him make *vorona rabov*. To what end?"

"Crow slaves make useful servants when properly controlled," Völundr replied on Ladislav's behalf. "Nobody looks twice at a crow flying near them. Besides, they are expendable."

"So are you," Vasilli hissed.

Ladislav ignored their bickering and approached the crow slave on the floor. He knelt down and took its head between his hands. It wept as Ladislav forced himself into its mind. By the time he was finished, blackish blood oozed from the creature's nose, ears, and eyes.

"Clean this up for me, Völundr." Ladislav waved his hand at the corpse. "And send some more to Paris to find Anyanka."

"As you wish." Völundr approached the corpse and waved his hand over it. The body dissolved into a fine white ash, and within seconds, two domovoi had cleaned up the rest of its remains, leaving no trace of it ever being there.

"Vasilli, Völundr will be taking over the search for Anya and your brother." Ladislav must have sensed the brewing storm in Vasilli, because he quickly added, "Only temporarily. They are in Paris, and Völundr has spent the past few months there. He knows the city, and you have been hunting in and out of Skazki for weeks. Rest. Restore your body and your power, and then, if they haven't been recovered, you can continue the hunt."

Vasilli's mind hazed with red rage as he fought to contain himself. Then, clear as a bell, he heard his mother's voice: *Let the sheep bleat and die first, Vas'ka. Hide like a wolf, and when your prey thinks that they have won the fight and are safe, you tear their throats out and feast on their bones.*

Völundr didn't have the power to take on all of Anya's companions—including the firebird—and live. Vasilli would let him do the hard work of finding them and wearing them down. At least if Ladislav thought he was "resting," his steely gaze would be focused elsewhere.

Vasilli willed his expression to relax and forced a charming smile to his lips. "You know, that sounds like wisdom itself. I'm tired of traveling rough and unwinding Baba Yaga's traps. You will let me know if you have made any progress, though, won't you?"

Ladislav smiled back, thinking he had won. "Of course, Vasilli. You are my most trusted advisor, a prince in this organization. If Völundr finds Anya, you will be the first to know. Yvan will not be far away."

Vasilli could just about smell the bullshit in the air. Still, he raised his glass of vodka to the old man, all the while imagining the many ways he could kill him.

25

THEY HAD BEEN BACK in Paris for two days, and Trajan couldn't put off feeding any longer. Early in the night, Cerise met him in the garage, dressed in scrubs with a small satchel over her shoulder.

Trajan took out his keys. "Are you ready? I want to get this over with."

"Of course I'm ready. I'm gagging for a drink. Relax, Trajan. We'll back within the hour. I told Izrayl where we're going, and Yvan isn't about to let anything happen to Anya. No matter how much you like playing human, you need to feed."

"Don't lecture me, Cerise." He climbed into the driver's side of his black sedan. It didn't matter what his common sense told him or that Anya would be eating and chatting with Yvan, Katya, and Izrayl while he was gone. His overprotective side had kicked into overdrive after he kissed her, and the fact that the Darkness had gotten onto Katya so quickly also put him on edge. He started the engine and pulled out of the garage.

"I know you'd prefer to keep this part of your nature in the shadows, but you can't shield her from it. Besides, she saw you kill Vasilli's monster for herself. I don't want to lecture you, but do yourself a favor and be as honest as you can with her. Human women are big on honesty."

"Because your experience with human women has been so extensive?"

"It's been a lot more extensive than yours, pet."

"Can we please not fight about this anymore?"

Cerise rolled her eyes. "We aren't fighting. We're *discussing*. What hospital?"

"The American, it's closest."

Cerise dug around in her bag, producing two ID tags as Trajan drove. When he parked, she clipped one onto the breast pocket of his jacket.

"I'll meet you back here in thirty minutes," she said. "Be a doll and send me down some freshies, would you? If you need me, I'll be in the morgue looking gorgeous."

Trajan watched Cerise move off, efficient and smiling as if she were there legally. Despite their hospital IDs, Trajan had never had the acting skill to pull off the deception as successfully as her. He went inside and ducked into the men's room. He faded, his human form melting away until he was invisible to the human eye and video cameras. Sometimes, he was spotted by someone attuned to the supernatural, but that didn't happen often. Being unanchored to a physical form was freedom itself. Trajan reveled in his true form, no longer bombarded by the needs of a human body.

Hospitals were the perfect hunting grounds for a thanatos. They were the gateways of life and death and could always provide what he needed. Sometimes, Trajan didn't even have to feed off individuals because so much life force residue hung in the air, which he could gather to him like a magnet. Tonight, he haunted the corridors, the silvery strands of soul absorbing into him like small sips of fine wine.

The cancer ward was a place of slow suffering, and Trajan moved toward it, following the call of so many lives begging for release. The first person he encountered was a woman who couldn't have been much older than Anya. Both of her breasts had been removed, and each breath was a struggle. Her pale blue eyes filled with tears as she sensed him move closer.

"Finally," she whispered through cracked lips.

Trajan pressed a kiss to her forehead and replied in the ancient language of the dead: "May you find your Elysium."

Then as her shade surrendered, he drew it into his body and exploded with energy. Like a drug addict finally getting their fix, Trajan sighed in relief and ecstasy before moving on to the next set of rooms.

In the morgue, Cerise tied a face mask on and flipped through the folders of the recently deceased. She didn't like to drink from just any old corpse. Clean body, clean mind applied to supernaturals as well as humans. If she wasn't careful and put trash in her body, it had all sorts of repercussions—flashes of memory that didn't belong to her and strange cravings, to name a couple. She was never affected by such trivialities as a full keres, but being free from her servitude and maintaining a human guise, the old rules had changed. She saw it as a parting 'fuck you' from Eris, because the goddess never liked to relinquish what belonged to her.

A man came in after dying during a triple bypass, and with one look at the corpse, Cerise decided against it. The man was grossly obese, and she would be able to detect the thick, sticky taste of fat in his blood. She would also crave every crap food the man had put in his body, and her thighs didn't need it either.

Cerise was just inserting a huge syringe into the heart of a twelve-year-old girl when two male orderlies wheeled in a fresh cadaver.

"We have three more on the way down—wait, who are you?" one of them asked.

Cerise flashed them her ID tag. "I'm on loan from the Hôpital Saint Vincent de Paul for the night." She pulled down her mask and smiled. "I'm Cerise."

They didn't question her further but chatted politely, then left to collect other bodies. Once they had gone, she went back to work. She had ten minutes, and she really didn't want to be there when they came back.

Yvan paced his rooms, trying to will his mind into silence. The streets below him were filled with vehicles and light and so much noise despite the late hour. This era was nothing like his own, and Yvan didn't think he would ever get used to it.

Earlier that day, Izrayl had shown him what television was, and it gave him such a fright he hadn't been able to bring himself to turn it back on again. Izrayl, on the other hand, had laughed until tears ran down his cheeks.

On top of the confusing technology, Yvan had to deal with an audience: Anya and Trajan, snuggling on the couch. They'd been so comfortable together that Yvan could barely stand to look at them.

Anya had told him that her heart was big enough for both of them, and he wouldn't be that asshole who couldn't manage to be happy for her. Anya deserved happiness wherever she could get it.

You know you only have yourself to blame. The firebird's voice dripped with arrogance as it rolled through Yvan's mind.

"Please shut up. I have enough to think about without your input," Yvan muttered.

You know I am speaking the truth.

"You know nothing. It doesn't matter anyway. Even Baba Zosia told me that she saw them together in her visions. It would've been pointless to try to intervene."

I am beginning to learn much about the human heart being inside of one. You didn't even try—

"Just shut up!" Yvan shouted. Flames spurted out of his hands, and he hurried to shake them out. He sat down, breathing heavily.

That is...new. The firebird didn't sound nearly as confident now.

Yvan studied his hands, his curiosity getting the better of him. They weren't burned, but he could still feel the tingling aftershock of the firebird's power riding him. "It's something we'll have to get control of if it's going to be useful." He held up his hands and worked on producing a small flame in his palm.

Out of his three brothers, Yvan was the most average. Vasilli had his magic. Dimitri had his brute strength. And Yvan had to rely on his wits and swiftness to outmatch them. Now *he* had magic, and he wasn't sure what to do with it or how to control it. If he could learn how to harness it, he would have the means to protect Anya himself. Maybe then he'd stop having nightmares about Vasilli's vicious thorns killing her slowly and painfully while he stood by, unable to help her.

I find it interesting that you have nightmares about something that didn't happen, but you never dream about the death of your wife. I can feel the pain of her betrayal deep within you, Prince. The grief—

Yvan ignited. Flames licked out from his skin as the magic reacted to his anger. "Never speak of my wife again," he hissed.

Before the firebird could berate him, a different pulse of magic hit Yvan hard in the chest, driving the air from his lungs and setting his nerves on edge.

"What the hell was that?"

Anya's power. Go now, Prince!

26

ANYA STOOD IN AN ancient forest, the smell of decaying leaf litter and earth hanging heavy in the air like smog.

"Damn it, not again," she muttered. Since Baba Zosia had torn apart what was left of Anya's memory spell, she'd been dreaming so vividly that she wasn't sure if they were memories or her own imagination.

Anya looked up at the branches above her. The leaves didn't move. There was no breeze, no chirping of birds or rustling of animals. Careful not to make much noise, she walked through the trees, searching for a path.

The trees were eerie, covered in moss and shadow, so when Anya saw a patch of sunlight, she ran for it. The pine and birch trees thinned out to reveal a large clearing and a small cottage built of stone and wood. Smoke drifted from the chimney, and well-tended gardens filled with vegetables, flowers, and herbs surrounded the house.

"In the middle of the big, dark forest lived an evil witch," Anya whispered as she approached.

Anya placed one foot on the steps, and the door opened. A woman stepped out with a sword raised high and pointed directly at her.

Anya raised her hands in surrender. "Whoa, I don't mean you any harm."

The sword didn't lower, and a pair of piercing, angry green eyes stared at her. She knew those eyes, as well as the silver hair held back in a messy braid.

"Who are you?" they both asked at once.

"I am Yanka, and you are trespassing on my land," the woman hissed, wearing Anya's famous glare.

"Shit. I'm Anya. I think—I mean I *am*—your granddaughter five times over." She edged back from the sword point.

After ten long seconds, Yanka sheathed her sword and studied her with narrowed eyes. She looked around thirty-five years old to Anya's reckoning. A scar ran along her neck down to her collarbone.

"What are you doing here?" Yanka finally asked.

"I'm dreaming."

Yanka shook her head. "This isn't the Land of Dreaming. It's the Land of the Dead."

Anya's heart tripped. "I think I would know if I were dead."

"Would you? I didn't. I thought I was dreaming too when I came to this place, yet I'm still waiting to wake up."

"I'm not dead," Anya insisted.

"You hope." Yanka crossed her pale, scarred arms, then pulled the sleeves of her dress down to hide them from Anya's gaze. "I need a drink," she said. She turned back toward the door. "Wipe your feet."

Anya followed her through the shadowy hallway and into a kitchen. It was similar to the one she had back at the farm, with wooden cupboards and benches along one wall, a pine table, and a cast-iron stove. Yanka wore a simple woolen dress and a soft leather girdle pressed with intricate designs. She opened a cupboard and brought out a large jar of a violet liquid.

"How long have you been in this place?" Anya asked, trying not to stare at her.

"Too long to remember properly now. I woke in the forest and found my way to this cottage. I repaired it and settled in to wait. The forest—"

"Is eerily silent," Anya said.

"I was going to say dangerous. You can't leave the cottage after nightfall. I tried once and got this." Yanka put the jar on the table and lifted the hem of her dress. Wrapped around her left leg was a long, curving scar.

"Der'mo." Anya cringed. "I'm sure I'll wake up by nightfall."

Yanka lowered her skirt and placed two squat pottery mugs next to the jar. She sat on one of the three-legged stools and gestured for Anya to sit on the other one. A small knife appeared in her hand, and she deftly cut the wax seal. "So you are of Ilya's brood? I forget what name he gave himself."

"Venäläinen."

Yanka's face screwed up. "And a Finnish name to insult me further."

Ilya's brood, not Yanka's *family*. Trajan said that she and Ilya hadn't been close, but Anya was surprised at the disapproval in her tone. "Ilya was my grandfather's grandfather," Anya said.

Yanka poured the thick liquid from the jar into the mugs. "You have some magical ability, yes?" She sipped her drink.

Anya did the same and was pleasantly surprised to discover it was blackberry vodka. "Yeah, though I only found out about it recently. I'm still learning."

Yanka's eyes flashed with annoyance. "You should've begun your teaching when you were three."

"Eikki, my grandfather, thought it would be best not to teach me. Something about wanting me to have a safe, normal life."

And because I was too much like you, she didn't add. Anya had known Yanka for a whole five minutes and was already intimidated enough to keep her mouth shut.

Yanka muttered a curse. "Fool! Magic isn't something you can leave undeveloped. It will control you and burn you up."

"Is that what happened to you? Baba Yaga said that your magic destroyed you—"

"Baba Yaga is a lying cow, but even I'm not sure what happened to me... Here, give me your hand."

"Why?"

"I'm going to show you something that your grandfather should have." Yanka reached across the table. "The future."

Anya drained her mug and took Yanka's hand. An electrical zap of magic sparked between their palms when they touched, but Yanka didn't let go. She whispered under her breath, and images flooded Anya's mind so fast she couldn't discern one from another.

Then came flames and blood and harrowing screams.

"Anya!" Yvan charged into Anya's room, which was engulfed in flames. She writhed atop the sheets, fire pouring from her skin. Yvan's body lit up with the firebird's flames, and he walked through the fire to reach her.

His hands brushed her face. "Anya, wake up."

These are not ordinary flames. This is magic fire, the firebird said.

"It doesn't matter what type of fire it is!" Yvan took her by the shoulders and shook her. "Anyanka! Wake up!"

"Yvan?" Anya opened a bleary eye. The flames still burned, and she recoiled in fear, twisting about in her sheets.

"It's okay, Anya." Yvan held her face in his hands. "Turn the flames off. It's only your magic."

Anya nodded and shut her eyes in concentration. Within seconds, the flames vanished, sinking back inside of her. The firebird withdrew into Yvan at the same time, until the room was back to normal and it were as if the flames had never been there. Anya collapsed in his arms, shaking and crying.

"You're safe, Anya. Don't cry." Yvan patted her back. "You're okay."

"Just a dream," Anya murmured against his shirt.

Trajan strode into the room, his coat and hair wet, Yvan guessed from the rain. "What happened?"

Anya let Yvan go with a jerk and ran into Trajan's arms for comfort. Yvan schooled his face as a sharp spike of jealousy pierced his guts.

Cerise's face was white with worry. "We saw the flames coming out of the window when we drove in. We thought the whole place was burning."

"No, just me," Anya replied, her voice muffled by Trajan's overcoat.

"How about we go downstairs and get you something warm to drink?" Trajan kissed her gently and drove the spike into Yvan a little farther. He leaned back, his brow furrowed. "Why do you taste like blackberries?"

Sitting with Trajan's arm around her and a cup of hot tea in her hands, Anya finally relaxed enough to tell them about her dream and what Yanka had done to her. She couldn't remember what the vision Yanka had forced into her mind was about—other than that it was apparently "the future"—but she still felt the horror and pain of it deep inside of her.

Dream Yanka was enough to scare the shit out of her. Anya could only imagine what she must have been like when she was alive, and she couldn't help but wonder if she would become like that when she learned her magic.

"Just how much paprika did you put in that borsch you made tonight?" Izrayl asked Katya, who sat beside him. They were both bandaged up and recovering from the fight, but it didn't stop their bickering.

Katya rolled her eyes. "Very funny. It's more likely that you put something in it when I wasn't looking."

"I don't know much about magic, but how do we know your dream was real?" asked Cerise.

"She tasted of blackberries," Trajan said. "Dreams can be powerful but not enough to physically alter reality. Vasilli's thorns would be another example."

"It was real enough to Anya that her body and magic reacted. Whether or not she found her way to the Land of Dreaming or the Land of the Dead is irrelevant," Yvan said. He had a dark look in his eyes that Anya had never seen before. They flashed red and back to blue. It seemed the firebird wanted to make his presence known.

"If it weren't for Yvan, I'd still be burning." Anya smiled at him, and his glare softened a little. "You scared me. I thought I had set you on fire."

"The firebird and I have been working on controlling its magic. You couldn't set me on fire if you tried." He got to his feet and started to pace.

"Getting back to whether you made it to the Land of the Dead or Dreaming…" Katya said. "I have shaman friends who can walk those paths. They need to prepare first—usually they put themselves in a trance—but it's possible you did it without preparation. I'll ring them and see if they can help. Aleksandra suggested I get in contact with them anyway. They would be good teachers for you."

Anya drank her tea, her head still full of fire and terror. Whatever Yanka had done to her hadn't affected her physically, but mentally, she was a mess from the future horror she had pushed into her head. Maybe Yanka had wanted to warn her, not scare her, but Anya doubted it.

"We need to think about whether or not you're going to set yourself on fire every time you have a bad dream," Izrayl said, an uneasy look in his golden eyes. "You and Yvan might be fireproof, but I'm not."

Katya elbowed him. "Shut up. You don't need to scare her more."

"No, he's right," Anya said. Panic rose in her chest. "I have no idea what this means from now on. I could wake up with the house in ashes. I could… Excuse me. I can't—"

Anya hurried back to her room, flames and blood flashing in her mind's eye as salt filled her mouth. She went into her bathroom and climbed in the dry bathtub. At least there was nothing in there she could burn. She swallowed down her tears and worked to steady her breath.

Every day she learned something new about her magic, and every day she felt more like a stranger in her own body. *You have to learn how to control it. If you could use it to beat off bullies when you were twelve, surely you can do it now.*

"Anya? Are you hiding in here?" Trajan tapped on the bathroom door.

She pressed herself down as flat as she could. His curly head appeared above her.

"I'm not hiding. I'm trying to think," she said.

"You don't want to do that somewhere more comfortable?"

Anya sat up. "I'm worried that if I get upset, I'll light up again."

"Okay, then scoot forward." Trajan kicked off his shoes and climbed in behind her. His legs came down around either side of her, and he pulled her back against his chest. Warmth flooded her, and she relaxed into him.

"You know Izrayl didn't mean to upset you."

"I know, but that doesn't mean he was wrong. I don't want to have to worry about lighting on fire every time I go to bed. I have enough trouble sleeping as it is." Anya wove her hands with his.

"It was out of your control, Anya. You can't blame yourself. Katya's friends might be able to tell you what in the dream triggered a physical response in you. We know it wasn't a normal nightmare. And it doesn't mean you're going to react the same way every time."

"But we don't know that for sure, Trajan. It could be like this from now on. Like I needed to be more of a freak."

"You're in good company, then. I can suck the life force out of any living thing; Cerise has to drink dead blood to survive; Yvan shares his body with a mythical bird that sets on fire; Katya has so many skeletons in her closet I can just about hear them dancing; and don't even get me started on Izrayl's kinks."

Anya was laughing before she could stop herself. "You make a good point, but I still need to sleep."

"I can watch over you tonight. I don't need to sleep much."

Anya turned to look up at him. "You'll stay with me?"

"If you don't mind. It will be a lot more comfortable than sleeping in this bathtub."

That's debatable. The thought of Trajan sleeping over made her body and imagination ignite in a very different way. He helped her out of the tub and led her back to the bedroom. Miraculously, none of her bedding had been scorched in her inferno, and she said as much to Trajan as she climbed in.

"Let's worry about the properties of magical fire tomorrow," he said as he tucked her in. He made to sit down on the chair next to the bed, but she grabbed his hand, tugging him back to her. His eyes shone red, then returned back to autumn gold.

"Are you sure?" he asked.

She knew he was referring to his fear of accidentally feeding on her if he let his guard down, but she wanted him close. "Trajan, if you're not worried about me setting you on fire, I'm not worried about falling asleep beside you." Anya moved over to make space for him.

He nodded. "Practice."

Tingles swept down her spine at the implications in the word. He took off his glasses and placed them on the bedside table before climbing in beside her.

"What if I really did go to the Land of the Dead?" Anya asked, her voice small.

Trajan moved closer and placed his arm around her waist. She curled into him, putting her head on his chest.

"I've been to the Land of the Dead, and what you described is very far from it." His lips pressed against her hair. "We will work it out in the morning. Now close your eyes and sleep."

✦

Trajan watched Anya sleep, a frown forming on his face. They were going to need more help than just Katya's friends. Shamans were all well and good, but they needed more warriors. He had planned on reaching out to Hamish, and he couldn't wait any longer. Katya's encounter with the Darkness was enough to warrant more security. It would only be a matter of time before Vasilli and Ladislav tracked them down, and he wanted to be ready.

Trajan untangled himself from Anya and moved to the next room. He scrolled through his phone for all the last known numbers he had for Hamish, who liked to travel and was never in one place or had the same number for long.

A woman answered. "Burnt Downs Station."

"Hello. I was wondering if Hamish Hudson would be available."

"You a copper?"

"I assure you, madam, I'm not the police. I'm one of Hamish's acquaintances."

"Sorry, you sound like a copper. Look, Hamish ain't in. He's out mustering and isn't due back to the station for another three days."

"Could you please tell him that Trajan rang? I need him to come to Paris. I'm calling in the debt he owes me."

"I need him to bring the cattle in first, then you can have him. Not for too long, mind you, because he works hard, unlike some of the other good-for-nothing bastards out here."

"Of course. Just tell him it's urgent and that if he needs money to call me."

"No worries. I'll let him know."

The phone went dead, and Trajan sighed. At least he knew where Hamish was. Now all he could do was wait.

27

KATYA WOULD'VE LIKED TO drink the day away on the couch, but the inactivity of the past few days had gotten to her. She had spent most of the morning going through all of her previous contact numbers for the twins, trying to find a number that was still connected. Anya's fire-starting antics meant she had to find the boys and soon. She had no luck with the phone numbers and was contemplating mind-linking with Aleksandra to see if she could reach out to them by magical means. Katya needed to be calm to do that, and at the moment, she was agitated from sitting still so long. She was used to hunting every day, not lounging about in luxury while she had healed, so she hit the treadmill in the gym downstairs.

Katya was hitting her fifth mile when her phone buzzed. The screen read: *Unknown Caller.*

"Katya!"

"Chayton? You've got to be kidding me! I was just looking for a number for you boys. Have you been spying on me in your crystal ball again?" She laughed and turned the machine off so she could catch her breath.

"Very funny, smart ass. You know looking at balls isn't my thing," Chayton said while his brother, Honaw, laughed in the background. "We saw you while we were dream-walking. What crazy shit are you up to now? And what are you doing with a *volk krovi?*"

"Yeah, Katya, what's going on with the wolf?" Honaw called from what sounded like a foot or so away from the phone. "I thought I was your only true love?"

Katya looked up as Izrayl came into the gym dressed in workout clothes. He raised a curious black brow. Of course, he would've been able to hear every bloody word from the stairs. Katya sat on the weight bench next to her and muttered a curse as her bandages pulled.

"How are the wounds?" asked Chayton.

"Great, so you saw that too, huh?" Katya unwrapped the bindings around her ribs.

"We did. You better start talking, hunter. We hear you're in Paris."

"I am," Katya confirmed. "I was attacked a few nights ago, as you saw. I'm with a girl—Anya. She's full of magic and has had no training. Get this: Yanka's line, gatekeeper, and has no fucking idea what do with her power. I need you and Honaw to come to help her."

"Like no training at all? Who's watching her gate?"

"No one. That's why I need you."

There was a rustle, and Honaw's more resonant voice came across the line. "We aren't gatekeepers, Katya."

"No, but you're shamans, and you can dream-walk, which she can also do. She's got no one to help her out."

"Dream-walking is boundaries magic. Perhaps she could adapt that and apply the same principles to gates…"

Katya could almost hear the wheels in Chayton's head turning.

"Or it won't work at all," Honaw suggested.

"There's something else you need to know..." Katya bit her lip. "Apparently there's also a prophecy kicking about that foresees Anya and the firebird defeating Vasilli." The words came out in a rush.

There was a long silence on the end of the line.

"We saw it had been reborn. Is the firebird still with you?" asked Honaw.

"Yes?" She didn't know if this would reduce the likelihood of them coming to Paris or not.

Honaw grunted. "Well—"

"More fun for us. You know, with all the danger and excitement," Chayton said. "We're in Vancouver, so we'll get on the next available flight. Once we assess Anya's abilities, we can talk about how we can help. Now, tell me about this wolf. You seemed pretty upset when he got hurt. You dating him, little one? I never thought I'd see the day where you were hanging with a *volk krovi*."

Chayton always called her "little one" when he was teasing her. It was clear she wasn't getting out of the conversation without talking about Izrayl. They knew her family's history with them, so their surprise wasn't unfounded. She risked a glance over to where the wolf in question was watching her with glowing, golden eyes.

"He's helping out with Anya, and he saved my ass, Chay," she said, hoping he would drop it if she was as vague.

"It's not your ass I'm worried about. It's that soft little heart of yours. If he breaks it, it will be his ass in trouble."

"You know I can handle him and his ass. That's not even a concern. We're..." Katya struggled to identify him. "Colleagues?" Except they had been circling each other since they met, and after the fight in the park, she'd almost kissed him more than once. *You're getting dangerously close to saying "friend I flirt with." Subject change.* "Let me know when you land, and I'll come get you. Okay?"

"Last time I saw you, you were riding a motorcycle. Have you got a sidecar for Honaw?"

Katya heard sharp protests in the background, and she laughed hard and loud. God, she had missed them. "Last time we hung out, I didn't have friends with fancy, expensive cars. Don't worry. We won't need a sidecar. Tell Honaw I'll let him ride in front with me if he's nice."

A deep growl from behind made her jump. Izrayl leaned over, his face appearing upside down. She hadn't even heard him move. Katya tried to push him away, but he stayed put. His gold eyes burned hot with wolf.

"Are you okay with us crashing with you and these fancy friends?" Chayton said.

"Of course. Trajan will want you close. He's worried about the Darkness and Anya setting herself on fire."

Izrayl moved around to the front of the bench. Katya desperately tried to concentrate on what Chayton was saying, but she felt like a rabbit about to be pounced on. The thought shouldn't have excited her as much as it did.

"...can be protective," Honaw was saying. "But I want to see Paris. I haven't been there in years, and I'm not going to take a ten-hour flight and see nothing. We are due at least one night out drinking, Katya."

"The last time you boys and I went drinking, I danced on a table, and we all ended up hungover for a week. I don't think we're going to have that level of freedom this time." Katya kept her eyes on Izrayl. He crouched down in front of her, placing his warm hands on her elbows where they rested on her knees. What was his problem now?

"Um, Chay? I gotta go," Katya said. "Text me your flight details, and I'll be there to get you. I promise."

"All right. Are you okay?"

"I'm fine. Bye!" Katya hung up and stared wide-eyed at the huge man in front of her. "And what do you think you're doing?"

"Proving that I'm never, ever going to be your colleague."

Katya's breath caught as Izrayl ran his hands up to grip her biceps, pulled her closer, and kissed her. Hot desire shot through her veins, the intensity of which surprised her. She whimpered as he deepened the embrace, his stubble rough against her skin. Katya brushed her tongue against his, savoring the taste of him: maple syrup and male. He growled against her lips, making her whole body vibrate.

What. The. Hell.

Izrayl broke the kiss. "See? I told you."

Katya was too stunned to speak, her brain hazed with lust and chanting his name.

Izrayl had been keeping watch over her since the night she was attacked, making sure she took her antibiotics and painkillers on time—and without alcohol. He'd been acting more like a fussy nurse than Cerise had. The wolf had a sweet side she hadn't expected, and it made him even harder to ignore. Her lips tingled, and she huffed out a breath. She knew he'd be a good kisser, but damn…

You're supposed to kill volk krovi, not kiss them, her father growled in her head. If he could see her from the afterlife, she was sure he was clenching his big, violent fists and shaking them at her. He had done everything he could to make her hate *volk krovi,* and now, she had made out with one.

Well, you always did like to provoke the old bastard.

"You're almost healed," Izrayl said when she remained speechless. He tilted his head to examine her ribs. "It must be one of the bonuses of being born in Skazki, right?"

"Yes. It also means I have no fear of busting anything when I do this." Katya shoved his chest hard, and Izrayl rocked backward onto the mat.

"What the hell was that for?"

"Kissing me without permission." She got off the weight bench, needing to put some space between them.

"You could've stopped me with a word, but you didn't. You act tough, hunter, but you like me, and you hate it." Izrayl moved toward her. "It unnerved you. *That's* why you're fighting me."

"Don't flatter yourself, you arrogant bastard."

"Just give it up, Katya. This hostile flirting thing you do only turns me on."

Katya reacted before he could get closer, kicking his legs out from underneath him. He fell onto his back with a curse. She stepped over him and made for the stairs.

Izrayl leaped up and tackled her fast. They flew through the air and landed in the pool with a splash. Katya popped up and pushed the hair from her face before Izrayl broke the surface beside her and laughed.

"You dick!" she shouted. She looked into the water beneath her. "I lost my shoe."

Izrayl dove down and retrieved her soaked sneaker. When he came back up, he offered it to her. "Cinderella."

"Thanks." She took it and tossed it from the pool, then treaded water for a few moments, looking at him thoughtfully.

"Are you thinking about how you could drown me?" Izrayl pushed his wet hair from his face.

"It's tempting. I'm still angry with you."

His gold eyes sparkled with mischief. "No, you're not."

"Stop laughing at me. I'm serious."

"You look it." His grin softened. "I've never seen a woman with as many scars as you."

"It comes with the job. If you don't like them, don't look at them." Katya wished she hadn't taken her shirt off.

"Don't be so defensive. I was only making an observation. I think they suit you. Your tattoos do too. What do they all mean?"

"They're protection symbols from just about every nation and religion."

"Do they help?"

"Sometimes. It depends on what I'm up against. I figure they can't hurt. And you can't give me a hard time about my scars. You have more than me."

"And I had some weird creature's fingers stuck in my back."

"Pretty gross," Katya agreed. Her legs were tired from running and now treading water. Unlike her, Izrayl could touch the bottom of the pool.

As if reading her mind, he stretched out a hand toward her. "Give your legs a rest. I'm not going to bite, Katya."

She took his hand so he wouldn't badger her anymore. The pain in her legs eased as he held her steady. She knew she should climb out of the pool, but for some reason, she didn't.

"You see, *volk krovi* aren't so bad after all." Izrayl frowned. "Is it true what you said about them killing your mother?"

Katya went still with shock. "I told you…?"

"Yeah, you may have mentioned it when you were drunk…"

"And you only bother to bring it up now?" Oh god, she couldn't believe herself.

"How was I supposed to know you didn't remember our conversation? And why would I bring it up again? Besides, I can't imagine it's a subject anyone would enjoy talking about it."

Katya rubbed at the scar over her eye and finally asked, "You really want to know?"

"Of course I do. Give me the short version if it makes you uncomfortable."

Katya got caught in the sincerity of his gaze and was talking before she even realized it. "I was eleven at the time. I barely remember my mother, only that she was a healer and looked at lot like Aleki. One night, she was sought out by the alpha of a *volk krovi* pack. His wife had had a difficult birth and wouldn't stop bleeding. My mother did everything she could with her herbs and her magic, but she couldn't save her. About a week later, my mother was out gleaning the forest and never came home. Her body washed up a day later with deep claw marks scored all over her body. I've never heard a sound of such despair and rage than my father's cries that day."

Izrayl didn't interrupt her, just held her steady.

"After that, he changed. He blamed the *volk krovi*, but the pack had moved on, and he couldn't confront them. He killed any he could after that, blinded by a rage that never went away. Most of the time, he took that rage out on Aleki and me. She looks so much like my mother that he couldn't stand the sight of her." Katya touched the scar on her brow that still throbbed whenever she talked about him. "This happened about four weeks after my mother's death. He was drunk and went after Aleki. I stepped in the way to protect her, and he hit me with a bottle. I would've lost this eye and probably my life if Baba Zosia hadn't turned up with some of the men from our tribe to pull him off me. After that, Aleki and I lived with her. When I was healed, I went back to training with him. He never apologized, and I never forgave him. He trained me to hate your kind, to kill and ask questions afterward. If he were still alive, he would be so horrified that I kissed you that he'd try to put a bullet in me too."

Izrayl's eyes burned with anger, but he didn't push her away, even knowing that she had killed other wolves like him. She wouldn't have blamed him if he had.

"You said he's dead?"

Katya nodded.

He tugged her closer and kissed her scar. "Lucky for him."

Katya tried to shrug off the emotion that clogged her throat. "He taught me what I needed to know. My family have always been the protectors and seers of the tribe. I became the hunter because Aleki was a seer from the moment she opened her three eyes. She's so much more powerful than she lets show. If you want to see the true talent in the family, look to her."

"I don't need to. I'm looking at some pretty great talent right now."

Katya laughed. "You really are an incorrigible flirt, aren't you?"

"Guilty as charged. It made you smile again, and that's what counts." Izrayl grinned. "Warming up to me yet?"

"You're going to have to wait to find out." Katya let go of him and drifted backward. "As for me, I'm going for a shower."

"Can I come?"

Katya pulled herself out of the pool. "You wish."

"Let me know when you change your mind. I'm an excellent back washer."

28

KATYA WAS SHIVERING BY the time she got to her bathroom. After peeling off her wet clothes, she stepped in and let the boiling water cascade over her, stretching out her muscles so they wouldn't cramp. A part of her regretted running away from Izrayl, but if she had stayed, she would've ended up kissing him again. Whatever was building between them was never going to be casual, and she needed space. She felt too raw and vulnerable after talking about her parents, and she didn't want to use Izrayl just to make herself feel better.

Katya's phone vibrated on the basin. She stepped out of the shower and dried herself with one of the thick towels. After slipping on a bathrobe, she picked up her phone.

ON A HUNT IN PARIS TONIGHT. CALL ME IF IN-
TERESTED. BEL.

"Shit." Isabelle Blackwood was a hunter and one of Katya's mentors. If she was asking for help on a job, she must've been worried about it.

Katya fired back another text asking for details and hurried to get dressed. She slipped out of her door only to be spotted by Izrayl from the other end of the hall. He looked fresh from a shower, wearing only jeans, and was in the middle of braiding his hair.

"Sneaking out again? Are you serious?"

"I'll go wherever I like. It's none of your business."

He closed in on her. "It is when I have to come and bail you out."

"Then come with me," Katya said, surprising herself.

Izrayl went from overprotective to curious in a blink. "Where are we going?"

"I have a hunter friend called Isabelle. She wants my help with a job."

"You've only just healed from your last…*outing*." Izrayl brushed a piece of hair back from her face. "Did you tell her that?"

"No, and she doesn't need to know. She never would have contacted me if she didn't really need my help."

"I don't like it, but I'm in. I can't let you go out by yourself again."

"My hero," Katya said dryly.

"Give me a second." He ducked back into his rooms, then reappeared wearing a three-quarter length black pea coat with a dark green shirt and boots.

"Are you armed?" Katya asked.

He opened his coat wide to reveal an arsenal almost as impressive as hers. "I might do this in human form so your friend doesn't try to hunt me too. You got that sword with you? You look pretty hot when you use it."

"Of course I have my sword." Katya's ringtone jingled, and she opened the message from Isabelle. "Do you know where this is?" She held up the phone for him to see the address in the 18th arrondissement of the city.

"I should be able to find it. We'll take my car."

They got into the elevator, and Katya's adrenaline kicked up as the doors slid shut, enclosing her in the small space with Izrayl's heat and masculine scent. She was never going to be able to concentrate if she didn't get this out of her system…

She hit the stop button and turned to look up at him. Izrayl raised a questioning brow as she rose on tiptoes and pressed her lips to his. A low growl rumbled in his chest as he deepened the kiss. Katya nipped at Izrayl's bottom lip and felt his self-control snap. He lifted her up and had her pressed against the elevator doors before she could blink. She wrapped her legs around him, her hands buried in his hair, and met his intensity head-on. She'd fought her urge for days like an idiot, but not anymore.

Katya's phone chimed again, obliterating the moment.

"We have to get going," she said, breathless. She pulled away from him and leaned down from his hold to press the button to get the elevator moving. It opened on the garage level, and Izrayl lowered her to her feet, his eyes still hot enough to make her second-guess going out.

She pulled out of his grip and headed for the car. "Stop looking at me like that."

"Not that I'm complaining, but do you want to tell me what that was for?"

Katya grinned and opened the passenger door. "Luck."

He cursed under his breath, and that only made her grin widen.

"Does Isabelle call you up out of the blue like this a lot?" Izrayl asked as he pulled out onto the street.

"Not often, but when she does, it's always last-minute. I didn't even know she was in France."

"Any idea what she's hunting?"

"Not a clue. I hope I don't get you killed."

"Just worry about yourself, little hunter."

They drove in silence for a few moments until Katya's phone pinged.

MEET ME ON THE ROOF. B.

"She really needs to learn to text without caps," Katya said. "Keep an eye out for a fire escape with a roof access."

Katya and Izrayl left the car a few blocks from their destination and continued on foot. It was a quiet night, and Katya could smell the water of the Canal de l'Ourcq in the air. Izrayl walked a few steps behind her, watching her back.

They scaled the building next door before making their way across to the roof of their destination. Katya didn't know who they were about to ambush, but the dilapidated building didn't appear to have any security. She nearly crashed into Isabelle as she came around a corner.

Isabelle Blackwood had been a friend of the family for years, and Katya hero-worshipped her. Rumors abounded about her in the hunter community, most speculating that Isabelle was half-vampire, a demon, or a supernatural of some sort. Katya could believe the half-supernatural rumor, because Isabelle hadn't aged the whole time Katya had known her. Isabelle looked about twenty-five years old, with long blond hair and violet eyes. Her obvious femininity was a deception; she could outfight, outshoot, and outhunt any of her male counterparts.

Isabelle had shown Katya many tricks of the trade, especially after she was old enough to get away from the tribe. The two of them caught up whenever they could. The first time Katya had seen her in action, she'd almost gotten herself killed standing there watching Isabelle slice, dice, and shoot. She was magic with a blade and damn frightening to behold.

Isabelle looked the same as she always did. Her honey hair fell to her waist in a braid and shone in scant light. Katya caught the glimmer of weapons strapped to her legs in holsters similar to her own. She wore the hunting gear Katya had seen her in most often: tight dark trousers, high lace-up boots, a dark blue shirt, and a many-buttoned governess waistcoat. She had a three-quarter length jacket over the top, which held, if possible, more weapons than Katya had.

"Thank you for coming," Isabelle said, her English accent crisp as the night air. She was in full hunter mode, her expression serious. Hugs and catch-ups would wait until later.

"It's good to see you. This is Izrayl." Katya nodded in his direction.

Isabelle gave him an appraising once-over before she offered her hand. He shook it with a smile. "Nice to have you along. Katya and I will try not to get you killed."

Izrayl grinned. "She said the same thing. You don't have to worry."

"Oh, I'm not worried. If you die, it's your own fault. Let's go. It's getting late."

"Belle, info. What are we up against?"

Isabelle turned on her heel. She had a look in her eye that Katya had never seen before—uncertainty. "I'm not sure. I've been staking this place out for a few days, and there hasn't been anyone coming or going, but the building is radiating enough darkness to set my teeth on edge." Isabelle pointed at the surrounding houses. "Why do you think these buildings are empty? In a suburb like this, these mansions should be filled with people. This place has scared them off. Even normals can feel evil. Sorry I don't have more to go on."

Katya nodded. Isabelle had unique talents, which gave her an edge. If she was this worried, it was enough for Katya to believe her without the proof. "Let's go take a look." Katya pulled out her gun and looked over at Izrayl. His eyes were glowing again, and she wondered if he was using his *volk krovi* senses to get a feel for whatever lay beneath their feet.

Isabelle reached into a pocket, pulled out two small strips of metal, and expertly picked the lock on the roof access door.

"They have minimal security, whoever they are," Katya said. "No electrical trips or cameras anywhere."

Izrayl pulled out one of his guns. "Perhaps they don't need them because people know better than to break in here."

They stepped into the stairwell, and the hair on the back of Katya's neck rose. A chemical smell in the air mixed with decay and sweat. Isabelle had her knives out and ready as she crept down the stairs in front of them. She opened another door, which led to the top floor. There wasn't a single sound coming from anywhere.

Overturned furniture and clutter littered the three rooms, showing signs of a hurried departure. Isabelle placed a hand on a wall and shut her eyes. Izrayl opened his mouth to say something, but Katya grabbed his arm. She had seen Isabelle in action before. She claimed she could sometimes read objects, and Katya had never questioned her abilities.

Isabelle jerked her hand away from the wall. "Beneath us. I'm sorry, Katya. I shouldn't have brought you." Without elaborating, Isabelle strode down the stairs to the next level.

Katya hurried to catch her and was almost bowled over by the smell of blood and decaying flesh. It filled her nose, making her dry gag.

"They were torturing them," Isabelle said from the far side of the room.

On a few old metal hospital beds, corpses had been left to rot. Around the room were chains on the walls, small tables littered with medical instruments, and what remained of a science lab. Plastic sheeting had been hung up as a divider, and Katya carefully lifted it with the barrel of her gun. It took her a few moments to recognize what she was actually looking at. Half of it looked human, but one arm was the broken wing of a bird. Feathers stuck out of it in odd places, disguising half of its face. Its liquid black eye blinked, and Katya jumped back. It made a glutinous sound, and she struggled to keep her nerve. The creature before her tried again, black fluid running from its mouth.

"Kill..."

"It wants you to," Izrayl said from behind her. "Do it, Katya. It's in pain."

Katya lightly touched the feathers on its deformed face as she placed the barrel of her gun under its chin and squeezed the trigger. "Let's find the bastards who did this." She pushed past Izrayl and looked around for Isabelle, who stood examining a slew of papers tacked to a wall. Some of it looked like family trees.

"These victims were from magical bloodlines," Isabelle said, her voice cold. "Obviously, they weren't getting what they wanted from them."

"But why leave the building like this?"

"Maybe they spotted me watching it and thought they were compromised." Isabelle handed her a piece of paper. The seal pressed in black ink was a sword with a snarling dragon around it.

"Fucking Darkness," Katya spat. "I wonder if they have something like this in mind for Anya if they get a hold of her."

Isabelle turned to look at her. "Who's Anya?"

"She's a long story. One I won't tell you about here."

"Very well." Isabelle collected some of the papers and stuffed them into the front of her waistcoat.

Katya turned away from the collage of bloodlines and spotted a small door, not even a meter high, on the far wall. Gripping her gun, she walked over to it. She slid the bolt across, and before she could pull the door open, something burst through, snarling and snapping, knocking her over as she fired a shot and missed. Whatever it was leaped on top of her, its legs squeezing the air from her lungs. There was a snarl, and a black wolf launched over the top of her, knocking the creature off. There was a wet shriek and then nothing.

Gasping for air, Katya rolled onto her side. Isabelle helped her up. Izrayl stood over what remained of the thing that had attacked her, his fur standing high and vicious. Patches of feathers grew out of the creature in places, and its black beak was filled with human teeth. Isabelle slammed the little door shut again and slid the bolt across.

"You ever seen anything like it?" asked Katya.

"No, though it looks like some kind of bird-human hybrid, like the others. Maybe this particular experiment was the closest they got to success." Isabelle looked over the body. She brushed her fingers over its shoulder and pulled her hand back. "Definitely made with magic, the fuckers."

Izrayl transformed back into a man, and Katya tossed him his coat to cover up.

Isabelle smiled. "You didn't tell me your friend was one of the *volk krovi*. How interesting this night has been."

"Surprise," Katya said numbly.

"It's time we left," Izrayl said with more growl than usual.

"I couldn't agree more." Isabelle snapped pictures of the creature on her phone before standing. "There's something I'd like to do first."

Minutes later, the three of them strode out of the building as flames engulfed the top levels.

"Come by this address tomorrow." Katya wrote Trajan's house number on Isabelle's hand. "We need to talk."

"I'll be there," Isabelle promised. She gave Katya a tight hug. "It *is* good to see you despite this shit show."

"You too, Belle."

Isabelle fixed Izrayl with her violet gaze. "Look after her tonight."

"I will," he said without hesitation.

Isabelle shot them a wink before melting into the darkness of the street.

They were silent on the drive back home, Katya's chest aching from what she had seen. Silent tears slid down her cheeks, and Izrayl was smart enough not to comment on them. It wasn't until they pulled into the basement garage that Katya felt she could finally breathe again.

"Katya—"

"Don't." She got out of the car and hit the elevator button over and over until Izrayl grabbed her hand. "Go on, then. Make a joke about the hunter who cries after a job."

"I wasn't going to say anything. Stop putting words in my mouth."

The elevator binged, and she stepped in. Katya hadn't had to do a mercy killing in a long time, and she had never seen fear and pain like she had tonight in that creature's eyes. When the doors opened again, she headed straight for her room.

Katya pulled off her boots and unloaded her weapons, placing them neatly on a table. "Don't you have your own room to go to?"

Izrayl pulled her close, and she started crying fresh tears. "Talk to me. I would think less of you if you weren't upset by the pure evil we saw tonight, Yakaterina. I've seen bigger men lose their stomachs over less. It's not a weakness to have compassion."

"I need a shower," Katya said brusquely. She unbuttoned her pants as she headed for the bathroom. "Coming?"

"Are you serious?"

"After a night like this, I really don't want to be alone. Usually, I'd go pick up some lucky guy and celebrate being alive. I thought I'd see if you're interested in showing me some of those back-washing skills you mentioned instead."

"You would have to be the most unpredictable woman I have ever met."

"Is that a yes?"

"It's a hell yes."

Katya turned on the shower taps and tried not to grimace as she pulled off her shirt. Two massive, deep purple bruises adorned either side of her ribs.

"It looks like you've been put through the wringer again." Izrayl ran his fingers along them.

"It's lucky there was only one of those creatures left to deal with if that's how good my form is."

"You're being pretty hard on yourself, considering that just over a week ago, I thought you were done for." Izrayl kissed the base of her neck where her first tattoo was, sending desire rippling down her spine. "You know, I never would have picked you as the sweet, girly underwear type."

Katya laughed. "We all have our weaknesses. Mine just happens to be underwear. What's yours?"

Izrayl's lips brushed her ear. "Tough hunters who wear girly underwear."

Katya turned to wrap her arms around his neck. "Good answer."

29

KATYA STEERED CERISE'S RED Jaguar through Paris's tight streets, driving like a demon through the traffic. She made a silent promise to be Cerise's slave for life for letting her use her car.

Bloody Izrayl! If it weren't for him, she wouldn't have overslept. Instead, she would've been waiting for the twins when they landed, not getting pissy texts because she wasn't there. She screeched into the five-minute parking and dialed Chayton's number.

"Hey, I'm here! I'll get out and wave my arms like an idiot until you see me." She left the Jag purring, climbed out, and looked around the car park for her friends. She spotted them almost instantly.

They were very handsome, very tall Native American men with brown skin and long black hair. What couldn't be seen with the naked eye was their immortality and status as two of the few Powers America had. They hated leaving America for too long, so Katya would owe them a hefty debt if they all survived the coming fight.

"I was wondering if you had abandoned us," Chayton said.

He and Honaw hugged her from both sides. She groaned under their weight but couldn't stop laughing. When they freed her, she kissed them both.

"I'm so sorry I wasn't here on time. I'm a terrible friend."

"Yes, you are. You smell like a wolf. What have you been doing?" Honaw asked. There was a very loaded silence that lasted a full ten seconds. "I change my mind. Don't tell me."

"Hallelujah, the drought is over." Chayton nudged her.

"Don't give Izrayl too much of a hard time. He saved my ass more than once in the past few weeks."

"Sounds like that's not the only thing he's been doing with your ass," Honaw muttered.

"Does he have jet lag or what?" Katya asked his brother.

"Ignore him. He's grumpy and hungry." Chayton gestured around the lot. "Which one is yours?"

Katya walked over to the red Jag and slipped into the soft leather driver's seat.

The twins stood gaping before struggling with each other for the front seat. Honaw, the bigger of the two, won out. "Holy shit, you've been a thieving hunter, haven't you?"

"It belongs to one of my new friends. She's got a thing for red, as you can probably tell." Katya eased the beautiful car out into traffic and hit the accelerator.

Chayton was sucked back against the seat. "She'll kill you when she finds out you've been revving in her car."

"I've seen her drive. Believe me, I'm taking it easy. She's a keres." Katya couldn't help but laugh at their expressions. "What? You didn't see that in your visions?"

"We just never thought we would see the day you would be friends with supes," Honaw said. "Or shagging a *volk krovi* for that matter."

"I'm a big girl, Bear. I don't need your approval."

"I'm surprised that you've finally gotten over your problem with his kind."

"I think it's great." Chayton placed a hand on Katya's shoulder. "It's good to see you've found someone to love."

Katya swerved, then swore.

"What the hell?" Honaw gripped the dash.

"Tell Chayton to stop scaring me!" Katya steadied the car. "Shut up about that sort of shit when I'm driving. Bloody hell, I barely know the guy. Sheesh."

Honaw tugged on her ponytail. "Yeah, but you like him. I can tell."

She batted his hand away. "And what about you? How's your love life going?"

Chayton laughed, and Honaw grumbled.

"None of your business."

"Yeah, that's what I thought."

Katya pulled into Trajan's driveway and then the underground garage. The twins climbed out and looked around with wide eyes and drooling mouths.

"Honaw, I think we need to make friends with these supes," Chayton said as he studied the Rolls-Royce.

"Come on, you two. You can look at pretty cars later." Katya took both their hands and pulled them into the elevator. She thought of the trip she had in there with Izrayl and grinned. The *volk krovi* sure could kiss.

"I see that smile, and it usually means trouble." Chayton gave her hand a squeeze.

"And you haven't even met him yet." The elevator door opened, and they were flooded with the warm, sweet smell of frying pancakes. "By the smell of things, he's cooking breakfast."

"No wonder you're in love with him. He's replaced Aleksandra with the prestigious position of keeping you well fed."

A dreamy look passed over Honaw's face. "Oh, Aleksandra. She can cook a meal that will make a man weep."

Katya's eyes narrowed. "Sounds like you aren't just sighing over her cooking. Don't be getting mushy ideas about her, or I'll have to kick your ass like last time."

She followed her nose to the kitchen and pushed through the door. Izrayl stood in front of the stove, dressed only in a pair of jeans. Butterflies and lust exploded in her stomach as he turned and grinned at her.

"Good morning." He wore a welcoming smile.

Katya's gaze lingered along the smooth pelvic grooves that disappeared under his loose jeans. She knew where they led and wanted to visit again.

"Boys, this is Izrayl. Izrayl, this is Honaw and Chayton," she managed.

"The wolf," they said together.

Honaw offered Izrayl his hand, and Izrayl shook it.

"That's me. I thought you'd be hungry after such a shitty flight."

"Honaw is always hungry. Don't you worry about that," Chayton said.

Katya's eyes traced Izrayl's mouth before she snapped her attention to the pile of pancakes he'd cooked. "I'm starving," she said, a bit too loudly.

She hustled the twins to sit and set them up with plates and toppings. Katya did her best to ignore Izrayl as she brewed them all strong coffee. He disappeared from kitchen for a few minutes, returning with a black T-shirt on. She couldn't have said why, but it was worse than his skin being bare. Izrayl brought the food over and sat next to her, his knee brushing hers.

"Did I tell you Isabelle Blackwood is in town?" Katya asked the brothers.

Both stopped eating to give her identical stares. "Seriously?"

"We went with her on a job last night—a really screwed up one too. We could use her help now that the Darkness is on our tails."

"You want to be careful that she doesn't make things worse for you. That girl draws trouble like ants to honey." Chayton placed a hand over Katya's. "Are you sure you're in enough trouble to risk it?"

"Trust me; we need her. She has a better idea of what's currently going on with the Illumination and the Darkness. You know she's obsessed with keeping close tabs on both."

"Only so she can stay out of their way," Honaw said. "She's not going to want to get into a head-on conflict with them."

"She might after last night. It was beyond fucked up. They've been experimenting on people from magical bloodlines and left them there to die from their transmutation experiments." Katya had been unable to get the strange, pain-filled creatures out of her mind. She stabbed a piece of bacon. "I don't know if the Darkness is planning something big or just wants to increase their numbers. Isabelle has been looking into it. She's supposed to drop in sometime today."

The twins had one of their silent conversations, consisting of frowns, expressive eyebrows, and a grunt from Honaw.

Katya leaned forward. "What? What have you seen?"

"War," Honaw said. "But we can't see when it kicks off. I hope you know what you're doing. I love Isabelle, but you know she doesn't play well with others."

"She certainly gave the impression of someone you'd want to avoid in a bright alley, let alone a dark one," Izrayl said. "She isn't all human, that's for sure."

"No, she isn't," Katya agreed. "But I won't be the one to talk about it, mainly because I've never had the guts to ask her. If the twins know, they will keep their mouths shut. Right, boys?"

"We don't have a death wish," they said. "Besides, it's all speculation."

Female chattering echoed through the house, and Cerise and Anya entered the kitchen. The twins stood respectfully with big smiles.

"Ladies." Honaw bent at the waist. "I'm Honaw." He nodded to his brother. "And that's Chayton, the less attractive brother."

"Hello, boys. I'm Cerise. When Katya told me there were shamans coming, I imagined old men. I'm glad to see how mistaken I was." Her blue eyes were pure mischief as she looked them over.

"It's nice to meet you. We haven't encountered a keres in a long time," Chayton said.

"There are a few of us hiding about. Don't worry, I'm retired." Cerise paused thoughtfully, then added, "Well, sort of. "

Anya held out her hand. "I'm Anya. Thank you so much for flying all this way." Her hand touched Honaw's, and there was a loud crack of static before they blew backward in opposite directions. Honaw hit the wall with an audible thump, Anya hit the kitchen counter, and the world turned to chaos.

Anya's head throbbed in pain, and her vision blurred as she tried to sit up. Honaw was on the other side of the kitchen. The wall was broken where he'd collided with it. "Oh my god. I'm so sorry."

"Holy shit." Honaw stared at her with wide eyes.

Anya winced and touched the back of her head. Her hand came away wet with blood. Panic and magic rushed through her, and she cried out as flames burst out of her skin. The flames went higher, responding to her emotions, and everyone backed away. The kitchen door swung open, and Trajan appeared beside her.

"Get back, Trajan," Izrayl said.

But Trajan leaned closer. "Anya, you're okay. It's just your magic."

Anya wrapped her arms around her knees and rocked. Through the dancing flames, her eyes locked on Yvan, who stormed into the kitchen and moved Trajan out of the way.

"I've got this one." Yvan's arm licked with the firebird's flames, and he reached out to take Anya's hand. "*Shalost*, look at me." Anya put her hand in his, and their flames mingled. "Calm your mind and turn the flames off. You can do this."

Anya nodded and closed her eyes.

Focus on your memory of the firebird, Katya prompted her.

Anya breathed deeply as the firebird in the night sky filled her mind. As her heart slowed, the flames began to fade, pulling back inside of her.

"That's it," Yvan said.

Anya's eyes opened, and she fell forward into his strong arms. "Get me out of here. I don't want them to see me cry."

Yvan scooped her up without questioning her. "Give us a moment," he said to the others. He carried Anya through the house, finally placing her on a soft couch in the library.

"Just shoot me now, will you?" she muttered.

He placed a blanket around her, then bundled together a wad of tissues and pressed it to the wound on her head. "You seem to be more than capable of hurting yourself without my help. You shouldn't be so hard on yourself. You're untrained and have a lot of power. These sorts of things happen."

"To who?" Anya sniffed, rubbing the tears off her face.

"When Vasilli first started learning magic, he blew up the top of a tower. All you did was set yourself on fire."

Anya groaned. "The poor twins. I make such a good first impression, don't I?" She dropped her head in her hands.

"The first time we met, you tried to hit me with a big stick," he reminded her. "They got off easy with the fire."

"In my defense, you were naked and sprawled out on my floor."

"And weren't you lucky?" Yvan smirked. "You'd best turn around so I can see this cut." He brushed her hair back over her shoulder and leaned in to inspect the damage just above her ear. "It doesn't seem to be very deep," he said, his breath tickling her neck. "The firebird can heal it if you like."

"Please. I'm meant to be learning magic. I can't do that with a blazing headache. Though I'll be surprised if I still have teachers after that introduction."

"You will. Don't be so dramatic. Now, hold still." Yvan placed two fingers on the wound, and a warm charge of power flowed over her skin. "Good as new."

Anya touched the healed skin. "That's amazing."

"The firebird doesn't like to see you in pain. I'm not keen on it either."

Anya turned and hugged him tightly.

He wrapped his arms around her and rested his cheek atop her head. "Anya? What else is wrong?"

Anya's sense of dread from earlier in the day washed back over her. She and Cerise had gone for a walk to alleviate the nausea her nightmares had left her with, but her obvious inability to control her magic had brought that feeling back tenfold. "I feel like something's coming for me. A darkness is closing in, and I don't know that I'll be able to stop it when it arrives. I'm afraid I'll be forced to watch you all die because of me."

"Battles *are* coming, but that's no reason for you to fall into despair," Yvan said gently. "What we do now is train, learn, and make our plans so that when the battle comes, we are ready for it. No sides in a war are without losses, but you can't shoulder that burden. You didn't ask for any of this. The ones who stand beside you are the ones who love you. You would die for the ones you love, so don't expect any less of us."

"What am I going to do?" Anya asked, her face pressed against him.

"You're going to wash the tears from your face and the blood from your hair. You're going to get your runes and your drum, and you're going to go to the twins and get some training. That's the only way you will feel more in control. Make yourself too busy with learning to think of anything else. Got it?"

"Yes, Prince Yvan." Anya kissed his cheek. "Whatever would I do without your good advice?"

Yvan smiled her favorite smile, the rare one he only ever seemed to show her. "I don't know—be really irresponsible? Go on, you'd best get moving."

Anya hurried upstairs to her room and into the bathroom to examine the fright that was her bloody hair. She turned on the taps and stuck her head over the bath.

"Do you need some help?"

Anya yelped in surprise.

"I'm sorry," Trajan said. "I didn't mean to scare you."

"You're far too quiet for your own good." Anya looked up at him through a tangled curtain of bloody hair.

"Let me help." He rolled up his shirt sleeves.

"You'll get all wet and—"

"It doesn't matter, Anya." He knelt beside her. "I feel useless enough as it is. At least I can do this."

Anya didn't argue as he began to pour the warm water over her hair. "You don't need to worry about the cut. The firebird healed it."

"It's a relief that Yvan is here to come to the rescue and carry you away," he said with a touch of coolness.

"I could've burned you if you'd tried to touch me. Just because I didn't burn the bed, doesn't mean my magic can't hurt you. Don't be jealous that Yvan stepped in. He was the only one who could help."

"I'm not jealous of Yvan." Then he laughed. "Okay, maybe I am a little. It's definitely a new emotion."

"Don't be. You know me and Yvan aren't like that."

Anya tried to relax enough for Trajan to finish cleaning the blood from her hair. He massaged conditioner in and detangled the strands as he went. No one had ever washed Anya's hair before. The act was strangely intimate, and the fact that he was touching her so casually made heat blossom in her chest.

Trajan dried her hair with a towel, and she peaked at him through her wet strands. He was wearing navy pinstripe pants and a pale blue shirt rolled to his elbows, which was slightly damp.

"What are you smiling at?" he asked as he continued to work the towel over her head.

"You."

He frowned. "I don't understand."

That only made her smile more. "Don't let it worry you. Thank you for your help."

Trajan found the fresh scar in her hair and slipped on his glasses for a better look. "I didn't know the firebird could heal like that." He studied it for a moment more before leaning closer, pressing his nose behind her ear. "I love the way your hair smells."

Goose bumps rose along her arms as he kissed the new scar. "For someone who claims to have limited experience with women, you're rather good with them."

"I read," Trajan replied. She felt him smile against her skin. "Voraciously."

Anya fought the positively salacious images that bombarded her and tried in vain to keep the blush from her face. "How promising…but I need to go apologize to the twins. I can't do that if you're determined to distract me."

Trajan smiled and kissed her forehead. "Remember to have fun. You loved your magic. You never feared it."

30

ANYA CHANGED HER CLOTHES and grabbed her drum, runes, and Eikki's journals. She didn't know if the twins would be able to make any sense of Eikki's notes, but it wouldn't hurt for her to ask. She took three deep breaths and tried to calm the nerves rushing through her. The twins had traveled across the world to help her, and that made her both grateful and wary. She was learning that the supernatural world ran on personal favors and debts, and she couldn't help but wonder what the twins would get out of helping her.

"Go and find out," she said aloud. Anya hurried out of her rooms before she lost her nerve. She found the twins settling into their rooms and tapped on the open door. "Hey, I apologize for shocking you before," she said to Honaw.

"Lucky you're so pretty. Otherwise, I would've had to blast you right back."

"It's hardly the first time someone wanted to throw him across a room," Chayton added, gesturing for her to come in.

Anya sighed. "Now you can see why I need your help. I can barely control my magic, and it likes to come at unexpected times—like when I'm asleep."

"You have a lot of magic, Anya. You'll have to be patient if we're going to teach you."

Honaw folded his big arms. "Actually, *extra* patient, because we aren't shamans of your people. We can only try to find some common ground."

"I have patience when I need to. I brought some things you might be able to give me a little insight into." Anya lifted the items in her arms.

Chayton shook his head. "All in good time. The first thing I need you to do is remove your shoes and sit with us." He sat on the thick cream-colored carpet while Honaw pushed the couches out of the way.

"We need some space to spread out if we're going to do some dream-walking," Honaw said, then sat down next to his brother.

Anya unzipped her boots and joined them in the small circle, placing Eikki's journals and her other gear in front of her.

"Katya tells me you dream-traveled back in time." Honaw lifted his brow and smiled.

"By accident. I talked to my dead grandmother."

"Yanka," said Chayton reverently.

"I see Katya has filled you in."

"A little. Yanka was an amazing Power."

"So I keep hearing." Anya toyed with her bag of runes.

"We don't need to talk about Yanka. We need to talk about you and figure out what your abilities are." Chayton offered her his hand.

Anya was afraid to touch it in case she sent another shaman flying. "Are you sure you want to risk it?"

"It will be fine, Anya."

Slowly, she placed her own palm over his. Nothing happened. The heat between their hands built.

"I have learned to block magic leaks. Honaw was unprepared for your reaction and how much power you had. When two people with magic touch, their power also touches. Sometimes it's very mild, like a faint tingle or static electricity—"

"Or sometimes you get blown across the room," Honaw added. Anya cringed, but he smiled as he said it.

"What else?" she asked.

"Power is hereditary, but it also changes with each child. Sometimes, an abundance of power is passed to one child, whereas their sibling receives no magic."

Anya nodded. "Apparently, my father had no magic."

"And yet here you are, bursting with it. Katya told us about your grandfather, the memory spell, and his reasons for doing it. I suppose we will find out if you have as much magic as Yanka soon enough," Honaw said. "Tell us about your childhood."

It was Anya's least favorite subject, but they had traveled too far for her to not accept their help. She told them about the farm, about the village, Eikki and the memories he had stolen. Chayton and Honaw looked thoughtfully at each other a few times, wordless messages passing between them. When she got to the problem of the gates, Honaw chuckled.

"What's funny?" Anya asked him.

"Eikki hid your memories but didn't consider that the farm itself was so drenched with power, you've likely felt its magic your entire life and thought it was normal."

"What do you mean? I told you Eikki hid everything from me."

"You grew up on a nexus of power. Double crossroads. Not only is your farm the crossroads of Russia and Karelia, but also Russia and Skazki," Chayton said. "It's no surprise your family established themselves there and never moved. It also explains the depth of power you have. Even the forest you grew up next to was magical. You ate the food grown in that soil. What Honaw is saying is that there's so much magic in every layer of you, it's always felt normal to you, even when you weren't aware of it." Chayton flicked through Eikki's journals, looking over the drawings with a delighted expression. "I think I would have liked your grandfather. Did he tell you stories?"

Anya leaned back against the couch. "Yeah, all the time before he put the memory spell on me. Myths and fairy tales and folk songs. Everything from the *Kalevala* to the *Poetic Edda* to Russian legend. Then there were things he composed himself. He was always whispering rhymes to the trees and singing to the wild reindeer that used to turn up."

"Our people are also great storytellers," said Honaw. He glanced at his brother. "Maybe that's our way in?"

"What do you mean?" asked Anya.

"Stories have power," Chayton said. "Your people have a long oral history. I'm sure you know some of the stories by heart. In the old songs and stories lay ancient wisdom and knowledge. We can teach you to harness the power of your tongue. We aren't talking about formulating spells; that's unnecessary. Magic is about not only innate power, but intent. Sometimes it's useful to have words to shape that intent. We can teach you how to use story to articulate that intent."

Honaw grinned. "It'll be fun. You can tell us the stories of your people, and we will tell you the stories of ours. I'm sure Trajan has copies of your legends if you need to brush up on them. The stories of your land call to your blood. Their magic is in you; you just have to remember them."

Anya thought it over. So much of Eikki made more sense every day. He would sing the *Kalevala* rune songs to her on dark nights and told her the importance of knowing the origin of everything in nature. If a shaman knew how all things came to be, like the great shaman Väinämöinen, they could command and manipulate those things to do their bidding.

"You know, the faculty you have for fire actually might explain why it was your power that prompted the firebird to hatch," said Chayton. "That egg was in your family for years. I'm sure they all would have handled it and maybe even tried to wake it up with their own magic, and yet it was in your possession for only a night, and boom! Firebird reborn."

Honaw grunted. "I feel fate all over this." He shrugged. "It doesn't matter. It was bound to happen at some point."

"Can I ask you both something? Why are you helping me? Katya said that you're Powers in America. Why come all this way to teach someone that isn't even one of your people?"

"The enemy of our enemy is our friend," said Honaw.

"Vasilli?" Anya guessed.

"The Darkness in general, but mostly Ladislav and Vasilli. Ladislav and the Darkness encouraged the Europeans to colonize America. They wanted to see what magic was there that they could exploit. They almost destroyed our people, our land, and our culture. We want revenge for that—for starters."

"There's also growing Darkness activity all throughout our country, and the Neutrals have been raising concerns with us," Chayton said. "We've seen the war coming, and the rest of the supernaturals are bound to suffer because of it. If you can stop Vasilli and the Darkness here in Europe with our help, it may save more pain in the future." Chayton put a hand on her shoulder. "Once it's known that you are a strong enemy of Vasilli with the firebird on your side, a lot of Neutrals will want to help you. You'll have allies everywhere."

Anya laughed. She couldn't help it. The thought that she could take on a man who could collapse a house with a twist of his hand was unfathomable. "I can't promise you that I'll ever be strong enough to take on Vasilli, but I'll do my best. I have to close the gates on my farm first. That's the most pressing deadline. After that, I'll do everything I can to stop Vasilli."

Honaw nodded. "That's a good enough promise for us. Gates magic is specific to bloodline. It will be tricky for us to teach you something useful."

"But dream-walking is crossing boundaries to other worlds, and so is spirit world walking," Chayton said. "We can teach you that in hopes that it can be adapted for your purposes. Simply put, it's all about sensing a gateway and getting through it and back again."

"Chayton can figure out the logistics of that, and I'll teach you some tricks to take the edge off the magical buildup inside of you. We can focus on the bigger stuff when you can think clearly." Honaw produced an apple out of thin air. "Let's start with levitating things. That can be handy in a fight, and there's no doubt one is coming for you, little shamanitsa."

Isabelle Blackwood stood in front of an elegant stone mansion and double-checked the address Katya had given her. She scanned the street around her before pressing the red intercom button.

The reply came almost instantly. "Can I help you?"

"My name is Isabelle Blackwood. I'm here to see Katya Domotetsky."

With a loud buzz, the gate swung open. Small cameras followed her as she made her way to the polished front door. It was opened by a tall, lithe man with curly chestnut hair. He was ancient. Power emanated from him so strongly Isabelle almost took a step backward.

"Katya will be along shortly," he said. "Welcome."

"Thank you." Isabelle held out her hand, and he shook it without any hesitation. There was something about him she couldn't put her finger on, but her senses were burning. Usually, she knew a creature's nature by looking at them, and yet she was drawing a complete blank.

"I'm Trajan. Please, come in." He took her coat and hung it in a small cupboard next to the door.

"What are you?" Isabelle asked.

Trajan's lips curled into a smile. "I'm a thanatos."

"Amazing. I've never met one of you before." She looked at him more closely, the hunter part of her scanning him for what could be a weakness.

"And you are?"

"A hunter who was bitten by something evil a long time ago."

"You have stigmata?" Trajan guessed.

"Something like that." His amused smile played around the corners of his mouth, and she found herself liking Trajan.

"Isabelle?" Katya jogged down the grand staircase, wearing tight black jeans and a purple top, her hair slightly disheveled. "I thought I heard your voice."

Izrayl sauntered down the stairs after her, pulling on a fresh shirt. He smiled at Isabelle, then added a wink. "I see you have met Trajan."

"Yes, we were just doing a little game of Get to Know Your Monsters."

"Fabulous. That saves me a lot of time." Katya hugged her. "Thank you for coming. Let's go talk in the library."

"I'll go round up the others. I'm sure Anya will be ready for a break by now," Trajan said. "Please excuse me." He headed up the stairs.

"Would you like some tea?" Katya offered.

"Yes, please. It's freezing outside."

"Izrayl will take you to the library. I won't be long."

As Izrayl walked past Katya, he brushed a hand down her back—a small but intimate gesture. Then he led Isabelle through the gorgeous home until they reached the double doors to the library.

"I must say I'm surprised to see Katya getting friendly with a *volk krovi*," Isabelle said as she sat down on one of the armchairs. "Her family doesn't have a good history with them."

"It must be my winning personality." Izrayl flopped down in the opposite chair and pulled his long braid over one shoulder.

"Or your beautiful body."

"You noticed." He grinned.

"You care about her?"

"Yes." Izrayl nodded. "And neither one of us has to hide our true natures." His expression shifted into a soft smile, clearly unable to hide his infatuation. "Not to get all sappy, but you know what I mean."

"I do." Isabelle tried to return the smile. Once, she thought she'd found the one, but her enemies always find a way to catch up with her. She hadn't been willing to put him in danger. Better for him to have a full, safe life. She had to let him go. "Katya has told you about her mother, hasn't she?"

He nodded. "Her past with the *volk krovi* isn't an issue."

"Good to hear it. She's been carrying the weight of her father's bullshit for too long. He was a good hunter, but god, he could be a bastard."

Katya appeared carrying a steaming mug. "Here we are—two sugars, no milk." She passed it to Isabelle before seating herself on the arm of Izrayl's chair. He rested his palm on the small of her back and gave Katya a look of such enchantment that Isabelle had to hide a smile.

A second later, Trajan strode into the library, leading a group of people that included two men she would recognize anywhere.

"Holy shit, it's the Thunder Twins!" Isabelle got up and threw her arms around them both. "I haven't seen you in how long?"

Chayton kissed her cheek. "1963, New York, I think."

"I must say, I'm surprised to see you here."

"Likewise. You know we don't like leaving America, but this was important."

They had all positioned themselves in a rough circle. Trajan held the hand of a blond young woman, who shimmered with enough magic that Isabelle could almost see it in the air. Talk about an odd and dangerous pair.

A tall, dark Russian stepped into her line of sight and offered her his hand. "I'm Yvan."

She shook his hand but jumped when his blue eyes changed to golden red and back again.

"It's nothing to be concerned about." He smiled, then sat down.

The red-haired woman watched her cautiously from just outside the group. "Cerise. I'm a keres," she said by way of introduction.

Isabelle gave her a nod. There wasn't a normal one among them.

"And I'm Anya," the ashen-haired woman said from her place beside Trajan.

"The troublemaker." Yvan grinned when she flipped him off.

Isabelle turned to Katya. "Okay, what's going on? Don't leave out a thing. My senses are going mental, and I need clarification. The Illumination and the Darkness are more active than usual, and that makes me nervous. What we found last night was beyond anything I've seen in years."

"What did you find?" Anya asked.

"I was waiting until we were all together so I didn't have to repeat myself a million times," Katya said. "Isabelle, if you don't mind?"

She nodded. "The Darkness was experimenting on the people of a magical bloodline. The Darkness, like the Illumination, hunt for old families who hold power or once held power. Both follow these magical families to find the best talent. The people here in the human world don't believe in magic anymore, which means they have no idea of their power. It's not uncommon for them to just disappear into the night, either recruited or kidnapped. Last night, we found the aftermath of a dark magic user's transmutation experiment on people with magic. They were twisted hybrid creatures left to died horribly and in pain."

Honaw groaned. "You really haven't changed a bit, Isabelle. Still blunt as ever."

"You all need to know, because this level of horror is increasing. The Darkness is building up their ranks and preparing for something. I just don't know what." Isabelle sipped her tea. "Now, tell me what this is all about and why the hell I should agree to help."

See the crow circling high over the Parisian suburb of Neuilly-sur-Seine. It swoops and dives over a gray stone mansion and lands on a windowsill. It cocks its head to one side as it studies the fair-haired human.

Warm, red magic pulses around her and lingers on the objects she touches. The crow flutters to a bathroom window that has been left ajar. Using its sharp beak, it works the crack open little by little until it can squeeze its feathered body through.

The crow hops down from the window, across the toilet's porcelain top, and onto the basin. It claws at the tangle of hair still trapped in the coarse bristles of a hairbrush. With a small bundle of silver firmly in its grasp, it pushes its way out the window and soars into the empty sky, searching for its master.

31

TRAJAN SPOTTED HAMISH AMONG the arriving passengers as he walked into the Charles de Gaulle Airport. He'd called Trajan from Dubai to let him know he was on his way and what time he was due in Paris. It was courteous behavior for Hamish, who tended to show up unexpectedly and leave just as quickly.

Hamish was unmistakable in a crowd, being six foot five and all muscle. His skin was a tanned a golden brown, which was almost the same color as his hair. His hazel eyes sparkled with mischief when he saw Trajan leaning against a sign with a newspaper tucked under his arm.

"Hey, pretty girl. You come here often?"

"I do if I want to pick up good-for-nothing cowboys," Trajan said. They laughed and gave each other a brief hug. "You seem to have dressed up for the occasion. You look like a cowboy who's finally discovered washing."

Hamish pulled down on the blue cowboy shirt he wore. His dark denim jeans had been ironed, and even his belt buckle was polished. Usually, when Trajan picked him up from a flight, Hamish was disheveled and drunk.

"Gladys wouldn't let me leave looking like a scruff."

"I didn't know you had a lady friend."

"An *old* lady. She feels the need to mother me, which is kinda nice, seeing how I never had a mother."

They walked through the brightly lit terminal and toward the exit signs.

"So, tell me what's going on," said Hamish.

Trajan condensed the situation as much as he could. Hamish already knew Trajan's history with Ilya and Eikki, but the last time the two had caught up, Eikki was still alive, which meant Hamish wasn't aware that Trajan had taken up guarding Anya again.

Hamish squeezed into Trajan's BMW. "You were watching her all this time, and she had no idea you were there? You never said anything to her?"

Trajan shook his head. "I thought it best if I didn't."

"You're an idiot. A massive, dumb idiot."

"Believe me, I know." Trajan told Hamish about Yvan and how they had turned up on his doorstep wet and bedraggled while he wove through the heavy traffic.

Hamish blew out a breath. "It's going to be wild meeting these people you've always talked about, especially Anya. She sounds like my kind of girl."

Trajan narrowed his eyes but knew Hamish couldn't help himself. "She won't tolerate your bullshit for a second. We are going to have a full house, so try to behave yourself."

"When have I ever not behaved?"

"Would you like the list alphabetically, by date, or the cost figure for the damages?" Trajan pulled into his house as Hamish filled the car with his booming laughter.

"Please, Hamish. There are ladies here, so no walking around without your trousers on."

"You just want to ruin all my fun, don't you? You afraid little Anya will switch camps when she sees what a real man looks like? You know, one who isn't afraid to touch her."

"I think we both know that neither of us are *real* men, and for your information, I have been touching her." Trajan led the way through the garage and into the elevator.

"Well, look at that—my boy is finally becoming a man." Hamish pinched Trajan's cheek. "About time you got a girlfriend. It only took a hundred years, you loser."

"You have no room to talk. If I recall correctly, your last love shot you in the ass when you first met." Trajan instantly regretted the remark. Hamish looked like he had been kicked in the guts. That particular woman had been killed, and for all of his flirting, Hamish hadn't gotten over it. "I'm sorry, Hamish. I didn't mean—"

"It was a long time ago. Maybe I should follow your example and find a hot witch to shack up with." Hamish's smile thankfully returned.

The doors opened to reveal Anya, who was waiting for them in her camisole and boxer shorts. She looked tousled, sleepy, and so adorable Trajan wanted to squeeze her.

"I thought I heard you come home," she said. "Hamish? I'm Anya."

"Yes, I thought you must be." He smiled extra deviously, and Trajan had an overwhelming urge to strike him.

"I need tea. You want some?" Anya asked.

"I'd kill for a cuppa."

Trajan rolled his eyes at Hamish's need to flirt with everyone he met.

"I bet after such a long flight." Anya yawned as she led the way to the kitchen.

Trajan switched on the kettle as Anya retrieved three cups from a cupboard. To Trajan's surprise, the sugar bowl floated over to him from the opposite end of the counter. A drawer opened, and a teaspoon appeared, then stuck itself into the granules.

"One or two?" Trajan asked, trying to hide his surprise.

"Two, please," Hamish said, and the spoon obeyed. "Are there going to be singing birds doing my laundry while I'm here too?"

"I hate to disappoint, but my skills aren't quite there yet. Though some of those birds would be handy when you think about it." Anya chuckled. "I bloody hate washing clothes."

"I see your lessons with the twins went well today," Trajan said.

"They did. Honaw taught me to levitate things, and it turns out, it really helps the buzzing in my head. I think that's why I'm so sleepy tonight."

"You always were a natural at magic. It's going to be good for you." Trajan kissed the top of her head. "I'm so proud of you."

"Baby steps." Anya gave him a pleased smile. She passed Hamish his cup of tea. "How was your flight?"

"Really long, but I'm kind of wired now."

"Trajan will keep you company. I, on the other hand, am dead on my feet, and the twins are going to start teaching me about dream-walking tomorrow." Anya snaked her arms around Trajan's neck and kissed his cheek. "I'll see you to-morrow."

"Where's my good night kiss?" Hamish eyed her expectantly.

"Sorry, Hamish. You're just not as handsome as this one." Anya patted Trajan's arm and smiled cheekily before wandering out of the kitchen with her steaming cup.

Hamish gave a snort of disbelief. "She's just saying that to make you feel better. I'm way better looking than you."

"Anya said it, not me."

"I still can't believe you haven't slept with her. She a virgin or something?"

"No, she's not. I'm just afraid I'll hurt her." Though the temptation to try was growing the more time they spent together without an incident. Trajan wanted to know what her warm, soft skin tasted like, how it would feel pressed up against his. His command on his abilities was good, but he wondered just how far he could go if he released some of his fear.

"Your control is amazing, Trajan. Give it a go. You might enjoy yourself for once and relieve some of that stress you're both under." Hamish released a filthy laugh.

Trajan rolled his eyes. "You're an animal."

"Ain't that the truth."

"We don't have what one could consider a normal courtship. I don't even know if that physical aspect would be possible."

"Anya doesn't strike me as the type who couldn't handle you or your quirks. Besides, from what you said about him on the drive home, I'm sure Yvan would murder you if you hurt her, so your remorse would be short-lived." Hamish's laughter broke off, and his nose went up into the air just as Trajan heard a woman scream.

"Anya..." He bolted up the stairs with Hamish close behind him. The tall windows in Anya's room were shattered. There was blood all over the floor, the curtains were slashed, and Anya was gone.

Katya woke to Anya's frightened screams echoing through the walls. She flew out of bed, grabbed her gun, and charged into the hallway. In Anya's room, Trajan was crouched on the ground next to a massive golden dingo. There was no sign of Anya.

"Who the hell is this?" Katya pointed her gun at the dingo. It let out a low, threatening growl, and a large black wolf moved in from behind her.

"Easy, Katya. He's a friend," Trajan said. He fingered a small piece of torn red material while studying a trail of blood along the carpet. Something feral passed over his normally placid face, and Katya's hand tightened instinctively on her gun. She had never seen him so angry.

"Where's Anya?" she demanded.

"They've taken her," Yvan said as he came through the doorway, his eyes burning like flames. "How did they get past your security systems?"

Trajan's voice betrayed no emotion. "I don't know."

Izrayl let out a small whine when he sniffed the blood trail.

"Settle down, Yvan. Blaming others won't help get her back." Katya turned to Izrayl. "What can you smell?"

Izrayl circled around the room before shifting back. "It's strange. There isn't much of a scent. It just smells like death, and it's dark." He shook his head. "It's unlike anything I've encountered before. It's like...despair."

Katya passed him a towel from Anya's bathroom. "Cover up."

"I could say the same to you." He glanced over her tank top and black panties.

Before she could muster a glare, the golden dingo shifted into a strapping golden man. "I should've bought another towel," Katya said, keeping her eyes focused firmly on his face.

"That's okay, love. I'm not shy." The stranger flashed a big smile. "Nice to see you again, Izrayl."

"Hamish." Izrayl shook his hand.

Trajan looked up from the smashed glass of the window. He ran his fingertips along the sill.

"So, what the hell are you? Some kind of were-dingo?" Katya asked.

"I'm just plain old cursed."

"Good to know." Katya rubbed at her scar, a headache already brewing. "I'm going to ring Isabelle and tell her to get her ass over here. She might be able to pick up something from the room that we can't."

Isabelle arrived at Trajan's within the hour. Katya was waiting for her in a pair of faded jeans and a shirt, looking wired.

"Morning, Belle. Welcome to my nightmare." Katya led her to the lounge room where everyone had gathered. Trajan stood with Izrayl and the twins while Yvan filled Cerise in on what had happened. Isabelle's eyes found a tall man standing in the shadows. He leaned forward into the light, and her world tilted on its axis. *It can't be.*

"What are you doing here?" she demanded, her shock robbing her of her manners.

The room fell silent. Hamish's mouth opened and closed a few times before his face flushed in anger. "I could say the same to you. You're the one who disappeared off the face of the earth." Hamish moved in on her. "I thought you were dead. You—you were human!"

"Not anymore." She stepped backward so he wasn't looming over her.

Trajan's voice sliced through the tension between them. "What's going on?"

"This is Belle Holland," Hamish all but spat.

She raised her chin and smiled. "Isabelle Blackwood, actually."

"Just what we need," Trajan muttered.

"You didn't even tell me your real name? Or that you're a supe?" Hamish shook his head. "You're a real piece of work."

Isabelle looked at the confused faces in the room, suddenly aware that they were making a scene, which went against her British sensibilities. She schooled her features and said coolly, "Now's not the time for this fight, Hamish."

He sneered at her. "This conversation isn't over."

"This conversation hasn't even begun," she snapped. "But we will have it in private," Isabelle turned away from him and looked pointedly at Izrayl. "You said something about death and despair?"

"I can't describe it any better than that. I'm sorry."

"It's all good news tonight." Isabelle sighed. "If I can have a look in Anya's room, I might be able to get a clearer picture of what happened."

"Show her, please." Trajan appeared calm on the outside, but Isabelle could feel the anger pouring off him.

Katya led her to the trashed bedroom, and Isabelle felt the dark presence as soon as she stepped inside. Her hand went to the rosary in her pocket. *Get it together. It's gone.*

"Definitely incorporeal." She touched the broken window and shuddered. "You won't find any prints or a trail. I think a nehemoth took her."

"I thought nehemoth were just some Jewish fable."

"No, they exist. Though I've never gone up against one.

"But how can a ghost be strong enough to not only break in, but carry away an adult woman?" Katya asked.

"Technically, nehemoth aren't ghosts. They could be classed as demons if you wanted to get down to the nitty-gritty. This one was definitely under someone's control."

"How can you tell?"

"They can only be summoned by a powerful magic user. They're hard to control, so usually, only someone strong can be its master. If Vasilli has enough power to control one, we're in deeper trouble than I thought."

"Do you know of any other buildings that belong to the Darkness where they might be holding Anya?"

"I've found three that could be used for their operations. After what we found a few nights ago, I'm sure they're still in the city somewhere. Just because they abandoned that building doesn't mean they don't have another lab set up elsewhere."

"We'll have to attack all of them. It will be the only way to find her in time and not alert the others that we're coming. I don't think they'll kill her, but she'll be made to suffer."

"I'd hate to see what the thanatos would do if they harm her," Isabelle said.

Katya released a heavy breath in wordless agreement. "So what's going on with you and this Hamish guy?"

"Our paths crossed a long time ago."

"Care to elaborate?" Katya asked, her smile crooked and cheeky.

Isabelle didn't smile back. "I shot him."

Hamish stormed into his room and restrained himself from punching a hole through one of Trajan's walls. The room was clean and exactly the way he had left it two years ago. He pulled on a T-shirt and boots, then opened his gun cabinet. He had missed these particular weapons when he was back in Australia. He'd left Europe on a drunken whim last time but knew that one day, he'd come back for them.

Hamish put on his gun belt and holstered his pearl-handled revolvers before reaching for his Winchester rifles. He slung leather holsters onto his back and slid them into position. They were long rifles, but Hamish was tall enough that they fit snugly between his shoulder blades.

Pulling on his Driza-Bone coat, he swore long and inarticulately. *Bloody Belle is alive.*

The top of his left butt cheek ached where he wore the scar from the bullet she'd put in him. And that wasn't even the scar that hurt the most. He thought of the ring still locked in a box on the other side of the world, and his guts twisted.

Hamish had been ready to tell Isabelle his darkest secrets, including the whole truth about his convict past, how he was cursed and responsible for the death of his wife. If she still wanted him after, he was going to marry her. But Hamish had gone to Isabelle's apartment to find it burning. He'd thought she had burned along with it and lost his mind in grief and rage.

And she hadn't even told him her real name.

"How are you holding up?" Trajan appeared in the doorway. He was dressed in his black trench coat, his face twitching from holding in his anger.

"Tip fucking top, mate. I'm more concerned about your well-being. You can't hide it from me. I know you're fucking fuming. Best keep it in check before that pretty human veneer you're wearing goes to shit."

"I'm doing my best. I still can't believe Isabelle is the girl who messed you up."

"I swear she was human when I knew her. I thought she was dead," Hamish said through gritted teeth. "I saw her building in flames... Christ, I found her bloody clothes." His hands curled into tight fists to stop them from shaking. He had tried to kill himself more than once after that, and Trajan had managed to pull him back from the darkness. He owed Trajan his life, and that was a debt that meant something.

Trajan rested a hand on his shoulder. "I'm sure she had a reason for doing what she did. Now you can finally find out. Maybe this is your chance to move on."

"I don't even care anymore." Hamish shoved Trajan's hand away. "Let's go find your girl."

In the 18th arrondissement of the city, a tall man in a navy leather trench coat watched as a team of Illumination investigators combed through the ashes of a destroyed building. Fire—deliberately lit—had been the cause of its destruction, but that wasn't what he was here to investigate.

"Excuse me, General, sir?" The sweaty young man pulled him out of his thoughts.

"What is it?"

"The team has uncovered some peculiar remains that could confirm this building was used by the Darkness."

"Show me."

Stepping over fallen beams and piles of ash, they came to a neatly pegged area.

"You see, sir, that's definitely a humanoid skeleton, but this section here? Well, that's a wing."

Aramis leaned down for a closer look. With a pale finger, he touched the fan of bones. Images bombarded him, and he pulled his hand back. "You are correct. This was a site used by the Darkness. I'd say this was a failed experiment. Were there any other bodies?"

"Three human and another experiment with bird features. Beak with teeth."

"Sounds intense. Can you find out if it's been mixed with bird DNA or if it was some kind of transmutation?"

"I won't be able to give you full details until we are back in the lab, sir."

"Very well. Organize the remains to be shipped for examination." Aramis pulled his vibrating cell phone from his pocket and answered it.

A curt male voice came over the line. "Aramis, we have a problem. I've just received information about a powerful witch in Paris."

"Is she one of ours?"

"She's neutral at this stage, but she has the potential to wreak havoc if we don't find her. The Darkness is already onto her, so be careful."

"Not a problem, sir. I'll organize a team to search her out and arrange a meeting."

"Oh, and Aramis? There's something else you should know."

"Yes?"

"She's a Venäläinen and of Yanka's bloodline, not by marriage. That won't be an issue for you, will it?"

Aramis paused for only a second before saying, "No, sir." He hung up the phone and tried not to drop it as he slipped it back in his coat. His hands shook as he tried to maintain a calm façade. *Yanka's blood.*

He had to find her and fast.

32

ANYA WOKE TO THE smell of chemicals and decay. Her vision blurred, and her eyes were scratchy and dry. A low, distorted murmur came from her right. Her head pounded from the blow she'd received from an invisible attacker.

What the hell happened? Anya rubbed her eyes until they grew accustomed to the darkness. She was in a large room with only one boarded-up window that let in small chinks of light. Iron manacles encircled her ankles, and she lay on a damp wood floor. Fear rushed through her, and she pulled at the chains, which were bolted into the wood and covered in runes that she didn't recognize.

"Don't move," a voice to her right half wheezed in Russian. "They will know you are awake."

Through the gloom, Anya made out the pale, naked figure of a woman shackled to the wall. Her long brown hair hung in ropey tendrils over her, concealing some of her nude figure. Her skin was covered in pearlescent blue fish scales that were peeling, and her lips were cracked and bloody. A large bowl of water sat on the floor a couple of meters from her.

"What are you?" asked Anya.

"I'm a shishiga," she whispered. "I don't have a name." Anya looked at her and then the bowl of water. "It's their idea of a joke. My chains aren't long enough to reach the water so I can have some relief."

"Who are they?"

"The Darkness, of course."

"I was afraid you were going to say that."

A rustling came from the shadows. "You should be afraid." What Anya had taken to be a pile of rags on the floor unfolded into a small gnomish creature that wouldn't quite reach Anya's knees.

"She knows that, ovinnik," the shishiga hissed. "She's the shamanitsa they have been hunting for."

He grunted. "She doesn't look like much of a shamanitsa to me."

Anya didn't take offense. "I don't feel like one right now. Why are you two here?"

"They want what they always want—our magic and our secrets," the grimy ovinnik spat. "Our blood and our souls. They want the secrets to my fire sprite nature, but I will give them nothing."

"Do you know where we are?"

"Paris, but exactly where, I don't know. There's a water canal close to us. I can smell it. If I could reach it, I would be free." Tears leaked out of the shishiga's black eyes. Where they fell on her cheeks, the pale blue skin healed itself.

Anya hugged her knees to her chest and didn't ask any more questions.

Katya? Katya? Anya tried to reach out with her mind, but she didn't feel a connection. A scream shook the walls, jolting her. The shishiga curled into a tight ball, her hair around her as a cover, and the ovinnik muttered curses as he, too, tried to make himself even smaller.

Anya stood to relieve her cramped legs and flinched. Her iron manacles clanked as they dragged on the floor, but it couldn't be helped. The fear and despair in the room threatened to choke her, but she couldn't allow it to. Trajan and Yvan would find her if she didn't escape first. She just needed to keep calm and be smart.

But that was easier said than done. Now that she was on her feet, Anya's head spun. She felt dopey like she had been drugged. She flexed her hands, and for the first time in weeks, she couldn't feel the magic running under her skin. Panic rose up through her, and she pressed a hand to her chest as she nearly doubled over from a lack of air.

The door to the room opened, and Anya stood straight and defiant. The most colorless person she had ever seen walked in. He was of average height and build, his fair hair cut short. His gray eyes were pale, almost white, and utterly devoid of all emotion. If eyes were the window to the soul, then no soul was home. Anya fought not to shudder under his gaze.

"Anyanka, we meet at last," he said, his voice holding touches of a Swedish accent. "I am Völundr."

"You're not who I was expecting."

"You thought Vasilli had managed to catch you at last? Clearly, he's more incompetent than I thought. I managed to catch you quite easily, didn't I?"

"What was that thing you sent after me?" she demanded. It had been man-shaped but made entirely of smoke and shadows.

"The nehemoth? That was a trick of Ladislav's sent from Moscow. I'm merely here in a delivery capacity, but I intend for you to be quite useful before I give you up."

"I'm not going to help you with anything, you sadistic bastard," Anya spat.

He grabbed her around the throat with a speed she didn't anticipate. She clawed at his hands, but Völundr held her firm.

"I may be under orders not to kill you, Yanka's blood, but that doesn't mean I have to deliver you undamaged." He let go of her with a strong push that sent her stumbling back against the wall. She fell to her knees, gasping for air. Something sharp pricked her neck, and the last thing she saw was Völundr standing over her with a syringe.

Water dripped somewhere. The steady sound pulled Anya from her stupor. Misty droplets from outside were being blown through the unevenly boarded window, and the shishiga next to her made soft mewing sounds as the moisture in the air revived her.

Anya clutched her head, a migraine pressing in on her. As her eyes adjusted to the darkness, she spotted the ovinnik shivering and shrunken.

"How long was I out?" Anya asked. Her mouth felt like it had been stuffed with cotton balls.

"About eight hours," the shishiga said. "I wouldn't fight them anymore. They will just keep putting poison in you."

Anya shook her numb hands and sensed a very low flicker of magic under her skin. She stretched her hand toward the bowl of water, and it shifted a little off the boards. She desperately needed something to drink. Anya tried again, and the power trickled out of her. The bowl lifted a few centimeters off the floor and floated over to her. She caught it and took a long sip. The water was stale but tasted good enough. Summoning what strength she had left, Anya floated the bowl over to the shishiga. The creature took it and sobbed with relief.

"They will know you did this," she whispered.

"Doesn't matter. If you can escape, do it."

The shishiga placed her manacled hands into the bowl. They dissolved and rematerialized without the iron around them. She did her feet one at a time until she was free.

"I won't forget this Yanka's blood."

"Hurry before they catch you," the ovinnik urged.

The shishiga stood by the broken window, where the rain seeped through the gaps in the boards, dripped down the wall, and pooled next to the ovinnik. She stepped into the puddle, and Anya gasped as she shone pale blue before melting into the water. The blue light pulsed as it snaked up the water on the walls, through the crack, and disappeared. The awe of the moment was shattered by heavy footsteps and loud shouts echoing through the house.

"Do you think she made it to the canal?" Anya asked.

"I hope so, because you may just regret helping her before the night is out."

"Doesn't matter," Anya repeated as the door was kicked in.

"You vindictive little slut." Völundr strode in and kicked the empty bowl across the room. "I don't know how you did that, but it seems I'm going to have to up your doses."

"When is Vasilli going to get here?" she asked, attempting a bored tone.

He grabbed her face and squeezed it. "Why? Do you wish for death already?"

"No, not death." She pulled her face away from him. "It would just be nice to deal with a professional with real power." Anya expected the blow, but it still rattled her. She managed to keep her feet and propped herself against the wall.

"I *have* real power, and I would enjoy proving it if I wasn't under Ladislav's orders. Oh, I would delight in making you scream, little girl. I'm tempted to tell them that I have you already just to see what they are going to do to you."

Anya wiped the blood from her mouth with the back of her hand. "What are you going to do with me?"

"I have a plan, and you are the key," Völundr said softly, his personality altering and becoming gentle. He touched her damaged face. "Don't you see, Anya? You are my bait."

"Bait for what?"

Völundr smiled, and a heavy weight settled in Anya's chest. "You are going to help me catch Death itself."

It had been twenty-four hours since Anya was taken, and the city's plans littered the thick carpet in Trajan's wing of the house. Isabelle had marked the areas she'd been suspicious of, but two had already come up empty. Yvan had barely spoken since they discovered Anya gone, and when Trajan tried to talk privately with him, Yvan had turned into the firebird and ignored him.

The others had finally given in to their need for sleep, leaving only Trajan to pace.

Isabelle walked in. "Have you slept at all?"

"Not exactly. Why aren't you resting?" There was something about the hunter that didn't feel right to Trajan. Unlike other humans and their bright souls, she was a blurred presence in his mind.

"I don't need a lot of sleep." She made herself comfortable on one of his couches.

"Why is that, Isabelle? What kind of bite turns someone into a supernatural creature?"

"The kind that's dead, so you don't have to worry about it. The important thing right now is finding Anya. I'm going to revisit some places I got a weird vibe from during my own investigations. I dismissed them at the time, but they're worth checking."

"Thank you."

"They might hurt her, but they won't kill her, Trajan. She's too valuable for that. They won't break her unless they have no other choice."

"I would like to say that brings me comfort, but that would be a lie."

"I know. It doesn't make it less true." Isabelle was a blunt and beautiful woman, and he could see why Hamish was so infatuated with her.

Trajan sat down on one of the plush chairs. "May I ask you something?"

"You may ask, but I might not answer."

"That's your right. Why did you break up with Hamish and then let him believe you were dead?"

The confidence Isabelle exuded seemed to abandon her. "I was being hunted, and they had seen me with him. I couldn't let them use him against me, so I left."

"He said he found your bloody clothes."

"The bomb I didn't expect. I was injured, and I thought if I left some kind of evidence behind, my enemies would be satisfied and leave Hamish alone." The hard edges to her voice softened fractionally.

"He mourned you for many years, just so you're aware."

Isabelle crossed her arms. "Why are you telling me this? To make me feel guilty?"

"I want you to know because he'll never tell you himself. Try not to be too hard on him. He is unsettled enough by your presence."

"I'll try to keep that in mind."

Trajan managed a smile. "Did you really shoot him when you first met?"

Isabelle laughed. "I put a bullet in his ass. That's what you get when you run away from a fight."

Trajan sighed. "Well, we aren't going to sleep, so we might as well be busy. I don't suppose you want to give me half of those other addresses of yours?" He thought Isabelle would protest in some way or try to talk him out of it, but she seemed pleased to be doing something other than waiting for people to wake up.

"Just promise me you'll call me if you find anything," she said as she passed him a list from her pocket and a card with her number printed on it. "Don't go charging in."

"Only if you promise to do the same. You aren't all human, but that doesn't mean you're invincible. As a hunter, you know that even immortals have weaknesses."

"It's a deal."

Trajan knew Isabelle lied, just as she knew that he did. They wouldn't risk waiting for backup. They would investigate for themselves before calling and wasting each other's time if their hunch proved groundless.

Trajan got his coat and disappeared into the streets of Paris, his blood boiling for vengeance.

⁘

Trajan was walking along the Hauts-de-Seine, making his way steadily toward one of the addresses on Isabelle's list near Le Port-Marly, when a flash of blue in the water caught his eye. He paused as the head of a woman bobbed up in front of him. He leaned closer over the railings for a better look. She was definitely there, but the other people walking past didn't seem to notice her. She was without a doubt a supernatural of some sort, but not one Trajan knew of.

"Can you see me?" she asked. "What manner of creature are you?"

"I'm a thanatos, and I don't mean you any harm."

Her beautiful face turned vicious. "Are you the Darkness?"

"No, I'm neutral. Why? Have you seen the Darkness around here? I'm trying to find someone they've taken."

Something flashed over the water creature's face. "Who is it you're searching for?"

"A woman about so tall." Trajan indicated where Anya's head reached the groove of his chest. "She has very fair hair—almost white—with green eyes."

Her dark eyes widened. "Yanka's blood. She said you would be looking for her."

"You have seen Anya?" he asked, no longer caring enough to keep his voice lowered so passersby wouldn't think he was crazy.

"She helped me get free of them last night in the rain." She looked like she was crying, but there was so much water on her face it was difficult to tell. "She risked the evil one's wrath and used her magic to get me to the water." The creature moved back and forth in distress.

"That sounds like Anya."

"I fear they will have punished her terribly for it. She shouldn't have done it, but I was so desperate. I was dying."

"Calm yourself. She would've known that she would pay for helping you. Is this why you haven't left Paris?"

"I am a shishiga. I owe her a life debt. I can't leave until I have repaid her."

"Tell me where she is being kept, and your debt will be repaid. I can save her."

33

ANYA HAD SPENT HOURS chained to the wall in a large living room Völundr had gutted for his workspace. She had been unconscious when they led her to this room, and now she didn't know what floor she was on or what part of the house she was in. Völundr clearly no longer trusted her in the room with the ovinnik, and he wasn't about to lose another hostage.

The physical pain in her aching arms was hard to bear, but having to watch Völundr work was worse. He created his crow slaves with a cruel efficiency, swapping their forms over and over for entertainment. He'd drawn a neat circle in chalk behind the door leading into the gutted living room and decorated it in symbols Anya didn't know or understand. When he cut himself and drew runes with his own blood, Anya thought she would vomit. The tickle of magic she could still feel inside of her recoiled from whatever ritual he was performing.

Anya had been staying quiet and drowsy-looking so they would think she was still heavily sedated. She couldn't fool them entirely, though, because an alarm would sound every two hours, and Völundr would inject more drugs into her.

Anya had tried to mind-link with Katya again, but her power was nowhere near strong enough, and the drugs left her with the opposite of a clear head. While falling in and out of consciousness, she dreamed of the farm and Eikki, of the firebird blazing in the night, Trajan smiling as he read aloud to her. Images of the past month flowed through her mind. She dreamed of Baba Yaga clack-clacking at her loom, Yanka walking through the forest or picking herbs from her garden, of a man with raven hair and golden eyes standing next to a tower on a green hill.

Shouting and commotion in the house drew Anya out of her dream. The door on the other side of the room burst open, and there he was: Trajan, full of fury and flecked with blood. He spotted her hanging from the wall, and his eyes turned red. Two guards rushed him. He grabbed one by the face and flung him hard at the wall. The other man he punched in the throat so hard his fist tore through his neck.

"Trajan, no!" Anya croaked desperately. "The floor—"

Trajan didn't hear her as he tossed the corpse aside and moved to rush to her side. As soon as he hit the first symbol on the floor, an invisible hand of power slammed him down and into Völundr's circle. Trajan hissed an otherworldly sound and smashed against the invisible walls, screaming as power electrocuted him, then collapsed. After a moment, he groaned and pushed himself up. He spat something black from his mouth. "Anya, are you all right?"

"Oh, you know, the usual." She gave him a weak smile. "Just hanging out and waiting for my rescue."

"I apologize for not being better at it."

"I'm glad you can admit that this was a ridiculous attempt." Völundr appeared, and Anya struggled at her manacles, her hands itching to wipe the grin from his face. "Now, now, Anya, you know what happened the last time you caused a fuss."

"He has nothing to do with this, Völundr. It's me Ladislav and Vasilli want. Let him go."

"No." Völundr stepped toward Trajan.

"Your magic circle won't hold me for long." Trajan's voice shifted, becoming deeper and distorted. The hair on Anya's arms stood on end.

"You don't frighten me, thanatos," Völundr hissed.

"I should."

Völundr's hand twisted, and Trajan clutched his head. "Now you will see him for what he truly is, Anya."

Trajan writhed in pain.

"Stop it, please," she begged.

Völundr didn't seem to listen or care. Trajan's clothes melted under the power pouring from Völundr's hands. Anya pulled frantically at her chains, trying desperately to access her magic. She screamed in fury, and Völundr glared.

"Shut her up, will you?" he told the nearest guard.

Anya thrashed, trying to fight off the guard's attack, but as soon as he hit her, her world went black.

Anya dreamed she was sitting by the fire in her small farmhouse. Eikki was in a chair opposite her with a kantele on his lap, plucking the strings with well-practiced ease.

"Remember this story, Anya," he said as he continued to play. "It lives in your blood with all of our ancestors, ready to help you when you need it." Then he sang in his strong, husky voice, and Anya let the *Kalevala's* familiar stories wash over her.

Steady old Väinämöinen, rune singer of unspeakable power, had been building a boat and wounded himself with an ax. He found a gray-bearded healer to help him with the wound. Väinämöinen told the old man about the Origin of Iron. He explained how iron was first created, how the magician had the power to control it. Väinämöinen sang his rune songs, and the iron had to obey. It lifted from the wound in his leg so it could be healed.

Anya jerked awake as someone hit her in the ribs. She opened swollen eyes and wished she hadn't.

"Wake up, Yanka's blood." Völundr kissed her busted lips. "Wake up and see what I have done."

Trajan—if she could still call him that—had been entirely stripped of his human form. His skin was now a shimmering dark gray, and wings of smoke and shadows protruded from his back. Although he covered his face, she could still see enlarged, deep red eyes between his hands.

"Let him go," Anya whispered. "Stop this. I'll give you anything."

"You already have. I wanted a thanatos, and now I have one."

"I'm going to kill you for this, Völundr." A deep calm settled within Anya. Her magic rose up in her. It seemed Völundr had been too preoccupied torturing Trajan to remember to inject her.

Völundr rattled her iron chains and laughed. "Oh, brave Anya. You aren't going to do a damn thing."

Anya's dream came back to her in hazy snippets: Eikki's stories, the Origin of Iron. The twins had told her the old stories have power and truth in them and that her aptitude for fire was one of her greatest strengths. The Origin of Iron. *It lives in your blood with all of our ancestors, ready to help you when you need it.*

Völundr had turned his attention back to Trajan, so he didn't see Anya find her feet and stand firm. He didn't see the fury in her eyes when she glared at the iron around her wrists. Instead, Völundr taunted his prey, telling Trajan in intimate detail what he would do to Anya, and then what Vasilli and Ladislav would do once they were told he had her.

Anya's power flared up in her, fierce and hot. She opened her mouth, and her whispered words came unhindered by any other thought in her mind:

"Iron that binds me,
iron that pains me,
iron that holds me
in cold, cruel grasp.

Remember your brother,
that frightening Fire.
Remember the touch,
of Ilmarinen's hammer.
Remember coals
burning heat
of Forge's Fire.
Rise and remember.
Release your brother.
The one that tamed you
into shape and into form.
Release his fury,
the heat of his anger.
Remember Mother's milk
that made you on Ukko's knee.
Return to earth now.
Flow like Mother's milk
into cold, dark earth.
Free Brother Fire from
cruel, cold grasp.
Let his anger flow out
onto those that bind me."

Flames, hot and blinding, burst from Anya's hands before spreading down her body. The iron manacles melted like plastic and dripped onto the ground. Anya was aware of Völundr shouting, but she couldn't make out the words over the roaring in her ears. He ran for the door, but Anya held out a hand, and it swung shut and locked.

"You should have let him go when I asked," Anya said.

The guard bashed against the door beside Völundr, trying to find a way out. Völundr began working spells against her, but they were only beestings against her skin. The fire poured out of her, setting the room ablaze. Her hands stretched toward the two struggling men, who screamed as they burned from the inside. With Vischto, it had been instantaneous, but Anya wanted these men to suffer. She stepped over them as they writhed, and she walked through the door, the walls catching fire as she passed. She kicked open doors until she found where the ovinnik was being held.

"Yanka's blood." Its eyes were wide in its gaunt face.

Anya gripped his chains, and they melted beneath her hands. She touched his face and smiled. The ovinnik smiled back, his body turning into something between a cat and a man as he lit up with her fire.

"Go through the house and do your work," Anya said. "If you find others, set them free."

He ran from the room, screaming and laughing, leaving trails of fire wherever he went. Anya went back to Trajan and punched a hole through the invisible force holding him. Völundr's circle shattered beneath her touch. The flames along her skin were fading now, but the fierce power still rode her.

Trajan was curled tight in a ball, covered in golden ichor from his wounds. Anya rolled him over. "Trajan?"

He turned his silver face from her. "Don't look at me, Anya. I'm too weak to shield—"

Anya gripped his arm, silencing his protest. "I can't move you on my own. Take what you need so you can heal. We need to get out of here before the Darkness is on us."

He shuddered. "No. I'll kill you."

"You won't. I trust you. It's freely given, so take it."

Despite his reluctance, the silvery smokelike substance was already seeping out of her skin and rushing into him. Anya sagged against him as the roaring, angry power in her veins slowly retreated. Trajan's skin shimmered and lightened—the first sign of his shift back to human—when Anya lost consciousness.

Trajan let Anya go, horrified at what he had done, the taste of her golden life force still lingering on his tongue. The house burned around him, blocking them inside.

"Trajan!" Hamish appeared in the flaming doorway. "I found him!"

Cerise came through the door, her face turning from fear to fury. "Trajan, what have you done?" she screamed. She pulled Anya from his arms and lifted her up.

Hamish's heavy coat dropped over Trajan's naked body, and he was hauled to his feet. Völundr's body twisted in the corner. Trajan could still feel the life in him fighting. He leaned over and placed a hand on Völundr's terrified face. "I'm going to send you somewhere very special for what you've done," Trajan said, and Völundr screamed as his soul was ripped from his body.

"No time!" Hamish shouted and tossed Trajan over his shoulder. Hamish carried him through the burning house and outside onto the street.

Izrayl and Yvan put Anya in the back seat of Cerise's car. Yvan climbed in after her and held Anya to him, his mouth moving with words Trajan couldn't hear as he tried to wake her. Trajan looked back at the burning house, sensing all the souls that had died in there. Spreading his arms, he pulled all of them to him.

"Trajan," Cerise said, coming to his side. "Trajan, don't take them. Don't put the souls of those assholes inside you for even a moment."

But he ignored her until there was nothing left. "I have no intention of keeping them. I don't want them left to wander this plane."

For the first time since Ilya saved him, Trajan opened the unseen door separating reality from the spirit world. It was where it had always been, in the corner of his eye, at the edge of his perception. Cerise stumbled away from the torn hole in reality and yelled at the others to keep back and cover their eyes. Trajan focused on the soul energy inside of him. First, he sent all the souls the Darkness had killed to the whatever afterlife awaited them and Völundr's operatives' straight to the Underworld. Völundr's he kept until last.

With an old efficiency, Trajan opened another gate leading to the seething, cold blackness of Tartarus. Summoning Völundr's soul, he sent it howling into the abyss. He shut both of the doors with haste. The threshold between worlds dissipated once more, and he was left standing in the wet, dark streets of Paris. Trajan turned just as Izrayl's massive fist connected with his jaw, knocking him out cold.

34

TRAJAN CAME AROUND FROM Izrayl's punch the following day, disoriented and raving, still feeling echoes of the magic Völundr had used on him.

Cerise was at his side, ready to ground him in reality. Gripping his biceps, she forced him to look at her, and when he was able to focus, she told him what had happened. He could barely remember anything about the last twenty hours. Apparently, Cerise had tracked his phone he hadn't returned to the mansion, and they had arrived just in time to see Anya turn the building into an inferno.

"You opened a gateway to fucking Tartarus, Trajan!" Cerise yelled in Greek before calming herself, chain-smoking worse than ever. "Can you imagine what would happen to this world if you had left it open? If something had tried to get through?"

"I'm sorry, Cerise." Trajan felt like a scolded child. He couldn't believe he had done it either. All he remembered was being in agony, Anya burning, and then nothing.

"It doesn't matter now. We have to make preparations to get out of Paris. Once the Darkness finds out what happened, we'll all be fucked. We have to assume that they know where we are now."

"Völundr hadn't told Ladislav that he had Anya yet. That could buy us some time. He was using her to get at me before he reported back to Moscow."

Cerise lit another cigarette. "Who the hell is Völundr?"

"He was the one holding Anya captive. From what I can guess, he was a liaison of Ladislav's." Trajan pressed the heels of his hands into his eyes as it all came back to him. "He was dead before I knew it. Anya will know more about him." He stood. "I need to see her."

"Good luck getting past Katya," Cerise said, but waved him on.

Trajan paced the hallway, trying to think of a way to convince Katya to let him in to see Anya. According to Cerise, she still hadn't woken, and because they were unsure whether to expect the Darkness to show up again, someone was guarding her room at all times.

Katya was wearing her handguns and leaning against Anya's bedroom door when he finally got the courage to approach her. She drew on him. "Go away, Trajan."

"Katya, please. I'm myself again."

"And what kind of comfort is that? I saw what you did yesterday. You think I'm ever going to get those screams out of my head?"

"I'm still the same Trajan you knew yesterday. Do you think Izrayl would've brought me back here if I wasn't? Do you think Yvan would've let me in the house?"

Katya lowered her gun but didn't holster it again. "I would still be careful of Yvan if I were you." She eyed him warily. "You can have ten minutes, and I'll be right outside the door waiting for you."

"I understand."

"I hope you do." Katya walked away, leaving him to sit by Anya's bed.

Anya was pale under the smudges of ash on her face and through her hair. She looked the complete opposite of the vengeful shamanitsa she had been a day before.

Trajan's memory of the previous twenty-four hours was hazy, but he would never forget the pure fury on Anya's face or the way she melted the iron holding her. Anya's fire magic had saved them both, and now she had seen his true form—as much as one could on this plane of existence. She hadn't been repulsed or scared. She had touched him and offered her life's energy to help him.

Trajan's insides cramped with anger at himself for being weak enough to take it. He should've been the one to save her, not the other way around. He was meant to be her protector, and he had failed her. Trajan's mouth watered just remembering the golden taste of it, and his self-loathing doubled. Now, because of what he had done, she hadn't woken.

"I'm so sorry, Anya," he whispered. He brushed the hair from her face, his fingers lingering on her cheek. Even if she did wake up, he didn't know how he was ever going to make amends for the unforgivable thing he had done.

"No, no, no," Anya croaked, lashing out at the sheets.

Hope rushed through him. "Anya? Wake up. You're having a nightmare."

Her eyes snapped open, then met his as he leaned over her. She screamed. Anya struggled out of the sheets and scrambled out of bed, backing away from him in terror.

Katya appeared in the doorway. Anya knocked her over and ran down the hall.

"What the hell?" Katya got to her feet, her jade eyes wide and locked on Trajan. "What did you do?"

Anya barged into Yvan's rooms and ran for his bathroom. She slammed the door behind her and turned the lock. Shaking and crying, she tore her dirty clothes off and managed to turn on the shower taps before her knees gave out and she crumpled on the tiles. Sobs escaped her in heavy, painful gasps, and she pulled her knees to her chest and rocked. Screams echoed in her head. The blood-and-ash taste in her mouth was strong enough to make her gag.

You killed all those people, and you didn't feel bad about it for a moment. She still didn't, and that made her feel even worse. *The first time you use your magic properly, and you use it to kill, just like those boys at the lake.*

"Anya?" someone called from the other side of the door. It burst open, and Yvan's dark head appeared around the shower door, concern written on his face. "Do you want to come out of there?"

She tucked her legs closer to her chest. "I c-can't m-move." She shivered from shock, although the water was hot.

Yvan kicked off his shoes and turned the water even hotter, then sat down beside her fully clothed. He draped an arm around her, and she leaned into him, sobbing. "You're okay," he whispered and stroked her hair. "Do you want to tell me about it?"

The whole confusing story tumbled out of her: the shishiga and her peeling skin, the imprisoned ovinnik, the crow slaves, Völundr torturing her and then Trajan.

Yvan held her tighter when she spoke about the huge amount of power that had taken over her. She couldn't remember anything after she urged Trajan to take her energy except for horrifying night terrors of hell, distorted crow slaves, and Völundr screaming in the darkness. When she'd woken to Trajan at her bedside, all she could see was his thanatos form looming over her.

Once her story turned to a ramble of words and images, Yvan said, "Anya, take a deep breath for me."

She did.

"I think the drugs Völundr injected you with are still wearing off. You're coming down from a long high. Right now, you need to relax. Vasilli and Ladislav weren't even aware that you were captured. That gives us a few days to get out of Paris, and by the time they realize what happened, we will be long gone. They aren't ever going to get their hands on you again, *shalost*."

"I killed them, Yvan. They were screaming, and I left them to die." The horror of it clawed at her insides.

"They would have done worse to you, Anya. Think of all the others they would have hurt and experimented on in that building. This is war. You survived. There is no shame in that."

Anya gripped him tighter. Her whole world had been turned upside down again, but Yvan was still her rock, the only thing keeping her from getting swept away in the madness. "I met two other fairy-tale creatures when I was captive, and now I'm here with you—a wonderful, cursed fairy-tale prince from Skazki. It's like I am trapped in a fairy tale of my own, but this one isn't going to have a happy ending, is it?"

Yvan chuckled. "I'm not much of a prince anymore. One thing I've learned is that we can never predict the future. You've been given a massive gift, and you have been using it for good. You gave a shishiga and an ovinnik a much happier ending than they thought possible. Think about them and the second chances they have now because of you. Don't think about the lives you had to take."

Anya nodded, then sighed. "What are we going to do now?"

"The first thing you need to do is get out of this shower. Then, when we are packed and ready, we're getting out of Paris. The others have been making the arrangements since we found you." He gave her a reassuring smile. "And Trajan woke screaming too, so don't feel bad about doing the same thing."

Anya flinched at the mention of Trajan. *Oh god, you screamed in his face.* "Can you do me a favor?" she asked.

"Anything."

"Can you talk to him for me? He's going to think I'm afraid of him. I was screaming because of the dream, and then he was looming over me, and I didn't know if I was asleep or awake—"

"And coming down off the drugs probably made the nightmares and the world in general that much more terrifying." Yvan nodded. "I'll tell him."

He stood and climbed out of the shower, then unfolded a massive towel and held it out for her, discreetly looking away as she stood, turned off the taps, and stepped into it. Yvan wrapped it around her like a little child and dried her face with a corner. "Go and get dressed. You need food. I'll talk to Trajan."

"Thank you, Yvan. You always know the right thing to say."

Yvan smiled and flicked the end of her nose. "Of course I do. I'm the hero, remember?"

"Now, don't go getting a big head. Just because an old woman in Skazki said that doesn't mean it's true." Anya grinned, feeling better by the second.

Yvan found Trajan in the library with Hamish and Izrayl, a whiskey by his elbow and his head in his hands.

"Anya's never been afraid of you, but she's been through a lot..." Izrayl was saying to him.

The three men looked up as Yvan joined them.

"I just rescued her from my shower. Anya is coming down off the drugs she was given. She was having night terrors, and she panicked when you woke her,

Trajan. That's all. She's embarrassed she screamed at you." He folded his arms. He was still pissed off at the thanatos for not calling for backup and then feeding on Anya, but him fighting with Trajan wouldn't help her, so he reined in his frustrations for her benefit.

"See? I told you not to beat yourself up." Hamish slapped Trajan on the back so hard his body jerked under the impact.

"What do you mean you rescued her *from the shower*?" A dark look settled in Trajan's eyes. "You went in there when she was naked?"

Yvan held his menacing stare, even as his heart rate went up.

"Trajan, cut it out." Izrayl pointed to the decorative house plants that had started to shrivel and die.

Trajan shook himself and looked away.

Yvan pretended to be unfazed as he poured himself vodka from the crystal decanter. He took a long sip before he said, "She was dreaming of hell when you woke her. She could hear Völundr screaming."

"Did you tell her what I did? That I opened the passages to Tartarus?"

"No, that's something you can explain to her, and you had best do it soon so she knows she's not losing her mind."

Hamish sipped his bourbon. "Shit happens, Trajan. You gotta move on from it. Anya's a cool chick. She'll get it. Hell, after what she just went through with that Swedish little prick, she'll probably praise you for it."

Yvan thought of the bruises on Anya's face. He had the urge to both resurrect and kill Völundr and take Anya in his arms and hold her.

She's not yours to hold, the firebird reminded him.

Yvan ignored him.

Isabelle came into the room, followed by Katya, Cerise, and the twins, breaking the previous tension and replacing it with strained but measured unease. Without preamble, she said, "We need to start a twenty-four-hour guard over the house until we can get out of Paris. If we're lucky, we might have some time before they become worried enough about their colleagues to send someone. I have a friend who's hacked into the Darkness communications network and is trying to find out where Ladislav and Vasilli are. We have to assume they'll come as soon as they are notified about the burned wreckage of their safe house. We aren't ready to fight them head-on, so our goal is to leave as soon as we've got everything in order and Anya feels well enough to move."

"Chayton and I have cast some protection warding around the grounds in case they send something magical after us in the meantime," Honaw said. His deep American accent had a smoky quality. A whiskey voice, Yvan had heard Katya refer to it as.

Katya nodded. "Everybody, stay on guard. It's not about if they'll come for her again—it's when. Ideally, we'll get out of here before then, but you know the Darkness." She glanced around the room. "They'll stop at nothing."

Anya sat on one of the cream-colored couches in Trajan's rooms, wondering if she was a coward for not going downstairs to see everyone. She still didn't feel right from the drugs and was scared she would have another meltdown if she had to deal with too many people at once. Her heart leaped when the door rattled and Trajan came in.

"Hey," she said softly.

"What are you doing hiding in here?" He closed the door and smiled, so that was a good sign.

"I'm not hiding. I just wanted to talk to you without an audience." Anya folded her arms around herself, wanting to go to him but too scared to. "I'm really sorry about screaming at you. I was still high and having nightmares. You know I'm not actually scared of you, Trajan."

"I know, but I thought after seeing my true form…"

She shook her head. "It doesn't matter. I was more frightened that you were being tortured than seeing your other side." Anya would never forget his cries of pain or the feelings of utter helplessness that had overwhelmed her.

"I should've been smarter and not fallen into the trap to begin with."

"You can't blame yourself for that. Besides, it doesn't matter, because I saved you." She smiled. "It's kind of nice to be the one that did the saving for once."

He laughed. "You certainly did that. Let's get some more light in here, shall we?"

He moved about the dark room, turning on the beautiful stained glass lamps and lighting the small fireplace. At the back of it, there was an engraved plate of a figure holding a spear that looked ancient Greek in origin. Like everything in the house, it was effortlessly elegant. Trajan fit in perfectly with his manners and habit of dressing in ties and waistcoats. His clothes would have looked like a uniform on anyone else, but on him, they looked comfortable and casual. The fire caught, the warm glow highlighting his shiny chestnut curls.

"What?" he asked when he noticed her staring.

"I was wondering if I was still high." She pulled her feet up. "You're handsome as hell in this light."

"You definitely must still be suffering from the effects of that poison." Trajan smiled just at the corner of his mouth, but Anya spotted it before it disappeared. "Can I get you anything? We have food downstairs."

"Don't fuss. I'm fine." Trajan sat down beside her, still looking worried and nervous. Anya took his hand and squeezed it. "I'm not afraid of what you are, and I don't regret helping you for one second."

"How can you really not be afraid, Anya? You saw what lives under this human form." Despite his words, his grip on her tightened.

She leaned into him. "You watched me burn people alive. You saw under my skin too. It was like that day at the lake with those boys. I went calm and let the rage and magic take over. You should be scared of me too."

Trajan shook his head. "No, you don't understand. I sent Völundr's soul to Tartarus—the worst place in the Underworld that I could possibly find. That's why you were having nightmares. The darkness of it touched you. I can't believe I was so foolish."

"Trajan, you had been tortured." She nudged him. "I can deal with the nightmares if you can."

Trajan tucked her hair behind her ears and held her face gently in his hands. "For one so young, you know and have seen so much." There was a tinge of sadness in his voice. "You've lived, and you have suffered and seen death and darkness, but your soul burns with light. Being close to a creature like me will only make it worse. You'll always be living with Death. I don't ever want that light in you to go out."

Trajan was so earnest that Anya leaned forward, ran her hands through his thick hair, and kissed him softly. His eyes widened in surprise before he pulled her down onto the floor with him and held her tight.

"I thought you were dead when I saw you hanging from that wall," he whispered against her hair. "I was so frightened that I was too late…"

"Don't talk about it." Anya reached up to stroke his temple.

The fine lines under his eyes crinkled. He kissed her cheek, then her brow. "Even after days of captivity, you are still so lovely."

"And you're a terrific liar." Anya grinned. She had seen her bruised face in the mirror earlier. "I think Völundr's games must have given you brain damage."

"I don't have brain damage. I can see you for what you are. Your soul shines like a supernova." Trajan stroked her damaged face. "The bruises on your skin don't diminish it, even a little."

"You really know how to make a girl blush."

"Not all girls. Just you." Trajan grabbed some pillows from the couch and propped them under her before covering her with a caramel-colored cashmere blanket.

She pulled him close again and ran her hands under the dark blue waist-coat he wore. "I promise not to wake screaming in your face if you sleep next to me tonight."

"Screaming or not, I'm not planning on letting you out of my sight for a long time."

Anya smiled at that, snuggling into him and breathing in his autumn scent, letting it calm her like it always did.

She soon fell into a dream, though it didn't feel dream-shaped or like a memory. Everything was too sharp and vivid. She could smell the forest, feel the land at her feet. *My land.* In the distance was the black scorch mark of what remained of her barn and a small house. She never thought she would see the day that she would miss the farm, but her heart soared to see it.

Anya froze when she spotted Vasilli standing next to a robust older man with silvery gray hair that hung to his waist. Neither of them looked her way or seemed to notice she was there.

"Have you heard from him yet?" Vasilli asked.

"Not yet, but the nehemoth has been released. It will use the hair we recovered to track her."

Vasilli scoffed. "And it should have already completed its task by now. It's likely back to wandering the spirit worlds already. You should have let me handle this, Ladislav. That piece of shit Völundr can't be trusted."

"None of us are to be trusted. He's loyal, though, and his loyalty is to me. You are loyal because you have no other choice."

Vasilli's fists clenched at his sides. "I am loyal."

"The only one you have ever been loyal to is the dead princess. Move on, Vasilli."

"Once Anyanka is caught, many things will change. She will come into her birthright quickly if she doesn't fight us, and then you'll have to watch your back. If she's anything like Yanka, she will surpass you within a year."

"I'm not concerned about Anya or her talents. I'm concerned about this." Ladislav held out his hand, and the invisible wall in front of him shimmered red for a moment. "It's weakening. Within a month, it will open, and if we can prevent anyone from interfering, we'll finally control it. The Darkness will claim both worlds, bringing a new age of belief and worship." Ladislav's voice was hungry and determined.

The men were silent for a long while before Ladislav shook himself. "Let's go, Vasilli. I feel too exposed here."

"It's the Venäläinen ghosts watching us," Vasilli said, taking obvious enjoyment in Ladislav's discomfort.

Ladislav grunted before heading back into the forest, and Vasilli followed him obediently.

Snow fell, and Anya shivered, curling her body inward to shield herself from the biting wind. She turned back to inspect the house's charred ruins and gasped when she saw they were whole once more.

A tall man walked across the field in front of her. His long, golden hair was tied back, and his green eyes shone with anger as he glared at the creatures that had appeared on the other side of the invisible wall Ladislav had just inspected.

Who the hell is that?

He turned and looked straight through Anya, and she knew who he was.

Ilya.

She had seen a picture of him before, in a locket she'd left behind. Strong power flowed out of him. She could feel the magic streaming through the air. He stopped beside her. She wanted to reach out and touch him. Now that he was closer, she could appreciate his high cheekbones and the golden stubble on his face. He looked like a lost Viking god.

"You will not enter," Ilya said, his steady voice carrying over the noise of the thrashing creatures on the other side of the barrier. "I am the keeper of these gates, and you won't pass into this world."

There was a terrible screeching sound as a horned beast burst through. Its face was faintly humanoid but covered in fur and sleek with sweat, and its long horns were smeared with blood. Anya cried out as it charged Ilya like a berserker. Ilya lifted his hand, and the creature soared off the ground. He made a simple twisting motion, and the beast began to choke and struggle. He dropped his hand again, and the body fell to the ground.

Ilya drew out a steel knife with a golden pine handle carved like a snarling bear. With quick movements, he made two shallow cuts on both of his forearms. Then he sang, but Anya couldn't make out the words. Ilya threw the bloody knife, and it landed in the earth where the two worlds touched. The ground trembled underneath Anya's feet, and she watched with a mixture of awe and terror as Ilya's left hand came down over the cut on his right arm and he scooped the flowing blood into his palm.

He crouched down and drew a line in the dirt. Then he poured the blood that had pooled in his hand into the groove. Sweat beaded his forehead as he worked. His words never stopped but try as she might, Anya couldn't make them out.

Ilya repeated the process with his opposite hand before returning to his feet. She could feel his exhaustion in every movement.

After scooping blood into both of his hands, he flung it out into the air. As soon as the crimson drops touched the barrier, the creatures straining against it were flung back with an almighty force. They flew through the air, hitting trees and earth. The remaining creatures turned and fled.

This is how he closed the gates, Anya realized. Maybe she could close them the same way.

Ilya's fine features were now ashen. He took a few strips of cloth from his pocket, tied them around his cuts, and retrieved his knife.

"Ilya…" Anya whispered.

He stopped and looked around as if he'd heard her. She reached out, and as soon as she touched him, he slipped away, and she fell into another dream.

35

ON THE OTHER SIDE of the mansion, Isabelle was down on the floor in cobra pose, trying to clear her mind and relax her muscles. She was edgy, unsure how she felt about being so caught up in the plots of the Darkness, even though she had agreed to stay with Katya and her crew. It wouldn't take the Illumination long to get involved either. All of her instincts told her to run, that this wasn't her fight, but if they went to war, it was going to be everyone's fight.

"Even you can't run forever," Isabelle murmured, her fingers flicking over her rosary beads.

Once they retrieved Anya and Trajan, Isabelle had emailed a contact in New Orleans to inquire about the nature of the nehemoth. If anyone could get her useful information, it was Harley and her friend Fox. Isabelle had been checking her email every hour but still hadn't heard back. She had never encountered a nehemoth before and didn't know how to ward the house against it returning.

Isabelle glanced through the thick curtains, worried that the Darkness would try to engage in a full assault on the mansion to get Anya back—and the firebird too. A golden flicker in the garden caught her eye. A dingo prowled through the plants. It seemed Hamish was out patrolling the borders and alone for once. She had to talk to him. They needed to get their frustrations out without an audience. Maybe then she would be able to get some sleep.

Isabelle grabbed one of her guns, then hurried out of the room and through the back kitchen door. The smell of ice and diesel fumes hung in the night air. Hamish moved along the fence line toward her, and she fought the urge to turn back. He was the one person who seemed to rob her of all her courage.

Hamish sat down in front of her, a droopy smile on his face. She crouched down beside him and resisted the desire to pat him.

"Can we talk?" she asked.

In response, Hamish lifted his leg, peed, and trotted off. Isabelle gaped at the wet stain on the front of her chest and pants. She stood, biting back a scream, and turned back toward the house. Hamish was clearly not ready to talk yet. She felt stupid for even trying.

Cursing, Isabelle stood on the back step and peeled off her soiled clothes. *Mr. Hudson, you just declared war.* She promised retribution as she bent down to pick up her pajamas.

"You've put on some weight since I last saw you from this angle." Hamish buttoned a pair of jeans, his head tilted to one side as he inspected her.

Isabelle bundled her clothes and threw them at him. They hit him in the chest with a satisfying splat. "Go screw yourself."

His eyes still looked feral after his recent change, and her trigger finger twitched. She took a step backward and opened the door to the kitchen.

"Isabelle..." he said in that soft, imploring tone that was so rare for him. She wasn't going to let it work on her. Not when he hadn't even attempted to talk to her since the night Anya was taken.

Isabelle whipped around. "What? You want to make another jibe about my weight like an asshole?"

Hamish hesitated a moment before asking, "Do people still say *jibe?*"

"If that's all you have to say to me after all these years, you're a bigger idiot than I thought."

His expression darkened as he advanced on her. "I wasn't the one who pissed off in the middle of the night. You left me, Belle. Remember? I tried hunting you down, and when I finally did, it was after the whole place had been blown to bits."

"I left to protect you, moron. I had enemies closing in on me. Do you think I could've sat back and watched them murder you to hurt me? I didn't matter you were immortal, that you were strong…I couldn't watch you die." Isabelle shook her head. "Every immortal has a weakness, and they would have found yours soon enough."

"I didn't need protecting," Hamish said, then scoffed. "And if you would have said goodbye and ended it properly, it would have been different. It would have been better than *this*. You weren't some random chick I picked up at the pub, and you know it, so don't pretend otherwise."

Isabelle folded her arms over her chest. Vulnerable, pissed off, and half-naked wasn't the way she wanted to have this conversation. "By the time the heat was off me, too much time had passed. I wouldn't risk it again. It's not that I didn't want to find you, but a lot had changed, and I didn't need the reputation of being a hunter who had sex with her targets instead of killing them."

Hamish rolled his eyes. "Don't bullshit me, Belle. You've never given a crap about what other hunters thought of you. What changed?"

Isabelle didn't offer an answer. God had a cruel sense of humor to let their paths cross again. She pulled her long hair down over her neck to hide the scar. She wasn't about to tell anyone about that.

Hamish offered her his clean, white T-shirt.

"Thank you." She slipped it over her head. "I'm going back to bed. I'll tell you some other night when I'm up to it. Tonight, I'm not, and you're just going to have to accept that. For what it's worth, I thought I was doing the right thing when I left you." She turned.

"Hey, Belle?"

She glanced over her shoulder at him.

Hamish cleared his throat. "About the weight comment. I'm sorry. I was an asshole. It looks good on you."

"Thanks for clarifying. I'll sleep better tonight."

"Look, I'm trying to apologize." He walked up behind her on the stairs. "I would like us to be civil, even if it's just for Trajan's sake."

Hamish's hand brushed hers where it rested on the banister, his skin hot on hers. She jerked her hand away.

"Yeah, whatever. Goodnight, Belle." Hamish pushed past her, leaving her standing there cursing the day she walked through Trajan's door.

The next morning, Isabelle woke to notification alerts on her laptop. She opened a tired, gritty eye and groaned. She had promised to train Anya on some basic hand-to-hand combat while the others made final decisions on their next moves, but the incident with Hamish the night before rushed back to her, and she buried her head under the pillows. She wasn't ready to deal with the world again.

The sound of motorbike engines revving erupting from Isabelle's phone—Harley's ringtone. With a sigh, she crawled out of bed and opened her message:

```
Read ur email. It's IMPORTANT. Luv, H.
```

Isabelle looked down at Hamish's T-shirt. She had been so upset the night before, she had washed the pee off her leg and climbed immediately into bed. Hamish's scent on his shirt was now assaulting her.

The nightmare continues. She pulled it off and dropped it onto the carpet.

Isabelle couldn't help but smile when she opened Harley's email. It was splashed with her shop's logo, the colors bright enough to make Isabelle's eyes ache. Legba's Ladies was a dominantly women-run motorcycle fabricator workshop in New Orleans, and the three men who worked there considered themselves the luckiest men in the world.

Harley had been born to two motorcycle mechanics. The story went that her father delivered her on the shop floor on his favorite Harley-Davidson jacket. She was christened Harley that night, and now she had taken over her parents' business, earning a reputation as one of the best.

Harley had made Isabelle's custom motorcycle that was down in Trajan's garage. It had all sorts of interesting features hidden from the naked eye, like a place for spare knives, and silver blades that shot out of her rims. That idea had been inspired by the chariots in *Gladiator*. Holy symbols had been stamped into different parts of the frame, and Fox had airbrushed a fierce, blond Valkyrie on the fuel tank. Fox wasn't just a talented artist, but the best hacker Isabelle had ever known.

Between them, Harley and Fox were the best researchers Isabelle knew, and they hadn't let her down yet. Isabelle scrolled through the email with a sigh, reading the research they'd found on the nehemoth and Harley's offer to fly over if Isabelle needed her. Harley was like a little sister and one of the few women Isabelle actually liked. This was big trouble, and there was no way in seven hells Isabelle was going to position Harley in the Darkness's line of fire.

A soft knock at the door drew her eyes away from the laptop screen.

"Just a minute," she called. She found a dressing gown and wrapped it around herself, then picked up Hamish's shirt and stuffed it under the blanket.

Trajan was waiting patiently outside of her door when she opened it. "Sorry to interrupt. Have you seen Hamish?"

Isabelle's hand on the door handle tightened as unexpected fear curled in her chest. "He's not in the mansion?"

He shook his head. "No, I can't find him anywhere."

She sighed. "We had a fight in the garden last night. I went to bed and figured he did the same. Do you think someone snatched him?"

"I doubt it, but everyone here knows not to leave the safety of the mansion."

Isabelle knew precisely why he would leave. Her. *Goddamn it.*

"I think I know where he might be. I'll go get him," she said.

"Thank you, Isabelle. Help yourself to any of the cars downstairs. The sooner he's back, the better. I don't want him causing a bar fight and drawing unnecessary attention to himself."

Hamish sat on a stool in the recently refurbished Dirty Rose Bar. It was where he'd met Isabelle fifty years before, and he had secretly hoped it would've been burned to the ground. He had been an immortal, shape-shifting soldier then, and she had been masquerading as a stunning bar singer that happened to say yes when he offered to buy her a drink. She was also human back then.

"Another?" the bartender asked.

"Yes, no ice."

The boy nodded and didn't say a thing. He was probably wondering how Hamish was still alive after all the alcohol he had consumed. Hamish loved a twenty-four-hour bar and was making the most of it. He'd been drinking steadily for nearly twelve hours and had no intention of stopping.

Hamish really couldn't understand why Isabelle was so angry at him. Surely, he was the one entitled to being angry after all the years he'd been left to think she was dead? He had never felt a connection like the one he'd had with Belle. He had looked for it, and nothing ever came close.

The bell on the bar door chimed, and there she was—a drunken man's dream made real. In his hallucination, she was dressed in tight black jeans, a lacy cream top, and a black leather jacket. Her long hair fell in waves over her shoulders, and she still had those perfect, kissable red lips.

The bartender placed the rum in front of him, and Hamish drank it straight down to clear the illusion away. He couldn't even get drunk without her ghost haunting him.

"Hamish." Her warm voice washed over him. Maybe he should stop drinking. Seeing and hearing things were usually signs to sober up.

Isabelle sat down beside him. "I thought I'd find you here. Trajan is worried about you." She turned to the bartender. "Martini, thank you."

He nodded and went to mix it for her.

"I can't believe the old place still stands," she murmured as she glanced around.

Oh great. She really was there. "Trajan is too wrapped up in the Russian witch to notice if I go out for a drink."

"Maybe if you hadn't been missing for nearly twelve hours, it would have been less obvious." Isabelle took her drink from the bartender, who blushed when she smiled at him. "This is weird, isn't it?"

"I don't know how I ended up here. I feel like I'm in the twilight zone, except you aren't singing."

She reddened at that, maybe surprised that he had remembered. The first night they met, she'd climbed up on a table and sang for a bar full of people. Later on, he found out that she was a hunter. He foolishly attacked her, thinking she had been sent to kill him, and she had shot him in the ass mid-fight. It turned out that she'd had no idea he was an immortal shifter. She'd wanted to drink with him because she actually liked him. It had been a hell of a first date.

"Do you still sing?"

"Only in the shower."

"I'll have to catch your show sometime."

Isabelle laughed, nearly choking on her drink. It surprised him. She had a great, big, filthy laugh, and it reminded him of the days when they didn't hate each other.

"I assure you, the sight isn't what it used to be." Isabelle tossed back the rest of her martini and ordered another one.

"I saw a bit last night, and it looked just fine to me." Hamish waved his glass at the barman, and he refilled it.

"Well, you still look exactly the same. Are you still finding wars and saving the day?" she asked, referring to his old pastime.

"I'm back home on a cattle station again. You get tired of killing men. It's too easy and disheartening. Supernaturals present much more of a challenge these days."

"Very true. I think that's why I'm staying around. Trouble flocks to that witch, and it's going to be a killer fight when it comes to a head."

"We might even get the chance to die in this one."

"Just for something different."

They both burst out laughing at that. The bartender looked at them with a perplexed expression, which made them laugh even more.

"Make me another, please." There was a glow in Isabelle's cheeks—the first sign of her getting tipsy. It made Hamish smile that she still couldn't hold her liquor. "We really should get back to the mansion after this round. Trajan is fretting like a mother hen."

"I have a better idea. How about we stay here, and you can keep on drinking? You're less hostile with vodka in your system." Hamish gave her a sideways grin over his glass.

She punched him in the shoulder. "I'm serious. They'll send out a search party for us soon."

"You'll protect me from any bad guys."

"What can I do to convince that drunken brain of yours to come with me easily?"

Hamish rubbed his chin. Finally, he got to his surprisingly steady feet and offered her his hand. "Dance with me."

Isabelle frowned at him, but there was mischief in her eyes. "Fine. One dance, then we're leaving."

The music in the bar hadn't changed much. It was still that sweet, nostalgic French jazz. Isabelle took his hand and placed her other hand on his high shoulder. Hamish swallowed and rested his hand on the small of her back. They were suddenly nervous teenagers on a first date.

"This seems familiar," Isabelle said as they moved to the music.

"Why didn't you come back all those years ago? What happened? You were human then. You aren't now. You haven't aged a day since I saw you."

"A demon I was hunting got the better of me and bit me. I'm still mostly human. I can just do things a little differently now. It happened not long after I left you, and I was so disgusted and frightened by what was happening due to the demon stigmata—I couldn't face you like I was. It's taken me a long time to accept it."

Hamish took the information in, and they moved slowly to the music, oblivious that the next song had started.

"I really did think I was protecting you," she said.

"I was crazy about you, kiddo."

"I'm sorry I hurt you, but I couldn't let anything happen to you. You deserved better than that."

They lapsed into a long silence again. Her body moving against his was driving him crazy, but not enough to stop.

"Please say something."

Hamish hadn't realized his silence was bothering her. "It's okay, Belle. I don't hate you, even if I'm still hurt over it. When you want to tell me more about that demon bite, I want to hear it."

Isabelle gave him a soft smile, but there was an old pain in her eyes. Whatever happened, it had been much worse than she let on, but he knew better than to press her for more.

"I don't want to be mad at you, and I don't want to fight anymore," he added. "What we had was rare, and we should remember that."

"I do remember." Isabelle stepped out of his arms. "But we really should head back now. There's more alcohol at the mansion if you want to keep drinking."

Hamish fought the urge to grab her and kiss her. "Okay, Mom. I'll behave and come quietly."

As Hamish was fixing up his massive tab, the barman whispered, "Now I see why you were drinking so hard."

Hamish gave him a large tip.

He stepped out of the bar and onto the bright street. "So, whose car did you steal?"

"Whoever owns the silver Aston Martin." Isabelle flashed him a grin before opening the driver's side door.

"Trajan might wring your neck for taking it."

"He told me to go find you, and I couldn't put you on the back of my bike. You're too big." Isabelle put her foot on the gas, and they squealed all the way down the road.

The alcohol sloshed around in Hamish's stomach. "Do you always drive like this?"

"Yes. I'm an immortal now, so crashing won't kill me."

"It would hurt like bloody hell, though."

"I know it does. I tested it more than once."

Hamish didn't reply. He'd been in that headspace when he was first cursed as a shifter. Isabelle had gone through her own transformation alone, just like he had, and he wished that he could've been there for her.

When they finally pulled into the driveway, Hamish was almost sick on the shiny dashboard. He stepped out of the car on wobbly legs and would have fallen if Isabelle hadn't caught him by the arm.

"Jesus, you're a heavy bastard." She worked to balance on her heels but slipped on the finished concrete floor, and they ended up in a heap on the ground.

"And you think I'm heavy," Hamish said as they untangled themselves.

She looked so beautiful sprawled on the concrete that before he could stop himself, he leaned over and kissed her. Hamish brushed the sides of her face with the pads of his fingers, marveling at the softness of her skin. When he pulled back, she had a soft, surprised look in her eye.

"Looks like we still got it, old girl," he whispered.

36

THAT NIGHT, ANYA GATHERED them together and told them of her vision of Vasilli, Ladislav, and Ilya. Ladislav had said the gates would break within a month, and she wanted to get there soon to try the magic she'd seen Ilya do.

"If the Darkness takes over the gates, they'll let whatever they like in from Skazki," Honaw said. "But they're idiots to think they will be able to claim both worlds completely without resistance. They might be able to recruit more members in Skazki, but even then, they will have a war on their hands."

"You'd think the Illumination would already be moving to prevent it," Anya replied. "I thought they were meant to stop the Darkness from doing this kind of thing?"

Katya let out a harsh bark of laughter. "Those assholes are clueless."

"Perhaps we should tip them off?" Cerise suggested.

Isabelle scoffed. "Why? So they can capture Anya as soon as they lay eyes on her?"

Cerise shrugged. "They should be the ones to deal with the Darkness, not a small group of Neutrals."

"First, we need to stop arguing," Chayton said before turning to Anya. "If the Darkness is successful in Russia, the idea will spread, and soon, we'll have the slaying of gatekeepers the world over. Gatekeepers are mostly neutral, but they'll be forced to take sides."

Hamish nodded. "So we head to Russia and kick their asses."

Yvan smiled wryly. "Only if Vasilli doesn't find us first. They must know that Völundr failed and will send another team for us."

"Aren't you as cheerful as ever?" Izrayl raised a brow.

"Realistic. The sooner we can get Anya to the gates, the better."

Anya rose early from her warm bed. Isabelle had been training her hard, and though she felt clumsy in comparison to the experienced hunter, she appreciated the lessons. She would have loved to explore the city with Trajan hand in hand, but after her kidnapping and Trajan's subsequent torture, she refused to leave the safety of the mansion.

Security within the mansion had been improved with a brand-new high-tech system. They were on a rotating roster to keep guard at all times and had emergency backpacks ready to go if they had to leave in a hurry. Passports with fake names were being forged for all of them in preparation for their departure. They had to assume the Darkness had ties with border security and Interpol.

Anya was still on farm hours; otherwise, she suspected her 6:30 a.m. training sessions would have been torture. Her days were taken up by self-defense sessions with Isabelle, then magic lessons with Chayton and Honaw. They'd been teaching her how to use her power instinctively and control her surroundings if she fell into another lucid dream. She couldn't stop thinking of the vision she'd had when she was captured.

It lives in your blood with all of our ancestors, ready to help you when you need it, Eikki had said. It had been enough to release her magic. Maybe it could help when she reached the gates.

"Do you think I'll be able to close the gates the way Ilya did in my dream?" Anya asked that afternoon.

"It makes sense that blood is the key," Chayton said. "Your ancestors have been bound to the gates for centuries, and that bond is stronger than you can imagine. Some gatekeepers say their gates call to them like living entities."

Honaw shrugged. "There's only one way to find out, and that's to go to the farm and see what you feel. It might be that you have to do some trial and error to find what way is going to work for you." He brought out his drum and looked at Anya. "You ready to feel for the boundaries of the Land of Dreaming again? Sensing ephemeral boundaries will help you find the ones on your farm."

Anya lay back on the floor, her head on a pillow, and closed her eyes. "I'm ready."

Chayton positioned himself beside her, ready to go in and help pull her out if she went too deep. Honaw beat on the drum in a steady rhythm. Anya's ears vibrated as she focused on the sound until her limbs grew heavy and she disconnected from her body.

In Anya's lucid dreams, they always began in a forest. She figured it was because the forest had marked the boundary between the farm and an otherworld her entire life, even if she hadn't always known it.

Chayton appeared beside her on the edge of a forest. "Good, Anya. You had enough control this time not to plunge straight in." He took her hand. "Tell me what you see."

Anya walked to the forest's edge and placed her hand over the tree line. Her skin trembled as magic swirled impatiently under her skin. The forest cleared, and she saw a signpost.

"There's a crossroads, but instead of four possible paths leading from it, there are eight," she said. "There's something written on the sign, but I can't quite make it out." She stepped in a little too far, and the crossroads dragged her inward.

Chayton grabbed her shoulders, then shouted a word she couldn't make out. She was slammed back into her body. Anya sat up, gasping for air. Chayton groaned beside her.

"What happened this time?" demanded Honaw.

"She stepped over the boundary."

"I only leaned in a little to see what the sign said." Anya rubbed her hands over her arms, her skin cold. "It grabbed me and sucked me in."

Honaw ran an irritated hand over his face before pushing the drum at Chayton. "Okay, it's my turn."

Anya drained her water bottle and settled back against the pillow. It was going to be a long day.

In Moscow, Vasilli lit a thin cigar and poured himself another shot of icy vodka, waiting for his team of mercenaries to make contact. After receiving no word from Völundr, Ladislav had sent Darkness operatives to check on him, and they found his operation in ashes and Anya missing. It took all of Vasilli's self-control not to rub it in the old prick's face. Vasilli was two steps ahead of him anyway, with his own people in place to raid the thanatos's mansion. His phone rang, and he put his drink down to answer it.

"Are you in position?" he asked.

The laptop screen in front of him flickered to life as a camera was turned on in Paris. A group of men in black gear assembled on a roof across from a mansion.

"Yes, sir. Your directives still the same?" Serge asked. "Get the girl and the firebird, kill anyone that gets in the way?"

"Yes, but if Yvan and Anya put up a fight, shoot to maim. Their powers are unpredictable, but a well-placed bullet will slow them down. You know where to take them. I'll join you after it's done."

"Enjoy the show, sir." Serge hung up.

Vasilli picked up his vodka and swirled the ice around his glass. The previous evening, Ladislav had invaded his dreams, showing off as he usually did when he wanted to press his authority. They had visited Anyanka's weakening gates, but Vasilli was well aware that the Darkness already had a team stationed at the village to keep an eye on it. There was nothing magical or intuitive about the information Ladislav "uncovered" during this trip. More likely, he'd received a report and used it as an excuse to remind Vasilli that he could slither into his mind at will.

"Idiot," Vasilli muttered, downing the vodka and pouring another. He leaned back in his chair and smoked, watching as his mercenaries moved in on the mansion.

If the raid was successful, he wouldn't have to put up with Ladislav's bullshit any longer. He would have so much power that no one could stop him from taking the Darkness for himself. Vasilli was looking forward to spilling the blood of those who were loyal to Ladislav. His weak rule couldn't come to an end soon enough.

37

ANYA'S MAGIC WOKE HER with a surge of heat and terror that slammed into her so hard she sat bolt upright. She sucked in a breath. The glass of one of her bedroom windows shattered, and a man dressed in black tactical gear was on her before she could shout. He grabbed her by the shirt and dragged her close, trying to reach her throat. Anya clawed desperately at his hands.

"Trajan!" she screamed. She tried in vain to kick the man away from her.

Trajan was there in seconds, his hands grabbing the man by his shoulders. Her attacker's eyes bulged, and the skin of his face shrank and shriveled as the life was pulled from his cells. Anya pushed this mummifying hands away from her and picked up the knife she bought in Skazki.

"We need to move." Trajan looked through the broken window. "They disabled the security alarms somehow. There will be more in the house."

Hamish crashed through the door, shirtless and carrying a Winchester in each hand. A revolver stuck out of the front of his blood-flecked jeans. "Fucker jumped me. I was going to say sorry for wrecking your carpet, but shit happens. We need to get the others and get outta here."

They rushed down the hallway, Hamish leading the way to Isabelle's room. They had heard the commotion before they got there.

Five men surrounded Isabelle and were closing in on her. One rushed at her with such speed he was a blur. Isabelle flipped over him and drove her knife into his back. As he fell screaming, she jumped again, hitting another in the chest. Hamish shot one in the head, spraying the couches with bits of skull and brain. Trajan killed the other two with a single touch.

Isabelle tightened her gun holsters and slid her long knives down the backs of her boots. "Let's find the others."

Anya froze as a ripple of power flowed through the mansion. "Yvan." She took off down the halls, fire licking her veins. She made it to Cerise's doorway, and someone grabbed her from behind and pressed a cold blade to her throat.

"Let her go, and I'll make your death swift." Cerise's keres form rolled over her skin, her human guise melting away. She looked like an ancient Grecian warrior in black armor, her sword in one hand.

"This little Russian witch is going to be my biggest payday yet." The man jerked Anya tighter against him. "I only want her. The rest will be spared if you let us take her."

Cerise raised her sword. "Not an option."

"You're not going anywhere with Anyanka." Yvan appeared in the doorway. His eyes glowed with the firebird's power, and flames spread out along his hands. He gave Anya a slight nod before shouting, "*Pozhar!*"

Anya exploded into flames, and the man holding her fell backward with a cry. She ducked as Yvan threw a ball of fire that hit the man squarely in the chest. He screamed only once before he burned up, leaving behind a near perfect statue of ash. Anya ran to Yvan and held him tightly. They burned as one for a few seconds before their flames died.

"Thank you." She released him.

"Are you cut?" He lifted her chin with a finger, checking her throat.

"No time for cuddles." Isabelle barged in. "We have to get moving. There's going to be more coming. The Darkness always works in two-team systems. They will have picked up that wave of magic a hundred kilometers away. Every magically sensitive person will have felt it."

"I need to get my runes and drum from the twins' room—"

"We already have them." Honaw dangled her belongings in the air and gave Anya a stern look. "You really have to stop throwing your power like that."

"It was Yvan!" she said quickly.

"His flames went through hers, so it probably doubled the power," Trajan said.

"Can we please argue about magical technicalities later?" Cerise snapped. "Everyone get their stuff and get downstairs. I'm going to get some supplies, and I think you should too, Trajan." She gave him a meaningful look, and he nodded.

Katya and Izrayl were already waiting for them by the time they got downstairs, Izrayl lounging against his car, Katya sitting on the bonnet.

"Never a dull moment with Anya around." Izrayl smiled, but it didn't quite reach his eyes.

"What's the plan?" Katya asked.

"We need to get Russia. To my farm," Anya said.

Trajan took her hand and gave it a comforting squeeze.

Katya nodded. "Russia it is. Into the lion's den."

"You aren't worried, are you, pup?" Izrayl pinched Katya's chin, and she batted his hand away.

"Do I look worried?"

Chayton smiled at Anya. "What an exciting life you lead."

"Reminds me of the old days," Honaw added wistfully. "Something about people trying to kill you really makes you feel alive."

Anya cringed. "Thanks, guys. That makes me feel so much better about putting your lives at risk."

"Don't worry about it." Chayton patted her shoulder. "That was some pretty impressive magic you did with Yvan. We're proud of you."

"Be proud when I close the gates." Anya sounded colder than she wanted. Now that they'd temporarily fended off the enemy, the shock of being attacked in her sleep and nearly having her throat cut was creeping up on her. She was doing her best not to show it. What she needed now was to get in the car with Trajan on one side of her and Yvan on the other, and have a nice drink of vodka as they put the city behind them.

Across the garage, Cerise tossed her bag into the back of her red Jaguar and climbed into the driver's seat, her human form back in place. "When you're ready, darlings!" She looked especially edgy as she lit a cigarette.

Yvan put his bag in her car and took the front seat. Anya's brow furrowed, and her urge to get drunk intensified as a strange barb of jealousy stabbed at her.

"I know you want us all to stick together, but I'm taking my bike," Isabelle said to Trajan. "There's no way I'm going to let some filthy lackeys of Ladislav get it."

Trajan put his hands up in surrender. "I wouldn't dream of asking you to leave it behind. Hamish can ride with me and Anya."

Isabelle's motorcycle roared to life, making them all jump. "Today, people! They are coming! I can feel it."

The twins climbed in with Katya and Izrayl while Trajan led Anya to a black Land Rover SUV. Hamish sprawled out on the back seat, and Anya sat in the front after shoving her bag onto the floor.

Trajan closed her door and strode around to the driver's side. "When we get to the border, we'll put the cars on a train. I don't want to get to the end of Russia with no transport. There are too many of us to carry now."

After their trip from Romania, none of them were keen on hitching rides through cold Eastern European countries, and Anya's farm was remote enough as it was. Trajan didn't believe in holding with the speed limit, and neither did the people they were with. Anya didn't care how fast they went. She wanted to be out of France before anything else came looking for her.

Aramis surveyed the wreckage and bodies in the mansion with as much passivity as he could. He opened his phone and dialed a number.

"I'm going to need a cleanup crew before the police arrive," he said, then hung up.

This was the third house they'd investigated in a fortnight, and he knew they were connected. He just didn't know how.

The second house turned out to be another building owned by the Darkness. Unlike the first fire, it had been lit by magic. The residue of fresh magic had been intense, and Aramis had known just by the feel of it that it had been started by Yanka's descendant. It had taken immense self-control to stay on the site, let alone the case.

"At least ten remains so far, sir," a faceless man mumbled through his balaclava. "The magic is off the charts again, and it was used to kill. There are four different magical signatures, but one in particular was on a larger scale."

"The same as the last building?"

"Yes, General. But I think it was more controlled this time around. There, it was an explosion, but here, I believe it was directed at the one target."

"Do we know who this target was?"

"Yes, but you should come take a look."

Aramis followed the man up the stairs to the remains. He had seen many strange things, but the man's perfect ashen figure was definitely a surprise. It reminded him of the bodies they had found under the ash of Pompeii.

"You can see why I wanted to show you. It creeped the hell out of our men when they found it."

"I can imagine." Aramis held out a hand to the victim's face. Without touching it, he closed his eyes. Her magic was all over it, but intermixed was something older and stronger that had killed. Whispering under his breath, he drew on his own magic, and the last seconds of the victim's life flashed through his mind.

There was a dark-haired man with a firebird glowing on his chest. The girl in the victim's arms ignited in a burst of flame. He dropped her, and she fell to the floor. Her face turned, and Aramis jolted out of the vision with a cry.

"Are you all right, sir?"

Aramis breathed heavily but nodded. "I'm fine. It's time we make contact with these people. This situation is getting out of control."

"With all due respect, sir, you know the family's history. Do you think she'll listen to us or blow us all to pieces?"

Aramis smiled grimly. "We'll find out soon enough."

PART THREE
THE BROKEN GATES

38

ANYA FIRST NOTICED THE tall stranger watching her at the Slovakian border. It wasn't unusual to see fair people in this part of Europe, but the stranger was striking with his silver hair, fairer even than hers. His blue eyes were made bluer by the navy leather trench coat he wore, on which he had the collar turned up.

Anya had glimpsed him for only a split second in the dining car before someone stepped in front of him, and then he was gone. He had looked directly at her, though, and in that second, her magic flared like a fever.

In the Czech Republic, they boarded a train and had their vehicles stored in the cargo carriages. Anya had always felt claustrophobic on trains, and the closer she came to Russia, the more agitated she became. After the first few days of traveling, Anya's body clock was so entirely out of whack that she lost the concept of time.

Trajan understood her anxiety and was doing his best to distract and calm her. He told her stories of her relatives he'd known and read books aloud as she lay in his arms. Anya suspected theirs was the strangest relationship in the world, but whatever it was, it was enough for her.

"Do you know that you are drinking too much again?" Yvan said behind her.

Anya sat in a booth in what she called the "vodka carriage"—the only place she could successfully hide and that conveniently had its own bar.

"And?" Anya made a point of taking a long swallow of her drink while keeping full eye contact.

Yvan's eyes narrowed at the challenge, and he came around to sit down opposite her. He had been playing cards and arguing playfully with Cerise for hours before, and while Anya was happy they were getting along, something about it bothered her. She didn't know where the streak of jealousy came from. She was with Trajan; she shouldn't care what Yvan did with anyone. But she still couldn't help the overprotective impulse that rose up in her.

"Is there a reason for all the drinking?" Yvan asked.

"Boredom. Nerves. Magic bugging me. You name it."

"Getting drunk every day won't help any of that, and you know it."

"How's Cerise?" Anya asked.

Yvan's eyebrows drew together in confusion. "Cerise? She's fine. Why ask me?"

"You two seem to be getting awfully friendly."

"I'm awfully friendly with everybody. How is your human-thanatos relationship working out?"

"It's working just fine."

Yvan smiled pleasantly at her. "How nice for you."

"It is, yes."

"If it's so great, how come you're hiding in the back of the train drinking by yourself?"

Anya scowled but couldn't think of a reply.

Yvan sighed and helped himself to her vodka. "I'm not going to argue with you, *shalost*. I just think there should be someone in your life who's not going to indulge you because they think you're the chosen one." He drained his vodka in one gulp. "You should be using the time on this train to practice your magic with Honaw and Chayton, not drinking the entire vodka supply. Get focused and stop wallowing." Yvan hesitated before he bent down and kissed the top of her head. "And get some sleep occasionally."

Yvan left her sitting there, drunk and ashamed. He was disappointed, and that killed her more than anything he could have said.

As soon as the carriage door shut, Anya burst into tears. She should've just told him the truth: she was drinking because the closer they got to Russia, the more afraid she became. Anya might have seen Ilya shut the gates in her vision, but she had no idea if that method would work for her. She didn't know what the words were that he'd spoken. She could turn up and cut herself to pieces, and the gate could remain open. *Chosen one, my ass.*

Anya ran the sleeves of her gray sweater down her face to wipe her tears away. When she dropped her arms back into her lap, she spotted the stranger again—tall, impossibly fair, and looking at her with a mixture of horror and surprise. He went to open the door to the carriage, but then stopped, turned around, and disappeared along the aisle.

Anya's chest filled with instant pressure, and she fought to push down the magic threatening to break out of her. Shaking and drunk, she got to her feet and hurried back to her compartment. *He probably didn't want to drink in there because you were bawling your eyes out.* Her surge of magic was surely just a co-incidence.

Over the next few days, Anya spent her time with Chayton and Honaw, as Yvan had suggested. They worked on teaching her how to use the drum she'd been given. Like Baba Zosia, they didn't dare touch it in case the symbols changed. They also tried dream-walking a few more times, but every time, Anya was drawn to something she shouldn't be and was pulled back out.

Anya wanted to tell them about the silver man she'd seen who had disrupted her magic. If it wasn't for the fact that she had been drunk both times she'd seen him, she probably would have.

No, she would keep the stranger to herself, at least until she saw him sober. Then Anya would send Isabelle and Katya to rough him up for scaring her.

"What is it?" Trajan's face came into focus in front of her.

They were eating in one of the dining cars, and the noise of clanking cutlery and people talking was almost deafening.

"Nothing, just thinking."

Trajan looked at her over the top of his glasses. "Are you and Yvan talking to each other yet?"

"I don't know what you mean."

"Come now, Anya. You haven't spoken to him all day. That's some kind of record. Usually, you two are thick as thieves. Did you have an argument?"

"Something like that. We'll get over it. Don't worry."

"I'm not worried, nor am I complaining about having you to myself for once. But still, don't let some squabble become an incurable problem. You care for each other too much for that."

Anya smiled, because only Trajan would say it like that: *an incurable problem.* He wore a burgundy scarf around his neck that set off his eyes and contrasted boldly with his dark curls. He pushed his glasses up the bridge of his nose, a nervous habit Anya didn't think he was even aware of.

Something pale flashed over his shoulder. Anya's phantom stranger sat at one of the end tables. Her breath caught, and magic rushed through her veins, trying to break free of her. It was like it wanted to reach out and touch him. She dug her nails into her palms and tried to hold it in so she didn't set herself on fire again.

The silver man looked at Trajan the way a gardener looks at a slug. He noticed Anya watching him, and his expression relaxed. He inclined his head in greeting, then tucked the paper he'd been reading under his arm and departed from the carriage. It wasn't until he was out of sight that Anya finally felt like she could breathe again.

"I think you're right." She got to her feet. "I need to go speak to Yvan."

Trajan opened his mouth to say something, but she grabbed him by the soft fabric of his scarf and pulled him in for a quick kiss before hurrying after her silver man.

By the time Anya moved into the next carriage, the stranger was gone, as if he'd vanished into thin air. *What the hell?*

Anya glanced over her shoulder a few times as she hurried to Yvan's compartment. Without knocking, she barged in to find the firebird in full flaming glory perched on the metal bar of the bed. Swearing, she pulled the door shut behind her before a curious passenger looked in.

Anya sat down on the bed beside it. "Hey, is Yvan in there? I really need to talk to him."

It cooed at her, and Anya got the distinct impression she was getting a cold shoulder. She released just a bit of her magic, and her hand lit up with its own fire. Careful not to startle it, she gently stroked the bird's back.

"I know he's annoyed with me, but this is important."

It ignored her, and too tired to fight, she lay down to wait.

She looks so peaceful when she sleeps, the firebird said. It looked down at Anya as her hand burned with magic, her flames dancing with its own as though they were one. Deep inside of it, Yvan squirmed. *If I let you out, do you promise not to upset her? Look how tired she is. She is fading under the strain. You are meant to be the one to stop that from happening. You promised to protect her.*

Let me out so I can! Yvan shouted.

The firebird's wing touched her cheek before it started to change. Yvan tried to hold in the cries of pain so as not to wake her, and he shifted until he lay naked and panting on the thin carpet. He looked up uncertainly, but Anya hadn't moved.

Yvan got to his feet and pulled on a pair of jeans and a shirt. The firebird was right. She did look drained. He had been harsh with her, but at least she'd stopped drinking so much. Yvan wondered if Trajan knew she had been sneaking off to the bar when everyone was sleeping. Probably not. Trajan could be clueless about the most mundane of things.

It's not up to him to take care of her. It's up to you.

Yvan ignored the firebird as he placed a spare blanket over Anya. He brushed her cheek with his fingertips before he sat down on the floor and rested his back against the bed.

Anya moved in her sleep, and her arm flopped down beside him. As he was tucking it back in, her fingers tightened around his and held them. Yvan left his hand there for a long moment, a sense of guilty weakness washing over him. Once she had settled, he carefully unlocked their fingers and pulled his hand back. He wasn't in the mood to torture himself.

Yvan remained preoccupied by his thoughts until Anya roused.

"Nice to see you," she said and rubbed her eyes.

"Sorry if I woke you."

"You didn't." She yawned. "I didn't mean to fall asleep. It just kind of happened."

"You looked like you needed it." Yvan moved to sit down on the edge of the bed beside her. "I'm sorry if I upset you last night."

"Don't be sorry. You were right, after all, and we have bigger problems." Anya sat up. "I think there's someone on the train who's following me."

Yvan cocked his head. "How do you know it's not just another passenger?"

"I thought that at first, but his gaze is too direct and he seems…aware. He's really tall, silver hair, and whenever I see him, my magic starts dancing like a little kid hungry for his attention." Anya toyed with the end of her braid.

"Have you told anyone else about him?"

"Just you. I know the others would probably freak out and start checking every compartment, thinking he was going to attack me."

Yvan did his best to hide that that was what he wanted to do too. "True. We seem to have collected a trigger-happy group who would rough up a passenger before asking questions." He managed his concern and tried for the level approach Anya came to him for. "He hasn't said anything to you, right? So he really could just be a random passenger."

"I want to think that, except how my magic reacts when I see him… I don't think he's Darkness, but he's something else. It's like my magic wants to reach out and touch him. It's never done that before."

"How do you know he isn't one of the Darkness?"

"I don't, but he doesn't feel bad. I don't think my magic would have reacted like that if he was. I've met both Vasilli and Völundr, and I never experienced
anything like it."

"He might just think you're too pretty to be drinking alone so often."

Anya snorted. "Yvan, if he was going to hit on me, he would have done it
by now. Maybe he's another magic user and is curious?"

"Do you want me to get Izrayl and do a search for him? See what he's up to?"

Anya pushed her hands through her tousled hair. "Yes? No. No, don't. This
could all be my nerves over closing the gates messing with my head."

"Okay, but if he approaches you and is threatening, blast the hell out of him
with your magic. I'll help you clean up the body afterward."

Anya laughed. "Thanks."

"I'm not joking." He really wasn't. "In the meantime, I'll keep an eye out
for someone matching his description and see what the firebird thinks of him.
He could simply be another magic user who is curious about you, but even in
that case, I don't love it." Yvan didn't want to be an overprotective asshole, but
he couldn't help it. "Maybe you shouldn't go anywhere by yourself, especially at
night. If you want to drink, come get me first."

Anya rolled her eyes. "I would, but your frown of disapproval would kill
my buzz."

Aramis watched Anya leave her male companion's compartment. Her magical
aura burned as bright as the sun. As he followed her, she glanced around as if she
sensed his presence. Her trailing magic left a red signature clinging to surfaces
wherever it landed. Any magically adept person could follow her if they wanted
to, which was going to make it harder to protect her. And there was no doubt in
his mind that she would need protection. Anya was so much like Yanka that any
of her old rivals would kill her on sight for that alone.

Aramis thought he would be able to perform this assignment with relative
ease, even with his history with her family, but one glance at those green eyes and
pale hair, and he had to fight not to go to her and tell her everything. It wasn't
Anya who he saw, though. It was Yanka. *She's dead.* But he could stop Anya from
meeting the same horrible fate.

Anya was already suspicious of him, and she had many powerful body-guards. He'd caught a glimpse of Isabelle Blackwood on the train—a legend even among the Illumination.

Then there was the thanatos, who was obviously her lover. Anger had washed through Aramis when he'd first seen them together. To get involved with a death spirit was to court death itself. Anya didn't seem nervous or repulsed, yet she would have to know what he truly was. How had she gotten so involved with all these creatures?

Aramis knew he was going to have to wait to get her alone to approach her. He'd almost done it the night he saw her drinking alone, but then those familiar green eyes had cut him to pieces and his courage failed him. She had to be approached carefully so she didn't spook before she heard him out. Aramis didn't like the thought of using compulsion magic on her to earn her trust, but he didn't see another choice.

Before leaving the carriage, Aramis gave a casual flick of his hand, and the trails of her scarlet magic faded away.

39

IT WAS AFTER MIDNIGHT when Anya pulled on her jeans and jacket and stumbled into the corridor. She'd felt better since she got some sleep and had a talk with Yvan, but when she tried to go back to her own bed, she was left wide awake and staring at the ceiling. Trains were never really silent, and no matter how hard she tried, she couldn't block out the clacking of the track beneath or the hum of the other passengers. Trajan was a creature of the night and had left her to sleep, but she'd twisted herself back into a ball of worry that had been momentarily eased by Yvan's presence.

Anya caught her reflection in the train windows and shuddered. Her hair was a wreck, and there were dark circles under her eyes. She pulled her hair back in a ponytail and rubbed her cheeks to get some color into them.

Pull yourself together, Anya.

She contemplated waking Yvan as he had asked her to do, but she didn't want to worry him. What could she say? That she was scared that she wouldn't be able to shut the gates and that she would fail them all? That she didn't think she was ever going to be able to take on Vasilli like Ilya's prophecy had claimed? Yvan already knew these things, and one thing Anya hated more than talking about her feelings was burdening someone else with them.

She made her way through the carriages to the bar. The tired barman smiled at her and handed her a glass of vodka before going back to reading his book. Anya sat down in one of the booths and watched the stars flash by above her. Her magic flared, and she looked up to see the silver man opening the door of the carriage. Anya glanced over at the barman, but he had fallen asleep on the counter. With no other doors out, she was trapped.

The stranger's blue eyes moved over her as he walked past and helped himself to the bar. "It would seem we are the only two people who can't sleep," he said in one of the most unusual voices Anya had ever heard—gentle but deep, with a touch of gravel and a lilting, unidentifiable accent.

"Trains are too noisy for me to sleep," Anya replied. He could just be a passenger. A normal, human passenger she'd just happened to notice. *You're not really dumb enough to believe that, are you?*

"I'm claustrophobic, so trains aren't my favorite form of travel either." He sat down opposite her. "Forgive me. I am Aramis."

"Like the musketeer?"

Aramis gave a pained sigh. "So I have been told."

"Anya."

Aramis offered her his hand, and hesitantly, she took it. Instantly, her magic flared and rushed to her palm. She tried to yank her hand back, but Aramis held it firm.

"Let me go! I don't want to hurt you!" she cried.

"You won't hurt me, Anya. Try to relax."

Her magic burst from her palm in two translucent, scarlet ribbons that twisted around Aramis's forearm. It held on to him, caressing him like a pet. Then, slowly, it retracted back into Anya and disappeared under her skin. He let go of her hand, and she clutched it to her chest.

Her power had never materialized like that before. It was rather always a sensation like static or fire. "What the hell are you?"

"I'm with the Illumination. I've come to protect you," Aramis said.

Anya tipped her head back and groaned. "Just what I need. What the hell do you people want from me?"

"We don't want anything from you, but I can help you if you let me."

"Why? I've done nothing wrong, and you don't even know me."

"That's where you are wrong, Anyanka. We do know you. The Illumination has kept files on your family since Yanka crossed into this world. We know who your parents were, how they met before you were born. Unfortunately, your grandfather kept the extent of your powers a secret from us."

"I wonder why he would do that?"

"Perhaps he was concerned we would take you away from him for proper training."

"Or he didn't want you using me like every other bastard wants to. The Darkness, the Illumination, the Powers. From what I can tell, you're all the same."

"We are on the side of good."

"That depends on which side you're standing on."

Aramis's blue eyes narrowed. "You are terribly stubborn, aren't you?"

"Yes, I am. And I'm extremely suspicious and not very trusting."

"I can tell." His lips curled up in amusement, and Anya began to feel the anger drain out of her. "Regardless, I have a team on board to assist if you're attacked."

"I don't need any more babysitters." Anya got up and went to the bar to get the bottle of vodka. "I've got plenty enough as it is, and I'm not interested in joining the Illumination either."

The bartender was out cold and slumped over the sink. Anya looked over to Aramis. He was tense, like he was ready to step in her way if she tried to bolt.

"Was this your doing?" she asked.

"I don't want us to be disturbed. He won't be waking anytime soon. Your file said you had a drinking problem." He looked pointedly at the bottle in her hand.

"My drinking is none of your business, just like everything else in that file, which you can shove up your ass." Anya sat back down and filled her cup.

Aramis took the bottle and filled his own. "I must admit, there wasn't a terrible lot of information about you. What we found in Paris will make an interesting addition."

"What is it you think you found in Paris?" Anya's heartbeat picked up. If they had been to Trajan's house, they would have seen the bodies they'd left behind.

"A man had been turned into a perfect ash sculpture. Only magic could have done such a thing."

"It was self-defense."

"I have no doubt. Can I ask who he was?"

"I don't know. I assume he was with the Darkness."

"Why is that?"

Anya's mouth opened of its own accord. "Because they're hunting me. First, they kidnapped and tortured me and my friend. Then, they broke into our house and tried to kill us. That man had a knife at my throat. He had it coming."

"How did you escape them when they kidnapped you? By burning their headquarters down?"

"How did you know about that?" She hated that she sounded afraid instead of angry.

"Your magic residue was all over it. Tell me what happened."

Anya folded her arms. "Why should I?"

"Because I'm trustworthy." Aramis smiled as he touched her hand.

Her power purred as a tingling warmth spread from him and over her skin. "What are you?" she whispered. "Why does my magic react to you like this?" She fought down tears as her magic was overwhelmed by the power pouring into her. "You want me to trust you, but you won't even tell me who you really are."

"I told you. My name is Aramis, and I am with the Illumination."

"What else are you?"

"If I tell you, will you tell me how you came to be on this train? Will you trust me and believe that I'm here to help you?" He stroked the soft underside of her wrist, his magic brushing against her again.

"Yes, I'll tell you everything," she found herself saying. A warm mist rolled over her, and the incessant flickering of power under her skin calmed.

"Very well. I am Álfr," said Aramis.

"An elf?" A cynical laugh escaped her lips before she could check it. "An elf with a French name."

"I'm not an elf like in your fairy tales. I am Álfr. It's Norse. As for my French name, Aramis is the closest I could get to my real name in the human tongue."

"Prove it. Prove that you're an elf...or Álfr. The legends call you the Fair Folk, but you look like your typical handsome thirty-something human man."

"It's a glamor. So I can blend in." He said it with such sincerity that Anya found herself believing him, but the cynical part of her still won out.

"Show me."

Aramis sighed, and a rush of power poured from him. The change started at the top of his head and flowed down his body in a ripple effect.

Anya had seen good-looking men before. Yvan was a fine example of male beauty—strongly built, long-limbed, and you could see him riding a horse and using a sword as well. Trajan was one step closer to refinement—well-groomed, well-spoken, and elegant in manners, but he was still human or human-shaped, with the slight flaws that came with it.

The man who sat opposite her was so far beyond anything she'd ever seen that her head filled with clichés: eyes as blue as sapphires, skin as pale as snow. Ethereal. Angelic. But none of those descriptions could ever explain Aramis. Yes, his eyes were blue, but they were so deep and so clear, Anya couldn't help but think that this blue was the first shade of blue God had ever created. The whiteness of his skin was unmarred and flawless. There was a sheen to it under the fluorescent lights, as though crushed pearls had been rubbed into it. He seemed to be lit from the inside. High cheekbones gave strong structure to his deep-set eyes, a straight nose, and smiling mouth. All of this was framed by thick, glossy silver-white hair. His true face wasn't terrifying like Tuoni's had been, but it was just as otherworldly.

"Wow. You're like Thranduil if he decided to slum it with humans." Anya reached across and touched his cheek in fascination, then pulled back quickly.

"Who?" he asked.

"Never mind," she said, embarrassed that she had spoken the thought aloud.

Aramis's human guise slid back into place. "Do you believe me now?"

"I believe you." She swallowed hard. "Is that why my magic acted like it did? Because you are Álfr?"

"What your *fródleikr*—your magic—did was quite unusual. We are a magical race, but I've never experienced that before. It's as if your magic recognized my true nature." Aramis brushed his fingers along the top of her hand, leaving trails of warmth. "Tell me what has happened, Anyanka. You won't regret trusting me."

"I better not, for your sake. I have lots of protectors already, and none of them are fans of the Illumination."

Aramis said nothing else but looked at her expectantly. Anya found she *wanted* to tell him despite her suspicious nature, so with a deep breath, she started with Tuoni's visit and moved on to how her world had turned its head. An empty bottle later, Aramis sat across from her wide-eyed.

"If your vision of Ladislav and Vasilli at the gates was correct, what the Darkness plans to do violates the treaty and could completely destroy Russia. It's a risk the Illumination can't take." His lips pressed into a thin line as he mulled this over. "Also, I now know more than ever that we need to protect you. Your power contains infinite potential, and you'll always be a target because of it."

"You can't be so naïve to think that the Illumination won't try to recruit me or whatever it is you do. I don't want to join them, and I doubt they will help me without me doing so." Anya folded her arms. "You won't convince me otherwise."

"I won't lie to you. The Illumination wants me to apprehend you—"

"I would like to see them try. The Darkness tried it and look at how it ended for them."

"I'm not threatening you, Anya," Aramis said. "You're the only one who can close the gate. They won't make a move until you do. The things they could teach you—"

"Stop it. I'm not interested. If you follow us to Russia, I can't stop you, but I won't be taken as a hostage again without a fight."

"There wouldn't be any force involved. It would be for your protection more than anything else." Aramis's gaze implored her to believe him.

"Yeah, I really doubt that. From what I hear of the Illumination, they aren't much better than the Darkness."

"Then your sources are incorrect. I won't let anything happen to you, Anya. Just let me help you and your companions. As for what happens after you close the gates…I'll endeavor to change my superiors' minds about it. Unless it is what you want. The Illumination isn't your enemy, and neither am I."

Aramis ran his fingers over the back of her hand. Anya didn't know why she trusted him or what he was saying, but she did. "It will take a lot of convincing to get the others to work with the Illumination, but I'll try."

Aramis smiled easily at her, and she found herself smiling back. She liked him, and he knew it.

"You should go off to bed. You need to sleep, and they'll panic if they can't find you," Aramis said finally.

Anya chuckled. "You aren't wrong about—"

The carriage door opened with a bang. Anya spun around just as Trajan stepped inside.

"It looks like they've already found us." Aramis got to his feet as black smoke began to pour from Trajan and his thanatos wings stretched from his back.

"Trajan, stop. He's a friend!" Anya shouted.

But the brown from Trajan's eyes melted into red, and Aramis's position changed to the defensive. Trajan vanished, then was on him in a heartbeat. Aramis glowed, and with a deafening crack, Trajan was thrown backward onto the stained carpet. Anya pushed Aramis out of the way and hurried to where Trajan lay.

"Are you hurt?" Anya fell to her knees beside him and checked him over. He looked up at her in a daze, blood trickling from his nose. She turned to glare at Aramis. "What the hell did you do to him?"

Aramis still hadn't taken his eyes off Trajan. "I defended myself."

Trajan sat up, clutching his head. "What the hell is he?"

"I am Álfr, and you will keep your distance," Aramis commanded. The power in his voice made Anya's hair stand on end.

"Álfr…"

"Long story," Anya muttered. "I told you not to attack him, Trajan."

"I didn't mean to. I saw him and…" Trajan seemed to be at a loss for words.

"It doesn't matter."

Trajan climbed to his feet. "I apologize," he said to Aramis.

"Accepted." Aramis gave him a nod. "I have to check on the security detail. Anya, please talk to your people and find out if an alliance is possible." He fixed her with his impossibly blue gaze and added more gently, "I will be close."

She nodded. "I'll find you."

As Aramis walked past her, his hand brushed hers, leaving her magic burning.

Anya shook her shoulders and focused on Trajan, who was still looking a bit dazed, rather than the way Aramis could ignite her magic. She wrapped an arm around his waist to guide him back to their compartment. In the hall, they were met by the twins and almost collided with Yvan.

Honaw moved to help shoulder Trajan's weight. "What's happened?"

Yvan rubbed his eyes. "How did I know you would be at the center of this newest disturbance, Anya?"

"Just help me get Trajan inside. He nearly had his brain knocked out." Anya was glad for the help. She was tipsy and shaky from the vodka and strange exchange with Aramis. Now that she was away from him, she couldn't believe the things she had revealed. Her knees wobbled, and Yvan grabbed her arm to steady her.

"It looks like you need to sit down. Some water couldn't hurt either."

Anya was placed next to Trajan on the narrow bed. Yvan fetched bottles of water while the twins positioned themselves on the carpet and eyed Anya expectantly.

Trajan slumped against the wall along the bed. "Tell them, Anya."

She didn't tell them that she thought he had used magic on her, but she told them of Aramis and the offer to work with the Illumination.

"Álfr…" Yvan shook his head. "Even in Skazki, they are a myth. I wonder how they ended up living here."

"There are two Álfr colonies in America that we know of," Chayton said. "We leave them alone. They leave us alone. Their existence isn't entirely secret, but they stick together and guard their privacy. We don't know much about them. It's surprising that one is working for the Illumination. They are highly magical, of course, but they don't get involved in the affairs of others." His thick brows drew together. "Strange."

"Another thing," Honaw said, "is that you'll have to restrain your nature, Trajan. Álfr are unlike humans or supernaturals. As a thanatos, you are Death, and they are pure life. You will always repel each other."

"What did he hit me with?" Trajan rubbed his chest.

"I don't know, but it was powerful enough to send us running." Honaw bit his lip. "There's something more pressing to worry about than that, though."

"What?" Anya asked.

"How are we going to convince Isabelle and the others to become allies with the Illumination—even temporarily? We're all neutral for a reason, and the Illumination isn't a charity. Their help will come with a price."

Anya rubbed her arms, trying to wipe the feeling of Aramis's magic off her skin. "I guess we'll find out."

40

IT TOOK UNTIL THE following evening for Anya to get everyone to agree to at least hear Aramis out. Anya was edgy but nowhere near what the others were. Trajan stayed closer than usual, one hand resting on her at all times. There was no way Anya could have talked them out of going unarmed, so she didn't even try. Katya and Isabelle appeared bulky beneath their overcoats, and Anya could only guess how many weapons they had between them. They didn't trust that they weren't walking into a trap, but they were willing to do it because they believed in Anya's judgement of Aramis. It made Anya queasy knowing that they were willing to make themselves vulnerable because she asked them too. She couldn't properly make sense of it herself, but she knew Aramis was important. She could feel it in her blood and in her magic.

Only the twins seemed calm and casual in their dark jeans and matching black T-shirts. Both wore their hair out, making it even harder to tell which was which. Their magical signature was the only thing Anya could tell them apart by, and she was glad they had taught her how to feel it out. To anyone else, they would be two very tall, very serious-looking, very identical men. The twins were the only ones who had any knowledge of the Álfr in the real world, and while Katya and Isabelle had scoffed at what they knew to be a myth, the others were curious. Anya suspected the hunters only agreed to the meeting because they wanted to confirm that Aramis was really Álfr.

"You two are the only ones acting normal tonight," Anya said to Chayton and Honaw.

They both smiled.

"We're not worried because you have enough power to take them all out if they threaten us," Chayton said. "Besides, it sounds like this Álfr is a fan of yours."

"I don't know about a fan, but he seems to genuinely think that the Illumination wants to help."

"Maybe Aramis wants to help, but that's not the Illumination's style," Honaw said.

Anya bit the inside of her cheek. "I don't think my magic would have reacted the way it did if I couldn't trust him."

"So trust your Álfr, but don't think for a minute that the others with him wouldn't betray you."

As they made their way to Aramis's carriage, Anya could only imagine what the other passengers thought of the group moving through the train. They looked like train robbers—especially Hamish in his long coat, boots, and shiny cowboy belt buckle. They were all tense and on guard. Anya wanted to remind them that they had all been traveling on the same train for quite a while now, so if the Illumination wanted to attack, they'd had plenty of opportunities already. One glance at Isabelle's face, and Anya decided not to mention it.

Two burly men in black guarded the doors to Aramis's private carriage. Izrayl and Hamish eyed them warily. There wasn't a lot of room to fight on the train, but Anya was sure they would have liked to pick one regardless.

"There will be no weapons past this point," said one guard. He had a thick Cockney English accent and a severely crooked nose.

"Leave our weapons with you? You're fucking dreaming mate," Hamish said, as eloquent as ever.

As they argued, Anya reached out with her magical senses like the twins had taught her. She found Aramis's presence glowing in her mind like a silvery star. It moved toward her, and then the doors behind the guards opened. Aramis stood in the threshold, serious and imposing. He was dressed casually in dark jeans and a gray shirt and was leaner under the blue coat he wore the previous night than Anya had expected.

"Is there a problem?" he asked.

"They are refusing to disarm," the guard replied.

"You can hardly blame them. Let them pass."

"I don't think that's a good idea, sir."

"Noted. Now let them pass." Aramis turned and walked back into the carriage.

Hamish lifted his middle finger at the guard as they filed in, and Anya was sure Isabelle hissed at one.

The carriage was roomy, with lounges and mismatched seats lining the walls. A massive desk sat at the far end, stacked with papers and a small laptop. There were two other men in the room waiting for them.

"You'll have to forgive the suspicious nature of my men," said Aramis as he sat down. He indicated that they should make themselves comfortable. Isabelle and Katya remained standing, but Aramis didn't seem to mind one way or another.

"Suspicion keeps you alive," said one of the strangers.

Aramis introduced them as Petyr and Ruben, commanders of the two Illumination teams on board. Ruben looked like he was in his fifties, with steel-gray hair and a frown like thunder clouds. Petyr at least tried to smile at them. Anya followed Aramis's lead and introduced her companions. When she reached Isabelle, Ruben grunted, and Aramis glared at him.

Isabelle ignored this and trained her gaze on Aramis. "So, what do you want?"

"We're here to help Anya. She explained the predicament with the gate, so we plan travel to Russia with you and assist in stopping anything from entering our world that shouldn't—and, of course, to stop the Darkness from taking control of the gates and destroying all of Russia."

Isabelle didn't look impressed. "I've never seen an Illuminator get their hands dirty out of the goodness of their heart."

Ruben scoffed. "At least we aren't baby killers. Right, Blackwood?"

Fury flashed over Isabelle's face, along with something else. If Anya didn't know her any better, she would have thought it was fear.

Isabelle took one step forward. "The fuck did you just say to me?"

Despite Aramis's warning glare, Ruben pressed on. "I was there that night thirty years ago. We had to clean up the little limbs of the children you ripped apart."

"That is enough," Aramis said, his voice like ice, but Ruben didn't seem to hear him.

"We were the ones who had to bury them. All those poor, innocent kids, who died in terror." Ruben got to his feet and moved toward Isabelle as he spoke. "Yet for all our efforts, the culprit remains unpunished. You fled, only to reappear years later, hailed as the greatest hunter in the world. How ironic."

"Hold your tongue, you fucking spark plug, or I'll rip it out." Isabelle's tone was so cold, Anya's skin broke out in goose bumps. She didn't think being called a "spark plug" was so bad, but the commanders bristled with offense.

Ruben pointed a finger at Isabelle. "I've no doubt that, in time, you'll show your true self, and we'll have to take you out. It's a dark day for the Illumination that we make an alliance with such a filthy monster."

Ruben only had a second to gloat before there was a blur of movement, and he was on the floor, blood pouring from his mouth where his jaw had been shattered. The attack hadn't come from where anyone expected. Hamish stood over him, fists still balled and poised for another assault.

"Don't you ever speak to her like that again," he said, his voice low and menacing. "If you do, all your specialist training won't amount to shit."

Isabelle moved to stand over the bleeding commander, one hand resting on the butt of her pistol. With the other, she reached up, jerked the shoulder of her coat down, and pulled her shirt away from her body so they could all see the mangled scar over her throat and shoulder. Ruben looked up at her with round eyes.

"I didn't kill those children. They weren't the only people who were attacked that night," she spat. "This is such a waste of my fucking time." Isabelle turned and headed for the door, yanking it open with enough force that it vibrated on its hinges.

"Stop her!" Ruben struggled to get up.

The two guards tried to grab Isabelle but caught air as she ducked. One made to grab her again, swinging low. Isabelle caught his arm one-handed and twisted it back, splintering the bones, and drove her other fist into his face. She kept walking.

"Hamish—" Katya began, but he was already heading for the door.

Ruben cursed as he held a wad tissues to his face, trying to staunch the blood seeping from his broken nose.

"You are relieved of your command," Aramis said. "At the next stop, you will remove yourself from the train and make your way back to London, where the Council can decide what to do with you. It's no wonder these people mistrust us when they have you for an example." He turned his sharp blue eyes on Petyr. "If you have a problem with our alliance with Anya and her people, I suggest you leave as well. If you stay, keep your mouth shut, or I'll seal it permanently."

Without protest, Ruben removed himself from the carriage, while Petyr remained.

After an hour of discussion, the uneasiness between Aramis and Anya's group began to alleviate, but Katya's guarded expression didn't change. Aramis answered all their questions without hesitation and in detail. Cerise chained-smoked to the point that Aramis wordlessly retrieved an ashtray for her. She had dressed up for the occasion, claiming that while some people wore weapons as armor, she wore fur and heels. It seemed to be working on Petyr, who was struggling not to look at her.

"We're getting some people in place to check the farm before we arrive," said Aramis. "If the Darkness is already there, we'll know about it. The last time we picked up on Vasilli was a week ago in Moscow."

"And what if they are there?" asked Anya.

"If they attack, we can defend you, but we can't act until they do. I won't break the treaty. There's a chance that our presence might be enough of a deterrent and encourage them to leave you alone."

Anya nodded. Her magic thrummed incessantly under her skin just from being near Aramis. It was almost as if her magic had a crush on him, and she fought the urge to start scratching at her arms like a junkie. His effect on her was that strong. The previous night, as soon as his magic had touched her, she'd felt like telling him everything he wanted to know.

Her eyes widened as she lost track of the current conversation.

Oh, Anya. You are so stupid.

Aramis hadn't just let his magic touch hers; he had been using it *on* her. Her hands tightened into fists, but she kept her cool. She wouldn't be the one to have a tantrum and ruin their chance of securing the Illumination as backup at the farm.

It was late when they drifted off to their beds, a tentative agreement between them.

"I'll meet you there in a minute," Anya said to Trajan. "I need to talk to Aramis."

Trajan glanced at the Álfr. "I don't like you being alone with him," he said under his breath.

"I'll be fine." Anya kissed him, and with a resigned sigh, Trajan followed the others from the carriage.

Aramis leaned against the front of his desk, smiling as Anya stepped toward him. "I think—"

Anya struck him hard across the face. "How dare you use magic on me! You tricked me into trusting you last night."

"I only used a bit of compulsion to make you feel comfortable around me. I genuinely want to help you, Anya, and I knew you wouldn't give me a chance in time." A red mark appeared on his pale cheek.

Anya had to suppress a shout of frustration. She did not like being manipulated. Aramis caught her hand as she raised it again, and translucent tendrils of power burst from her skin and wrapped around him. They pulsed like a heartbeat as they entwined with his magic.

"Why does it do that?" Anya grumbled, pulling her hand away.

"I don't know, but we can work it out together. I'm sorry I used magic on you, but my intentions were honorable. Just trust me." He stood only a hair's breadth from her now.

Anya stepped back. "You want me to trust you? Don't use your magic on me again, and don't lie to me." She folded her arms so she wouldn't touch him again.

"I promise. I would like to also offer my assistance in training you. This isn't the Illumination offering, but me."

"The twins are already training me. I don't need your help."

"The twins are Powers in their own lands, and they will need to return to them. And I'm assuming your magic doesn't react to them like it does to me. It's something I've never seen in my considerably long life, but I know others who might understand it."

Anya gave him a dubious look. "You work for the Illumination. I really doubt they're going to let you train me without my commitment to join you."

"Who said they need to know?" His blue eyes flashed with a streak of mischief she didn't expect.

Anya couldn't help it; her resolve loosened just a bit as her curiosity won out. "Maybe a few lessons, just to see how I feel about it. But I really don't need another babysitter."

"I'll never be one. Let's have a lesson tomorrow when we get off the train." He gave her a conciliatory smile. "Sleep well, Anya."

"Yeah, I'll try." But she really doubted she would. Her mind was on fire, and her magic had been spun into a tizzy from so much time around him.

Anya's compartment was empty when she got back, and she figured Trajan had gone to have a drink with the others. She grabbed the leather bag holding her drum, determined to calm her magic down. Anya yelped as the drum shocked her with static.

"Bastard." She sucked her stinging finger. She tipped the bag upside down on the bed and flipped the drum over. Her teeth closed hard on her sore finger.

There was a new symbol on the top half of the drum—the heavenly realm. Unlike the others inked in dark brown, this was a shining silver leaf drawn in intricate detail. Anya knew without question what it meant. "Bloody Aramis."

Anya didn't know how or why, but Aramis was important. She had been around enough magic users by that point to know that the way her power reacted to his was not normal. Now he had turned up on her drum, where until then, the only other symbol that represented someone close to her was Yvan and the firebird.

Maybe it's destiny, the way meeting Yvan was.

The only way to find out was to trust Aramis and hope like hell he didn't betray her.

41

ISABELLE RUSHED THROUGH THE aisles and headed for the storage carriages to get her motorcycle. At the next stop, she was riding off this damn train. She wouldn't work with the Illumination and let them treat her like she was some kind of monster.

Ruben had made her so angry that she felt the dark part of herself move about underneath the surface. If Hamish hadn't intervened, she would've killed him. Her hand was itching to go back and put a bullet in the spark plug's skull.

In the cold cargo carriages, the musty odor of damp canvas and motor oil filled the air. She found her bike closest to the large sliding door and pulled the blanket off it. A sob caught in her throat, and she gripped the leather seat as she leaned forward to breathe.

You know the truth about real monsters. You couldn't have saved those children. You could barely save yourself from that beast. The truth didn't stop the horror of the night from coming back to her. She could still smell the blood and fear in the air, see the toys and tiny bodies littered across the floor…

"Where do you think you're going?" Hamish's voice cut through the noise of the train, making her jump. "I never picked you for one to bugger off in the middle of a fight."

"I'm not running. I'm getting out of the way so I don't kill someone. I won't work for the fucking Illumination."

"You're going to stay and talk to me about what happened back there, Belle." Hamish reached over and pulled the clutch cable out of her handlebars.

"I don't need the bike to go, cowboy." Isabelle slid the door of the carriage open, and rain poured in over her. She jumped but not quickly enough. Strong hands grabbed the back of her coat and ripped her back in.

"Let me go!" Isabelle turned and scratched out at him, but Hamish didn't loosen his grip. He lifted her and dumped her on the bonnet of a nearby car.

"You think I'm going to let you go when I've only just found you?" Hamish shook his head. "You aren't leaving until I get some answers. Tell me about that scar. You didn't have it when we were together."

Isabelle leaned forward and put her head in her hands. The only way she could get away from him was to hurt him, and she couldn't do it. She wiped the rain from her face and looked up at him. Hamish's hazel eyes bored into her, full of worry and concern. Another sob rose in her throat. If there was one person in the world that might understand, it was Hamish.

"It was after the bombing." Isabelle swallowed hard as the smell of the place hit her again. "About thirty years ago, I was outside Budapest hunting a possessed child. I followed it to an orphanage, but by the time I got there, it had slaughtered everyone in the building. I'd never been up against a demon before. I didn't even know that was what I was hunting until it was too late. It just about ripped my throat out."

Hamish leaned against the car, his arm going around her waist. "Fuck, Belle. How did you get away?"

Isabelle sniffed and wiped at her face. She knew she shouldn't, but she leaned into his warmth anyway. It had been so long since someone had tried to comfort her. "I was saved by a priest called Vadim, who was also a hunter. He killed the demon and took me back to the church. I would've been as dead as all of those kids if it weren't for him. I lived but not without a price." She paused before her voice broke. "I've had to live with a demon stigmata ever since."

Hamish's expression softened enough to make her heart ache. "Why didn't you find me? You knew I was immortal. I was always around. I could've helped you, Belle."

"It took me a long time to deal with it." *Monster.* That word had been like a mantra in her head back then. "I thought I had lost my soul. I couldn't bear to look at myself in the mirror, let alone see if an older lover would still accept me after all of *that*."

"I would have understood," he said firmly. "You shouldn't have had to go through that alone."

"You thought I was dead, and I didn't want to put you in danger again. You saw that guy tonight; they all think I did it." She took his hand. "Look, for what it's worth, I am sorry for letting you believe I died in that explosion. I really did think I was doing the right thing."

"I know that now, but I lost my fucking mind." His grip on her tightened. "You know why I got sent to Australia as a convict back in 1790? It was over a woman—my wife, the love of my life—and when a bunch of English bastards tried to rape her, I beat the shit out of them."

"You never told me that." God, the secrets they had kept from each other.

"I planned on telling you everything about me the night you disappeared—the night I thought you died. I was tired of keeping secrets, and I trusted you. I figured if you could accept it all, I was going to marry you."

Isabelle felt like she'd been kicked in the gut. "Really?"

"Truly. I was crazy about you, even if you did put a bullet in my ass," he said with a small smile. "A scar that still pains me when it rains, just so you know."

She tried to smile, but her heart was breaking at how stupid she'd been to walk away from him instead of just being honest. "What happened next, when you were sent to Australia?"

"They knew I was good in a fight, so they made me their killer. They transported my wife over there too. If I didn't do their bidding, they would kill her. The English were determined to claim land for their colony, and they killed any indigenous tribes who tried to resist. I know it was wrong to carry out their orders against the tribes, but the one time I tried to refuse, they beat my wife so badly, she miscarried our baby." Hamish's voice cracked with loss and rage. "Then I was cursed by one of the tribe's elders. I turned into a dingo, and the manacles slipped from me for the first time in four years. I killed every single one of the English bastards who'd been holding my leash, but I was too late to save my wife. As soon as they heard of the attack, they knew it was me and shot her. I was out in the bush trying to figure out how to change back into a human, and while I fucked about, they killed her."

"Jesus, Hamish. I'm so sorry." Isabelle didn't know what else to say. She just held his hand until the anger rolling off him calmed.

"Can you see why I lost my mind over you? I was too late to save you too. You were the only woman I'd met since my wife that I thought might actually accept this side of me." Hamish took her face in his hands. "I won't lose you again. Not over a squabble with these Illumination bastards for a crime you didn't commit."

"I'm sorry I put you through all of that, Hamish. Really, I am." Isabelle covered his hands with hers. Tears fell down her cheeks—the first time she'd cried in over a decade.

He brushed away her tears. "Don't cry, baby. It breaks me up."

"I can't help it. As soon as I get around you, I get bloody emotional."

Hamish kissed her forehead. "It's good for you. You've been so cold since you turned up. That closed-off person isn't the Belle I remember."

"The demon killed that Belle."

"I don't believe that for a second. You're still her. You just need to let the right people around you to bring her out again."

Maybe he was right. She had kept people at arm's length for so long because everyone she loved always died. Except him. She looked up into his hazel eyes, and warmth sparked inside of her.

"Why do the Illumination think you killed the kids?" he asked.

"They saw me enter the building, and when they finally got the balls to follow, everyone was dead and I was gone."

"You know the truth, so why give a shit what they think? I can't make you stay, but it's going to be a good fight, and I'd feel better having you fighting at my side." When she raised a brow, he amended, "Okay, I might tie you up to make you stay, but I'll feel bad about it."

Isabelle laughed, knowing he would do it too. "The Illumination won't let Anya go, you know. They'll pretend they're on her side, but when the dust settles, she'll be taken down."

"Anya trusts this Aramis guy, and that's enough for me. If they betray us, we'll deal with them." Hamish pulled her closer. "Stay for the fight, stay for Anya, or just stay for me. Please, Belle."

"It's not going to be a fight. It's going to be a fucking bloodbath." Isabelle ran her hands over his chest.

He grinned. "Then I'll buy you a rubber ducky."

"God, I hate you." She shook her head and smiled.

"Liar," Hamish said and kissed her.

42

AS SOON AS ANYA'S feet touched Russian soil, a tremble of power rolled up through her and made her bones shake. They were about twelve hours from the farm, but even so, it was like her magic could feel how close they were. She'd never felt a sensation like it before. It was if the ground were trying to pull her magic down through her feet. Aramis appeared beside her in the dark as the others helped unload the vehicles.

"What was it?" he asked. Aramis took her hand, and her magic stopped trying to escape and latched onto his instead.

Anya clutched her head. "I don't know. It's like my bones and magic are shuddering."

"Come with me."

Anya followed him toward a group of trees.

"Anya!" Trajan called, but she waved him off.

When they reached the trees, Aramis took off his blue coat and handed it to her. "Hold this. I want to check something." He crouched down beside her and pushed his hand into the dirt. He shut his eyes while Anya watched in fascination as his silvery magic shimmered out of him and into the earth. Aramis gasped and pulled his hand out so quickly that dirt sprayed everywhere.

Anya touched his shoulder. "Are you okay?"

"The earth is…screaming. Take off your shoes. I need to show you something."

Aramis took off his shoes, and Anya slipped out of her boots and pulled off her socks. Aramis ran a finger up her pale foot, and the cold evaporated from them. He stood up and put his jacket back on before taking her hand. Ribbons of magic fastened to her where she touched him, and the heady taste of his power flowed through the rest of her body. It was like drinking silver light and springtime. Anya sighed as it coiled around her own magic.

"I want you to close your eyes and bury your feet in the earth," he said. "Then I want you to reach out like you do when you're searching for a magical aura like the twins taught you. Reach into it. Feel the energy all around you. Concentrate. Feel it roll up through your feet and into your body. Feel it in every part of you."

Anya dug her bare feet into the soil, closed her eyes, and reached out, trying to find what Aramis was describing. Her heartbeat slowed, and then magic rushed up into her. A high-pitched wave of pain and panic tore its way through her brain, and she crumpled to her knees. Images flashed through her mind: the burnt farm, a scarlet aurora, blood rising from the soil, a chanting chorus of voices.

She gasped. "I hear it." Tears fell from her eyes as Aramis knelt down beside her. He released her hand so she could run it through the loose earth. The sound moved through her again, calling out to her for help. "Oh god. What is it, Aramis?"

"The gates. They are weakening. You can hear and feel them because you're tied to them through blood and magic. They are sending out a warning."

"How come you can hear it too?"

"The Álfr have a connection to all living things. It's earth magic." He extended a hand to her. "The closer you get to the gates, the more you will feel it."

Anya's legs wobbled as he helped her stand. "I can't say I'm looking forward to it."

Aramis held her steady while she put her boots back on. "I've been thinking a lot about your dream about Ilya and the ritual he performed. You said he had a knife with a carved bear handle?"

Anya nodded.

"It could be a ritual knife specifically used to close the gates. If we can find it, we'll know for sure. Without it, you might not be able to perform the magic properly. We should check the house ruins when we get to the farm."

"Vasilli burned it to the ground. I doubt anything would have survived, and I never saw a knife like it lying around."

Aramis smiled. "If it's important, there would've been magic protecting it, and the fire wouldn't have damaged it. If we find no knife, it means any will do."

Trajan walked over and took Anya into his arms. "Are you okay?"

She nodded her head, determined not to worry him when he was already suspicious of Aramis. "Fine. A little woozy. It turns out the gates can talk to me." She swayed on her feet.

Aramis brushed the dirt from his clothes. "I know we were planning on staying in Anya's village, but I'm afraid that will be too dangerous if the gates keep screaming at her. It will drive her mad. We'll try the next village over, where hopefully they won't call to Anya so strongly."

Anya straightened, her nausea passing. "Will you let the others know?" she asked Trajan. He looked like he would argue but instead gave a nod and walked back to where the cars were parked.

Aramis watched him go. "He doesn't like me being anywhere near you."

"I think he might be worried that you're going to magic me away to join the Illumination." Anya's hands were burning and filthy from their contact with the earth.

"Trust me, Anya. If I really wanted to magic you away, there isn't a thing he or the Illumination could do to stop me."

After twelve more hours of traveling, they drove into the small town Anya called *Otverstie*—or Hole—situated on the other side of the forest bordering her farm. They paid for rooms at the town's only tavern. Roya, one of the barmaids, didn't recognize Anya even though they'd gone to school together.

I hate this fucking place. Anya missed the farm, but the people and places around it? Not even a little bit. The farmhouse was no more, and Anya knew she couldn't go back to her old life even if she wanted to. But she was a gatekeeper, and she'd always be tied to this place, whether she hated it or not. It wasn't a cheerful thought.

Aramis had been right about the gate's distress affecting her the closer she got to them. It took all of her effort to drown out the sound of drums, the chanting of voices, the taste of blood and magic on her tongue. She was being torn apart by a longing to go to them and the urge to run as fast as she could in the other direction.

Under Aramis's instruction, everyone had gone out to scout the surrounding forest between them and the farm, but Anya had been forced to stay behind. As Aramis had explained, the gate was bound to her bloodline, and now that her power had been released, it would recognize her and try to draw magic from her to repair itself. It hadn't done it to her previously because Eikki's magic was still sustaining it after his death. According to Aramis, they couldn't risk it latching onto her like a leech before she was ready to shut the gate herself.

Still, Anya did not like being told where she could and could not go, especially when she was the only one being relegated to the tavern while everyone else went out.

"We need to do this properly and be prepared for anything. If you connect to the gates without people ready to protect your back, you're going to make yourself vulnerable to a potential attack from the Darkness," Aramis had said.

It wasn't until Yvan had come to calm her down that she'd backed off. He had managed to soothe her temper, but not enough to stick to her current no-alcohol rule. She'd tried to keep calm and use her power a little to dull the noise of the gates, but as soon as Aramis and the calming influence of his magic was out of sight, the drums and chanting had kicked up to a deafening roar. Anya had all but ran to the bar for a drink.

Some shamanitsa you're turning out to be.

Anya sat at a table hidden from view of the other patrons. She didn't want any inconvenient questions from anyone if they happened to recognize her. A pleasant numbness was just starting to creep along her arms when Katya found her.

"No big surprise finding you hiding in the bar." She sat down opposite her.

"Nowhere else to hide." Anya offered the half-empty bottle of vodka. "Drink?"

"Don't mind if I do." Katya took a hearty swig and passed it back to her.

"Why aren't you out with the others?"

"I finished up the section Aramis gave me to scout and came right back to make sure you had someone close to protect you. We can't have you disappearing. Yvan and Trajan are already having a competition to see which one can stress about you the most."

Anya raised a brow. "You weren't worried I was going to run off, were you?" Despite not knowing if she could shut the gates at all, she was going to try her best.

Katya shook her head. "No, I was worried someone was going to run off with you. I know you wouldn't run from your gatekeeping duties."

Anya scoffed and drank some more. "You mean like Vasilli sneaking up and jumping me?"

"Well, you wouldn't be able to put up much of a fight in your current state. But I wasn't thinking of Vasilli. I had someone a little closer in mind."

"Who, then? Aramis? You think he's going to hurt me?"

"I've seen the way he looks at you. Trajan has noticed too. He might be in the first relationship of his life, but that doesn't mean he's completely clueless."

Anya reached forward and took the bottle from her. "You're imagining things. Aramis isn't interested in me that way." At least, she didn't think he was. He had never overstepped with her; he'd never hit on her or gave any indication that he might want to. Magic was the thing that drew them to each other, and as far as Anya could tell, that was it.

Katya tapped her fingers on the table. "Maybe not, but I still want you to be cautious around him. I think he's interested in more than just protecting you."

"He's been a perfect gentleman, and he understands what I'm going through and wants to help. He's going to assist me with the gates, then go back to the Illumination. If he's interested in anything else, it's the way my magic reacts to him."

Katya chewed on her lip. "I hope so. Just know that I'll be there if he tries anything. I don't care who he is. I'll gladly kick that perfect ass of his."

The tavern door opened, and the rest of Anya's companions filed in. The people in the bar shot them suspicious glares. They were probably the most strangers they'd seen all year. Trajan looked cold and tired, but he still managed one of his gut-wrenching smiles when he saw Anya.

He sat down next to her and kissed her cheek. "Hitting the hard stuff again?"

Aramis joined them. "Does it help muffle the noise of the gates?"

Katya's eyes narrowed as he took a seat.

Anya nodded. "It does, but not much. The drums and the voices are getting louder. I don't know how else to stop it. None of my other exercises are working." Her shoulders slumped. "Did you find anything out there?"

"No one is in the immediate area, but I believe they are camping close to the outskirts of the farm," Aramis said. "I suggest that you and I go for a closer look tomorrow and see if we can find Ilya's knife."

Trajan's hand found hers under the table. "No. Anya isn't going anywhere near the farm. The Darkness will grab her or worse."

Anya patted Trajan's hand to calm him. "Won't going that close make it easier for the gate to connect with me?"

"I have something that will dull your magic down so it can't be accessed—a potion with only a short period of efficacy. Plus, a small amount of close exposure may help you prepare for the potency of the gate's magic. Either way, we need that knife, and you're the only one who will be able to find it."

Anya put down her glass. "Okay, I'll go with you. I know these forests better than any of the Darkness, and we can get around them."

Aramis shook his head. "I can use my magic to cloak us. I won't risk us being detected. Not yet."

"Can I talk to you upstairs, please?" Trajan whispered to her.

Anya was going to argue with him, but the concern in his eyes made her pause. She nodded. "I'll see you tomorrow, Aramis."

Trajan helped her out of her chair. She wasn't drunk enough to need help walking, but he still held her tight until they were back in her rooms with the door closed.

She sat down on the bed and kicked off her boots. "What's wrong?"

"I don't want you alone with Aramis." Trajan took off his coat and sat down beside her. "I know you trust him because of how your magic interacts with his, but I don't. Not with you."

"Is this jealousy or your thanatos side talking because it's incompatible with the Álfr?"

Trajan dragged a hand through his hair. "It's neither, Anya! It's the fact that he conveniently turned up when you were most vulnerable and is trying to swoop in like some valiant knight to rescue you." He made a sound of frustration at the back of his throat. "I don't know. Maybe I am jealous. I don't want to share you with another person. Yvan's bad enough."

"You *are* jealous." Anya took his face in her hands. "Don't be. I don't see Aramis as my knight in shining armor. I see him as a means to an end. Yes, my magic reacts to his, and I want to know why. That doesn't mean that any other part of me reacts to him."

"I'm sorry. I'm not used to feeling this way, and I don't—"

Anya kissed him. No one had ever been jealous over her before, and it made her feel strangely cherished. Trajan's arms came around her. He pulled her down onto the bed and pinned her beneath him.

Trajan broke the kiss and stared down at her. "I don't want to come across as an overprotective asshole, but be patient with me." He stroked the lines of her face, eyes still full of conflict. "I love you too much to lose you now."

Anya's hand stilled in his hair as her heart tripped. "You love me?"

"If love is this sick, scared sensation under my ribs, if it's my heart feeling like it's going to give out when I look at you—then yes, I love you."

Joy bubbled up through her. Trajan, the one who made her skin ache and heart pound, loved her. "Yeah, that's love." She twisted her fingers into the hair at the nape of his neck. His breath was warm against her smiling lips. "I love you too."

Trajan's face broke into the most heartbreakingly beautiful grin she had ever seen, and then he kissed her until she was breathless.

"I still have to go with Aramis to the farm," Anya said as she curled up in Trajan's arms. "I have to search the wreckage for Ilya's knife."

Trajan's fingers wove through her hair. "I just don't like the way he looks at you."

She rolled her eyes. "You and Katya should start a club."

"Perhaps you should start listening to what we're saying."

"I need to get the knife. Then I'll never have to be alone with him again, and you won't have to worry about it."

Trajan shook his head. "I have a valid reason to be concerned. I fear him trying to take you away from us. The Illumination has always hunted the most gifted to place among them. In many ways, they do exactly what Ladislav and his people do. I understand they are needed to control the Darkness if you can't close the gates, but I worry that now that they know you, they'll hunt you as strongly as Ladislav and Vasilli."

"I won't go with them, and Aramis knows it. I have no interest in being a prize of the Illumination. As soon as the gates are closed, I want to get as far away from here as possible."

Trajan leaned down and kissed her cheeks. "If you don't return within two hours tomorrow, I'll come after you. I don't care if Yvan burns the forest down, and the Darkness swarms us. I won't let him take you."

Aramis's phone rang angrily in his pocket. He knew it was an elder—one of the three that ruled the Illumination from on high—but he was trying to put off answering their calls, especially any from Lord Ainsley.

Aramis walked into the woods to get away from the tension in the tavern. Too many supernaturals under the one roof caused friction, and he was surprised they'd all managed to live together in Paris without killing each other. The phone rang again. He dug it out of his pocket with a small sigh and answered it.

"Aramis, what the devil is going on over there? You haven't reported in two days."

"I apologize, sir. The reception here isn't the best."

"There are other ways for us to communicate," said Ainsley.

"The situation here is precarious. I do not wish to use any kind of power that could be detected by the enemy."

There was a long pause on the other end of the phone.

"Tell me about the girl."

Aramis hesitated. "She's amazing, sir. A wealth of untapped power. More than I have ever encountered since Yanka. After this situation with the gates is sorted, I'd like some time off from my regular responsibilities to stay and train her."

"That won't be necessary. We have another assignment for you."

Aramis's blood went cold. "Oh?"

"Bring her to us, Aramis. We can teach her."

"With all due respect, she would never come with me. She's too closely tied to her companions and won't leave them."

"I didn't say *ask* her to come to us. I said, *bring* her to us."

Aramis tried to keep the anger and dread roiling through him from his voice. "Anya wouldn't react kindly to force, and I find the thought of hurting her unsavory. Her magic tends to rise up and protect her. She would be a force to reckon with if I attempted to pressure her."

"You do it, Aramis, or I'll send another team to extract her, and they won't be so delicate. I'll leave the choice up to you. You told me her lineage wouldn't be an issue, so stop making this personal."

The line went dead, and Aramis fought the urge to throw his phone into the forest and be done with it. The Illumination had given him purpose during the hardest period of his life, but some of his debts ran deeper than his loyalty to them—debts that Aramis might finally have a chance to repay so that his battered soul could finally mend.

He turned back toward the tavern. *Get the gates closed first, then worry about how to get out of their orders.*

43

ANYA, TRAJAN, AND ARAMIS stood at the edge of the forest in the freezing morning mist. Anya had slept poorly, even wrapped in the warmth of Trajan's arms and the glow of his confession. She'd never felt so loved and safe, even with the threat of the weakening gates hanging over her head, but it didn't quite diminish the nervous energy streaking through her veins. With any luck, the hike through the forest would wear her out enough to sleep tonight.

"You have two hours, and then I'm coming after you," Trajan told Aramis. His eyes had nearly shifted to all red when Anya squeezed his hand. Trajan turned and kissed her cold nose and lips. "Be safe."

"I will be. Don't forget this forest is my home. I'll be back soon." She nudged him. "Enjoy the peace and quiet."

He smiled, but it didn't reach his eyes.

"We'll return soon, Trajan," Aramis promised.

"If anything happens to her, I'll hold you responsible."

"Okay, we're leaving now," Anya said to stop another inevitable argument. She stood on tiptoes and kissed Trajan long and hard.

Aramis cleared his throat.

"I'm coming." Anya let go of Trajan's hand before following Aramis into the forest.

Anya didn't realize how much she'd missed her forest until they were under the heavy pine branches. She hadn't explored this eastern side for a long time, and she'd missed the berry-picking season while she was away. There wasn't a cloudberry to be seen, and it made her feel sad and nostalgic for her childhood. Eikki had spent a lot of time with her picking berries, mushrooms, and wildflowers. He'd named the types of trees they passed until Anya knew them by heart. Pine, birch, aspen, and rowan grew wild and thick around her.

Eikki would sometimes run a callused hand over them and greet them. *"Hello, Grandfather Birch. Grow strong, old friend,"* he would say cheerfully. Anya thought this was normal practice until she greeted an aspen tree on her first day of school and a boy threw a rock at her.

"Do you know that your boyfriend is very intense?" Aramis asked, dragging Anya out of the flood of memories. "If I didn't know better, I would say he's insecure."

Anya grinned. "Trajan's not insecure. He just doesn't like you. He's also under the impression that you're going to try to kidnap me."

"Why would I want to kidnap you? You have to close the gates, remember?" Aramis held her hand as he helped her over a slippery tree trunk. Her magic rushed into him. He smiled but didn't mention it.

"He knows that. It's what happens after that he's concerned about." Anya took her hand back and fought to reel her power in.

"One problem at a time." Aramis reached into his pocket, pulled out a silver flask, and offered it to her. "Drink some of this. It will dull your magic and make it easier for me to shield you when the time comes."

Anya took the flask and sniffed it with a smile. "If you're trying to drug me so you can kidnap me without a fight, it won't work."

He raised a brow. "What makes you so sure?"

Anya remembered what he'd said about no one being able to stop him if he wanted to take her away, and goose bumps crept up her spine.

"When the nehemoth took me, Völundr drugged me to dull my magic, and you know what happened? When I saw what he had done to Trajan, it burned straight out of my body."

"Then you really have nothing to fear, do you?" Aramis's teasing smile widened as his silver hair tangled in the wind.

He really does look like a silver knight.

Anya shoved the thought away and took a long swig. It had a most unusual taste, like some kind of sweet berry liquor. She tried to identify the flavor, but it kept changing until it finally evaporated with a tingle on her tongue. The buzzing under her skin quieted almost instantly, and the drumming in her head faded until it was like it was never there.

"Wow, that's some amazing liquor. I wish you would've given me some of that a few days ago. It would've stopped me from hitting the vodka so hard." Though the absence of her flickering power made her feel unusually empty.

"It's typically not given to humans. It becomes too addictive. Let's keep going. It will wear off soon."

Anya followed after him. "How are you going to shield our presence from the Darkness if they're hiding out here?"

"Like this." He waved his hand over his face and was gone. Anya could see slight movement in the air, like heat waves above hot pavement. She swiped her hand through it and caught the fabric of his shirt. Fingers touched her face, and Aramis materialized in front of her. She looked down at her feet and found they were no longer there.

"Don't panic," he said. "You're just under the shield."

Anya did her best to unclench her death grip on his shirt. "It's a shame you couldn't make a car invisible so we didn't have to walk. That would've given us a lot more time to find Ilya's knife."

"Cars are too complex. Besides, just because they can't see us doesn't mean they can't hear us. Is a thirty-minute walk through the forest with me such a trial?"

Anya didn't know if he was teasing or not. "I have to keep a close eye on you in case you try to kidnap me, remember? That's exhausting."

Aramis's smile slipped. "Have you thought about coming to the Illumination for training and guidance?"

Anya shook her head. "Sorry. It sounds too much like school to me—that and imprisonment. They would expect the debt to be repaid in some way, and the price will always be too high."

"For someone who knows nothing about us, you are extremely perceptive."

"I might not know everything about the supernatural world and its politics, but I know how the human world works. Nothing is free, and no one is going to have that kind of power over me."

"That's true in many ways, but you could do with more training. The twins can only remain with you for so long. You are Yanka's granddaughter. The sky is the limit for what you're capable of. She was one of the greatest Powers the world has ever seen."

"You say that like you knew her."

Aramis didn't respond but picked up his pace.

Anya grabbed his sleeve and pulled him back. "You *did* know her, didn't you?"

"Anya, please lower your voice. Remember, they can still hear us."

"But you knew her. You knew Yanka."

"Yes. Now can we go?"

"Will you tell me about her?" Anya pressed. Why hadn't he told her about Yanka to begin with?

"If you really want to know, I will. But let's focus on the task at hand first." Aramis looked like he was a world away, lost in his memories, and it seemed none of them were pleasant. He shook his head and walked on.

"Will you at least tell me if she was terrifying? She was scarier than I imagined when I dream-walked and saw her. She made good blackberry vodka, though. I could taste it for days."

Aramis took her arm and pulled her to a stop. "You dream-walked and saw Yanka?"

"I told you I did. I'm sure of it."

Aramis dropped her arm, his face paling. "No, you said you had a dream about Yanka. Not that you dream-*walked* with Yanka."

"It's the same—"

"It doesn't matter. Yanka is dead. I saw her body." Aramis ran a hand over his face. "Let's keep going before that potion wears off."

Anya bit down on all the new questions she had and followed him.

They reached the edge of the forest and surveyed the open field that stretched out before them. The black charcoal skeleton of her house and barn marred the otherwise perfect land. Anya's chest grew tight at the familiar sight. *Home.*

"I don't see anyone," she whispered.

"They are there. Look along the forest line, just past the house."

Anya squinted but still couldn't see anything. "I don't have supernatural sight, remember?"

Aramis dug around in his pockets and handed her a rifle scope. She took it and rescanned the tree line. Men patrolled the forest, and a few were definitely not human judging by the grace of their movements and the disconcerting look about them.

"Can they see us?" Anya handed him back the scope.

"No, but they might be able to sense us if we take too long." Aramis drew a knife from the inside of his coat and kept it low. Its blade was thin and as long as Anya's arm with a silver edge engraved with elegant swirling designs.

"Are you going to need that?"

"You never know."

Anya took a deep breath and stepped out into the open. There were no cries of alarm, so she strode across the familiar fields and toward the black rubble of her house.

"I'll give you a minute," Aramis said as Anya walked into the ruins.

Vasilli had done an extraordinary job of destroying the place. If it weren't for Yvan, she would have died in that fire out of sheer stupidity, because for some reason, she'd thought Vasilli wasn't going to hurt her. She suddenly wished Yvan and the firebird were there to tell her everything would be okay, that he would keep her safe from his brother's wrath. Except now she had to protect him. Anya knew the only way to keep Yvan safe from Vasilli was to put the evil bastard in the ground.

Only the stone fireplace still stood. She thought of all the bizarre family tokens that had filled the home. Perhaps if she had known about her dormant magic, she could have seen the magical objects from the mundane.

"I can't even remember seeing the knife. Not once," she said finally.

"If it's important to the ritual, it would have been hidden someplace where it would be safe from any sort of disaster."

"Then we're screwed, because the house is wrecked. It could be at the cabin, but I don't remember seeing it there either."

Anya walked around the wreckage, occasionally recognizing objects in their burnt and mutilated forms. What she had left of the family jewelry had melted in one giant blob. A silver locket with Ilya's portrait painted in it was blackened and slightly bent but otherwise okay. She pocketed it, thinking of him as he'd appeared in her vision.

Anya squatted down on the hearthstone of the fireplace and ran her fingers through the ash. The chimney had half collapsed, but the mantelpiece was still intact. Her ashy fingers throbbed, and her subdued magic sparked in her veins, then danced across the stone.

"What did you just do?" Aramis asked in a forceful whisper. "I can feel your magic."

"I don't know. There's something here…" She got back to her feet and ran her hands along the top of the mantelpiece, magic tingling in her fingertips again. Anya ran her hands over the fireplace until they stopped on a brick in the center of the mantel. The concrete seal around it was cracked and loose. She grabbed at it with her fingers and pulled it out of place.

"I found something!"

Aramis hurried to her side, and Anya lifted the brick the rest of the way out and flipped it over. It was hollowed out, and inside was a bundle wrapped in oiled leather.

"It would be the safest place if you wanted to keep something hidden. A protection spell must have been shielding it from me, but it likely recognized your magic." Aramis braced himself against the mantle as Anya unwrapped the leather and Ilya's knife tumbled into her hand.

The snarling bear looked up at her. It tingled in her hands. Anya swayed as the chanting rose up in her head and her mouth filled with ash.

Aramis steadied her. "We need to go. Your magic is spiking."

Anya wrapped the knife and stumbled out of the house ruins. Still holding her hand, Aramis led her across the fields toward the cover of the forest.

Anya reached the tree line and sagged over her knees. "Oh god, Aramis. The drums, the blood…they're calling me." She stepped back toward the field, but Aramis pulled her forward and hung on to her until she stopped struggling.

"Fight it, Anya! The gate is trying to link with you." He swore. "Touching the knife made it worse." Aramis released his power and let it wash over her until she could think straight again. "We have to keep moving."

He held tightly to her hand as they jogged through the forest. The gate called out, and Anya slid in the leaves to look behind her, only to find men in tactical gear moving through the trees thirty meters behind them. "Aramis…"

"I know. I see them too. When they make their move, I want you to run as hard and as fast as you can. Get back to the tavern. I'll hold them off."

"Why aren't they shooting at us?"

"They need us alive," he muttered and pulled out his long knife.

There were five of them, and they attacked from all sides. Aramis's knife was a blur, taking down one in the first sweep. He was mesmerizing as he ducked their blows, moving in the space around the bodies, slashing and lunging, dancing to some beautiful music only he could hear.

"Go, Anya!" he shouted, jarring her out of her trance.

Anya only got a few meters when another man in tactical gear appeared in front of her.

"The witch," he spat. He pulled a gun on her. "I don't want to shoot you, girl, so do as I say and come quietly."

Anya's magic surged, turning her blood to fire, and she gave herself over to it. The gun glowed bright red, and the man dropped it with a startled yelp. He swore and went for her, hands outstretched like claws. Anya lifted her hand, and black ash burst from his mouth. He collapsed, crying out as his organs burned inside of him. A shout behind her made her turn to where Aramis battled three men at once, the others already fallen by his blade. She raised her hand again, then Aramis spotted her.

"Anya! Don't!"

But the men had already collapsed, screaming as ash burst from their mouths and withered their skin. Aramis looked at them, then at her and back again, his face white with shock.

"I told you to run." He grabbed her hand, yanking her out of surge of the power riding her.

"I'm sorry, but I'm done letting other people fight my battles," Anya snapped, but bile filled the back of her mouth even as she said it. "I let my magic protect me…" She looked down at her hands. Those men were dead now, and allowing her magic to kill them in self-defense had been as easy and natural as breathing.

Like the men you set on fire in Paris and the boys you almost drowned. Anya pushed down her horror.

Aramis gripped her hand. "We can talk about it later, but we need to get out of here before more arrive."

So they ran.

Aramis saw Anya safe in Trajan's arms before he went up to his bedroom. The door was barely shut behind him before he ran to the bathroom and threw up in the toilet. She'd barely lifted a finger, and the men in the forest were dead. They hadn't stood a fighting chance.

Aramis heaved again until he had nothing left in his stomach, then washed out his mouth and slumped down onto his bed.

"Killed them, just like that," he muttered. "Too much like her."

Watching Anya kill those men was Yanka all over again. She had the same glow of vengeance in her green eyes, the same darkness seething inside of her.

She's not Yanka. He could save Anya. He would wait until the gates were shut, and then he would tell her everything. He'd make her understand the danger she was in from her own power. He would explain what happened when she killed with magic, that it ate away at her soul.

Aramis's cell phone rang, and he knew what he was going to be asked to do. He picked it up and crushed it, the plastic and glass shattering in his hand. He would have twenty-four hours at the most before they slapped a rogue label and a bounty on him. After what he saw today, that didn't matter anymore.

She's not Yanka. You can keep the light in her alive.

If Anya didn't close the gates, the Illumination would have a war on their hands and would be too busy to hunt him. If she did, they would expect him to take her back to England to force her to join them. His stomach turned, already knowing that he wouldn't be able to do that to her against her will. In twenty-four hours, no matter what, Aramis would have Anya far away.

Aramis stood and returned to the bathroom to splash water on his face. He cupped his hands and let them fill up before drinking down a cool gulp of water. As the liquid hit his stomach, his head snapped up, and he met his own wide gaze in the mirror.

Blackberry vodka. Anya said she had tasted blackberry vodka for days after dreaming about Yanka.

Aramis reached for his bag and pulled out one of his burner phones. He dialed a number and hoped it hadn't changed.

"*Bună seara*, Aramis. What are you doing calling me on a burner? And after such a long time, I might add."

Aramis smiled. "There are too many listeners on the others, Silvian. Besides, you know what would happen if I was caught talking to a Rogue."

"Then why are you talking to one?"

"I need you to look into something for me."

There was a long silence at the end of the line. "Why come to me?"

"Because you're the best, and because they won't be able to trace you."

"You sure know how to kiss my ass when you need to. What do you need, Aramis? I owe you a favor, and you know I can't turn you down."

"It's about Yanka."

"Aramis, you can't—"

"Shut up, Silvian. I need everything the Illumination has on her. Especially concerning how she died."

"You doubt what the Illumination told you?"

"I'm growing skeptical."

Silvian laughed—a deep, joyful sound. "My, my. It's taken you long enough. Do you really want to be digging around in the past? You know how long it took to get over it the first time. What's it been? A hundred years? What brought this on?"

Aramis gripped the phone tighter. "Have you ever heard of someone who could dream-walk into a dead person's dream?"

"No, but I'm assuming you have."

"Yanka's granddaughter has walked with Yanka."

"Fuck."

"She has no idea what she's done. There was no preparation. She just…went to sleep."

"How much time do I have?" Silvian asked, his tone now gravely serious.

"Not a lot. She has to close the family gates tomorrow. I have no doubt that she'll do it, and once she does, I'll need to keep the Illumination from taking her back to London."

"Good idea. Keep her away from them. You might play general, but deep down, you know what they do to people they think could be a threat one day." Silvian would know; he'd been their assassin once, after all. "If this girl is Yanka's blood, there's no telling what she could do. I'll dig deep, Aramis, see what treasure they're hiding. Is this cell safe to call you back on?"

"Yes."

"Leave it on, and I'll contact you when I know something. One question before I go," Silvian said with a thoughtful pause. "What if what you're thinking is correct, and they've lied to you about what really happened? What will you do?"

"I'll be joining you on the rogue blacklist and killing whoever was responsible."

Aramis hung up, his mind already moving to the dark, cold place of his past. The glamour on his skin shifted, and his Álfr tattoos snaked up one arm and over his chest and face—the physical markings of the position he'd once held among his people.

Silvian wasn't the only one who had been an assassin.

44

ANYA WAS SITTING ON her bed with her head in her hands when Yvan knocked on the door and slipped into her room.

"I heard you killed some people today." He crouched down in front of her. "I wanted to make sure you're okay."

Tears slipped down Anya's cheeks. "I did it so easily, Yvan. Every time I let my magic take over, it lashes out and kills. What kind of magic is that?"

Yvan put his warm hands over her tightly clenched fists. "The kind that's trying to protect you. The only time you let it take charge is when you're being hurt or attacked. Magic is not evil; it's the most neutral force in the world. It's what's inside of you that influences it."

"I know, and I use it to *kill* people. Maybe that's what's inside of me!" It was her worst fear.

The firebird's soothing flames rose out of Yvan's hands and curled around her arms. "I've seen real evil, Anya, and trust me, you're not it."

Anya looked into his eyes, at the fire dancing in them. "I'm scared, Yvan. It's not just about closing the gates; it's what I'm becoming. I'm not 'chosen one' material, and I'm going to disappoint everyone when I can't be that person for them."

"Fuck everyone," Yvan said, making her eyes go wide in surprise. "I'm serious, Anya. You're not responsible for anyone's bullshit expectations. You've had nothing to do with the supernatural world. You didn't start the fight between the Illumination and the Darkness. You aren't responsible for cleaning it up."

Anya's hands tightened over his. "But what if I am? What if this is my destiny?"

"Tuoni told you the firebird egg was your destiny, and here I am." Yvan grinned. "This is the only destiny you need to be worried about."

"You're right, Vanya. I blame you entirely for this mess you dragged me into." Anya laughed as he cringed.

"I hate that nickname."

"Too bad. You're stuck with it now." She took out Ilya's knife. "Do you think the firebird can tell me if this is magical?"

Yvan sat down beside her and took the knife, then slid it out to examine the blade. His eyes flamed bright, and he said in a voice not quite his own, "The blade is tied to the gates by the blood that's fed the steel. The blood of your ancestors resides in it, and it's all about blood and power in the end." Yvan sheathed the blade and passed it back to her.

Anya's magic purred in her veins as she touched the bear's head on the pommel. She shoved the knife back in her bag. "I learned something else today. Aramis knew Yanka."

Yvan blew out a breath. "That makes a lot of sense."

"What do you mean?"

"I've been going over his sudden appearance and eagerness to win you over. The twins said the Álfr keep to themselves, so why would one turn up and do everything he could for you? It's not just about closing the gates and foiling the plans of the Darkness." Yvan shook his head. "No, Aramis has a secret. Something that he feels he needs to atone for."

"You can't possibly know that. He may have just been friends with Yanka and wants to help out her clueless descendant."

Yvan gave her a patient look. "If that were the case, he would have said it in the beginning. He's carrying shame for something, and once you find out what, you'll know why he wants to help you."

"Shit." Anya flopped back onto the bed. "Do you think I can trust him?"

"For the moment, while he's helpful. I suppose he'll prove what his motivations really are in the long term."

"Let me close the gates first. Then I'll corner him and get him to admit what the hell he's all about." She liked Aramis, and the thought he was using her hit her where it hurt.

"Good idea. You need to sleep, Anya. And don't worry about the gates. I'm sure you and your magic will know what to do when the time comes." Yvan gave her hand a final squeeze, and the firebird dropped one of its flames to dance along her hand.

Anya gasped as it melted into her skin and a small drop of its magic raced into her veins. It was like ancient wildfire and adrenaline, the freedom of skies and worlds pulsing inside of her.

"He says it's for luck," Yvan said.

Anya got up in a rush and put her arms around him, pressing her face into the firebird on Yvan's chest. "Thank you. I'm honored that you'd share some of your power with me."

Yvan's arms tightened around her. "We're always going to be here for you, Anya. To whatever end. Both of us."

In the heart of the forest, Vasilli crouched down and touched the burnt husks that remained of his men. He knew without reading the feel of her magic that it was Anya's doing.

She's getting stronger, Vasilli mused and smiled a little. Serge failing to retrieve her in Paris had irritated him even as the footage of her intrigued him. He had wanted to strip the magic out of her, but the ease with which she killed made him rethink that. If he could turn her to his side, maybe she would be more useful as another soldier in his coup against Ladislav. It would all depend on how willing she was to serve him. If she wasn't, he would take her power. His phone rang, and he groaned before answering it.

"Tell me what's happening," Ladislav demanded. "I sent you to monitor the gates, yet I just got a message from Sven saying that they've been in distress all day. Explain yourself, Vasilli."

"Sven wouldn't know what gates in distress look like." Vasilli made a mental note to slit the fucker's throat as soon as he could. "I didn't call you because there was no need to. Anya and Yvan have arrived with the Illumination in tow, and I've been scouting their numbers. Unless you want to break your precious treaty, you're going to have to let me handle this my way."

"No, I'm coming to you. This is too important to risk you screwing it up, and I don't trust you to do everything you can to get me the firebird. He's your brother, after all." Ladislav hung up, and Vasilli fought not to slam the phone into the nearest tree.

He growled through his teeth. "Fuck."

Vasilli had planned on letting down the magical shields smothering his power and capturing Anya and Yvan while they were busy with the gates. Then, flush with magic, he planned to go back to Moscow and tear Ladislav apart. He kicked the dirt, sending it sprinkling over the corpses of his men. Vasilli wasn't ready to reveal his true power to Ladislav, and now he would have to keep it buried and watch as the old bastard took his prize.

He cursed the Sudjaye for weaving such bullshit into his destiny. Every time he got close to victory, they fucked him.

Change your destiny. Be the wolf, his mother told him. Vasilli attempted to clear his head and the rage from his heart. If Ladislav no longer trusted him, he would need a shadow cloak to protect him from being stabbed in the back as soon as he arrived.

"Be the wolf," he murmured. He would rather Anya shut the gates than allow Ladislav to have their power.

Vasilli pulled his knife from his belt, cut his palm, and drew a blood circle on the forest floor. Then he sat inside of it and let his power cascade out of him to gather the shadows he would need for protection.

45

A NYA ROUSED BEFORE DAWN to a gentle stroke of fingers on her face. She groaned and moved to bat them away.

"Get up, Anya. The gates need you."

Anya cracked open an eye. A man with golden hair and green eyes stared down at her.

"Ilya?" she murmured.

Anya sat bolt upright, now wide awake, but the apparition was gone. Drums and voices roared in her head, and she bit down a scream. Trajan woke beside her, his eyes shining crimson.

"Anya? What's wrong?"

"The gates. We need to get to the gates." Anya pulled herself out of bed.

"I'll wake the others and get them ready." Trajan steadied her as she swayed. "Are you going to be—"

"I'm fine. Just go." Anya pushed him away and ran into the bathroom. She made it to the sink before dry heaving.

Ilya, where did you go?

Anya washed her face and drank handfuls of water, then stumbled back into the bedroom and got dressed. Her hand curled around Ilya's knife, and her magic flickered impatiently. The voices grew louder in her head, but she still couldn't make out anything clear in the cacophony.

"I'm going, I'm going," she told them, then hurried downstairs to where Trajan had assembled everyone by the cars.

"Anya, you look pale as death." Aramis went to take her hand but then let his fall back to his side. His concerned expression melted away, and his general face replaced it. "Don't forget that when you were captured, your magic flowed by using words, not blood. From what I've seen other gatekeepers do, you'll only need to sacrifice a little blood so that the gate recognizes you as its keeper."

"I'll remember," Anya said, one hand going into her pocket to grip Ilya's knife.

Yvan didn't offer her any words of comfort. Instead, he took her hand and let the firebird's power seep into her cold body. Deep inside her, the flame it had passed on to her flared hot, stilling her nerves and giving her courage.

Cerise brought her into a tight hug and kissed her forehead. "Good luck, sweetie. Try not to get too damaged. I'm a nurse, not a miracle worker."

"Just don't drink my blood if I die."

Cerise laughed. "No promises."

Chayton and Honaw gave her identical smiles. "You got this, Anya. You focus on the gates, and we'll protect your back."

"The Illumination won't want to break the treaty, but they have promised to keep the Darkness from attacking you," Aramis added.

"Yeah, I'll believe it when I see it." Katya buckled her gun belt. "Are we going or what?"

They piled into the cars, with Anya wedged between Aramis and Trajan, and Katya and Izrayl in the front. Yvan went with Cerise and the twins, and a flash of panic went through her as she was separated from him and the firebird. *It's only for the drive. It will be fine.* Anya fought not to clutch her head and focused on breathing.

Trajan put an arm around her. "Tell me how I can help."

She leaned into him, breathed in his autumn scent. *Safe.* Tears filled her eyes. "Just get me there so I can get this noise out of my head and shut these damn gates."

"Don't worry. Your abilities far outweigh your training," Aramis said. "Your ancestors could do it, and they only had a fraction of the power you have."

"They had the blessing of being taught what to do." She had gone over and over her vision of Ilya, trying to find meaning in his movements so she could recreate them, but it still felt like she was going in blind.

The closer they got to the farm, the more Anya could feel the gates heaving and screaming, like an extra pulse beating out a rhythm in her brain.

"We've got company," Izrayl said.

Anya turned. Men in black gear on motorbikes were closing in on them.

"Darkness or Illumination?" Trajan asked.

They ducked as gunfire peppered the night and hit the back window. Isabelle and Hamish drove up beside them, and Hamish's big Winchesters boomed. One of the motorbikes went down.

"Definitely Darkness. They don't care about attacking us when there's no one here to see it." Aramis typed on his phone. "I'll send word to the Illumination close by to get over here as a deterrent. That was what was agreed on."

"They could have changed their minds." Katya opened the sunroof. "Don't worry, spark plug, I'm happy to be the deterrent in the meantime."

"Watch yourself, hunter," Izrayl growled.

Katya kissed him on the cheek before popping up through the roof and firing.

"Get down, Anya." Trajan covered her with his body.

Adrenaline pumped through her veins as she worked to manage her breathing. Beside her, Aramis lit up with silvery light and placed his hand on the window. Magic that tasted like starlight and spring washed over the vehicle. Katya cursed above them.

"What the hell, spark plug!"

"It's a shield to keep you from getting your face blown off!" Aramis shouted. She kept on firing.

"Thanks," Izrayl said gruffly, not taking his eyes off the road as they pulled into the farm.

Anya's magic roared in her ears, and she bit her tongue hard enough to taste blood. "Stop the car. Stop the car!"

Izrayl pulled up in front of the remains of the barn. Trajan got out first and all but lifted Anya out. As her feet touched the ground, an aurora of light streaked out of the forest and across the field. She gasped.

The gates.

They looked like the ones she had seen before but were scarlet where the others had been blue.

"Do you see them? I never thought they would be so beautiful." The magic in the earth wrapped around her feet.

"No, I can't see anything," Trajan said.

Anya turned away from the wall of light and breathed him in, trying to imprint his scent and the feel of his body onto her in case anything happened.

"You've got this, Anya." He tilted her head up so their eyes met. "You were born to do this, my love. Don't forget that."

"I wish I had your confidence." Her voice shook with the nerves that were chewing at her insides.

"You don't need it." Trajan brushed a kiss against her lips. "Be careful. I love you."

Anya stared up into his wine-colored eyes as the drums echoed in her mind. "I love you t—"

The men in black-and-red gear ripped into the field, dropping their bikes and lifting their guns.

"No time left," Aramis said. "I'm sorry. I can only hold these shields for so long."

The pale silvery light of his shield now stretched around them, and the twins' bronze-colored magic joined to reinforce it. Now that day was breaking, Anya could make out more ranks of soldiers wearing the crest of the Darkness at the edge of the forest. They crept forward at the sight of Anya and their fellow operatives trailing her.

Anya glanced at Aramis. "I thought you said they wouldn't attack to avoid breaking the treaty?"

Instead of answering, he nodded across the field. A fleet of Jeeps appeared and crawled closer to the gates before men in in bright gear piled out. Over their uniforms, they wore shining silver chest plates, and each of them carried a sword.

Anya stared for a moment, then looked back to the tree line. The Darkness operatives slowed their advance, lowering their weapons an inch. Those that had pursued them on motorbikes paused midstride.

"The Illumination have finally arrived," Isabelle said, reloading her guns. "I see their knights-in-shining-armor complex is still going strong."

Aramis drew out his long knife. "They won't move unless the Darkness openly attacks us in plain sight. Ladislav will have to be insane to break the treaty."

Hamish snorted. "I don't know about you, but it feels like the day for some insanity to me."

Anya didn't hear what else they said. Their voices grew muddled while the gates reached out and touched her magic with scarlet vines. Everything seemed to fade into the background as Anya approached the shimmering aurora in the middle of the field, her eyes on its frayed edges that touched the land. There were tears in the aurora, and through them, Anya saw the dawn sky of Skazki.

Please show me what you need, she begged the gates when she reached them. She could feel the expectations pressing in on her, knew that her friends and enemies were all watching her. She pushed all of that aside. Only the gates mattered now.

With a shaking hand, Anya pulled out Ilya's knife and ran the blade over her palm. Blood pooled in it. She placed her hand on the aurora and released her magic.

As her blood and magic mingled and fell to the earth, Ilya appeared beside her, then his son, Ahti. Anya gasped as more specters rose from the ground and stood around her. She didn't recognize most of them, but she knew who they were: her ancestors, who had lived and died on the land. They were all around her.

Then she saw Eikki. Tears welled in her eyes. He joined her and mouthed words she couldn't hear. The voices in her head moved in time with his lips until she could make out the echoing words: *I'm sorry. Be safe. I love you.* Anya tried to reach for him, but her hand slid through him. Eikki's green eyes filled with warning, and he mouthed the word *Murdered* and pointed to his chest. *Trust no one.* Anya only had time to nod before Ilya's hand rested on her shoulder, and the chorus of voices silenced, then rose together in one voice.

Do not be afraid. Your ancestors stand with you. Feel our power in your bones and blood and the earth at your feet, they said to her. *It's at your fingertips, waiting for you to use. You are not alone. You never were. Feel the magic calling out to you. Draw it up from the bones and blood that have protected this land.*

Anya's feet pulsed with power, and she closed her eyes and drew the hot magic up from the earth. "I feel it," she whispered as her own magic tied itself to the land. Then she exhaled and let it take control of her.

Anya knelt down and drew a line in the earth where the light of the gate touched it. She squeezed her hand and let her blood flow into the ground. Her ancestors chanted, the power of their rune songs racing through her veins and biting her tongue. She stood and opened her mouth to release their voices.

"I am Gate's strong keeper,
Rune singer, and Magic wielder.
Door to Dreamland,
Land of Heroes, Land of Stories,
I stand on your threshold
between the spaces of the world.
I stand on your threshold
and offer all that I am.
I stand on your threshold
and hold your door shut.
That space to Hero Land
I hold closed
to those who are unworthy.
They cannot pass.
I am Gate's strong keeper,
Rune singer, and Magic wielder.
My magic, my blood, my voice
command you,

tell you to close.
With blood spilt over,
where Gates have broken,
join like flesh together
and bless it into its place.
With words and blood
I command you."

The aurora flared bright as Anya's magic roared out of her and filled it. The frays and tears began to mend and seal, shielding Mir and hiding the glimpses of Skazki. Her power rode through her as the aurora faded, and the power in the land, in the forest, in the rising sun—all the magic of the world—sang to her.

A note of discord broke the song apart, and Anya's attention snapped to the tree line. A man emerged from the forest on her side of the gate. A cloak of shadows and night flared around him, and Anya could sense the fear and darkness of his power in the space between. He smiled at her, and her insides turned to ice.

"Vasilli…"

Aramis stared in wide-eyed wonder as Anya slipped deep into the gate's magic and went to a place none of them could follow. He kept his shields up around her, just in case bullets began to fly.

"What's happening to her?" Trajan demanded.

"I'm not sure, but don't touch her whatever you do." Magic pulsed through the earth under Aramis's feet.

The twins laughed aloud and in sync, their faces filled with glee.

"She's drawing on the power of her ancestors," said Chayton. "There are apparitions all around her."

Whatever Anya was doing, it was working. The gates shuddered as their power was replenished. The Illumination and the Darkness eyed each other from either side of Aramis and the group, weapons drawn and ready, waiting for orders. Katya and Isabelle hadn't lowered their guard for even a second, and the shadows of Cerise's true form danced in her eyes as if she could feel the battle coming.

"Vasilli…"

Aramis's head snapped up at Anya's voice. He followed her gaze to where Vasilli stepped from the trees in a cloak of shadows.

Yvan moved up beside Aramis. He glared across the field at his brother, and the firebird rolled flames out over his skin. "How can I help?"

Aramis stared at the shadows pouring from Vasilli, panic creeping up his throat. "I—"

"You're too late, Vasilli! The gates are shut!" Anya shouted, her words reverberating with the sound of her ancestors' voices.

"I'm not here for the gates, witch. I'm here for you!"

The shadows rose out of Vasilli and raced across the empty field. They hit Aramis's shields, burning through them in seconds, and hit Anya. Aramis cried out in pain as his shields were cut off. The power that had been stirring in the earth roared up through Anya, and white light exploded out of her. It wrapped itself around Vasilli's shadows and pushed them back.

"We have incoming!" Isabelle called.

The Darkness operatives raced across the field toward them. There was a shout from the Illumination side, and they hurried to meet their charge.

Aramis froze where he stood. "They're breaking the treaty…"

Katya shook his shoulder. "Just focus on putting that shield back up so we don't get riddled with bullets in the crossfire!"

Aramis spun back to where Anya held back Vasilli's shadows. The two moved toward one another as their vortexes of power clashed and tangled between them.

Holy gods. What is she?

The Darkness descended on them, drawing Aramis's gaze away from Anya and back to the fight.

Bullets ricocheted off the twins' shields. They each drew bladed weapons and charged their way through, their shields and the others in the group moving with them. Aramis cut down two men before they had the chance to defend his attack. A wild laugh exploded out of Cerise as she moved within the bounds of the shield, her ancient armor gleaming black and silver and wreathed in shadow as she cut her way into their enemies.

Aramis hung back, separating his shield from the twins' and joining Yvan and Trajan as they took up positions at Anya's back and sides. He wrapped his shield around them, and his magic shuddered as she began to siphon more of the magic from the earth. Anya screamed a wordless sound of pure rage and released a burst of power that jarred Aramis as it exited his shield and burned hot through Vasilli's shadows, lighting them on fire. Vasilli roared as it hit him, striking him down with a blow so powerful Aramis staggered.

Anya gasped. "I did it." She shimmered softly with magic even as she swayed. She turned to smile at them and didn't see Ladislav come out of the trees, blood smeared on his bare chest, face, and arms. Aramis ran toward Anya, eyes wide.

"No!" He leaped as the resounding boom of Ladislav's spell exploded around them. Aramis caught Anya as she flew backward through the air. Both of them hit the ground hard, his shield disintegrating.

"Get her!" Ladislav shouted, and the world around them became a tangled chaos of gunfire and screams.

Aramis's ears rang, the sounds of battle drowning and distorted around him. There were too many of them—light and dark. While the Illumination were defending them now, they would stop at nothing to get Anya. There was no way they could take on both sides, especially not with Anya down. Trajan hauled Anya into his arms as Yvan helped Aramis to his feet.

"Retreat! Head for the cars!" Isabelle yelled, shoving Aramis out of the way as she shot an attacker in the face.

Beside her, Hamish smashed a Darkness operative in the nose with the wooden butt of his rifle. Blood gushed down the man's face before Hamish twisted the gun around and fired a bullet into his chest.

The twins covered Isabelle, Hamish, and Cerise with their shields as they retreated from the fight and ran for the parked vehicles. Ahead of them was Trajan, Anya dangling limply in his arms, and Yvan, who kept them encircled in flames so that no one dared approach them.

Next to Aramis, Katya's firearm clicked, and she holstered it, then drew her long blade from her thigh sheath. A black wolf collided with the Darkness operative advancing on her. A spray of blood misted Aramis's face as Izrayl's fangs tore through flesh and bone.

Aramis stumbled, too weak from sustaining a shield that had been blasted time and time again with powerful magic. He wove through the fighting Illumination and Darkness operatives, his focus trained on the cars. He summoned enough energy to throw a blast of magic behind him, knocking back their attackers from both sides.

Izrayl transformed midstride, and his naked limbs disappeared around the driver's side of one vehicle. It and the other vehicle were encircled by a large, bronze shield radiating from the car in front, where the twins were crammed into the back seat with Yvan and Cerise. Hamish sat behind the wheel, Isabelle still firing bullets through the passenger side window.

"Let's move!" she shouted.

Katya hoisted herself into the passenger seat next to Izrayl just as Aramis gripped the back door handle and climbed in beside Trajan. Only when he closed the door and settled into the seat did he realize that his body was going numb from the backlash of Ladislav's spell.

Trajan clutched Anya's still body to him, weeping and shaking. "Come on, Anya. Wake up. Please, wake up."

Aramis focused on her chest. It rose and fell. He groaned in relief. *Still alive.*

Hamish's engine revved, and the vehicle in front of them lurched forward. Katya tossed a jacket over Izrayl's bare lap before directing her firearm out the passenger side window.

Izrayl shifted the vehicle into drive. "Where are we going?"

"Just go!" Aramis said.

Izrayl slammed on the gas and tore through the field. Anya jostled in Trajan's lap as they barreled over bumps and divots. A sick feeling brewed in his gut at the sight of her. His burner phone rang as they caught air, then sped up the driveway and onto the road.

"What?" Aramis shouted down the line over the roar of Katya's gunfire.

"The Illumination just put out a death order for you and everyone you're with," Silvian said, his voice urgent and staticky. "It's being broadcasted over every channel of communication—human world tech as well as psychic and magical links. I was in their system when the call went out. Do you understand? They're hunting you now, Aramis. And you aren't going to believe what I found."

Aramis hung on to the door as Izrayl took a corner hard. "Tell me, Silvian!"

"It's about Yanka, why the girl can dream-walk with her…"

"What about it? Hurry up!" Aramis looked across at Anya. Whatever color she had was gone from her, and she still hadn't regained consciousness. Trajan had buried his face in the crook of her shoulder and was sobbing. There was silence at the end of the line as the phone reception dropped out.

"Spit it out! I have the Darkness *and* Illumination on my ass right now."

"Yanka is still alive, Aramis." Silvian's voice crackled. "Did you hear me? Yanka is alive!"

EPILOGUE

LOOK THROUGH THE FOREST to Baba Yaga's ugly bone cottage standing high on its chicken legs. *Clack, clack!* goes the loom as the iron-toothed witch works with her withered nimble hands. She whispers the words of power, adds the threads, and searches within the weave.

Baba Yaga dips a hand into her ratty robe and pulls out a radiant fire-bird feather. Magic beats through the cottage and radiates into the forest. Birds screech overhead, and ground animals hide deeper in their caves and burrows. She weaves the feather into the pattern, her bony arms shifting up and down, her fingers moving deftly as she hums. Next, with special care, she takes out a single strand of fair hair.

"Oh, Anya. If only you weren't so stubborn like Yanka. Things could be so different."

Into the weave the hair goes. It glows against the dark threads. The firebird's feather lights up at the same instant, and like magnets, they shoot through the weave toward each other.

"No! No, no, no!" Baba Yaga screeches with fury.

When the objects finally meet, white light explodes, throwing the witch across the room like a pile of rags and bones. The light sears deeper and deeper inside of her until, finally, it dissipates, and she feels like she can breathe again.

With a groan, Baba Yaga rolls over. The weave, which has taken so much power from her, is now ash. Her magic loom still stands, good as new. The feather and the hair are gone. She stares at the smoldering mess for a long while.

In the corner of the room, the crate that holds the ancient game begins to thrum, and she backs away from it until it settles. There is only one reason for it to behave like that: it's finally coming back into play.

"At last!" Baba Yaga shouts, her mad laughter echoing in the world around her.

The battle she's been dreaming about, the war she's been longing for with her shriveled, black heart, has finally come.

ABOUT THE AUTHOR

Amy Kuivalainen is the author of the Magicians of Venice (*The Immortal City*, *The Sea of the Dead*, *The King's Seal*) and the Firebird Faerie Tales.

A Finnish-Australian writer who is obsessed with magical wardrobes, doors, auroras, and burial mounds that might offer her a way into another realm, she enjoys mashing up mythology and lore into unique retellings about monsters and magic.

Amy enjoys practicing yoga and spending time in the beautiful city of Melbourne, where she is working on her next novel.

CPSIA information can be obtained
at www.ICGtesting.com
Printed in the USA
LVHW010512171221
706394LV00017B/652/J